A Girl's Guide to the Birds & the Bees

By the same author:

The Naughty Girls Book Club

A Girl's Guide to the Birds & the Bees

SOPHIE HART

Bookouture

Published by Bookouture

An imprint of StoryFire Ltd.
23 Sussex Road, Ickenham, UB10 8PN
United Kingdom

www.bookouture.com

ISBN: 978-1-909490-56-7
eBook ISBN: 978-1-909490-55-0

Chapter 1

'Sex is part of nature. I go along with nature'
– Marilyn Monroe

'So, don't forget, this week is all about embracing the difference. You can try anything – as long as it's something you've never done before, and both of you are comfortable with it. Sex on the kitchen table, or in the back of the car; a little light bondage or some dressing up; cover each other in whipped cream or melted chocolate…'

'I like the sound of that one,' Jennifer giggled.

'Whatever floats your boat,' Annie smiled, standing up behind her desk. 'Just make sure you shake things up and keep your sex life fresh. It's so easy to get stuck in a routine when you're in a long-term relationship, so every now and then you need to make the effort to break out of your comfort zone.'

The couple seated opposite her, in the large Chesterfield armchairs, stood up too and they all shook hands.

'Thanks so much, Annie. You're really making a difference,' said Jennifer, a professional-looking woman in her mid-forties.

Her husband, Richard, wrapped his arm around his wife and squeezed her to him, as Annie opened the door for them.

'You're very welcome. Have fun, and I'll see you both next week.'

'Bye, Annie!'

They walked off down the corridor towards the exit. Annie could hear them talking and laughing, the sound of Jennifer's heels echoing in the empty building.

Annie let the door close and slowly exhaled, rolling her shoulders back and stretching her neck to release the tension. Glancing up at the clock, she realised it was just after nine pm. No wonder she felt tired.

Richard and Jennifer had been her final clients of the day, so all that was left to do now was lock up and go home. Annie picked up the empty coffee mug from her desk then paused, staring around her office. The room was small but homely; given that she often worked twelve-hour days, it needed to be. The shelves were lined with psychology textbooks and bound copies of journals, whilst all her diplomas and certificates hung in gold frames on the cream-coloured walls. Behind her armchair was an old-fashioned standing lamp, and in the centre of the room was Annie's pride and joy: the antique, solid-oak desk that she'd bought at a local auction, with its shiny brass handles and leather-covered top. She was extremely proud of everything she'd achieved in her career, but couldn't help but feel that her life was a little lonely sometimes.

Annie Hall was thirty-four years old, and a qualified sex therapist – a profession which was far less exciting than everyone assumed. She had her own practice on the outskirts of Norwich, and rented an office in a purpose-built building in Sprowston which leased space to lots of different businesses. Across the corridor from her was an internet-based craft company, whilst down the hall was a chiropractor, and there was even a shoe designer on the upstairs floor.

At this time of night, everyone else had gone home. Annie was often the last to leave the building; she regularly worked unsociable hours – early mornings, late evenings, or even weekends – as they were the only times many of her clients could fit in their sessions. Consequently, her social life was pretty much non-existent.

Annie picked up her overflowing handbag and locked the door, then headed down the corridor to the communal kitchen. As she got closer, she could hear the sound of hoovering, and turned the corner to be greeted by Celeste, the cleaner.

'Annie, how are you?' Celeste beamed, bending down awkwardly to turn off the vacuum. She was a large lady in her late fifties, originally from Jamaica, and her knees weren't as good as they'd once been.

'I'm fine thanks, Celeste. And you?'

'Oh, not bad, can't complain. Another late night for you, is it?'

'You know what they say – no rest for the wicked.'

Celeste threw back her head and laughed heartily. 'They do indeed. Time for you to be getting off home now, hmm? You've no doubt got some lovely young man waiting for you, pretty girl like you.'

Annie blushed, looking down at the floor.

'No need to be so shy,' Celeste grinned slyly. 'Your boyfriend's a very lucky man.'

'Boyfriend?'

Celeste nodded wisely. 'With what you do for a living, I bet you can show him a really wild time, hey?' She let loose another peal of laughter, a real guffaw that seemed to bounce off the walls in the otherwise deserted kitchen.

Annie smiled awkwardly, wondering whether to correct Celeste, and confess to the fact that her love life was nowhere near as exciting as everyone assumed. It was a common misconception – people supposed that because Annie spent her days giving relationship advice and talking freely about sex, she must be some sort of man-eating tigress in her personal life. It couldn't have been further from the truth.

The reality was that Annie didn't have a boyfriend, and it was years since she'd been in a serious relationship. She'd made mistakes in her past, finding herself attracted to the wrong men for the wrong reasons (well, one man in particular), and since then she'd vowed to focus on her career without the distraction of a hectic love life.

So far, the plan seemed to be working, and Annie was happier than ever with how her business was going. She loved meeting a wide variety of people from all different walks of life, working with them to resolve their problems, and ultimately helping them to achieve their happy ever after. Despite her professional success, Annie's sister, Holly, was always trying to set her up with unsuitable men, and Annie had endured more than her fair share of speed dating events and online matchmaking sites. But all she'd encountered were freaks, geeks and outright creeps.

No, Annie realised, there was no way she could admit all of that to Celeste. Because of her job, everyone expected Annie to be dating a super-hot stud-muffin, using every trick in the book to leave him panting for more. It was more than a little embarrassing to admit that, despite being something of a guru when it came to other people's relationships, she seemed to be incapable of holding down one of her own.

'Well, I'd better get going,' Annie said brightly, changing the subject as she rinsed out her mug and stacked it neatly in the dishwasher. 'Have a good night, Celeste.'

'You too, Annie,' she replied, a twinkle in her dark eyes. 'Take care.'

As Annie walked off, she heard the vacuum burst into life once more, followed by the rich, throaty tones of Celeste belting out 'Respect' by Aretha Franklin. Annie smiled, as she turned back to see Celeste wiggling her hips, dancing along the corridor with the Hoover as a partner.

Outside it was dark and drizzling, a typical late January evening, and a thin sheen of frost was already beginning to form. Annie hurried over to her trusty Mini Cooper, her brown bobbed hair bouncing on her shoulders, as she gratefully climbed in out of the cold. It was a short journey to her house, round the ring road to Hellesdon, and the traffic was light at this time of night.

As she turned into her street, all of the houses seemed to be ablaze with light. Some had left their curtains open, and she could see the families inside – cuddled up on the sofa watching television, munching a late night snack, or trying to get the kids to go to bed. Annie's home, in comparison, was deserted and devoid of life, the only dark house in the entire street.

'Hi Harry! Hi Sally!' she called out, as she bustled in through the front door, dropping her bag and hanging up her coat.

She headed through to the living room, where her two pet goldfish (named after her favourite rom-com characters) were swimming contentedly round and round their bowl, utterly oblivious to the fact that their owner had arrived home. Annie sprinkled a few flakes of food on the surface of the water and watched as they chomped happily, swimming in tandem around one another.

Great, even her *goldfish* could hold down a relationship better than she could, Annie thought with a sigh as she walked through to the kitchen and pulled a microwaveable risotto out of the fridge. She set it spinning, then checked her phone to find a missed call and a text from her sister, Holly:

> *Hi sis, tried to call but u must have been at work, u workaholic! I've found a great man 4u, can't wait to fix u up ;) Call me xxx*

Annie rolled her eyes, deciding to ignore the message and pour herself a nice glass of Merlot instead.

Holly was five years younger than her, and happily married to her childhood sweetheart, Greg, who now worked for an insurance firm. Despite Holly's busy career as a journalist for a local magazine, she still seemed to have plenty of time to meddle in Annie's love life (or lack thereof). The results hadn't been hugely positive so far, Annie reflected: there'd been Kevin, aka The Octopus, who had a severe case of wandering hands; Owen, the recent divorcé, who'd spent the evening gushing about his ex-wife and was clearly still in love with her; and Jack, who took Annie to a Michelin-star restaurant, only to announce that he'd 'forgotten' his wallet when the bill arrived.

Why was everyone so concerned with her single status anyway? Annie wondered, as she carried her risotto through to the living room and switched on the TV. She flicked through the movie channels until she came across one that was showing *Notting Hill*.

Perfect! Annie thought delightedly. She'd seen it before – dozens of times, in fact – but she could always watch it again. Right now, it was the dinner-party scene, where Hugh Grant had taken Julia Roberts to meet his friends and everyone was trying not to freak out. The familiarity made Annie feel all warm and fuzzy inside.

Annie had been raised on the movies – even her name was inspired by Woody Allen's Oscar-winning film, *Annie Hall*. Her mother, Pamela, had met Graham Hall the same year that the movie had been released. She'd fallen in love with the film – and with Graham – and vowed that their first daughter would be called Annie. Even Annie's younger sister was named after Holly Golightly in *Breakfast at Tiffany's*.

Annie had grown up on the classics, watching everything from *Gone with the Wind* to *Casablanca*, graduating onto *Pretty Woman* and *Dirty Dancing* as she hit her teenage years. She was still a sucker for a romantic comedy, and the simple, satisfying storylines had left her with a belief that everyone could – and should – find their own happy ending. Helping people achieve that had become the goal of Annie's career.

On screen, Julia Roberts walked out of the front door and everyone inside let out a huge scream of disbelief. Annie smiled as she pulled her big diary out of her bag, leafing through it while she ate. Tomorrow she had another early start, seeing Michael and Carolyn before they went to work, but Annie didn't mind as they were a great couple. Michael was a mortgage advisor and Carolyn worked for a local charity, but since the death of her grandmother, to whom she'd been extremely close, Carolyn had completely lost interest in sex. It was a scenario Annie had come across many times before, and she knew that grief often resulted in a loss of libido. But they were both making strides, and Michael was wonderfully patient and understanding.

When she'd finished eating, Annie quickly washed her plate and then jumped in the shower, staying in there until the water ran cold. As she blow-dried her hair afterwards, she mentally re-played the conversation she'd had with Celeste, and realised she'd never got round to texting Holly back. Oh well, she could do it tomorrow. It was highly unlikely that this man was going to be any more suitable than all the others her sister had tried to pair her off with over the years.

It wasn't that Annie didn't want to meet someone; she'd love to be in a relationship with a man who was kind, clever, funny… and tall and handsome too, if that didn't make her sound shallow! She just hadn't found anyone that was right for her yet, she reflected, as she climbed under her duvet and switched off the bedside light.

Lying alone in the darkness, the double bed large and empty without a lover to fill it, the same question kept flashing across Annie's mind: if she could fix everyone else's love life, then why couldn't she fix her own?

Chapter 2

'No woman gets an orgasm from shining the kitchen floor' – **Betty Friedan**

Nick Crawford was deep in concentration, staring hard at the computer screen in front of him. Struck by a sudden burst of inspiration, he began typing furiously, his hands flying over the keyboard. Then he leant back in contemplation, re-reading what he'd written, and made a few small changes before he was off again, the words pouring out of him.

Nick worked in advertising, and he was currently writing a pitch for a local brewery that was launching a fruit-flavoured beer. He was determined to win the contract and was going all out to nail this presentation, ensuring it was as professional and polished as it could possibly be. Right now, Nick was on a roll, the buzz words and key phrases flowing effortlessly from his fingertips, as he slotted in statistics and carefully targeted market research.

On his desk, his phone vibrated, jumping noisily across a pile of documents. Nick tried to ignore it and continue with what he was writing, but the light was flashing insistently and he was losing his train of thought.

With a sigh of frustration, Nick snatched it up and saw that he had a message from his wife, Julia. Although he was ashamed to admit it, his heart instantly sank. And when he read the text, his heart sank even further:

I've taken the afternoon off – do the same. Meet you in the bedroom in 30mins. I'll be wearing the black lingerie you like ☺

Nick exhaled slowly, his head dropping into his hands as he massaged his brow. He was thirty-two years old, but today he looked closer to forty; there were deep bags under his pale blue eyes, frown lines etched into his forehead, and recently he'd been alarmed to start finding strands of grey in his thick, dark hair.

Nick read through the text once again, an uncomfortable feeling gnawing at the pit of his stomach. He really needed to finish this presentation – he'd promised his boss it would be with him by close of play today. Plus he needed to start brainstorming ideas for the Norfolk Cottages campaign, prep with his colleague, Anthony, about the new client they were meeting tomorrow, touch base with his team on where they were all at with their current projects… Julia's text was the last thing he needed.

But he knew how furious she'd be if he didn't come home. There would be tears, tantrums and arguments, followed by days of sulking and silent treatment… For a minute or two, Nick was torn, staring unseeingly at his computer. The image on the screen showed an attractive, professional-looking couple sitting outside a country pub enjoying their fruit-flavoured beer, but Nick's thoughts couldn't be further from his work right now.

Reluctantly, he made his decision. He saved the document and logged off, pulling on his jacket and throwing his mobile into his work bag. Then he headed across the room to his boss, Gerard's, office, and knocked softly on the door.

'Come in,' Gerard called.

Nick entered to see Gerard sitting behind his desk, opposite a woman Nick didn't recognise.

'Sorry,' Nick apologised hastily. 'I didn't realise you were busy.'

'Not a problem.' Gerard waved away his concerns. 'I was going to make the rounds shortly and do the introductions. Nick, this is Nina, and she'll be starting with us officially next week as our latest junior account executive.'

'Good to meet you,' Nick said, extending his hand. Nina was young – in her mid-twenties, he would have guessed – with long, dark hair that hung straight down her back, and large brown eyes.

She shook Nick's hand firmly, and gave him a warm smile. 'You too. I'm looking forward to working with you.'

'Well, now that's out of the way, what did you want to see me about?' Gerard asked.

'Oh, yes. Sorry…' Nick pulled a face, looking uncomfortable. 'There's been a bit of an emergency at home. Julia's just called and needs me there right away. Is it okay if I leave early?'

Gerard frowned, eyeing him suspiciously. Nick felt himself literally grow hot under the collar, beads of sweat forming along his hairline. He'd been asking for a lot of time off recently, and wondered how much longer Gerard's patience would hold.

'I can have the Broads Brewery presentation to you by ten am tomorrow,' Nick began, aware that he was gabbling. 'And Maria can lead the meeting this afternoon. I'll ask her to email me the minutes tonight so I can look over them at home.'

'You're making something of a habit of this, Nick.' Gerard's tone was disapproving.

'I know. I really am sorry. I wouldn't ask unless it was extremely important.'

'Fine,' Gerard agreed eventually. 'But you'll need to make up the hours, and check that Maria's happy to cover for you.'

'I will. Thank you,' Nick replied, visibly relieved. 'See you next week, Nina,' he added, as he dashed out of the door.

Nick took the stairs two at a time – no point in waiting for the lift – and hurried across the car park, sliding into the five-door, silver BMW 3 Series that he'd bought a few months ago. It was large, comfortable and – most importantly – a *family* car. Julia had insisted on it.

The traffic was light in the early afternoon, and the drive home was uneventful, but Nick could feel his anger growing with every mile he covered.

He would have to speak to Julia, he decided firmly, and tell her that she couldn't keep doing this – dragging him out of work and insisting that he come home for yet another session in the bedroom. It was okay for Julia; she was self-employed, running her own business as an events planner, so she could take a few hours off whenever she felt like it. But it was different for Nick. Gerard was clearly annoyed and, in the current financial climate, aggravating his boss really wasn't a clever idea. Nick enjoyed his job and wanted to keep it; it wasn't worth risking for a quickie with his wife.

The traffic lights turned red and Nick hit the brake, drumming his fingers impatiently on the steering wheel as he thought about his situation. He and Julia had been trying for a baby for almost a year now, and Julia was becoming increasingly desperate with every month that passed. Take last night, for example – almost as soon as they'd eaten their evening meal, Julia had been eager to get Nick into bed. He would happily have crashed out on the sofa and watched an episode or two of their *Breaking Bad* box set, but Julia wasn't taking no for an answer. Then, around five am, Nick woke blearily to find Julia's hands snaking into his pyjama bottoms, insistent on round two. He'd done his best to oblige but today, quite frankly, he was exhausted.

With a pang, Nick thought back to when he and Julia had first made the decision to start a family. Together, they'd discussed the idea of becoming parents, wanting to wait until the time was right and they were financially stable, certain that their days of wild partying were out of their system and that they were ready to cope with sleepless nights and dirty nappies.

Those first few weeks of trying to conceive were simultaneously thrilling and terrifying, their love-making charged with an extra intensity. They weren't fooling around any more – they were actually trying to create a whole new person, one who would irreversibly change both of their lives forever.

Every month, Nick and Julia experienced the thrill of waiting to see what the outcome would be, regularly finding themselves huddled together over a pregnancy test stick, watching for that double line to appear.

But it never did.

Every time, the test was negative and, every four weeks, Julia's period arrived, as regular as clockwork.

Their love-making took on a more frantic quality, their initial excitement gradually giving way to frustration and recrimination. Julia began reading books on fertility and following faddy diets. She was forever wandering around the house with a thermometer under her tongue, taking her temperature to determine the optimum days for conception, and—

A car horn blared, and Nick looked up in alarm, realising that the lights had turned green. He revved the engine and set off in a rush.

Almost before Nick's eyes, Julia had begun to change from the woman he'd married into someone else – someone irritable, emotional and obsessed with getting pregnant. In turn, Nick had changed too – he was defensive, angry, withdrawn – and he didn't like the person he'd become. The worst part was that he had no idea how to change things for the better, how to rediscover the sense of fun and freedom that he'd so loved when they'd first started dating just a few short years ago.

Julia had been a joy back then. Nick had been utterly mesmerised by her, remembering the way they would stay up until the early hours, sharing a bottle of wine and making plans for the future, or how she would look at him across a crowded room and instantly make him feel like the luckiest man alive.

Now, everything had changed. Nothing was fun, nothing was spontaneous. Julia's only focus was on getting pregnant; her only topics of conversation were natural birth versus an epidural, baby names, Lamaze classes and C-sections.

As Nick pulled into the driveway of his house, he noticed that, despite the fact it was barely two pm, the bedroom curtains were drawn. Out of the corner of his eye, he saw the living room blinds twitch and realised that Julia had been watching out of the window, waiting for him to come home.

Nick turned off the ignition and sat for a moment, mentally preparing himself for what was about to happen. He yawned widely, his bodily utterly shattered. Then, knowing he couldn't put it off any longer, he got out of the car and walked towards the front door.

He'd barely had a chance to put the key in the lock when the door swung open. Julia's hand reached out and grabbed him, pulling him inside. As promised, she was wearing sexy black lingerie – a lacy all-in-one number, with red bows and cut-out panels – but the look on her face was angry.

'What took you so long?' she demanded.

Nick opened his mouth to reply, but Julia cut him off. 'Never mind, just get upstairs.'

Nick followed her dutifully, mesmerised by the wiggle of her semi-naked bottom as she climbed the stairs in front of him. He reached out to caress it, but Julia slapped his hand away.

'Stop it, Nick,' she snapped. 'There's no time. According to the test, I'm ovulating right now.'

She dragged him into the bedroom and Nick saw that she'd switched off the overhead light, just the bedside lamp turned on to illuminate the room.

'Right, let's get on with it.' Julia's tone was brisk as she slipped out of her underwear, letting it drop onto the fluffy carpet. Nick watched her – his beautiful wife, her full breasts swaying, her dark blonde hair falling seductively across her face. He moved across to kiss her, but Julia looked at him in alarm.

'What are you doing? Why aren't you getting undressed?'

Nick let out a barely audible sigh, wondering how it had come to this. He'd sneaked out of work for a fast, frantic afternoon quickie with a woman who was desperate to get him into bed. It should have been the ultimate fantasy, but instead it was rapidly turning into one of the unsexiest moments of his life.

'Julia,' he began, wanting to try to explain the way he was feeling. But the look she gave him shut him up immediately, and Nick decided it was easiest just to get on with the job at hand. He bent down to untie his laces, stepping out of his work shoes and unzipping his trousers. Moments later, he was fully undressed, and Julia pounced.

'Come on, big boy. Show me what you're made of!'

Despite his reservations, Nick was a red-blooded, hetero-sexual male, and at the sight of his gorgeous, naked wife, his body naturally responded. Julia smiled wickedly, pushing him back onto the bed and climbing on top of him.

'I've been doing some reading, and new research suggests that girl-on-top might be surprisingly effective when look-ing to conceive,' she informed him matter-of-factly, as she wriggled around, trying to get comfortable.

'Uh huh,' Nick replied, wondering when his sex life had become as thrilling as watching a documentary on the potato famine. Everything about the experience seemed cold and clinical, with both of them merely going through the mo-tions. There'd been no kissing, no foreplay, no indication at all that this was a loving act between a happily married cou-ple. Nick was starting to get the uncomfortable feeling that Julia saw him as little more than a convenient sperm donor.

As his wife moved robotically on top of him, Nick found himself staring in frustration at the cracks in the ceiling, his mind wandering to the pitch he should have been writing that afternoon. Maybe he could add in a paragraph about national patterns of beer consumption, jazz it up with a few more photos from Shutterstock, then—

'Hurry up, Nick,' Julia barked, interrupting his thoughts. 'Are you nearly there yet?'

Her voice startled Nick out of his daydreams, and he sud-denly realised with blinding clarity that they couldn't carry on like this. Sex (it certainly couldn't be classed as love-making any more) with his wife was no longer enjoyable. It had become a chore – a task to be endured, rather than cherished and sa-voured. It wasn't fun, it wasn't healthy and it wasn't enjoyable.

Something needed to change – and fast.

Chapter 3

*'Sex and golf are the two things you can enjoy
even if you're not good at them'* – **Kevin Costner**

There was a tentative tap on Annie's office door. She jumped up from her desk, quickly hiding the copy of *Cosmopolitan* magazine she'd been reading, and dashed across to answer it. 'Hello, you must be Ray,' Annie smiled warmly, extending her hand.

The man was in his late fifties and of average height, with thin grey hair that was completely bald on the crown. He was wearing a pair of golf trousers, with a bulky waterproof jacket over the top.

'Yes. And you're Ms Hall?' he queried, shaking her hand.

'Please, call me Annie. Do come in, and make yourself comfortable.'

She closed the door behind him, as Ray nervously took a seat in one of the large armchairs, unzipping his coat to reveal a garish diamond-pattern jumper.

'I haven't… I mean, I've never done this kind of thing before…' he began, before trailing off and looking pleadingly at Annie, as though willing her to understand.

'Neither have ninety-nine percent of the people who come through my door, so you're not alone,' she said reassuringly. 'You've made a great first step by coming here. It's a very brave thing to do.'

Ray nodded uncertainly, not looking convinced.

'And you've come here on your own today,' Annie prompted him.

'Yes. My wife, Linda, she thinks I'm out at the driving range,' he explained, gesturing apologetically at his clothes. 'I didn't want her to know where I was going. I just wanted to see what this was all about, and whether or not you could help us, before I mention it to her.'

'I completely understand,' Annie assured him. 'Why don't I tell you a little more about what I do, and the way that I work. Then, if you want to, you can tell me about the reasons you came to see me today.'

'Okay,' Ray agreed hesitantly. 'That sounds… fine.'

'Can I get you a drink at all before we start? Tea or coffee?'

Ray chuckled. 'Do you have anything stronger? A large Johnnie Walker might make this easier.'

'I'm afraid not,' Annie laughed. 'Two sugars in your tea are about the most extreme thing I can offer.'

'Then I'll have to make do with that. And a splash of milk too, please.'

Once Ray was settled with his drink, and looking slightly less like he might bolt straight out of the door, Annie sat back in her chair and began to speak:

'I like to work in a very informal way. I want you to feel as comfortable as possible whilst you're in this room, and free to say whatever you want. Sometimes people find it easier to talk to someone they don't know, who has no preconceptions about them or their relationship, and who can be impartial. I don't judge, or tell you what you should and shouldn't be doing. I can give you advice, based on my knowledge and experience, and I can give suggestions – but it's up to you whether or not you follow that advice.'

Ray took a sip of his tea and nodded, his eyes wide.

'As I said, it's great that you've decided to come here today,' Annie continued brightly. 'I know from what you said on the phone that you clearly care very much about your relationship with your wife, and want to make it better. What is it in particular that's brought you to see me?'

Ray set his mug down on a coaster and swallowed thickly, clearly wondering whether or not to confide in Annie. It was a reaction she was accustomed to – people were always so anxious the first time they came to see her, but a few sessions down the line and they were chatting away like old friends.

'Well,' Ray began slowly. 'Linda and I... As you can see, we're a bit older. I'm fifty-nine and Linda's a year younger. We both work part time – you know, slowing down as we approach retirement.'

'And what do you both do?' Annie asked, as she scribbled notes on a pad.

'I'm a driving instructor,' Ray explained. 'And Linda has her own business, running a flower shop. Well, our eldest daughter, Rose, manages it now – like I said, we're supposed to be semi-retired – but Linda still goes in most days.'

'How many children do you have?'

'Three. As well as Rose, there's her sister, Marianne, and then Robbie, our youngest. He's just graduated, and lives in Manchester now, so we don't see him as much. Rose and Marianne are nearby, and they've both got little ones, so Linda and I are grandparents now. We look after the children a lot...'

He trailed off, and Annie waited for him to continue. She sensed that he was getting near to talking about the reason he'd come to see her, and experience had taught her that if she remained silent, her client would often fill the silence by talking about what was really on their mind.

'Sometimes I can't believe I'm a granddad. Where did the years go?' Ray asked, with a soft chuckle. 'And I know that, strictly speaking, I'm well past middle age. When kids in the street look at me they probably see an old man. But the thing is, I still *feel* young. Yes, I might get a few more aches and pains than I used to, and I can't see further than the end of my nose if I don't have my glasses on, but I don't want everything to just… stop,' he finished awkwardly. 'And some things have. Stopped, that is.'

'You and your wife have stopped being intimate?' Annie asked softly.

Ray turned crimson, colour infusing his face. He nodded, making a strangled sort of noise that Annie took for a yes.

'And when was the last time you and Linda made love?'

Ray was squirming in his seat, looking as though he'd rather have a wisdom tooth pulled without anaesthetic than answer Annie's question. Finally, he spoke, his voice dropping to a whisper. 'About a year ago.'

'And is there any particular reason for this, that you know of?'

Ray shrugged sadly, shaking his head.

'This is a very common issue for older couples, as I'm sure you're aware,' Annie began gently. 'If it's a mutual decision, then that's fine, but if one partner is still hoping to enjoy an active, regular sex life, it can cause a problem. Plus, at fifty-nine, there's no reason to be slowing down just yet.'

'I know,' Ray agreed. 'I accept that we're not as young as we once were, but there's life in the old dog yet, as they say. I don't want to think that that side of things is completely over.'

'How old was your wife when she went through the meno-pause?' Annie asked thoughtfully.

'The…? I…' Ray's mouth flapped open and closed in bewilderment. Annie might as well have asked him the square root of 142,078 and he would have had more chance of answering accurately.

'Never mind,' Annie insisted. 'It doesn't matter for now.'

'I love her, you see,' Ray burst out. 'Always will. I still remember the first date we ever went on, clear as day. I fell head over heels that night.' He smiled wistfully. 'And it's not just the… the physical act,' he managed finally, looking bashful once again. 'I miss the intimacy. The closeness. We're not like we used to be.'

Seated in the chair opposite Annie, Ray looked desperately sad all of a sudden, his shoulders bowed, his mouth drooping.

'Do you think Linda would be willing to come here?' Annie wondered. 'To come to these sessions with you, and talk to me?'

'I don't know,' Ray admitted. 'Would we… I mean, how does it work? Would we have to take our clothes off?' he whispered, looking terrified. 'Do you watch us while we… you know… and tell us where we're going wrong?'

Annie couldn't suppress the giggle that was building up. 'No, not at all,' she chuckled. 'I don't know why people always think that, but I promise you, no one will be getting naked. At least not until session three.'

Ray's head jerked up in alarm, then he saw that she was joking.

'Oh, right,' he managed to laugh. 'Well, that's a relief.'

'I'll talk to you both, and find out if there's any identifiable reason for the loss of intimacy,' Annie explained. 'You'll also get homework from me – exercises to work on and put into practice every week. And I don't just focus on the physical. It's all about rediscovering the love in the relationship.'

For the first time since Annie had met him, Ray seemed relieved. 'Good,' he exhaled. 'That sounds good. I'll speak to Linda, and see if she'll come with me.' His eyes were sad as he looked up at Annie. 'I just want things back to how they used to be. I want us to be happy again.'

❋ ❋ ❋

'Annie! Over here!'

Annie heard her sister's voice and looked across the crowded pub to where Holly was waving frantically, a huge grin on her face.

'Hey, Hols,' Annie beamed, as she slid her slim body through the tightly knit groups of after-work drinkers, and plonked herself down in the seat beside her sister, who'd somehow managed to secure a coveted corner table in the King's Arms.

The two women hugged, their easy intimacy giving away the fact that they were sisters, despite the fact they were very different in terms of looks. At five foot nine, Annie was tall and slim, with a sporty figure that meant she very rarely gained weight, no matter what she ate. Holly, however, was a head shorter, with soft curves and full breasts that Annie had always envied. Annie's neat brown bob was in sharp contrast to her sister's bouncy blonde curls, and Holly had always had the more outgoing personality of the two; lively and vivacious in contrast to Annie's shy and studious nature.

'I got you a G&T. I thought you'd probably need it,' Holly beamed.

'You're right. Mmm, delicious,' Annie sighed in satisfaction, as she took a sip of the crisp, sharp liquid.

'So how's everything at work?' Holly asked, as she settled herself into the comfy seat. 'I'm surprised you managed to get away so soon.'

'My last appointment was at six, so it's a fairly early one for me,' Annie agreed. 'But everything's going well. I had a new client today – a guy who's nearly sixty, and concerned that he and his wife aren't being intimate any more.'

'Bloody hell, I hope I'm still having sex when I'm sixty,' Holly burst out, with a giggle. 'Maybe that would make a good article – "Sex Lives of the Over Sixties",' she suggested, moving her hands in the air in front of her to indicate the headline splash.

'A little bit racy for *Norfolk Living*, isn't it?' Annie teased, referring to the local magazine that her sister wrote for. Its usual content was more church fêtes and wedding fairs than saucy columns about spicing up your sex life.

'True,' Holly conceded. 'It's hardly *Cosmo*. I've actually been out on a story this afternoon – I had to rush to get here, as the traffic was murder coming past the airport. I was up near Aylsham interviewing a dairy farmer who's convinced that his cows are the most photogenic in the county. He's actually had a calendar made! You get fifteen percent off if you order a copy through *Norfolk Living*.'

'Tempting,' Annie grinned, taking another swallow of her drink.

'You should go for it. Between you and me,' Holly lowered her voice conspiratorially, 'Myrtle the cover girl is an absolute stunner!'

The two sisters burst into giggles, and Annie found herself thinking how she needed to do this more often. Work wasn't everything – she should make sure she finished early a couple of nights a week and go for a drink with Holly, or some of her friends. Or even, heaven forbid, out on a date…

'So how's Greg?' Annie said, asking after her sister's husband.

'He's good. He's got a new obsession with vintage cars at the moment. You know his dad's got that old Triumph rusting in the garage? Well, they've decided to do it up,' Holly explained, shaking her head to indicate exactly what she thought of the idea. 'It's a father-son bonding exercise, I think. Anyway, they've spent every weekend tinkering with the engine, or whatever it is they do, and visiting all these scrap yards and classic car places to try and source the original parts. But it's keeping Greg entertained, so I guess that's a good thing.'

Annie nodded, knowing what was coming next and hoping to avoid it. But Holly wasn't going to let her off the hook that easily.

'What about you?' Holly asked slyly. 'Any secret love interest that you're dying to tell me about?'

Annie rolled her eyes. 'No. Nothing happening on that front.'

'I really wish you'd let me sign you up for Mysinglefriend.com. I could write you an amazing profile! Or maybe you should go on Match.com – that's how Martin and Anya met. They've been together for three years now, with a baby due in April.'

'That's not really my sort of thing, Hol.' Annie was squirming uncomfortably.

'Come on, sis, you've got to put yourself out there, otherwise you're never going to find anyone.'

'I don't know if I want to find anyone! I'm quite happy as I am, thank you very much.'

'Annie, you've basically been single since Mark. You can't let one bad experience ruin the rest of your life. Besides, that was years ago – you need to move on.'

'I *have* moved on,' Annie insisted. 'It's just… oh, I don't know,' she finished lamely, the mention of her ex's name dredging up all sorts of conflicting emotions.

She'd met Mark when she was at university, studying psychology. He was older than she was, working towards his master's degree, and the attraction was instant. Annie fell fast and hard – the chemistry between them was electric, and physically they couldn't get enough of each other.

Mark proposed on her twenty-first birthday, and Annie ecstatically accepted. Her parents, however, were less ecstatic, both fearing (correctly) that she was far too young and everything was happening too fast. But Annie didn't want to listen, wrapped up in her whirlwind romance. She'd watched enough films to know that this was what love was supposed to be like: passionate, dramatic and all-encompassing.

Annie had been utterly dazzled by Mark, by his charm, his intelligence and his good looks, so when he suggested that they get married in secret, Annie immediately agreed. Standing at the front of the registry office, with a couple of strangers they'd pulled off the street as witnesses, Annie felt that she was living out her own movie-style love affair. They were like Romeo and Juliet, or Heathcliff and Cathy – young, in love, and misunderstood by everyone around them.

Encouraged by Mark, Annie dropped out of uni just before her final exams, abandoning her career aspirations to play the role of devoted wife instead. Within a few months, she realised that she'd made a huge mistake. After all the hormones and lust had evaporated, she and Mark had little in common and, on their one-year anniversary, Annie asked for a divorce.

She had been twenty-three when the *decree absolute* was granted, and Annie felt foolish and ashamed of the whole experience, embarrassed by her naivety, and wondering how she'd been so blind to what everyone else could clearly see. It made her seriously question her own judgement, realising that she'd been more concerned with finding her Hollywood-style epic romance than making sure she'd picked the right man to spend the rest of her life with.

In the wake of the divorce, Annie re-enrolled at university, throwing herself into her studies, before finally setting up her own therapy practice. She'd dated tentatively over the years, but there'd been nothing serious, and she was terrified of making another big mistake.

'Listen,' Holly began gently, seeing Annie lost in her memories. 'There's this new guy that's started work with Greg. He's called Tom, and he's single, and Greg's told him about you…'

'Holly,' Annie sighed. 'I really don't know if—'

'Where's the harm?' Holly cut her off. 'Just go for one date. If you don't like him, you never have to see him again. If you *do* like him… badda bing, badda boom!'

Annie couldn't help laughing at her sister's enthusiasm. 'What's that supposed to mean?'

'I don't know really,' Holly giggled. 'But it's definitely a good thing. So what do you say? Hang on, let me find him on Facebook. He's friends with Greg, so I should be able to…' She scrolled through her phone, a look of intense concentration on her face. 'There,' Holly finished triumphantly. 'Not bad-looking, is he?'

Annie took the phone from her sister and scrutinised the photograph. The guy in the picture had dark hair and a square jaw line, and he was grinning at the camera, his dark eyes sparkling. Annie was pleasantly surprised. 'He looks okay, actually. What's the catch?'

'Maybe there isn't one. Maybe he just hasn't met the right woman yet.'

'Or maybe he's a mummy's boy who still wets the bed, and calls all women "princess",' Annie suggested dryly. 'Oh, no, he can't be, because I've already been out with him – Trevor from King's Lynn, remember? *And* he had that medical issue with the overactive sweat glands.' Annie shuddered at the memory.

'So what do you say?' Holly pressed, ignoring Annie's outburst. 'Can I tell Greg to pass on your number?'

Annie took a deep breath and closed her eyes, unable to shake the feeling that, once again, Holly had managed to wear her down and get her to agree to something she didn't want to do.

'Okay then, you win,' she shrugged, as Holly let out a cheer. 'You can give him my details. Just don't get your hopes up.'

'We'll see. You'll be thanking me at the wedding,' Holly winked.

Chapter 4

*'Women need a reason to have sex.
Men just need a place'* – **Billy Crystal**

'I still don't know what we're doing here,' Julia muttered irritably, her eyes darting around the small waiting room.

Nick sighed. 'We've been over this, Julia. You agreed to come. For my sake.'

'Well, I think it's bloody ridiculous. We'd be better off going to a *real* doctor to find out if there are any problems,' Julia continued, with a pointed look at Nick's crotch, 'than some quack who's going to talk to us about our *feelings* and probably never—'

The door swung open and Julia quickly stopped talking as Annie strode towards them, her arm outstretched.

'You must be Nick and Julia,' she smiled, as they all shook hands. 'Please, come through.'

They followed her through into the office, noting the degree certificates, the neat pile of papers on the desk and the open laptop.

'Do take a seat. Can I get either of you a drink?'

'We're fine, thank you,' Julia cut in quickly. She didn't intend to stay for long, so saw little point in making herself at home.

'No problem. So, Nick, you spoke to me a little on the phone about your reasons for coming here,' Annie began, noting the way that Julia's gaze darted suspiciously to her husband. 'Julia, why don't you start, and tell me how you view the situation.'

'There isn't a *situation*,' Julia replied, sounding frustrated. 'I don't even know why Nick wanted to come here in the first place. We've been trying for a baby for almost a year now, and I haven't got pregnant yet,' she continued, carefully avoiding Nick's gaze as she spoke. 'The way I see it is that we just keep trying until it happens. And if it doesn't, then we'll go to see a *proper* doctor.'

Annie nodded, deciding not to acknowledge Julia's insult. She could see that this woman was hurting badly, that she was angry and lashing out. Annie knew it was nothing personal.

'If you do think that there's a medical problem, then I would definitely advise you to go and speak to your GP. Obviously that's not what I'm here for. My role is to help you identify, and hopefully overcome, any issues affecting your sex life.'

'We don't have any issues,' Julia responded defensively. 'If you must know, we have sex almost every day, so I don't really understand what this whole thing is about.'

'Okay,' Annie said thoughtfully. This was clearly going to be a tough case, but it wasn't the first time she'd dealt with a tricky couple – clients were often in denial at first, and didn't make significant breakthroughs until a few weeks down the line. 'Nick, you obviously *did* feel there was a reason to come and see me. Can you explain what that was?'

Nick turned to Julia; she was glaring at him, her expression furious, and he wondered how best to proceed. 'I feel…' Nick began, pausing as he tried to think of the right words. 'I feel as though you don't care about me any more. It's like you're obsessed with having a baby, and that's all that matters to you.'

Julia rolled her eyes. 'Oh, grow up, Nick. The world doesn't revolve around you. If this is what you're like now, how are you going to feel when we actually *do* have a baby, and I'm run off my feet looking after it?'

'That's not what I meant!' Nick looked stung. He glanced over at Annie who nodded, encouraging him to go on. 'I'm not some child who's desperate for your attention, so don't treat me like that. All I want is for us to have a normal relationship, like we used to. But look at us – we barely talk these days. Yes, we have a lot of sex, but there's no connection there. I feel like if you could reproduce on your own, then you would, but unfortunately you need me there too.'

'Don't be so ridiculous,' Julia snapped. She was clearly livid, and the tension hung heavily in the air.

'Julia,' Annie pressed gently. 'How would you describe your sex life?'

'There's nothing wrong with our sex life! It's good. It's certainly very regular.' Julia turned triumphantly to Nick. 'I have friends who sleep with their husbands once a week, once a fortnight – sometimes even once a month. You get it practically every day, and you're still complaining.'

'It's not about how often,' Nick protested. 'I'd be happy with once a week if it seemed like you actually wanted to be there. We don't even bother with foreplay any more – you just want to get the whole thing over with as quickly as possible.'

Julia let out a slightly manic, high-pitched laugh. 'Have you ever heard a man complain about that before?' she demanded, turning to Annie. 'Too much sex and not enough foreplay? What a joke.'

'There's no right and wrong with what either of you want, and you need to remember that,' Annie told them firmly. 'But it's about finding a happy medium that suits the both of you. It's about compromise, and listening to the other person.'

Neither of them spoke, and Annie continued, 'I think the way forward is to take the focus off getting pregnant for a while – just for a few weeks or so – and back onto the two of you. Onto reconnecting, and rediscovering the reasons you fell in love in the first place. Julia, what made you fall for Nick?'

Julia's expression softened for the first time, her eyes brightening. 'He was so handsome, and so funny too. He really made me laugh.'

'Great,' Annie smiled, pleased with her response. 'Nick, what about Julia?'

'She was – is – absolutely gorgeous. I fancied her so much. And then when I spoke to her, she was so feisty and opinionated. She was definitely a challenge, but in a good way.'

'Julia, you said that one of the things that drew you to Nick was that he made you laugh. That's wonderful, and a shared sense of humour can be hugely important in a relationship. When would you say is the last time the two of you had a really good laugh together?'

Julia frowned, momentarily looking confused. 'He… I can't remember exactly. I mean, we've both been very busy – we both work long hours and… That's a stupid question! Why would I remember something like that? It's like asking whether or not I brushed my teeth this morning. It just sort of… happens.'

But Nick was shaking his head. 'No, it doesn't just happen. Not these days, anyway. Let's face it, we're both bloody miserable. I can't seem to make you happy like I used to. And that's why I wanted to come here, to these sessions.'

Julia said nothing. There was another long, uncomfortable pause, before Annie eventually broke the silence.

'I appreciate both of you being so honest with me, and I think we've made a very positive start. What I'm going to suggest that you do – and this may sound a little odd, but give me a chance to explain. I want you not to have sex for the next week.'

Julia's head snapped up in alarm. 'What? But I'm at my most fertile on Friday! If we miss this window, I've blown my best chance of getting pregnant for a month. No, I'm not do-ing it. Absolutely not.'

'The reason I've suggested this,' Annie continued, in mea-sured, soothing tones, 'is that I genuinely think it would help the two of you to strengthen your relationship. It would be one week without the pressure of trying to conceive, and during that time you can really focus on each other. I'm not saying don't go near each other. In fact, the whole point is to do everything *but* have intercourse. You can treat each other to a nice massage, spend time exploring each other's bodies, even enjoy oral sex. Just find other ways to pleasure each other.'

Julia's lips were pursed into a tight line, her whole body language indicating that she didn't have the slightest inten-tion of going along with Annie's suggestion.

'Do you remember how exciting it was to kiss when you were a teenager?' Annie tried again. 'The joy of lying for hours on the sofa, having a good old snog, knowing that things were unlikely to go any further than that? Well, why not recreate that? Go to the cinema, sit in the back row, and miss half of the film.'

'We're not teenagers,' Julia protested, rolling her eyes. 'We're grown adults, and I want to have sex!'

'I think Annie might have a point,' Nick spoke up. 'A sex-free week might be just what we need. We can go for dinner somewhere really nice – maybe even go away for the weekend. I can run you a nice bubble bath and—'

'A nice bubble bath isn't going to help me conceive, is it Nick?' Julia snapped. 'How am I going to have a baby if we don't have sex, hmm? It's basic biology! The stork isn't going to leave one under a gooseberry bush for us to find, is it?'

'Julia, I don't want you to think about getting pregnant, just for seven days.' Annie's voice was calm, yet firm, as she tried to explain, but Julia wouldn't listen.

'No!' she exclaimed, jumping to her feet. 'I don't want to do this. I don't know why we came, and I want to leave. Now!'

'Jules, please.' Nick tried to grab his wife's hand, but Julia tugged it away.

'No, I'm leaving, Nick. I don't know why I ever let you talk me into this.' And with that, Julia ran out of the door.

Nick stood for a moment in absolute shock, uncertainty written across his face as he tried to decide what to do for the best.

'Sorry. I'm so sorry,' he blurted out to Annie, before running out of the door and after his wife.

❄ ❄ ❄

Annie sat in stunned silence for a moment, slowly blowing out the air in her cheeks. She waited for a few minutes, but it seemed apparent that Nick and Julia weren't coming back. It was such a shame, Annie reflected. She'd seen situations like this time and time again; both partners hurt and angry, throwing away what they had because they were too stubborn to consider their other half's point of view.

What she really needed now, Annie decided, was a nice, calming cup of tea. She stood up from behind her desk and headed down the corridor to the communal kitchen, thinking about what she could possibly do to help Nick and Julia. She wondered whether they would come back. She hoped Nick would call her at least, then she could check that everything was okay with them, maybe make some suggestions to—

'Someone's having a tough day.'

Annie looked up, startled, to see Jamie Kennedy sitting at the kitchen table, a cup of coffee in his hand and a magazine open in front of him. Jamie worked in one of the other units and ran a software design company with his brother, Matt, working on everything from business programs to video game development.

'I was in my own world,' Annie admitted, feeling embarrassed. 'I didn't see you there.'

'Charming,' Jamie retorted with a grin. He was in his early thirties, with dark blond hair and blue eyes, and he was currently dressed in grey suit trousers and a creased shirt, the sleeves pushed up past his elbows. His body language was relaxed, his long legs stretched out under the table.

'Catching up with *Take a Break*?' Annie teased, as she walked past and saw what he was reading.

'What? Oh!' Jamie laughed. 'We really need to get some more masculine reads around her,' he told her, deliberately lowering his voice a couple of octaves. 'Ones with sports cars and bikini-clad women and… bloke stuff!'

'Nah, you love it. "I caught my husband naked with the neighbour",' Annie read over his shoulder, as Jamie slammed the magazine shut.

'I thought that sort of thing was more your department,' he commented wryly.

'I don't know if anything's my department,' Annie sighed, thinking of how badly the session with Nick and Julia had just gone.

'Why? What's happened?'

'Oh, just a tough first session with a new client,' Annie replied, as she turned on the kettle then reached into the biscuit tin for a chocolate HobNob. 'Sometimes people can be their own worst enemy. You wouldn't think it would be so hard to communicate your feelings to the person you married, would you?'

Jamie smiled indulgently. 'Don't you ever get tired of listening to other people's problems?'

'Not really. Everyone's different – no two cases are the same – and I always want to find a way to help if I can. It's very satisfying. I guess I'm just a sucker for a happy ending,' she confessed. 'How about you? How's everything with your business?'

'Busy, believe it or not. I know it might not look like it,' Jamie grinned, nodding at his coffee and magazine. 'I'm just taking a screen break. Your eyes go square after a while.'

'So what are you working on at the moment?'

Jamie raised an eyebrow. 'If I told you I'd have to kill you. Nah, we're designing a new app for a travel company. It's pretty cool, actually. You put in your budget, and the kind of holiday you want – beach, city break, culture, etc. – and it brings up the top deals for you.'

'Sounds great. Is it going to make you a millionaire?'

'Fingers crossed. I don't know whether it's quite as catchy as *Angry Birds* though.'

'Shame,' Annie replied, helping herself to a second HobNob. Before she could put the lid back on, Jamie had sneaked up behind her and snatched one out of the tin.

'Biscuits help you think more clearly. It's a fact,' Jamie told her, his blue eyes sparkling.

'Hmm, I'm not sure that's very scientific, but I choose to believe you,' Annie retorted, taking a bite.

Jamie ate his biscuit in two mouthfuls, washing it down with the last of his coffee. 'I'd better get back to it,' he said reluctantly, glancing up at the clock.

Annie followed his gaze. 'Me too. I don't have long until my next appointment, and I want to catch up with some paperwork before then.'

'Roll on retirement,' Jamie smiled.

'You know you love it really,' Annie teased him. 'Anyway, don't you just sit around all day playing games on your Sega Mega Drive?'

'Xbox One actually. You're so 1990s.'

'Don't the kids these days still play Tetris?' Annie wondered, feigning confusion.

'If they don't, they should. Pure genius, that game.'

'Ah, memories,' Annie sighed.

'Well, I'd better run,' Jamie said, stealing one final biscuit before heading for the door. 'Have a great day, Annie.'

'Thanks, Jamie,' she smiled. 'You too.'

Chapter 5

'Nice girls like sex too' – **Hugh Hefner**

'Hi, babe! Happy birthday!'

'Thanks,' Zoe grinned at her boyfriend, Simon, as he swept her into his arms and kissed her, oblivious to the stares of passers-by on the street. At six foot one and almost sixteen stone, he was a huge bear of a man, and Zoe loved the fact that he could scoop her up and throw her over his shoulder as though she weighed nothing. His size made her feel secure and protected, and she was pretty keen on the way he could throw her around in the bedroom too…

'Have you been waiting long?' Simon asked. In the distance, the church bells were chiming six.

'No, only a couple of minutes. Are you okay? You look a bit weird.'

'I'm fine,' Simon insisted, smoothing back his sandy hair. His large, heavy-set face was flushed and shiny, his hazel eyes glittering. 'I've just been rushing around. I didn't want to leave you standing here alone on your birthday.'

'Let's head in, it's freezing out here.' Zoe slipped her gloved hand into Simon's, and they made their way into Blue Mango, their favourite Thai restaurant, on Exchange Street. Inside it was warm and cosy and smelt delicious, the air heavy with the aroma of lemongrass, chilli and ginger.

Only a handful of the tables were occupied, and the waiter rushed over to greet them, seating them at a window table.

'Wow, you look gorgeous,' Simon exclaimed, practically salivating as Zoe shrugged off her coat. She was wearing a dark blue wrap dress, which perfectly showed off her petite figure and pale skin. Her long, copper-coloured hair was left loose, and she'd added just a touch of make-up to emphasise her clear, blue eyes.

'You don't scrub up too badly yourself,' Zoe grinned, thinking how handsome he looked in his smart grey trousers and a pale blue shirt – a real contrast to the casual overalls and hoodies he usually wore for work.

The two of them placed their orders: Pad Thai with prawns for Zoe, and chicken jungle curry for Simon, with a bottle of white wine to share.

'Happy birthday to my gorgeous girlfriend,' Simon toasted, when their drinks arrived.

Zoe found herself blushing as a couple of people overheard what he'd said, turning round to smile at them. 'Thank you,' she murmured. 'And thanks for my earrings. I love them,' she added, indicating the sparkly studs in her ears.

'You're very welcome,' Simon replied, as she blew a kiss at him across the table.

It was Zoe's twenty-fifth birthday, but despite hitting the quarter-of-a-century milestone, she and Simon had both had to work that day. To make up for it, Simon had surprised her with breakfast in bed that morning, accompanied by a pile of presents. There'd been the latest book by Jojo Moyes, half a dozen cupcakes from her favourite bakery, and some lush smellies from The Body Shop. Zoe's heart had begun to race when she'd unwrapped the blue velvet jewellery box – she and Simon had been together for three years now, and everyone kept asking when it would be their turn to walk down the aisle – and when she'd opened it she'd found the beautiful earrings nestled inside. If Zoe was being completely honest, she couldn't help but feel a stab of disappointment.

'So how was your day?' Simon asked solicitously.

'It was good. Busy as usual. We had a Persian cat with a seizure – Patrick suspected it was epilepsy – and we had to run tests straight away, which was pretty hectic, but the cat's recovering well and they sorted out medication, so that's good.'

Zoe worked as a veterinary assistant. Originally from Chester, she'd studied Veterinary Nursing at Norwich University, and stayed in the city ever since.

'And then Jackie got me a card, and a Colin the Caterpillar cake from Marks and Spencer's, which was sweet of her,' Zoe continued. 'We shared it amongst everyone on our tea break, and it was scrummy.' She frowned at Simon, who appeared to be staring off into space, giving him a playful nudge under the table. 'Are you listening to me?'

He looked up, startled. 'Sorry, yes. Persian. Seizure. Colin the Caterpillar. Scrummy. See?' he replied smugly, reaching across the table to take her hands. 'I'm the perfect boyfriend.'

'I don't know about that... Pretty close though,' Zoe smiled, weaving her fingers through his.

After three years together, the two of them were blissfully happy and still madly in love. Their sex life was great – regular and experimental – and neither of them was exactly shy in the bedroom. Or the living room. Or the bathroom.

Their friends were always teasing them, telling them to 'get a room' when they got a little too amorous in public, but both Zoe and Simon were eager to make sure that their sex life stayed fresh and exciting. In fact, tonight Zoe was wearing a brand new set of underwear that she knew Simon would love; even though it was *her* birthday, she wanted to give *him* a treat as well.

'Your Pad Thai, madam,' announced the waiter, and Zoe found herself blushing, as she snapped out of her naughty thoughts.

'How was work?' she asked Simon, as she speared a forkful of her food.

Simon shrugged in reply. 'Okay, I suppose. Obviously the season hasn't really got going yet, so I'm just doing general maintenance and repairs at the moment, making sure everything's ready for when we start getting busy. We've got a few bookings in for half term, but it won't really take off until Easter.'

Simon worked for his father, Brian, who ran a boat hire company on the Norfolk Broads. They rented out narrowboats and cabin cruisers for tourists to explore the maze of canals and waterways for which the county was famous. The business was hugely popular in the summer months, with families and groups of friends lured by the prospect of a week messing about in boats, stopping off at pubs along the way, and being lulled to sleep at night by the gently lapping water.

Zoe and Simon would sometimes borrow a vessel for the weekend, cruising the river by day and making passionate love in the tiny cabin at night. It was incredibly romantic.

'A couple of the boats are in for repairs at the moment, and I think I'm going to completely repaint the *Big Dipper*. She's looking a bit old and scruffy,' Simon continued.

'The *Big Dipper*? I thought you said your dad had sold that one, at the end of last summer?'

'Did I? Oh yeah, I meant the *Carolina*,' Simon corrected himself.

Zoe frowned. Her boyfriend was *definitely* behaving weirdly. He seemed oddly distracted, zoning in and out of their conversation. As Zoe watched, he pulled back his shirt cuff and checked his watch – for the second time in as many minutes.

'Sorry, am I keeping you from something?' Zoe asked sweetly.

'What? No, just making sure we're there on time for the show. We have to collect the tickets by seven thirty.'

As part of Zoe's birthday present, Simon had arranged for them to go and see *Grease* at the Theatre Royal, and Zoe was beyond excited.

'Relax, we've got plenty of time. It's not even half six yet,' Zoe reassured him. 'Mmm, this food is delicious. Is yours okay? You've hardly touched it.'

'Oh, it's great,' Simon assured her, digging in heartily. 'I'm just not that hungry, I suppose.'

'That's unlike you,' Zoe laughed. Being a big guy, Simon was known for his hearty appetite. 'Did you have a late lunch? Or maybe you're coming down with something. You look a little feverish,' she added worriedly, taking in the sheen of sweat on his forehead, and his flushed complexion.

'I'll be fine,' Simon insisted, breaking out into that grin she loved so much. 'And nothing will stop me from seeing the show tonight, don't worry.'

'Good!' Zoe exclaimed. 'I know I keep going on about it, but I absolutely love *Grease*. It's one of Mum's favourite films, so we watched it all the time when I was a kid. Me and my friend Claire, from back home, used to make up dance routines to the songs. She was always Sandy, and I had to be Frenchy, because of my hair,' Zoe giggled, indicating her russet-red waves.

'Mmm,' Simon replied distractedly.

'What's wrong with you tonight?' Zoe demanded, dropping her fork with a clatter.

Simon looked up in alarm. 'Nothing, nothing. I'm so sorry, babe.' He reached out across the table, taking her hands once more and softly stroking her palms with his fingertips. 'Nothing's wrong. I just want to make sure everything goes perfectly on your birthday, that's all.'

'Aww, that's so sweet,' Zoe murmured, her anger disappearing as quickly as it had arrived. 'But you don't need to worry. Everything's going to be amazing.'

'I hope so,' Simon replied, blowing out the air in his cheeks. 'I really hope so.'

❄ ❄ ❄

Zoe couldn't tear her eyes away from the stage, a huge grin plastered across her face as she watched the talented performers bring to life the world of *Grease*. The show was nearing its finale, with the cast singing about how they were always going to be together. It was a whirl of colour and energy, the girls twirling in their fifties-style skirts, the boys looking hot in their T-Bird leather jackets. Zoe couldn't help singing along to the familiar tunes, and a quick glance around told her that she wasn't the only one; the audience were clapping their hands and tapping their toes as they joined in.

Zoe glanced over at Simon to see if he was enjoying it as much as she was but, to her surprise, he looked terrible. He was staring off into the distance, his face deathly pale. He'd been acting strangely all evening; during the interval, he'd treated them both to a glass of champagne, but every time Zoe tried to talk to him he seemed distracted and on edge. After a few minutes he disappeared to the bathroom and didn't come back until the interval was almost over, leaving Zoe alone, self-consciously sipping her birthday fizz.

'Are you okay?' she whispered anxiously.

Simon stared at her, his eyes wide. 'Stay here. I'll be back soon.'

He went to stand up, but Zoe grabbed his arm and pulled him back down. 'What?' she asked in confusion. 'Are you ill? Shall I come with you?'

'No!' Simon practically snapped. 'Stay here. I'll be okay.'

He clambered over the feet of the people seated next to them, hastily making his way into the aisle and bolting through the exit doors.

Zoe watched in disbelief, wondering what she should do. Back on stage, *Grease* was reaching its climax, the audience cheering as Danny and Sandy drove off in a specially designed red Cadillac. The cast came forward to take their bows, but Zoe barely noticed. Her hands moved mechanically, joining in as everyone around her clapped wildly, but all of her attention was focused on the door through which Simon had sprinted, wondering whether or not she should follow him.

The audience gradually quietened down, as the actors playing Danny and Sandy held up their hands, calling for silence. Zoe was only half listening as the pair began to speak.

'We hope you all enjoyed our show tonight, and we'd like to say a huge thank you for coming to see us. Danny and Sandy found their happy ever after, but tonight we're hoping to make someone else's dream come true. We've got someone here who'd like to say a few words.'

The cast stood aside, and a man made his way through the middle, his bulky frame dominating the stage. He looked terrified, his eyes bulging like a rabbit caught in the headlights, as he took in the hundreds of people in front of him, all watching him expectantly.

Zoe looked up and gasped, her hands flying to her face in shock. It couldn't be, could it? But it was! It was Simon. What on earth was he doing on stage with the cast of *Grease*?

As Zoe watched, he turned towards where she was sitting, his eyes seeking her out in the mass of people. When he found her, he seemed to relax a little. Then, clearing his throat, he began to speak.

'Happy birthday to my gorgeous girlfriend, Zoe. I love you so much, and I wanted tonight to be truly memorable for you.'

His voice was shaky to start with, but his confidence was growing with every word. Out in the audience, people were twisting around, trying to work out who his speech was directed at. Zoe's heart was thumping, and she could feel that her cheeks had turned red.

'Which is why I wanted to ask…' Simon continued.

Suddenly, Zoe knew what was coming. She let out a cry as Simon got down on one knee, a ring box in his hands. His gaze was focused directly on her, and at that moment it seemed as though they were the only two people in the entire auditorium. There were gasps from the audience then the entire room fell silent.

'…Zoe Miller, will you marry me?'

Time seemed to slow. Everyone on stage was now staring at Zoe, the packed audience craning their necks to try to catch a glimpse of her.

Zoe opened her mouth to speak. 'Yes,' she whispered. The word came out as a croak, her voice barely audible, and she had to repeat herself. 'Yes!'

'She said yes!' shouted a man nearby.

The crowd took up the cry, relaying the message to Simon. 'She said yes, she said yes!' Then the applause broke out again, people whooping and cheering as the cast beckoned for Zoe to come and join Simon. The crowd parted as she made her way along the aisle, her legs shaky as she walked up to the front. Someone helped her onto the stage, and then Zoe fell into Simon's arms, the spotlight beaming down on them as the crowd oohed and aahed. It felt like an incredible dream.

Simon wrapped his arms around her, and Zoe realised that tears were streaming down her face, as he covered her with kisses and pushed the ring onto her finger.

'It matches your new earrings,' he teased, as Zoe looked down to see the glittering diamond on the silver band.

'I can't believe it,' she stammered. 'I can't believe you did all this.'

'I wanted it to be something you'd never forget. I love you, Zoe.'

The curtain fell around them, shielding them from the prying eyes of the audience and finally giving them a moment of privacy. Zoe looked up at her new fiancé and kissed him, long and hard, snuggling into his arms. The moment couldn't have been more perfect.

'I love you too, Simon,' she told him, when they finally came up for air. 'I love you so much, and I can't wait to be your wife.'

Chapter 6

'You know that look women get when they want to have sex? Me neither' – **Steve Martin**

'Hi Rose,' Ray smiled, the bell tinkling as he walked into the flower shop. Named 'Expressions', it was small, but extensively stocked, and he inhaled the glorious scent of lilies, freesias, dahlias and sweet peas, all standing round in silver buckets.

'Hi Dad, how are you?' Rose asked, coming out from behind the counter to give him a kiss on the cheek. She was medium height and slim, with thick brunette curls tied back in a ponytail.

'Oh, not bad, you know. Is your mum around?'

'She's just out the back – I'll give her a shout. Mum!' Rose yelled. 'Dad's here.'

'So how's everything with you?' Ray enquired, as they waited. 'How are the kids?'

'Great. Running me ragged as usual. Josh's best friend at school has just got a guinea pig, so he's been driving us mad asking for a pet. I don't know whether I've got the time to look after an animal, but it seems mean not to let him have something. It might be a good way to teach him about responsibility.'

'Do you remember when you and Marianne got that hamster?' Ray chuckled. 'You were so disappointed because it slept all day, and only woke up after you'd gone to bed.'

'We took it out to play in the garden and it ran away,' Rose remembered guiltily. 'I'm sure next door's cat ate it.'

They chatted easily and, after a couple of minutes, Linda emerged. She had shoulder-length wavy hair, which was dyed a flattering shade of ash blonde, and a softly curved body that had long since given up the fight against middle-age spread. Right now, she looked flustered, her arms full of beautiful dusky pink peonies.

'Ray – I didn't expect you here today.'

'I thought I'd surprise you,' he replied cheerily.

'I see.' Linda sounded distinctly underwhelmed. She seemed distracted, glancing round the shop before laying the flowers down on the counter.

Ray cleared his throat, trying to stay positive. 'I wondered if there was any chance of you knocking off a bit early? I thought we could go grab a bite to eat or something.'

'I don't know about that.' Linda frowned. 'We've got a lot on here, and I'm right in the middle of doing this display for the Guildhall. You could have rung and given me a bit of warning.'

'It wouldn't have been a surprise then, would it?' Ray said lightly. 'What about the St Giles for afternoon tea? You used to love doing that.'

'What's come over you, Dad?' Rose teased, picking up one of the peonies and twirling the stem between her fingers.

Ray shuffled awkwardly, looking embarrassed. 'Nothing. I just thought I'd treat my wife for once. Make an effort.' He turned back to Linda, feeling as though he was issuing a challenge. There was no real reason for her to turn him down, but he got the distinct impression that she didn't want to go. 'So, what do you say?' he pressed.

'Well… I don't know…'

'Oh, go on, Mum,' Rose encouraged. 'We're quietening down now, and I can always finish that Guildhall arrangement.'

Linda felt cornered. She looked from Ray to Rose, and then back again. 'Okay,' she agreed finally. 'I'll just put in the gypsophila, then grab my coat.'

As she headed through to the back of the shop, Rose grinned at her father. 'Trying to recapture the romance?'

'Something like that,' Ray admitted, aware that his daughter was uncomfortably close to the truth.

'Good for you,' she beamed. 'It's nice for you two to spend a bit of quality time together. And Mum could certainly do with a treat, after today.'

'Have you been busy?'

'Yeah, it's been manic. All the Valentine's orders are starting to come through, and it's only going to get worse over the next week. You know we're always rushed off our feet at this time of year.'

Ray smiled sentimentally. 'And of course, your mother's the only woman I know who *doesn't* want an enormous bouquet on Valentine's Day.'

'No, Mum's always sick of the sight of them,' Rose laughed.

Expressions was a family business, established by Linda almost thirty years ago. When her three children – Rose, Marianne and Robbie – started school, Linda found herself at something of a loose end. She'd always dreamt of owning a flower shop and, using a small inheritance she'd received, coupled with a loan from the bank, she scraped together enough to buy the tiny shop on Pottergate. With hard work and a lot of love, she converted the property from an old fishmongers into the pretty little florist's, and over the years she'd seen it flourish into a thriving business.

As the kids grew older, they took turns helping out at weekends and school holidays. Rose discovered that she'd inherited her mother's creative flair, as well as her passion for flowers, and when she left college she came to work for the business full time.

Now Expressions employed a Saturday girl, Katie, and Linda had planned to cut down her hours in recent years, but somehow that hadn't quite happened. Almost every day, she could still be found creating beautiful bouquets in the little workshop out the back, or serving her regular customers in the shop. Having built the business up from scratch, Linda was reluctant to let it go.

'By the way, I checked with Mum, and she said it'd be fine for you to have Josh and Harry tomorrow night,' Rose continued. 'Adam's offered to take me out for dinner. It's our date night, so I couldn't really say no.'

Ray nodded thoughtfully. Between babysitting their grandchildren, working part time in their respective jobs, and looking after Linda's elderly mother, it sometimes felt as though he and his wife barely got to see each other.

Linda emerged from the back, fastening her thick woollen coat. She pulled on her gloves – there was a bitter wind today – and settled the strap of her handbag on her shoulder.

'Now are you sure you'll be all right, Rose? Because I don't mind staying on.'

'I'll be fine. You get off and have a lovely afternoon. Make sure to bring me back a slice of cake,' Rose replied, only half-joking.

'See you later, love,' Ray called, as he opened the door for Linda and followed her outside.

'So what's all this about then?' she asked suspiciously, as they set off walking towards St Giles Street.

'It just seemed like a while since we'd done anything special together. I thought I'd be spontaneous,' Ray explained, reaching out to take Linda's hand.

The gesture felt awkward and unnatural, and Ray realised that he couldn't remember the last time they'd held hands in public. Come to think of it, he couldn't remember the last time they'd displayed any kind of physical affection towards one other at all. It was one of the many things that seemed to have fallen by the wayside, leaving them as little more than long-term acquaintances who happened to share a house. They communicated about whether they were running short of milk, and who was going to take the car for its service, or what was on the television tonight, but it was years since they'd talked about anything significant. Ray hoped that today would mark the start of a change between them.

They strolled along briskly, making small talk, until they reached the beautiful baroque building that was the St Giles House Hotel. Ray rested a hand on his wife's back as they walked up the front steps, heading across the black and white parquet floor and into the cosy lounge.

'Table for two, for afternoon tea, please.'

'Certainly.' The young waitress smiled at them as she showed them to a table by the far window. 'I'll bring your tea and cakes over shortly.'

'Well, this is all very nice,' Linda commented, looking slightly cheerier as she took off her coat and glanced around the room. It was smartly decorated in shades of burgundy and chocolate brown, and piano music was playing quietly in the background. Half a dozen of the other tables were occupied, and there was a low buzz of chatter, a tinkling of crockery.

'I'm glad you like it.'

'Oh, Rose asked if we could have the boys tomorrow night,' Linda remembered. 'I said it wouldn't be a problem.'

'Yes, she mentioned it,' Ray nodded. 'Adam's taking her for dinner, apparently.'

'Well, you're only young once, aren't you? It's good for them to have some time on their own, away from the kids.'

Ray nodded again, but couldn't seem to stop the words from bubbling up inside of him: 'What about us? When are *we* going to have some time alone together?'

His tone was resentful, and Linda looked shocked.

'We're having time alone together now, aren't we? Surely you don't begrudge Rose and Adam a night out? She works so hard in the shop.'

'It's not that,' Ray began earnestly, stopping short as the waitress came back over carrying two large pots of tea. She set them down, returning moments later with a three-tiered cake stand laden with sandwiches, fresh scones and delicate bite-size desserts.

'Mmm, this all looks delicious,' Linda remarked, helping herself to a triangular-shaped cucumber sandwich with the crusts cut off.

Ray took an egg and cress one, although he could rapidly feel his appetite deserting him. He hoped Linda would be open to what he had to say, but the thought of broaching the subject of therapy with her was truly terrifying.

'We should do this kind of thing more often,' Ray suggested, as he blew across the surface of his tea to cool it. 'Don't you think? Just you and me, taking time for ourselves, without the kids or the grandkids.'

Linda made a non-committal noise, and Ray pushed on, 'I mean, once we both took semi-retirement, I thought we'd be able to treat ourselves more often, but that flower shop seems to take up as much of your time as it ever did.'

Linda put her cup down sharply; there was a loud chink as it hit the saucer. 'Is that what this is about?' she demanded, her eyes flashing angrily. 'The fact that I'm still working in Expressions? I built that shop up from nothing, as well you know, and I *enjoy* working there. It gives me a sense of purpose that I wouldn't get from playing golf,' she finished pointedly.

Ray ignored the insult and pressed on. 'But there doesn't seem to be time for *us* any more and, quite frankly, I miss it. I miss the closeness, I miss the intimacy, and most of all, I miss *you*,' he finished softly, sliding his hand across the table to take hold of Linda's.

She snatched it away furiously. 'Oh, I see what this is *really* all about. The *closeness*, the *intimacy*,' she parodied him. 'It all comes down to S-E-X with you, doesn't it?' A half-eaten miniature éclair lay discarded on her plate, as Linda pursed her lips tightly.

'It is important to me, yes,' Ray acknowledged. He kept his voice low, even though the room was largely empty and the nearest people to them – two women in their mid-twenties – were three tables away and not paying the slightest bit of attention as they giggled and gossiped over a bottle of champagne.

'Yes, well, I'm fifty-eight. I'll be drawing a pension in a few years. Excuse me if I'm not swinging from the chandeliers every night,' Linda hissed.

'I'm not expecting that – just now and again would be nice. I'm fifty-nine, not dead,' Ray shot back.

The two of them glared at each other, the tension heavy in the air between them. Without speaking, Linda stabbed a scone, deftly slicing it in two and smothering it with cream and jam. She began eating in silence, completely ignoring her husband.

Finally, Ray let out a long sigh. 'I've been thinking that maybe we should go and see someone.'

'See someone? What on earth are you talking about?'

'Someone like… a counsellor. Or a therapist.'

There, he had finally said it! Ray swallowed nervously, waiting to see what Linda's reaction would be.

'I do *not* need therapy.' She looked furious, and Ray felt glad that they were in a public place where Linda couldn't make a scene. 'Maybe *you* need to be a little more understanding.'

'I *have* been understanding. But this isn't a healthy situation, love. I'm trying to do something about it, not ignore it until it's too late and we're both old and unhappy.'

'I'm perfectly fine, thank you very much.'

'No,' Ray said gently. 'You're not. *We're* not.'

Linda fumed silently, thinking about what Ray had just said. Finally, she burst out: 'So you want me to go and see someone? You want me to stand around in my underwear while some strange man pokes and prods at me? I've never heard anything so ridiculous!'

'It's not like that,' Ray insisted. 'It's more about talking – working through whatever issues we've got, and then being given exercises to try at home. Annie said that we—' Too late, Ray realised his mistake, and quickly shut up.

Linda looked at him sharply. 'Annie? Who's Annie?'

'She's… she's a therapist,' Ray admitted, realising that he'd dug himself into a hole. 'Specialising in relationships. I went to see her last week.'

Linda's mouth fell open. 'You did *what*? You went to see a stranger, and you told them our private business?'

'Linda, it's—'

'You told another woman that you weren't satisfied with our marriage?'

'Please, love,' Ray begged. 'It wasn't like that. She's there to help us. We can have individual meetings with her, and she also runs group sessions at the weekend—'

'Group sessions?' Linda looked outraged. 'What exactly are you expecting from me, Raymond? You want me to participate in some kind of orgy, is that it? That's the most disgusting thing I've ever heard.'

'No, no, it's nothing like that,' Ray explained hastily. 'It's more like group therapy, apparently, and Annie thinks it could be really helpful for us. But we don't have to do anything you don't want to…' He trailed off, his expression desperate as he looked over at his wife. 'I just want us to be how we used to be. I don't even… I don't even know if you love me any more.'

Ray's voice cracked on the final words, and he looked thoroughly defeated. His head was bowed, his hands resting limply on the tablecloth beside his untouched plate of food.

Linda stared at him across the table. Her face was stricken, her eyes wide and shiny with tears. 'I… I don't know either,' she admitted, and her voice was little more than a whisper.

Chapter 7

'No sex is better than bad sex' – **Germaine Greer**

Annie cautiously approached the man standing at the bar, quickly taking in his appearance. Smartly dressed in relaxed jeans and a fitted T-shirt, his hair was freshly washed and his shoes shiny. At first glance, there were no obvious flaws, and he was definitely attractive.

He said something to the barmaid, and she laughed – apparently he was funny too. So why did Annie feel as though she wanted to run away, a sinking sensation in her stomach accompanied by sweaty palms and a mild feeling of nausea?

Oh, why had she ever agreed to this? She could be sat at home right now, watching *The Great British Bake Off*, while Harry and Sally swam contentedly beside her.

Is that what you want? a voice inside her head demanded. *To grow old and alone – not even a crazy cat lady, but a crazy* goldfish *lady?*

Taking a deep breath, Annie strode over to the man, a bright smile plastered on her face.

'Tom?'

'Annie! Lovely to meet you,' he exclaimed, kissing her on the cheek. 'How did you know it was me?'

'I recognised you from your Facebook photo,' Annie admitted. Then, realising that it might sound as though she'd been stalking him, she quickly added, 'I mean, Holly, my sister – Greg's wife – showed me your picture.'

'Yeah, Greg showed me yours too,' Tom nodded thoughtfully, continuing to stare at her. 'You know, you look different, somehow, from your photo.'

'Do I?'

'Yeah.' Tom frowned, and Annie couldn't help but feel slightly disconcerted.

'I'm not sure why,' she laughed. 'It *was* taken a couple of years ago, but I don't think I've changed that much.'

'Right,' Tom smiled, his eyes crinkling at the corners in a way that was definitely appealing. 'Would you like a drink?'

'Yes, please, that'd be lovely. I'll have a glass of red wine.'

'Good choice. Why don't you grab a table and I'll bring it over?'

'Thanks,' Annie smiled, as she made her way over to a high round table with two stools. So far it was going pretty well, she reflected. There were no fireworks or crowds of angels singing, but he was a good-looking guy, and she was willing to give him a chance – for Holly's sake, if nothing else.

There was a mirror opposite where she was sitting, and Annie surreptitiously checked out her appearance. She wasn't vain, but she thought she looked nice tonight; her bobbed hair was shiny and bouncy, and she'd taken time over her make-up, experimenting with black kohl for a smoky-eyed look. Black skinny jeans and a pretty lace top completed the look.

The bar was filling up, and she saw Tom making his way through the crowd carrying a glass of wine and a pint of lager. At least he hadn't tried the old 'forgotten my wallet' trick, Annie thought, warming to him even more.

'Thanks,' Annie smiled, taking a sip of her wine. It was fruity and delicious, and she could tell he hadn't simply picked the cheapest one on the menu. Another point in his favour.

'So, you work with Greg?' she asked, by way of an opener. 'At Huntington Mutual?'

'Yeah,' Tom nodded, running a hand through his dark hair. 'I'm actually more senior than him, but don't tell Greg I said that, will you?' he chuckled. 'I've only just started there. I took a couple of months off to go travelling before that.'

'Really?' Annie brightened. 'Where did you go?'

'The usual route – New Zealand, Australia, then up to Malaysia, Thailand and across to Cambodia then Vietnam.'

'Wow!' Annie was genuinely impressed. 'That sounds amazing.'

'It was pretty incredible. Do you want to see some photos?' he asked, pulling out an iPhone, as Annie nodded enthusiastically.

'Sure.'

Tom scrolled across the screen, turning his phone around to show Annie a classic Thai beach shot, all pure white sand, dazzling blue water and lush green mountains rising in the background. But it wasn't the scenery that attracted Annie's attention; in the centre of the photo, Tom was posing in nothing but a pair of Hawaiian board shorts, and Annie had to admit that his body looked amazing, all tanned and buff.

'Gorgeous,' she murmured under her breath. 'Thailand, that is,' she added hastily, while Tom grinned as though he knew exactly what was going through her mind.

'And this is the Golden Temple in Bangkok,' he went on.

Annie nodded as she looked at the picture, thinking that Tom just seemed to get better and better. He was cultured, well travelled, looked amazing without a shirt on… Maybe Holly and Greg had done a good job after all.

'Bangkok was extreme – I saw things there that would blow your mind,' Tom continued. 'They've got these women there who can shoot a ping-pong ball right out of their—'

'Yes, I've heard about those,' Annie cut in quickly, but Tom was already scrolling onto the next photo, which showed him with his arm around a pretty Thai girl.

'Shit,' he exclaimed, hastily snatching the phone back. 'That was just a… um… what you'd call a holiday romance.'

'Right,' Annie said neutrally, taking a sip of her wine and mentally reassessing Tom's suitability as a potential boyfriend. Maybe Holly and Greg's matchmaking skills left something to be desired after all.

'So, what do you do for a living, Annie?' Tom asked, trying to steer the conversation back onto safer ground.

'I'm a therapist,' Annie announced, unconsciously holding her breath and praying that Tom wouldn't say anything inappropriate.

'Yeah, that's right.' Tom clicked his fingers and pointed at her. 'Greg mentioned you're some kind of sex worker.'

Annie winced. 'No, not exactly. Sex worker tends to imply… never mind.' She forced a smile. 'I'm a qualified therapist. I help couples who are having problems in their relationship.'

'By having sex with them?' Tom pressed. He took a gulp of his drink and looked at her expectantly. Annie realised that his question was genuine.

'No, not by having sex with them,' she explained slowly. 'I counsel them. Offer them a safe place to talk through their issues.'

'Okay. Because I'm totally not judging you,' Tom said easily. 'That's one of the really great qualities about me as a person. In fact, when I was in Thailand, I thought about becoming a Buddhist.'

'Did you?'

'Yeah. I didn't want to have to stop going to the gym though.'

Annie's eyes narrowed in confusion. Following Tom's train of thought had suddenly become very difficult. 'Are Buddhists not… Can Buddhists not go to the gym?' she tried again.

Tom shook his head. 'I'd have to develop that little Buddha belly, wouldn't I? But I like my six-pack too much. See?' He pulled up his T-shirt to show off those impressive abs.

'Oh, I see,' Annie replied, trying very hard not to laugh. 'Buddhism's probably not for you then.'

'I think you're right,' Tom sighed, as he let his T-shirt drop again. 'So, Annie, are you a fan of the gym?'

Annie wrinkled her nose. 'I'm not much of a gym bunny, no. But I do like to go running every now and again – it really clears my head, especially when work gets stressful.'

Tom was frowning. 'You need to go the gym, Annie. Especially at your age – you need to start using weights, and building muscle mass.'

'At my age?'

'Yeah,' Tom nodded, not appearing to notice her outrage. 'I mean, what are you? Forty?'

Annie was taken aback. 'I'm thirty-four,' she replied, through gritted teeth.

'Really? Wow.' Tom looked shocked. Suddenly, his eyes widened, and he clicked his fingers once again. 'That's why you look different from your Facebook photo!' he exclaimed. 'You look much older in real life.'

It took all of Annie's willpower not to slap him round the face. Instead, she drained her glass of wine then stood up from the stool. 'Would you excuse me a moment?' she asked politely. 'I'm just going to the ladies' room.'

'No worries. I'll get you another drink. Same again, yeah?'

'Yes please,' Annie agreed, thinking that the only way she was going to get through this date was by drinking copious amounts of red wine.

In the safety of the bathroom, Annie took a few calming breaths, clutching onto the side of the sink so tightly that her knuckles turned white.

What on earth had her sister been thinking, setting her up with Tom? Just because Annie was single didn't mean she was desperate! And how on earth had her first impressions been proven so wrong? Yet again, Annie found herself worrying that her judgement was way off when it came to men. In a professional setting, she was undoubtedly an expert at dealing with relationships and emotions, but in her private life she seemed to mess it up every time.

Annie stared at her reflection in the mirror, scrutinising the fine lines around her eyes, the occasional silver hair nestling in her brunette bob. Had she really aged as rapidly as Tom said? Annie knew that she wasn't eighteen any more, but she didn't want to be either. She was happy with her looks, and comfortable in her own skin, but comments like Tom's were bound to make her question her appearance.

Reapplying a fresh coat of lipstick, Annie wondered what to do next. Her first idea was to climb out of the toilet window and escape, but she didn't think that was an option. If nothing else, she'd left her coat at the table, and she wasn't leaving without that. Maybe she *should* give Tom another chance, Annie told herself. After all, she'd promised Holly that she'd give this date a fair try, and leaving after one drink didn't really constitute that. Plus Tom didn't seem to be deliberately malicious, just… incurably stupid.

Annie shook out her hair, quickly running her fingers through it, then walked back through to the bar. She was delighted to see a glass of red wine waiting for her, and it was a moment before she realised that Tom was no longer sitting at the table. He was standing up with his back to Annie, chatting away to a girl who barely looked old enough to legally drink.

The girl was wearing the shortest, tightest dress that Annie had ever seen, and kept hopping from foot to foot, clearly uncomfortable in an enormous pair of heels. Annie sighed, suddenly feeling very middle-aged, as she realised that all she wanted to do was give the girl a pair of nice, comfy flats and a cosy jacket to keep her warm.

Tom and the mystery girl had their heads bent close together, and she was laughing at something he was showing her on his phone. The next moment, he casually slipped an arm around the girl's tiny waist, and Annie decided it was time for her to leave. There was a limit to how much she could take, and Tom had plainly just exceeded it. Plus, if she was quick, she might even catch the end of *Bake Off*.

Annie moved closer to grab her coat, overhearing Tom's conversation as she did so. 'Yeah, I work out a lot,' he was saying to the girl, who was looking at him with an expression of rapt fascination. 'Check out my abs,' he invited her, as he pulled up his T-shirt.

The girl's eyes widened in awe, and she cautiously reached a hand out to touch his washboard stomach, before collapsing into giggles.

'What did you say your name was, princess?' Tom asked casually.

The girl was winding a strand of long, fake hair around her finger. 'Gemma.'

'Hi Gemma,' Tom said, as Gemma giggled once again.

Annie had heard enough. She turned to leave when Gemma said something that caught her attention.

'So are you on your own tonight? I thought I saw you talking to someone earlier.'

'What?' For a moment, Tom looked panicked. 'Oh no, that wasn't anyone important. To be honest, I was just doing a favour for a friend by taking this woman out. She's thirty-four and single, so it's nice for her to get out of the house now and again.'

'Thirty-four!' Gemma repeated incredulously. 'That's just… weird.'

'Yeah,' Tom agreed. 'I like to think of it as charity work. Doing my bit to help the elderly,' he confided, bending his head closer to Gemma's as the two of them started laughing.

Annie's mouth tightened into a grim line, her heart pounding in anger. She felt humiliated and absolutely furious, a red mist appearing in front of her eyes. Acting purely on instinct, with no time to rationalise or think sensibly about what she was doing, she snatched up the glass of red wine on the table. Holding it over Tom's head, she tipped it up and poured…

Chapter 8

*'Only the united beat of sex and heart together can create ecstasy' – **Anaïs Nin***

'I have to say, you're somewhat younger than my usual clients,' Annie smiled warmly at the young couple sitting in front of her. They'd bounded through the door with youthful enthusiasm – a stark contrast to the reluctant entrance and worried glances of her usual first-timers.

Zoe and Simon grinned back excitedly.

'I'm twenty-five and he's twenty-eight,' Zoe informed Annie, her eyes dancing. 'And we just got engaged – look!' She thrust her left hand across the desk for Annie to see.

'Congratulations. What a beautiful ring,' Annie enthused, admiring the small diamond on the narrow silver band. Now she felt even more confused. Why on earth would a young, newly engaged couple require her services? It was usually couples who'd been together for a long time and found themselves stuck in a rut, or those whose relationships were in danger of imminent breakdown, that came to see her. Annie had learnt to be an excellent judge of people over the years, and these two looked extremely happy and in love.

Not wanting to disclose these thoughts to them, she asked simply, 'So what brings you to see me today?'

Zoe and Simon looked at each another anxiously, both expecting the other to speak first. Eventually, Simon cleared his throat.

'I'm not sure whether you'd be the right person to help us. We've had a pretty crazy idea, and it might not be something you want to deal with.'

'Okay,' Annie nodded, more intrigued than ever. 'Try me.'

'We've decided – I mean, we've talked about it a lot, and we've come to the conclusion that...' Simon took a deep breath and turned to his fiancée.

'We've taken a vow of celibacy!' Zoe burst out.

She looked so excited that Annie couldn't help laughing. 'Tell me more.'

'We're getting married in July,' Zoe explained, gabbling away excitedly. 'Well, we think it'll be July – we haven't set a date yet, and we need to start looking at venues and everything because I know it's really short notice, but we want to do it quickly if we can.'

Annie nodded, letting Zoe continue. She was speaking so fast that it was hard to keep up.

'And we just thought: how can we make our wedding day as special as possible? Well, our wedding *night* in this case. So we've decided that we're not going to have any sex until the wedding, haven't we, Simon?'

Simon nodded in confirmation. Annie looked at him carefully, trying to read his expression.

'And is this a mutual decision?'

'Yes, it is,' Simon replied. 'I mean, it was Zoe that came up with the idea, but I'm happy to go along with whatever she wants. Obviously I'll miss – well, you know – but I think it will work out for the best, in the long run.'

He was gazing at Zoe adoringly, and Annie thought once again what a sweet couple they made. Simon was so big, physically, and built like a rugby player, his jean-clad thighs almost taking up the whole width of the armchair. He was clearly besotted with his pretty fiancée, who looked even younger than her twenty-five years in casual clothes and the bare minimum of make-up, her long copper hair trailing down her back in a messy plait.

'Can you imagine how amazing our wedding night will be?' Zoe said dreamily. 'All that build up, and months of anticipation, before we finally… Ooh, it's going to be explosive!'

'I'm sure it'll be spectacular,' Annie smiled. 'So you've obviously been having regular sex already?'

'Yeah,' Simon nodded.

'*Very* regular,' Zoe added, with a naughty little grin. 'All over the place too. And we like to experiment.'

'Zoe!' Simon exclaimed. 'You can't say that.'

'Why not? Annie doesn't mind, do you? You must hear stuff like this every day.'

'I'm pretty unshockable,' Annie assured them.

'See! I told you,' Zoe said triumphantly to Simon. 'Actually, this one time we had sex on a train,' she giggled, turning back to Annie. 'It was a bank holiday, and we'd gone to Cambridge for the day. We caught the last train back, and there was no one else in the carriage. We'd been drinking, so we were both a bit tipsy, and we snuggled up and got a little too frisky. We had these coats over us, so no one would see, and then we'd literally just finished when the ticket inspector walked into the carriage. It was incredible!'

'Too much information,' Simon muttered, looking hugely embarrassed. 'This is only our first session, remember?'

Annie smiled at Zoe's candour, as she scribbled some notes on her pad. 'It sounds as though lack of excitement is the last thing you need to worry about in your relationship! Now, do you mind if I ask you a few questions? Firstly, how long have you been together?'

'Three years,' Simon replied, relieved to finally be on a safer subject.

'And four months,' Zoe couldn't resist adding.

'Great. You're obviously very strong in your relationship. Very secure, and committed,' Annie told them, linking her fingers together and resting her elbows on the desk as she sat forward. 'If you don't mind me saying, I'm not really sure what you need me for. You clearly don't have any major issues – unless there's something I'm not aware of?'

'Like Zoe said,' Simon began, 'We want to make our wedding night as special as possible. And, whilst it'll be great to finally have sex again, we want to make it amazing.'

'The best sex *ever*,' chimed in Zoe. 'So we've talked about it, and we want to discover everything about each other. To know each other intimately – inside and out,' she couldn't resist adding.

'So these next six months will be like… one big foreplay session?' Annie mused, finally understanding where they were going with this.

'Exactly!'

'And we thought that rather than just doing this ourselves, we should get a professional involved to make sure we're doing everything right, and maybe give us a programme to follow or something.'

'But make it fun,' Zoe added hastily. 'Not like homework, or a chore or anything.'

'Absolutely. Sex – or, in this case, the build up to it – should never be a chore,' Annie agreed, smiling at the couple in front of her. They were so young and so in love that she couldn't help but be reminded of her relationship with Mark. The difference with Zoe and Simon was that these two seemed to have their eyes wide open and their feet planted firmly on the ground. They'd clearly thought long and hard about marriage, and were doing everything they could to prepare for it, and lay a solid foundation for the future.

Annie sometimes wondered whether she and Mark would have stood a better chance of staying together if they'd spoken to a counsellor or visited a therapist. Then again, if Annie had been making rational and sensible decisions, she would probably never have married Mark in the first place.

'So, can you tell me a little bit more about you and your relationship?' Annie asked, shaking her head slightly to clear her thoughts. 'How did the two of you meet, for example?'

'In a taxi,' Simon replied, glancing over at Zoe for confirmation. 'It sounds ridiculous, but that's how it happened.'

'We were both out in town,' Zoe explained. 'I'd just been to Mojo's – the nightclub – with my friends, but I wasn't having a great night so I decided to leave early. I was knackered after a long week at work, and there were no decent-looking blokes in the club. Little did I know I was about to meet the man of my dreams…'

'I'd been in the Prince of Wales pub,' Simon took over. 'I had to be up early the next morning, and wasn't really up for going to a club, so when the pub chucked us out I decided to go home. I wandered down the street for a bit, then saw a taxi and tried to hail it—'

'But it was the same one I'd seen,' Zoe cut in, and Annie smiled at how seamlessly they switched telling the story from one to the other. They'd clearly reminisced about this moment many times before. 'It's not a long walk back to my flat, but my feet were killing me – I had these massive heels on – and I was desperate to grab that taxi.'

'We both got there at the same time. I was being the chivalrous gentleman, as ever, so I told Zoe that she could take it.'

'But he looked like a sad little puppy standing there,' Zoe cooed. 'It was starting to rain, and I felt bad about nicking the taxi—'

'*And* she clearly fancied me, of course.'

'I did, actually,' Zoe grinned. 'Who wouldn't? He didn't seem like an axe murderer, so I suggested that we share. We got chatting, swapped numbers…'

'I overwhelmed her with my charm, and the rest is history,' Simon grinned. 'So what do you think?' he continued, a worried shadow crossing his face. 'Do you think you can help us?'

Annie sat back in her chair, looking at the attractive young couple in front of her. They were so eager, so enthusiastic. She'd certainly never come across a situation like this before – this was a first, in her professional experience. But it showed great maturity, and a real desire to make their relationship last. Working with these two could be a lot of fun…

'Yes,' Annie smiled, her eyes twinkling as she looked at them. 'I think I can.'

❄   ❄   ❄

After Simon and Zoe had left, and Annie had set them their first 'homework', her mobile started ringing. She heard the vibrations deep in her bag and rooted around inside, trying to find it before it went through to the answer phone.

Triumphantly, she pulled it out, and saw 'Sister' flashing on the caller display. Annie pulled a face. She knew exactly what Holly would be calling about. For a second, she thought about letting it go to voicemail, but she knew that would only delay the inevitable.

'Hi Hol,' she said, brightly.

'Don't you "Hi Hol" me!' came the retort, as Annie grimaced and moved the phone away from her ear. 'What on earth did you *do*, Annie! Tom's telling everyone who'll listen that you're a crazy psycho. Greg is completely embarrassed – it's all around his office – and he's saying that he'll never try and set you up with anyone again.'

'Well, good,' Annie shot back, going on the defensive. 'I don't want him to set me up with anyone if that's the best he can do. Seriously, Holly, the guy was a complete idiot.'

'That doesn't mean you can throw a glass of wine over him! You're not Sharon Osbourne on the *X Factor*!'

'It wasn't a big glass,' Annie muttered petulantly. 'And it was humiliating, Hol. He was chatting up another girl right in front of me. And when I say girl, I mean it – she didn't look old enough to be out past ten pm on a school night, let alone drinking in a bar. And he kept going on about how old I looked, and how he was such a macho man down at the gym. Seriously, sis, he was a grade one dickhead.'

'You're too fussy, that's your problem,' Holly chastised her. It was a refrain Annie had heard many times over the years, and it always made her furious.

'I'm not *fussy*, I just have *standards*,' she huffed. 'There's a difference.'

'Is that what you advise your clients to do?' Holly demanded. 'If they're having problems in their relationship, they should start throwing things at each other? Honestly, what if one of them had seen you? You can be so irresponsible sometimes.'

Annie's anger was partly motivated by the fact that she knew Holly was right. It had been an extremely childish and unprofessional thing to do – albeit deeply satisfying – but if one of her clients had seen, she could have lost business. And if word got back to one of them... Norwich was only a small city, and she didn't know how many people Tom knew.

'Urgh. I suppose I need to ring him and apologise, don't I?' Annie said, feeling the slightest hint of regret.

'That would be appreciated. I'm only looking out for you, Annie,' Holly continued, her tone softening. 'You're your own worst enemy sometimes.'

'Yeah, yeah, spare me the lecture. You sound like Mum.'

'Oh, that reminds me,' Holly began, and Annie was grateful for the change of subject. 'Are you going round to Mum's next week? Sunday lunch?'

Annie hesitated. As much as she loved seeing her parents, she sometimes hated the traditional Sunday lunches with her mum, dad, Holly and Greg, as Annie got pushed to one end of the table next to the dog, and interrogated about why she didn't have a boyfriend.

'Yep, I'll be there,' she said finally.

'Okay, Annie, I'll see you then. Take care.'

'You too, sis. You too.'

Chapter 9

'Sex is God's joke on human beings' – **Bette Davis**

It was dark outside, and seemed to have been that way for hours, the rain pattering lightly on the windows. The office was lit with unflattering overhead strip-lights and the dull green glow of idle computers. Nick stifled a yawn as he glanced at the clock in the bottom corner of his screen – 9.16 pm. He was working late again tonight, trying to catch up on some of the things he'd missed while he was busy catering to Julia's demands. The Norfolk Cottages pitch was coming up, and Nick needed to be on top of his game for that.

The office was deserted, with all of his colleagues having long since left for the night. Well, almost all of them. Nina was still here; she'd been assigned to work with Nick on this proposal, and was insistent that if he was staying then she was too.

Right now, Nina was sitting beside him, staring at the screen with a frown on her face. She looked tired, her dark hair working loose from where she'd pinned it up. The smart black shift dress she was wearing had become crumpled and creased, and Nick couldn't help but notice that she'd unconsciously kicked off her heels under the desk, her shapely legs encased in sheer black stockings.

'Look, why don't you get off home,' Nick offered kindly. 'We're almost done here. I'm going to wrap up soon anyway.'

'It's no problem,' Nina shrugged. 'I don't mind staying until we're finished. Anyway, I was just going to suggest that this paragraph could be re-phrased.' She held up a manicured nail and tapped on the screen, her hands slender and elegant. 'We've already used "chocolate-box cottages", so how about if we say "picture-perfect properties" instead?'

'Yes, that sounds much better,' Nick agreed, deleting the original text and adding in Nina's suggestion. Despite being new to the company, Nina was learning fast, Nick thought admiringly. She was consistently coming up with strong, original ideas, and clearly had a great work ethic.

'And here,' she continued, leaning in towards him as she took hold of the mouse and scrolled down. Nick caught the scent of a musky perfume, and hastily moved away. 'It says that return clients make up twenty-three percent of business, but I think the figure's wrong. Shouldn't it—'

Nina broke off as Nick's mobile vibrated on the desk. Julia's name was flashing on the caller display, and they both stared at it.

'Do you need to get that?' Nina asked eventually.

'No,' Nick replied dismissively, pressing the button to send it to voicemail. 'It's only my wife.' As soon as the words were out of his mouth, he realised how terrible they sounded. 'Oh, I didn't mean it like that.' He forced an awkward laugh. 'What I meant was—'

'It's fine,' Nina assured him, looking up at him curiously from beneath her long, dark eyelashes.

'Um... Where were we?' Nick cleared his throat and turned back to the computer screen, but he couldn't seem to concentrate. The document seemed to be a jumble of words and numbers; it might have been written in Swahili for all the sense it was making to him right now.

Trust Julia to mess things up again, Nick thought in frustration. She was probably calling him to nag him about coming home, wanting to jump into bed because she was ovulating, or because she'd read about some new technique, or because Saturn was in Venus rising and her horoscope said conception was guaranteed.

For a crazy moment, Nick considered confiding in Nina about his problems, but quickly decided against it. She was only twenty-three, and a sly glance at her empty left hand told him she wasn't married, so he doubted she'd empathise with the intricacies of a long-term relationship.

Ah, to be young, single and fancy free! Nick felt a sudden stab of envy for Nina's carefree lifestyle, a longing for his bachelor days and a time before mortgages and bills and pregnancy tests and—

'Nick?' Nina's soft voice cut into his thoughts.

'Sorry,' he apologised, his head jerking up in alarm. 'Were you saying something?'

'Just that I think the correct figure should be thirty-two percent. I think it's a typo and the numbers are the wrong way round, but I can look it up…'

Nina reached across the desk for a thick folder and began leafing through the pages, as Nick rubbed his hands tiredly across his forehead.

He and Julia had barely spoken since the argument in Annie's office. They'd had a furious row afterwards, both of them tossing vicious and cruel words at each other, and the atmosphere in the house remained fraught with tension. Nick had been dealing with the situation largely by avoiding it; he left early in the morning, working late into the evening to limit the amount of time he had to spend with Julia. He wondered what she'd been calling for just now…

'You know what, Nina? Let's leave this for tonight. We'll come to it fresh tomorrow morning.'

'Sure,' Nina agreed easily, slipping her shoes back on and piling documents into her work bag. 'I'll have a think about target demographics too, and email you if I have any bright ideas.'

'Great. Thanks, Nina, you've been amazing as always,' Nick told her as they left the office and rode down in the lift. Outside, the stars were bright in the clear, cold night sky, their voices loud in the deserted car park.

'Well, I'll see you tomorrow,' Nick said, as they reached his car. He saw Nina glance admiringly at the silver BMW.

'Sure, see you tomorrow. Goodnight, Nick.'

Nina set off across the car park, her heels clicking, her thick woollen coat belted tightly to show off her slim waist.

Nick shivered suddenly, hastily climbing into his car and turning the key in the ignition. He watched in the rear view mirror, waiting until Nina had sped off, then he slowly pulled out of the car park and drove home.

❄ ❄ ❄

'Nick, is that you?' Julia called, as she heard the front door open.

Nick grimaced, instantly feeling on edge. He really didn't want another night of petty arguments, going over and over the same old issues before lapsing into frustrated, angry silence.

'Yeah,' he replied lightly, as he took his jacket off.

To his surprise, Julia came rushing through from the living room. She looked cute and cosy in a pair of checked pyjamas and fluffy boot-style slippers. Her blonde hair was freshly washed, and her face was bare of make-up, making her appear younger than her thirty-one years. She looked nervous, yet hopeful, unsure what reaction to expect from her husband.

'Hi,' she said timidly.

It was the friendliest Julia had been towards him for days. Gone was the tight-lipped, furious expression that had been a permanent fixture recently, and in its place was a tentative smile.

'Hi,' Nick replied warily, bending down to kiss her on the cheek. A look of hurt flashed across her eyes, and Nick could tell that she'd been hoping for more. But he wasn't ready to forgive and forget just yet. He'd gone out on a limb trying to repair their relationship by arranging the session with Annie, yet Julia had thrown it back in his face.

'How was your day?' she asked, with forced brightness.

'Fine, thanks. You?'

'Good. I won a new commission, for a ruby wedding anniversary, so…'

'That's great. Well done,' Nick said distractedly, his voice sounding flat. 'Anyway, I'm going to head up and have a shower.'

'Sure. I'll put some food on. You must be starving.'

'You don't have to bother. I'll grab something easy when I get out.'

'It's no trouble,' Julia insisted. 'You need to eat something when you're working such long hours. I tried to call you earlier, but…'

The sentence hung, unfinished, in the air between them. Nick didn't reply. He opened his mouth to respond, then closed it again, turning his back on Julia and running up the stairs. He didn't see the way his wife crumpled at his coldness, her eager expression giving way to one of dejection. She stared after her husband for a moment, then turned around and trudged into the kitchen.

❋ ❋ ❋

When Nick came back downstairs fifteen minutes later, freshly showered and dressed comfortably in jogging bottoms and an old T-shirt, he found Julia had set a place for him at their kitchen table. She'd cooked steak, with char-grilled tomatoes and asparagus, and had poured him a glass of red wine.

She looked up and smiled as she saw him, and Nick cautiously smiled back. He had to admit that the food looked wonderful. He'd been living off takeaways and toast for the last few nights, with Julia barely acknowledging his presence in the house.

'Aren't you having any?' he asked.

'I ate earlier, but I thought I'd cook yours fresh. It's nicer that way, and it only takes ten minutes.'

'Thanks,' Nick said grudgingly, realising that she was making an effort.

Julia left him to eat, quietly moving around the kitchen as she tidied up, stacking the dishwasher and wiping down the surfaces.

As Nick finished the last mouthful, he put down his knife and fork and pushed his chair back, saying, 'Thanks, Jules. That was delicious.'

Julia came hurrying over. 'You're welcome,' she told him, placing her hands lightly on his shoulders.

Nick tensed involuntarily, and Julia frowned.

'You're so stiff,' she murmured, letting her fingers roam over the tight muscles of his shoulder blades. 'You're working too hard at the moment.'

Julia began working her thumbs into the knots in his back, making small, circular movements through the thin fabric of his shirt. In spite of himself, Nick closed his eyes, feeling himself start to relax.

'Ahh, that's good,' he sighed, letting his head drop forward as Julia's hands moved upwards on either side of his spine, brushing over the short hairs at the base of his neck and making him shiver with pleasure.

'Honey, I'm sorry… about everything…' Julia told him, as she continued to knead his back, her hands slipping underneath his T-shirt for skin-on-skin contact. She bent down, kissing him lightly on the top of his head, burying her face in his still-damp hair before letting her hands slide round to his chest. Her breasts were grazing his back as she began to kiss Nick's neck, his ear, his cheek, moving round to find his lips.

Nick's eyes were closed, his body heavy and warm, as he was lulled into some kind of trance by the rhythmic, soothing movements of Julia's hands. The edges of her fingernails grazed his skin and he felt the first stirrings of arousal, as Julia kissed him languidly. She must be genuinely sorry, he realised, as her tongue slid into his mouth and she swung her body round so that she was straddling him, pressing against him as his excitement grew.

Nick grabbed hold of her bottom, feeling the soft, inviting flesh as he pulled her closer, his hands roaming over her thighs and—

'No!' Nick snapped suddenly, his eyes flying open as his head jerked back. He moved so quickly that Julia lost her balance, almost falling off his lap and steadying herself against the table.

'Nick, be careful!' she yelled, looking shocked.

'No,' Nick repeated, wriggling out from underneath her. 'I know exactly what you're doing, Julia – the food, the massage. You're not sorry at all, are you? I'm being bloody *seduced*!'

From the guilty look on Julia's face, he knew he was right, but she wasn't going to back down without a fight.

'You know, *some* men wouldn't complain about being seduced by their wives,' she shot back tartly. '*Some* men might actually enjoy it, instead of acting like it's the crime of the century.'

'But it's not about me, is it? It's about your bloody obsession with getting pregnant.'

'It's what we *both* want,' Julia protested. 'We agreed.'

Nick shook his head in defeat, wondering how his marriage had ended up like this. 'I don't know what I want any more.'

Julia moved towards him, her arms outstretched, but Nick backed away hurriedly.

'Just leave it,' he told her angrily. 'I'm going to bed. And I'm sleeping in the spare room.'

'Please, Nick,' Julia began, but Nick didn't want to listen. He stormed out of the door, and stomped up the stairs, striding across the landing and slamming the spare room door firmly shut.

❋ ❋ ❋

Julia let him go, deciding it was best not to follow him. She sat down in the chair he'd just vacated, staring off into space as she tried to figure out what was going wrong between them.

Did Nick even want a baby? They'd discussed it endlessly before they started trying, and he'd seemed wildly enthusiastic, gushing about the prospect of a newborn son or daughter to carry on the family line. He'd happily gone along with Julia's suggestions as she browsed the internet for the perfect crib, or picked out colours for turning the spare room into a nursery. They'd even talked about expanding their family further in the future; neither of them wanted to stop at just one.

But now… Julia let out a sigh of frustration. It was as though Nick had completely shut down about the idea, whereas for Julia, having a baby had become the most important thing in her life, the thought that occupied every waking moment. And in order to make a baby, she and Nick needed to have sex. It was blindingly obvious to Julia, but Nick didn't seem to see it that way. How was she supposed to get pregnant if he insisted on sleeping in separate bedrooms?

Every day, Julia saw mothers in the street pushing their babies in prams, or passed harassed families doing the school run, or read articles in the newspaper about couples with sixteen children crammed into a three-bedroom house, and the desperate longing inside of her would reawaken with a vengeance. How was it that they had all so easily achieved the one thing she wanted most in life?

And now Nick was bleating on about how their relationship was suffering, wanting to go and see that busybody counsellor woman. To Julia, it just didn't make sense. What husband wouldn't long for sex all day and every day, as often as he wanted and then some?

He'd seemed genuinely angry tonight, Julia reflected. She really hadn't been as calculating as he'd suspected – she'd simply tired of all the arguments and wanted to make up, figuring that a delicious, home-cooked meal and, yes, a long, steamy session between the sheets would get everything back on track. But once again, communication had broken down between the two of them, and the evening had ended in a row.

Wearily, Julia got to her feet and switched off the kitchen light, heading upstairs to bed. As she'd suspected, the door to the spare room was firmly shut; across the hall, she could see the unoccupied bed in the master bedroom. Julia stared at it for a moment, biting her lip in thought. Then she made her decision, reaching for the handle of the spare room door and quietly pushing it open.

The light from the landing shone into the room, a narrow strip illuminating the carpet and the single bed. Julia could make out Nick's familiar body shape beneath the duvet. He was perfectly still, his breathing even, but she doubted he was asleep.

Padding across to the far side of the bed, Julia peeled back the cover and slid in behind him, spooning his body and letting one arm snake around to find his warm, bare chest. He tensed beneath her hand, his muscles rigid, and Julia immediately felt guilty.

She kissed his neck softly, snuggling closer and murmuring in his ear. 'I'm sorry, honey. I really am. I know things aren't right between us, and that we need… We need to do something about it. If you really want, I'll come to therapy with you. Contact Annie and… I'll give it another try.'

Chapter 10

'If sex is such a natural phenomenon, how come there are so many books on how to do it right?' – **Bette Midler**

Zoe and Simon were both stark naked in their tiny little living room. The old-fashioned gas fire was turned up to its maximum setting, and they'd switched the overhead lights off, illuminating the room with some thick pillar candles that Zoe had bought a couple of months earlier in the January sales. The curtains had been carefully drawn to ensure that no one could see in, despite the fact that their flat was on the first floor, and now they sat cross-legged on the carpet, facing each other.

'I don't know how I'm going to last six months,' Simon groaned, as he gazed lustfully at Zoe's body. 'Are you *sure* this no-sex thing is a good idea? I think I'm regretting it now.'

Zoe giggled. 'Si, we haven't even gone a fortnight yet, and you're already struggling.'

'I know.' He looked up at her with a puppy-dog expression. 'Maybe we should bring the wedding forward.'

'Forward?'

'Yeah. To next week,' Simon suggested hopefully, as Zoe smiled.

'No,' she told him firmly, swatting his hand away as it began to creep up her inner thigh. 'We're going to do this properly.'

'Okay, you win,' Simon conceded. 'What did that worksheet say again?'

Zoe jumped up, heading over to their second-hand coffee table where she picked up the set of papers that Annie had given them. She was completely at ease with being naked in front of her fiancé, and saw no point in being shy – after all, he'd seen it all before. Like any woman, Zoe knew she had her flaws, but Simon had never given her the slightest indication that he didn't completely love her body – on the contrary, he couldn't seem to get enough of it – and Zoe was grateful for the confidence that gave her.

'"Erogenous zones are areas of the human body",' Zoe read out loud, as she took her place back on the floor in front of Simon. '"Which when stimulated in some way – for example, being tickled, sucked or licked – result in the sexual arousal and potential orgasm of the individual."'

'I'm aroused with you just talking about it,' Simon growled, glancing pointedly at his crotch.

Zoe's eyes widened. 'So I see!'

'I'm not sure how I'm going to be able to cope when you start tickling or sucking or licking.'

'You'll just have to exercise some self-restraint,' Zoe told him, her eyes sparkling. 'Now, carrying on, it says that: "As well as the obvious areas, such as breasts and genitalia, most people have many other erogenous zones which, when stimulated, result in differing degrees of arousal. These include, but are not limited to, the scalp, ear lobes, clavicle, armpits" – Ew!' Zoe broke off. 'I'm not licking your armpits! "...the inside of the elbows, knees, lower back, feet and toes."'

'I'll take all of those please,' Simon grinned.

Zoe ignored him and carried on speaking. 'So, Annie said we're supposed to focus on the less obvious zones and discover which ones turn us on the most. We have to take time to stroke and caress each other's bodies, and then rate the different areas from one to three, depending on how much we like it. One means we're not too fussed, two means we like it, and three means that we love it and can't get enough.'

'Sounds good.' Simon's eyes roamed hungrily over Zoe. 'Do you want to be the strok*er* or the strok*ee*?'

Zoe grinned. 'I don't mind. I'm easy.'

'Ah, how I wish that was true,' Simon sighed, as Zoe giggled. 'Okay then, I'll go first,' he declared, lying flat on his back and closing his eyes.

'Oh, I almost forgot!' Zoe leapt to her feet once again, and rushed over to the saggy blue sofa where she'd left her handbag. She rifled through and pulled out a long, sleek, stiff feather in a shimmering shade of teal, twirling it admiringly. 'Isn't it pretty?'

Simon opened his eyes to see what she was talking about. 'So does that mean you're not licking or sucking?' he asked, unable to keep the note of disappointment out of his voice.

'Not this week,' Zoe shook her head, as she brushed the feather experimentally against her palm, enjoying the pleasant tickling sensation. 'I got it on my lunch break, from that little craft shop on Elm Hill. The woman in the shop was chatting away, asking me what I planned to do with it. I panicked and told her I was making a hat!'

'A hat? Very inventive.'

'Oh, shut up and close your eyes,' Zoe retorted. Simon did as he was told, a lazy grin playing on his lips.

'Right,' Zoe murmured, looking thoughtfully at his naked body. 'Where do I start…?'

She was beginning to feel fairly aroused herself at the sight of Simon's broad shoulders and strong arms, the dark hair on his chest and his powerful, rugby-player thighs. Not to mention his impressive manhood…

It would be so easy to tear up Annie's worksheet and forget the pact that they'd made, Zoe reflected, biting her lip in frustration. She could climb on top of Simon right now, straddle him and slowly slide down onto his big—

'Are you still there?' Simon asked worriedly, half-opening one eye.

'What? Oh, yes, sorry,' Zoe replied, looking flustered. 'I got distracted there for a second. Close your eyes again.'

'I feel very vulnerable here,' Simon confessed. 'You'd better not be taking any dirty pictures and sending them to your friends. Or your mum.'

'Great idea – I hadn't thought of that,' Zoe chuckled. 'You know my mum thinks you're the best thing since sliced bread. She'd probably love it!'

'Can we *please* not talk about your mum right now? It's really inappropriate timing!'

'Okay, fair point,' Zoe laughed. She fell quiet, trying to recapture the mood. Then, tentatively reaching forward, she very gently trailed the feather over Simon's stomach. She brushed it across his navel, letting it catch in the dark, wiry hairs leading to his groin, then swished it out towards his hip bones.

Simon shivered, goose bumps appearing along his arm. 'Mmm, that tickles.'

Zoe smiled. 'You like?'

'Sort of… I'll give it a two,' Simon replied, scrunching up his face. 'Nice, but no wow factor.'

'Okay,' Zoe nodded, already selecting her next target. 'Hmm…' She crawled a couple of paces forward until she was level with his feet. They were typical male feet – unloved and uncared for, with nails that needed clipping and a tuft of dark hair sprouting from each toe. Slowly, Zoe ran the feather along the underside of Simon's right foot, dragging it from the heel to the ball, then sliding it along his toes.

Simon flinched, jerking his leg away. 'One!' he yelled. 'Zero, even. I didn't like that at all. It made me feel a bit sick, actually.'

'So you definitely don't have a foot fetish?'

'Not for *my* feet – yours might be a different story…'

'Well, we can both keep away from your feet in future then. I don't want to go near them again – not until you've had a decent pedicure.'

Simon frowned. 'I don't think you're very good at this game,' he teased. 'I think you need to concentrate on finding some zones that are going to blow my mind.'

'I'd be careful with that attitude,' Zoe replied, raising an eyebrow in warning. 'In case you've forgotten, you're in a very vulnerable position here. One false move from me, and our chances of having kids could be over.'

Simon quickly shut his mouth, lying quietly as Zoe moved to the other end of his body. She trailed the feather languorously up and down the side of his neck, over his collarbone, then back towards his earlobe.

'Grr, three,' Simon purred happily.

Zoe smiled, leaning forwards until her lips were almost touching his skin, before blowing lightly on the sensitive area around his neck and ear.

'Five… Ten… A hundred!' Simon cried out, his whole body tingling with pleasure. He opened his eyes and, seeing Zoe so close to him, couldn't resist reaching out to kiss her.

Zoe acquiesced, closing her eyes as Simon's large hands gently cupped her face, delighting in the familiar taste of his mouth, and the delicious warmth of his body. She lay down on the floor beside him, their legs entwining as things gradually became more heated, until Simon reluctantly pulled away.

'Are we allowed to do this?' he wondered. He was breathing heavily, his expression intense as he focused on his fiancée.

Zoe nodded. 'Yes. We're not having sex, are we? So it's fine.'

'It's not fine.' Simon rolled away from her with a groan. 'It's so frustrating! And if we carry on like this, I can't be responsible for my actions. Now give me that feather and let me have a turn!'

'Are you sure you don't need a cold shower instead?'

'Probably,' Simon agreed, as he plucked the feather from Zoe's hand and rolled her onto her stomach. 'Now, marks out of three for the lower back…?'

'Ooh, three,' Zoe sighed happily. She rested her head on her hands, her eyes catching on the diamond engagement ring sparkling in the candlelight. She still couldn't quite believe that it was hers, and that she really was going to marry her gorgeous fiancé. Then she turned her face to the side, settling down contentedly as Simon went about his task.

He continued to brush the feather across Zoe's bare skin, moving from her neck and shoulder blades down over the soft curve of her bottom, along the backs of her thighs, her calves, and finally sweeping across the soles of her feet. It felt utterly blissful, and Zoe sighed in delight, announcing that everywhere was a three.

'So your whole body is basically one big erogenous zone?'

'Makes life easy for you, doesn't it?' Zoe quipped, gazing lovingly at Simon.

'Hey, you shouldn't have your eyes open, that's cheating!' he exclaimed. Then a sly smile stole across his face. 'I've got an idea…'

Simon jumped to his feet and walked out of the room, Zoe admiring his firm, round bottom as he went. Due to all the manual labour he did at work, his body was in great shape.

In the bedroom, Simon was opening drawers and rifling through cupboards.

'What are you looking for?' Zoe shouted, propping herself up on her elbows.

'Never you mind,' Simon shouted back as he continued to search, the noise drifting through to where Zoe lay in the living room. The two of them lived in a small flat above a furniture shop on Magdalen Street, which Zoe had rented along with her friend, Hannah, when they left university. A few months after Zoe had met Simon, Hannah decided to move out and Simon decided to move in, in an arrangement that suited everyone perfectly. Now Zoe and Simon were saving up for their own place, but with a wedding and honeymoon to plan, money was tight. Zoe sometimes wondered whether they would ever be able to afford a home of their own…

'Found it!' Simon called triumphantly, as he came back through to the living room gleefully waving a tie. It was lilac-coloured, and the only one he owned; Zoe had chosen it when they'd attended a friend's wedding together last summer. 'I knew it would come in handy one day,' he grinned.

'What are you planning to do with that?' Zoe asked, her eyes dancing as she thought of what Simon might be intending to try. She was sitting up now, her long, titian hair hanging down past her shoulders and over her small breasts. Her skin was pale and smooth, her body slender.

Without saying a word, Simon bent down and looped the tie around her head, pulling it taut over her eyes and tying the ends in a knot.

'Can you see?'

Zoe shook her head, her excitement building. She felt a little nervous, but there was something incredibly sexy about giving up control, relinquishing all power to Simon.

'How many fingers am I holding up?'

'Three?' she guessed.

'Trick question,' Simon murmured, his lips close to her ear, his breath tickling the skin on her neck, disturbing the stray wisps of hair. 'I'm not holding up any. Now lie back…'

Zoe did as Simon commanded, her body on fire with anticipation. Simon couldn't take his eyes off her, as he picked up the feather and began to trace light circles around her pale pink nipples.

'Three,' Zoe whispered, her voice catching in her throat.

Simon exhaled heavily, waves of lust crashing over him. 'I don't know how I'm going to survive these next few months,' he told her again. 'Seriously Zoe, I'm so horny, I think I'm going to explode.'

Zoe contemplated his words for a few moments, the tension hanging heavily in the air between them. 'You know,' she began finally, her voice low and husky. 'We've only agreed not to have sex before the wedding. That actually leaves a whole lot of other things we can do… if we use our imaginations.'

Simon paused, thinking about what she'd just said. He was so turned on that he could barely breathe. 'I like the way you're thinking.'

Zoe sat up, sliding the tie off her head and looking Simon straight in the eye. 'What do you think?' she murmured suggestively. 'I'm sure we can come to some arrangement that's… mutually satisfying.'

Simon grinned, as he realised exactly what she was implying. 'I knew there was a reason I asked you to marry me,' he growled, as he pushed her back down on the floor and passionately kissed her.

Chapter 11

*'I don't know the question, but sex is definitely the answer' – **Woody Allen***

'Hello and welcome! It's great to see so many of you here today, and some new faces too,' Annie beamed, as she looked around the room, spotting Zoe and Simon and, surprisingly, Nick and Julia, seated in the semi-circle amongst her regulars.

'Now, as those of you who've been before will know, these Saturday morning sessions are very different to your individual sessions with me. We won't be referring to the specific reasons any of you come to visit me, and you absolutely don't have to do or say anything you don't feel comfortable with.'

She smiled round, as everyone nodded and murmured in the affirmative. There were a dozen people altogether – six couples – of varying ages. Some sat close to their partner, holding hands and glancing at one another occasionally, whilst others kept their chairs apart and looked straight ahead, avoiding eye contact with their other half.

'These group sessions are intended to be more fun and less intense than the one-on-one meetings, but hopefully you'll all still learn something valuable that will be of use to you in working on your relationships,' Annie continued. 'As there are some newcomers today, can we start by going round and having everyone say their names, then we can all get acquainted. Zoe, would you like to go first?'

Zoe and Simon were sitting on one end, and were one of the couples whose body language indicated they were in a very happy relationship.

'Okay,' Zoe agreed, looking a little nervous. She leant forward into the semi-circle, so that she could see everyone, and said brightly, 'Hi, I'm Zoe, and this is my boyfriend – well, fiancé – Simon.'

'Hi everyone, I'm Simon, and my wife-to-be very often speaks on my behalf,' Simon joked, making the others laugh as Zoe, realising what she'd done, blushed bright red.

Nick came next. 'I'm Nick,' he announced, with a brief, awkward nod.

'Julia,' said Julia shortly, the expression on her face indicating that this was the last place she wanted to be right now.

Nick had called Annie earlier in the week to explain the situation and say sorry for Julia's previous behaviour. Annie had suggested that they might like to attend one of her Saturday morning group sessions – to take the focus off the two of them, and also show Julia a lighter side of therapy – and Nick had eagerly taken up her offer. They'd arrived early and, with Nick's prompting, Julia had made her way over to apologise to Annie.

The other couples followed suit with the introductions; there was Richard and Jennifer, Michael and Carolyn, Hardeep and Shamila, and David and Brigitte.

'Perfect,' Annie smiled, once everyone had spoken. 'Now, I'd appreciate it if you kept anything that happens in here today confidential. I want this to be a safe place for people to learn in, and not have to worry that something they say might end up online, or passed round your friends as a piece of gossip.'

Once again, there were nodded agreements, and a little nervous laughter from Zoe.

'As you've probably noticed, there are some strange objects set up in the room today,' Annie continued. She'd hired the boardroom in the same building as her office – the largest space available – and pushed the table back against the wall to give them the biggest possible area to work in. At one end of the room was the semi-circle of chairs where everyone was now sitting, and directly in front of them was what appeared to be a mini obstacle course.

Miniature traffic cones had been set up in a line, followed by a low hurdle, then an exercise trampoline, a children's paddling pool full of water, and finally a low table with a hand bell on it.

'What we're going to do today is an exercise in listening to your partner and placing your trust in them. I'm not going to tell you much more for now… Who'd like to go first?'

Some of the couples immediately looked away, trying not to catch Annie's eye; it was like volunteering for PE class in school.

'Come on, you're all going to have a go eventually!'

Glancing round at the others, and seeing that no one seemed particularly enthusiastic, Zoe thrust her hand in the air. 'I will!' she exclaimed. 'That is – we will.'

'What did I say about you making decisions for me?' Simon said in a stage whisper, but he got to his feet nevertheless.

Annie looked pleased, as she produced a thin black scarf from her bag. 'Now, Simon, I'd like you to tie this over Zoe's eyes and ensure that she can't see.'

With a grin, Simon took the material from Annie. 'This is familiar,' he murmured. He looped it around Zoe's head and she giggled delightedly.

'Nice and tight – but make sure it's not restricting the blood flow,' Annie chuckled. 'Okay, Simon, what's going to happen is that you're going to guide Zoe round the obstacle course using only your voice – in and out of the cones, over the hurdle, onto the trampoline where she'll bounce three times, then avoid the water before she finally picks up the hand bell and rings it to show that you've finished. You need to be very clear and precise in your instructions, as Zoe is relying entirely on your voice to guide her. And Zoe, you need to listen very carefully to what Simon is telling you.'

'There's a first time for everything, I suppose,' he quipped, as the others laughed. Then they all fell silent, and Simon cleared his throat, aware of everyone watching him intently. 'Right, Zoe – can you hear me okay?'

'I'm blindfolded, not deaf!'

'Okay, okay,' Simon conceded. 'Be nice to me or I might accidentally send you into a wall.'

Annie looked at him. 'It's great that you have a very… ahem… playful relationship, but I need you to start the exercise now. There are a lot of couples to get through.'

'Of course, sorry,' Simon apologised. 'Right, babe, take two large steps forward…'

Tentatively, Zoe did as he'd instructed.

'Perfect, just like that. Then a small step to your right – right! That's your left!'

'Sorry! I always did get those two confused.'

'Never mind, we're back on track. Another half step forward, and then a step to your left – the opposite to last time, yeah?'

'I know that, smart arse!'

They carried on in much the same manner – Simon guiding Zoe round the course with lots of good-humoured banter between them. When Zoe eventually picked up the hand bell and triumphantly rang it, the watching group burst into spontaneous applause. Zoe pulled off her blindfold with a huge grin, before running straight to Simon who scooped her up in a cuddle.

'Well done, babe,' he congratulated her, bending down for an impulsive kiss.

'Great job, you two,' Annie enthused, as they went back to take their seats. 'Do the rest of you have any observations on how that went?'

'You clearly have a great relationship,' Michael spoke up. 'In fact, I'm not sure what you're doing here,' he joked. 'You worked very well together, and you weren't afraid to challenge each other.'

'But it was all done with good humour,' Shamila chimed in. 'There was never any frustration or bad temper.'

'I completely agree,' nodded Annie. 'The two of you worked wonderfully together, and any problems that you did encounter – like the hurdle, Zoe – you managed to overcome together. Who'd like to go next?'

Richard and Jennifer put their hands up. This time, Richard was blindfolded, and Jennifer guided him round the course. Despite Richard knocking over one of the traffic cones, and almost losing his temper at the trampoline, they made it round without incident – albeit more slowly than Zoe and Simon.

Next came Nick and Julia's turn. Julia reluctantly agreed to be blindfolded, as Nick gave the instructions. They immediately got off to a bad start when Julia tripped over one of the cones and almost sprained her ankle.

'I told you not to go that way!' Nick snapped, as Julia angrily pulled off the blindfold and sat on the floor, massaging her foot.

'You were shouting left,' Julia insisted. 'So I went left.'

'I said forward and then left, not left straight away!'

'This whole thing's bloody stupid anyway. I don't know why I agreed to come back.' Julia looked close to tears, and Annie stepped in.

'How's your ankle, Julia? Do you think you can walk on it?'

'I'll live,' Julia muttered sourly.

'Why don't you two go and sit back down,' Annie suggested. 'And someone else can have a turn. If you feel up to it later, you can try again at the end.'

'It's fine,' Julia snapped, shooting Nick a dirty look as she stood up once again. 'We'll carry on.'

'Why don't we swap over, and you can direct me?' Nick suggested. He looked furious at the way Julia was behaving, but evidently didn't want to make a scene in front of everyone.

'Fine.'

Julia took a seat, while Annie helped Nick to tie the scarf around his head. Julia's directions were short and terse:

'Forward. Left. Left. Forward. Right – no, not that far!'

Nick was white-lipped and livid as he made his way around the course as quickly as possible. When he rang the hand bell, there was no clapping. He tugged off the blindfold and stormed back to his seat, folding his arms across his chest. He and Julia didn't make eye contact, sitting with their bodies turned away from one other.

This time, Annie didn't ask for comments from the other couples. It was heartbreakingly obvious that Nick and Julia's relationship was not in a good place, and Annie desperately wanted to speak to the two of them on their own. She hoped that they would come back for another individual session with her; she really thought she could help them, but it was going to take a lot of work.

Michael and Carolyn went next, followed by Hardeep and Shamila. Last up were David and Brigitte, who were utterly hilarious as they took on the makeshift obstacle course and had everyone laughing, easing the tension that had existed ever since Nick and Julia's turn. By the end, the group were in hysterics at David's refusal to get off the trampoline as he was enjoying it so much, before Brigitte deliberately led him dangerously close to the paddling pool, claiming that he needed a bath.

Just as David finished the course to a chorus of cheers and wolf-whistles, there was a sharp rap on the door, which made everyone jump. Annie hurried over, and opened it to find Jamie standing there. As it was the weekend, he was dressed casually in jeans and a polo shirt, sandy-coloured stubble peppering his jaw line.

'Annie!' he exclaimed, a grin breaking out across his face as he saw her. 'I wondered who was making all the noise.'

'I'm so sorry,' she apologised, looking horrified. 'I didn't realise anyone else was in the building. It's usually deserted on a Saturday.'

Jamie smiled ruefully. 'Too much work, I'm afraid. I've had to come in today to get on with some things.'

'And you could hear us in your office?' Annie marvelled, knowing that Jamie's cubicle was at the other end of the building.

'Nah, I was just taking a break, and went for a walk round to stretch my legs. Then I heard all this going on.'

'Well, we'll try and keep it down,' Annie assured him. 'We've almost finished anyway.'

Zoe, who had been watching the exchange with interest, called out, 'Annie, why don't you have a go at the course?'

Annie looked startled. 'Me? No, I don't think so...'

'You could have a go with your friend,' Jennifer smirked, nodding at Jamie. 'If he's taking a break.'

'What's that?' Jamie looked interested, stepping fully into the room to hear what Zoe and Jennifer were saying.

'We've been doing an exercise,' Annie explained, starting to feel increasingly trapped. 'Focusing on listening and communication. It's an obstacle course, as you can see,' she said, waving her hand at the peculiar mix of items behind her. 'And one person does it blindfolded, while the other guides them. But it's meant for couples, so…'

'I don't mind giving it a go,' Jamie shrugged easily. 'If you want to test it out.'

'Go on, Annie,' Zoe cheered.

'Yeah, you should find out what the rest of us have been going through,' Simon added good-naturedly.

Annie looked round at the expectant faces, conceding that they had a point; if she was making them go through all this, then maybe she should experience it too.

'Well… I suppose so…' she agreed reluctantly, as Brigitte grinned and passed the scarf over to Jamie.

'What's your name, by the way?' Zoe spoke up, with a cheeky grin.

'Oh, I'm Jamie,' he smiled shyly, turning round to give the group a little wave.

'Hi Jamie,' came the chorus of replies.

He turned back to Annie, asking casually, 'Do you want to be blindfolded?'

'Sure, why not?' Annie replied, trying to sound calm when in actual fact she was wondering what on earth she'd got herself into.

As Jamie looped the scarf around her head, she felt the warmth of his fingertips against her skin, his hands brushing lightly over her hair as he carefully tied the scarf in place.

'So I just direct you around the course?' he asked, and Annie felt his breath against her neck as he spoke.

She swallowed, her heart thumping in her chest. 'That's right.'

'Great. Well, take two steps forward, and then a small step to the left. Hey, this is just like computer programming,' he grinned.

'So what does that make me?' Annie retorted. 'A string of code?'

'No talking please,' Zoe piped up. 'Jamie, you should only be giving directions, and Annie, you need to stay quiet and listen. It's all about the communication,' she parodied.

Jamie smiled. 'Okay, Annie, take another step forward…'

The room fell silent, everyone watching the two of them negotiate the obstacle course. Jamie's voice was calm and clear, and Annie followed his instructions exactly, expertly making her way around the course in record time.

She felt a huge sense of achievement as she rang the hand bell and pulled off the blindfold to see Jamie smiling at her from across the room. The rest of the group burst into applause, before Zoe quietened them down by asking, 'So does anyone have any comments to make?'

'I thought the communication between the two of you was excellent,' Simon spoke up.

'I agree,' added Jennifer. 'There are clearly no problems in your relationship.'

'In fact,' Carolyn put in, a glint in her eye, 'I would go so far as to say that the pair of you make an excellent couple.'

The group burst into laughter once again, as Annie felt her face flame. When she finally dared to meet Jamie's eyes, he was grinning at her.

Chapter 12

'Good sex is like good bridge. If you don't have a good partner, you'd better have a good hand' –
Mae West

'Knock knock, is anyone home?' Annie called out, as she pushed open the front door of her parents' house and stepped into the familiar hallway, with its comforting clutter of wellington boots and walking shoes, overcoats hanging from the old-fashioned stand and golf umbrellas propped up in the corner.

Her parents lived in a beautiful detached country-cottage-style house in the pretty little town of Aylsham, around half an hour from Annie's home. It wasn't the house she'd grown up in – her parents had downsized after she and Holly moved out – but she loved its cosy feel, and the familiar objects from her childhood in every room.

'Hello, boy,' she grinned, as her parents' dog, Romeo, an eight-year-old golden retriever, came barrelling towards her. She bent down and petted him, burying her hands in his fur, as Romeo let out an excited bark and tried to lick her face.

'Annie, there you are!' her mother, Pamela, exclaimed, as she came rushing through to greet her. An attractive woman in her early sixties, with a shoulder-length bob and sparkling blue eyes, Pamela was wearing a Cath Kidston apron over her clothes, and carrying a glass of rosé wine. 'Come through, come through,' she insisted, ushering Annie into the kitchen. 'Holly and Greg are already here.'

'Mmm, it smells delicious,' Annie commented, as she was hit by the mouth-watering aroma of her mother's Sunday lunch.

'Well, I'll be dishing up in ten minutes, so help yourself to a glass of wine.'

'Annie, lovely to see you,' her father, Graham, cried, getting up from the bar stool he was sitting on and coming across to give her a hug. At seventy-one, he was almost a decade older than her mother, and Annie couldn't help but notice the way he moved more slowly than he had the last time she'd seen him, his body stiffer, the lines on his face more pronounced.

'You too, Dad. The garden's looking beautiful,' she told him, looking out of the patio doors to the well-kept back garden beyond. The spring flowers were in full bloom, tubs of daffodils and tulips providing a riot of colour, whilst the borders were dotted with snowdrops and crocuses.

'We had a few plants killed off by that late frost, but everything seems to be blooming now,' Graham replied.

'Hey sis, I thought I heard you,' Holly grinned, rushing through the kitchen door and enveloping Annie in a hug. 'I was just showing Greg the new blinds in the living room.'

'Hi Hols. Hi Greg,' Annie beamed, kissing her sister's husband on the cheek. He was about the same height as her, with curly brown hair, and today he was wearing smart trousers and a pale blue shirt. Whilst he was undoubtedly attractive, he wasn't Annie's type at all – fortunately! Greg and Holly had been together since they were teenagers but, if Annie was being honest, she found him a little uptight and dull. There was no doubting that he loved her sister though, and the two of them seemed just as besotted now as they did when they were first dating.

'Can I get anyone a top up?' Annie asked, as she grabbed a wine glass from the cupboard and pulled the rosé out of the fridge.

'Go on then, just a splash,' her mother winked. 'I've been working hard all morning.'

'Holly?'

'I'm on the lemonade – I'm driving.'

'I wouldn't mind another beer, Annie,' Greg said, and Annie handed him and her father a bottle of Peroni.

'How's the classic car stuff going?' Annie asked Greg, all too aware that she'd thrown a drink over one of his colleagues in the not-too-distant past, and anxious to make amends with him.

'Good thanks.' Greg brightened. 'Would you believe that yesterday Dad and I drove all the way to Colchester just to pick up original hubcaps?'

'Wow,' Annie responded, not really sure how she ought to reply. 'That's dedication.'

'Oh, don't get him started, he'll never shut up,' Holly warned, as she affectionately cuddled up to her husband.

'Right, sit down, everyone, the food's on its way,' Pamela announced, as everyone took their places around the large, wooden dining table in the conservatory. Soon there were steaming heaps of roast beef, Yorkshire pudding and vegetables slathered in gravy on the plates in front of them.

'Can you pass me the roast potatoes, Dad?' Annie asked, helping herself to three as he did so.

Pamela raised an eyebrow. 'Careful, Annie, you need to watch that figure of yours.'

'Oh, don't be ridiculous, Mum,' Holly defended her sister. 'Annie's as skinny as a rake! I wish I could eat what she eats.'

'I'm just saying, it gets harder to keep the weight off once you're in your thirties. Believe me, I know. And if you want the men to take an interest, then you need to stay slim and attractive.'

Annie glanced at Holly and rolled her eyes, but her mother saw the gesture.

'I'm just saying,' Pamela continued, spearing a forkful of spring cabbage. 'It might seem all fine and dandy being a career woman now, but you've got to think about when you're older and need someone to take care of you.'

'I wouldn't have thought you'd be so keen for me to settle down after what happened last time,' Annie shot back, unable to resist.

'Oh. Yes. Mark,' Pamela said, pursing her lips into a fine line. 'Well, the less said about that episode, the better. But we've all moved on from it now, haven't we? That was just a silly, youthful mistake, and it's about time you found someone else, don't you think?'

Annie stared hard at her plate and carried on eating, carefully not looking at her mother. She didn't want to start an argument, but didn't trust herself to speak.

'Well, Annie *is* dating,' Holly spoke up, breaking the silence. Pamela turned to look at her, and Annie's head snapped up, wondering what Holly was doing. 'She went out on a date with a friend of Greg's,' Holly continued, sounding more uncertain now. 'Didn't she, Greg?'

Greg remained silent, until Holly jabbed him in the ribs. He fixed Annie with a hard look. 'Yes. Yes she did.'

'*What are you doing?*' Annie mouthed silently at Holly.

Holly looked panic-stricken. '*Sorry! Trying to help,*' she mouthed back.

'Did you now?' Pamela said, looking distinctly more impressed. 'And what was this young man's name?'

Annie cleared her throat. 'Tom. He was called Tom.'

'He sounds nice,' Pam replied, and Annie couldn't help but wonder what criteria her mother was basing this on. 'And will you be seeing him again?'

Annie hesitated, glancing across at Greg who had a face like thunder. 'No, I don't think I will. He… He wasn't my type,' she finished lamely.

Pamela put her fork down, disappointment written across her face. 'Oh, Annie. You're just too fussy, you know that.'

Annie opened her mouth to retort, but her father came to her rescue. 'You know, Annie, I didn't marry your mother until I was thirty-six. I was seen as a confirmed bachelor in those days, but then Pamela swept me off my feet,' he finished, smiling across at her.

'Yes, but it was different for you,' Pam insisted.

'Why? Because he was a man?' Annie shot back.

'Yes, exactly, darling. More wine, anyone?'

'Mum!' Holly burst out in exasperation, despairing at her mother's outdated views. Pamela merely shrugged, her face a picture of innocence as she refilled their glasses.

Annie opened her mouth to fire back a sarcastic retort, stopping in her tracks as she felt a wet nose snuffling at her feet and looked down to see Romeo. He was gazing up at her adoringly, with those huge brown eyes.

At least someone loves me, Annie thought wryly, smiling sweetly at her mother, as she smuggled Romeo a piece of Yorkshire pudding and he chomped happily underneath the table.

'Are you sure you don't want just one glass?' Pamela was asking Holly. 'I know you're driving, but so's Annie, and one glass is okay.'

'I'm fine thanks, Mum,' Holly replied. She sneaked a sideways glance at Greg, who almost imperceptibly nodded his head. 'Actually, there's something we need to tell you all.'

Annie's heart began to beat faster as she looked at her sister, noticing the glow that seemed to surround her, the way she was beaming at her husband.

Pamela seemed to sense it too, quickly sitting down at the table, one hand on her chest in anticipation.

'I'm pregnant,' Holly burst out. 'We're having a baby!'

'Oh congratulations,' Pamela cried, looking close to tears. 'That's wonderful news – Graham, break out the champagne!'

'Hey, that's not fair, I can't have any,' Holly protested, as everyone laughed.

Annie leant across to hug her sister. 'I'm so happy for you,' she said genuinely.

Holly looked back at her, her eyes dancing. 'You're going to be an auntie!'

'Auntie Annie?' Annie replied, pulling a face. 'I'm not sure about that.'

'You'll get used to it,' Holly grinned. 'Unless you want the baby to call you Auntie Wotsit,' she teased, picking up on Annie's teenage nickname which stemmed from an unfortunate incident with some fake tan.

'Annie's fine,' she replied hastily.

'So how far along are you? When's the baby due?' asked Pamela, dabbing her eyes with a tea towel.

'We've got our first scan on Thursday, so it's a little early still,' Holly explained. 'But we just couldn't wait.'

'Here, I'll let you do the honours,' Graham said, as he passed a bottle of champagne to Greg, who promptly popped the cork to a round of applause and filled four flutes.

Pamela raised her glass in a toast. 'To Holly and Greg, and their new little one. And to being grandparents.'

'And to Auntie Annie,' Holly couldn't resist adding.

'To Auntie Annie,' they echoed, as Annie blushed and took a large gulp of her champagne.

❄ ❄ ❄

'I'll never let go, Jack. I promise…'

Annie was curled up on the sofa in her onesie, cuddling a pillow, as she tried to stop the tears from flowing. Kate Winslet was clutching Leonardo DiCaprio's hands, giving them one final, tender kiss before he plunged into the icy waters of the Atlantic Ocean.

Annie's snuffles turned into full-on sobs, as the final scenes of *Titanic* played out, and she grabbed a tissue from the box on the coffee table. Her goldfish, Harry and Sally, watched disinterestedly as she dried her eyes and blew her nose.

As the titles rolled, and Celine Dion began to sing, Annie flopped backwards on the sofa and let out a sigh.

Maybe her mother was right, she thought dispiritedly. Maybe she *had* become too fussy when it came to men. But was it so very wrong to want a love like Jack and Rose – and a man who looked like Leo?

If anything, it was her mother's fault in the first place, for bringing her up on films like *Brief Encounter* and *Casablanca*. Annie wanted a strong, sexy, yet sensitive hero, who could defend her honour but talk about his feelings too.

If Annie was being honest with herself, she knew it was the news of her sister's pregnancy that had thrown her feelings into sharp relief, and caused her to come home from her parents' house and instantly stick *Titanic* on the DVD player. Of course, she was ecstatic that Holly and Greg were having a baby, and she couldn't wait to be an auntie… But Annie couldn't shake the feeling that nothing in her life was going to plan, while Holly was doing everything perfectly – marriage to her childhood sweetheart, a good job, settling down with a baby, and all before she hit thirty. All Annie had was an extensive DVD collection and a job which people sometimes confused with prostitution.

But no, she was just being silly, she told herself, as she hauled herself up from the sofa and threw the empty Ben & Jerry's Phish Food tub in the bin. The right man would come along eventually, she felt sure of it, and when he did she would *know*. It wouldn't be like the last time – she wouldn't misread the signs, or rush into anything she shouldn't, swept up in a romantic fantasy that had little to do with the reality of the situation. But it would only happen when the time was right.

One thing Annie had learnt from all the couples who came to see her – and from all the romantic comedies she'd watched over the years – was that you couldn't fake chemistry. Anyone who'd ever seen Elizabeth Taylor and Richard Burton together in *Cleopatra* knew that – the screen practically melted, the electricity between them was so hot.

Annie had often counselled couples who, on the surface, were as different as chalk and cheese, appearing to have little in common. One might be a six-foot burly male with a WWE obsession, married to a five-foot-nothing mousy type who preferred to spend time reading romance novels; or a go-get-'em alpha female with a guy who was quite happy to stay at home and be a house husband; but once you spoke to them, the chemistry between them was undeniable. Annie just helped them to rediscover it.

No, she resolved. Despite what her mother said, Annie didn't intend to settle for anything less than a man who could turn on her body *and* her brain. She would dry her eyes, cheer up and get back out there. After all, as Scarlett O'Hara might say, tomorrow is another day.

Chapter 13

*'My wife is a sex object. Every time I ask for sex,
she objects' – **Les Dawson***

'Linda, it's so good to finally meet you,' Annie smiled warmly, ushering Ray and his wife into her office.

Linda looked distinctly less enthusiastic. She kept her coat wrapped tightly around her, like a layer of protection, her lips pressed together in a thin line as she stared around Annie's office.

'Ray, how are you?' Annie asked, as she closed the door behind them.

'I'm well, thank you,' Ray replied politely, although his expression betrayed just how nervous he was at the prospect of what lay ahead. Annie suspected it had taken an awful lot of convincing just to get Linda to turn up today, and she knew she had to tread carefully if she was going to get Linda to return and work through their issues.

'So, Linda, what has Ray told you about these sessions?' she asked brightly.

Linda glanced angrily at her husband, before meeting Annie's gaze. 'Not very much. I know he thinks we have various… problems that he thinks you can help us with.'

Annie rested her elbows on the desk, lacing her fingers together. 'And have you had the opportunity to talk about these problems?'

'A little,' Linda offered, still looking as though she didn't want to be there. 'I know that it's all about our… well, about our *lack* of… Oh, this is ridiculous!' she burst out, standing up and turning angrily on Ray. 'I don't know why on earth you brought me here. I don't mean to be rude,' she said to Annie, 'and I'm sure you mean well, but there's absolutely no way this is going to work.'

'Linda,' Annie began, jumping to her feet.

Ray stood up too, placing his body between Linda and the exit. 'Please, love,' he said desperately. 'We've come this far. At least give it a fair go.'

Linda hesitated, looking from Ray to Annie and back again.

'We absolutely don't have to discuss anything you don't want to,' Annie assured her. 'You can let me know immediately if you're not comfortable with anything, and we'll change the subject.'

Mutinously, and without saying a word, Linda sat back down. Annie silently exhaled, meeting Ray's eyes in a mutual glance of relief.

'So perhaps we should start by talking more generally about your marriage – where you met, and how you first got together. Who'd like to start?'

Ray nodded encouragingly at Linda. 'Go on, love.'

Linda raised her eyes to the ceiling then took a deep breath. 'We first met in a club, back in 1979. The Empire, it was called, on Red Lion Street. It's not there any more. They knocked it down, and built that big Debenhams.'

'I'd gone with my mate, Jim, for his stag do,' Ray explained. 'He was getting married the following week, but I was still single.'

Linda shrugged. 'That's about it really. He came over to chat to me at the bar, and then we had a dance.'

'She caught my eye straight away,' Ray grinned. 'She was wearing this tiny little tartan mini skirt, with these knee-length socks, and a tight polo neck that showed off her fantastic boobs and her tiny waist.'

'All right, all right.' Linda rolled her eyes. 'You make me sound like a tart!'

A flicker of hurt crossed Ray's face. 'I didn't mean that at all. You looked wonderful.'

'Clearly things have changed a bit since then,' Linda said, with a wry glance at Annie.

'Not at all,' Ray insisted. 'You still look amazing.'

Linda snorted in disbelief. 'You can see why I fell for him, can't you? He had all the right lines,' she spat, and her tone was resentful.

Annie frowned, wondering why these memories didn't seem to be as happy for Linda as they were for Ray. 'Can you tell me about your wedding day? Ray, how did you propose?'

At this, both of them looked uncomfortable. Ray's leg began to jiggle anxiously, as Linda bit her lip and looked down at the floor.

'What happened?' Annie pressed.

'It wasn't… It wasn't a traditional sort of proposal,' Ray said carefully. 'Well, maybe it was sort of traditional – I'm sure we're not the only couple to get engaged under those circumstances. What I mean is, it wasn't really a hearts and flowers occasion. I was working at Rowntree's, the chocolate factory, at the time. Linda said she needed to talk to me, urgently, and she came and met me on my lunch break…'

'I was pregnant,' Linda burst out, tired of Ray stringing out the story. 'I'd got up the duff with our Rose, so Ray said he'd marry me. That's about the size of it, isn't it?' She turned to him accusingly.

'Well, not exactly…'

'Isn't it? Do you mean to say you'd have married me if I wasn't pregnant? I know you'd been sniffing around Susan Townsend. Pretty little Susie, with her perfect blonde hair and her fancy clothes from London. But instead you got lumbered with me because you wanted to *do the right thing*.' The bitterness in her voice was shocking. Ray looked as though he'd been slapped.

'Is that what you think? All these years, is this what you've believed?'

Linda nodded. A tear slowly rolled down her cheek, and she swiped it away angrily.

'That's just… It's just not true!' Ray protested. 'You really think I'd have stayed with you all this time, had our Marianne and Robbie too, if I wasn't absolutely, completely, head over heels in love with you?'

Linda raised an eyebrow. 'Making the best of a bad job, I think they call it. But it's fine – I had the kids and the shop, and they gave me a sense of purpose. No one can ever say I was a bad wife to you either; I always had your food on the table, and gave you what you wanted in bed too. But now I'm done. I don't want to live a lie any more.'

'Live a lie…?' Ray looked utterly baffled. 'So all these years when I thought everything was fine between us – that we were happy and in love – you're saying that was some kind of sham?'

'I don't know what I'm saying!' Linda was getting more upset with every word. Annie sat back quietly, instinctively feeling that she shouldn't speak at this point. Right now, Linda and Ray were being more honest with each other than they had been for years, and she needed to leave them to it.

'I don't know what to do, other than to lay my cards on the table,' Ray said eventually. 'You know it's not easy for me – I'm not a man who's big on talking about his emotions and feelings. But needs must, I suppose. I've been absolutely mad about you since the first moment I saw you. When I clapped eyes on you in that bar, you were hands down the most beautiful woman I'd ever seen, and something happened to me, right here,' he continued softly, clasping a hand over his heart, his voice sounding choked. 'And nothing's been the same since. I knew from our very first date that you were the girl I wanted to marry, and nothing has changed for me. Nothing. I don't know where you got that ridiculous story about Susan Townsend from.'

'Angie O'Brien told me, just after we got married.'

'Angie O'Brien was a nasty little stirrer with a vicious tongue. You really want to believe her, over me?'

'I don't know what to believe any more,' Linda said helplessly.

'Look, why do you think I'm always going on at you to work less hours in that damn shop? It's because I want to spend time with you. I want us to do things together.'

'What, like play golf?' Linda shot back.

For the first time, Ray looked across at Annie, his expression pleading.

'Linda,' Annie interjected softly, but Linda cut her off, abruptly getting to her feet.

'Thank you, Annie, but I think we're done here. I don't think this is for me.'

But to Annie and Linda's surprise, Ray jumped up too, saying defiantly: 'No, Linda, I need you to make a decision.

We've talked more honestly in these last thirty minutes than we have in thirty years. I don't know whether or not you believe me, but I've always loved you. *Always.* If you want to salvage this marriage then I believe that seeing Annie is a good thing, and that she's the only one who can help us. So you need to make a decision, and you need to make it now. Are you in, or are you out?'

Chapter 14

*'Among men, sex sometimes results in intimacy;
among women, intimacy sometimes results in sex'* –
Barbara Cartland

It was 9.30 pm and Annie was still in her office. The standing light behind her desk was switched on, the rain pattering lightly against the window. Annie stifled a yawn, stretching out her back which was aching from being hunched over her desk for so long. Then she leant forward and began writing once again, filling pages of A4 in her small, neat handwriting.

Annie kept case notes of every couple she worked with, detailing after every session the topics they'd talked about and the exercises she'd set them, noting down any particular positives or negatives, as well as ideas to try with them in future. In spite of the modern, shiny Samsung laptop that she owned, Annie preferred to handwrite all of her notes, before filing them away in the large silver cabinets in the corner of the room.

She was just writing up her observations of Ray and Linda's relationship when there was a knock on the door. Annie jumped. At this time of night, there was usually no one else around. Perhaps it was Celeste, the cleaner, wanting to tidy Annie's office, or come in for a chat.

'Jamie!' Annie exclaimed in surprise when she answered the door.

'Hi Annie, I wondered if you'd still be here. I know you often work late.'

'Yeah, unfortunately,' she grinned, wondering what he wanted. He was dressed in dark trousers and a navy blue sweater, with a white shirt peeking out from beneath, and he looked tired but exhilarated.

'Have you got time to take a break? I was wondering if you could help us out with something?'

Annie was instantly intrigued. 'I'd love an excuse to get me away from my desk. But what do you need me to do?'

'Come and see,' Jamie grinned, as he began to walk away down the corridor.

Annie stared after him in confusion. 'Do I need to bring anything?'

'Nope. Just yourself.'

She hurried to catch up with him as he strode past the kitchen, his long legs quickly covering the distance.

'I didn't realise anyone else was still around,' she told him.

'We've been putting in a few late nights of our own,' Jamie replied. 'Working hard on our latest project.'

'Oh, is that the one you mentioned before? The holiday finder app?'

'No, we finished that one, and the client loved it. This is a new game,' he announced, his blue eyes twinkling as he pushed open his office door with a flourish. Annie stepped in and glanced around. The unit was a similar size to her own space, but furnished completely differently. The walls were decorated with a couple of framed prints – a black and white photo of the New York skyline, and a dramatic shot of waves crashing around a lighthouse – whilst a spiky-leaved spider plant stood on the window sill. Other than that, the room seemed devoted to technology: two desks were pushed back to back, with a computer and multiple screens on each, as well as a laptop, an iPad, a couple of phones and a plethora of other gadgets. An empty takeaway pizza box was resting on a spare chair, and Jamie hastily folded it up and pushed it in the recycling bin.

'Sorry about that,' he apologised, looking shame-faced. 'Like I said, we've been working a lot of late nights.'

'No worries,' Annie smiled. 'Hi Matt, how are you?' she asked, greeting Jamie's brother, who was lounging in his swivel chair. Matt had the same blond hair and slim figure as his brother, although his hair was shorter, and Annie didn't think he was quite as attractive as Jamie. Right now, Matt also wore that same expression of exhausted exhilaration.

'Great thanks, Annie. So you're here to try out our new app, are you?'

'Am I?' Annie shrugged helplessly. 'I'm not really sure what I'm here for.'

'Annie Hall, you are in the enviable position of being the first person *ever* to try out *Coconut Shack*, the incredible new smartphone game that's about to take the world by storm,' Matt informed her. 'Do you realise just how lucky you are?'

'I don't think I do, no,' Annie replied honestly.

Matt looked at Jamie, and the pair of them shook their heads in disbelief, which made Annie giggle.

'Right, sit down here,' Jamie told her, indicating an unoccupied chair which she assumed must be his. He placed his hands on her shoulders as she sat down, and Annie felt her skin tingle at the warmth of his touch.

'Have you done much gaming before?' Jamie asked, appearing not to notice her reaction.

'And by gaming, we don't mean "Have you spent hours trying to complete *Grand Theft Auto 5*",' Matt clarified. 'More like the apps on your phone – *Plants vs Zombies*, that kind of thing.'

'I did have a bit of an *Angry Birds* addiction for a while back there,' Annie admitted. 'And I've played *Bejeweled* and a few others.'

'Perfect! Then you know exactly the kind of thing we're aiming for. You can try it on the Mac for now,' Jamie suggested, leaning over her to press a couple of buttons on the keyboard. A brightly coloured screen popped up, bearing the title 'Coconut Shack'. The graphics were bold, simplistic and childlike, but Annie could see how they would have mass appeal.

Jamie passed her a black pad, which was plugged into the side of the computer. 'This works the same way as the touch-screen technology on your phone,' he explained. 'So you'll play it through this for the moment. Ready?'

Annie looked panic-stricken. 'Aren't you going to explain what I have to do?'

Jamie shook his head. 'Nope. We want to see how intuitive the game is, so if you can pick it up without being told the rules, then we'll know it's worked. It has to be really easy and simple, yet addictive.'

'Okay,' Annie agreed nervously. She tapped on the pad to start, and the title graphic was replaced with a Hawaiian-looking backdrop. On the left of the screen was a helicopter, next to it was a giant coconut, and along the bottom were palm trees and pink hibiscus flowers. As Annie moved her finger on the keypad, the helicopter began to fly. It seemed obvious that she had to pick up the giant coconut, so she hovered low over it, and it quickly attached itself to the bottom of the helicopter. Then she flew off, over the palm trees, the background scrolling along behind. When she flew over a flower, the helicopter got tangled and crashed.

'Oh!' Annie wailed in disappointment. 'Can I have another go?'

'Go ahead,' Jamie nodded, smiling at Matt.

This time Annie knew what she was doing. The palm trees boosted her flight, giving her longer in the air, but she had to avoid the flowers as they could crash the helicopter. When she flew over a crab, she jabbed at the touch-pad and the coconut dropped, landing on the crab and crushing it. A message flashed up on the screen saying that she'd passed Level 1 and won fifty points.

'Hurray, I won!' Annie cheered, looking triumphantly at the brothers. 'Can I carry on?'

'Sure,' Jamie agreed.

The game continued in the same simple yet addictive format. As Annie passed through the levels, there were more coconuts to load and more crabs to crush, and each episode was slightly harder with the introduction of more obstacles. Every time Annie died, or finished a level, she promised herself 'just one more go'. Over an hour later, she was still sitting in the chair, telling herself that she would put it down in a minute. Matt had already left, explaining that he'd promised his girlfriend he wouldn't be home too late, which left only Jamie to supervise Annie's progress.

'Come on, Annie. You can do it!' Jamie cheered, as she cleared the final hurdle and made it onto Level 12.

'I'll just play up to fifteen,' she said casually, already absorbed in the game.

'Well, you'll have to stop at twenty, as we've only built that far. Aargh, watch out for that hidden flower! Oh no, you didn't listen to me,' he sighed, as Annie crashed once again.

She looked up briefly to glare at him, then carried on playing. They were sitting close together, their bodies almost touching, and Annie couldn't help but be aware of his presence beside her. His skin was warm, and he smelt of coffee and lingering traces of aftershave.

When she failed the same level three times in a row, Jamie looked at her pityingly and asked, 'Would you like me to complete it for you?'

'Would you like to shut up and let me concentrate?' Annie narrowed her eyes in mock-annoyance, and Jamie burst out laughing.

'I love a woman with attitude,' he teased. 'See, this game is turning you into a monster. Maybe you should stop playing?'

'Not yet,' Annie begged. 'Just five more minutes.'

When she finally hit Level 15, almost twenty minutes later, Annie sat back and glanced up at the clock. 'Woah, how did it get to eleven o'clock? I can't believe the time went so fast.'

'That's a good sign,' Jamie smiled. 'I'm glad you enjoyed it.'

'It's addictive,' Annie confessed. 'Honestly, you've made a really good game.' Her eyes were shining, her adrenaline pumping.

'Thanks. Do you have any suggestions on how to improve it?'

Annie thought for a moment. 'Not really. It's great as it is.'

'How about the name?'

'*Coconut Shack*? It's good. I always like alliteration though. How about something like… *Coconut Cracker*?'

'*Coconuts & Crabs*? *Crab Crusher*?'

'*Coconut Crush*?' Annie suggested.

Jamie stared at her, his eyes growing wide. 'Yes! That's absolutely perfect, Annie.' He looked as though he might throw his arms around her, but then thought better of it. 'If we had one, I'd crack open a bottle of champagne to celebrate. I don't suppose you fancy the cold dregs of a mug of coffee?'

'Not really,' Annie giggled, looking around. 'This place is a mess,' she stated, matter-of-factly. 'Do you ever let Celeste clean it?'

'Nope. There are all sorts of important things in here, we don't want them messing up. Besides, we might lose the creativity if everything was too ordered.'

'Hmm.' Annie looked sceptical. 'Is this what you're like at home?'

'Not exactly,' Jamie admitted. 'To be honest, I spend most of my time here, so my house is pretty tidy. Although I love to cook, so on my days off the kitchen's always full of clutter.'

Annie raised an eyebrow in surprise. 'You love to cook? You sound like the perfect man,' she said without thinking, then immediately regretted it, her cheeks flushing pink.

'Well, I wouldn't exactly say that…'

'Do you live on your own?' Annie asked, attempting to change the subject, then realising it looked as though she was prying even further into his personal life.

'Yeah,' Jamie nodded, not seeming to notice. 'I do now. I used to live…' He trailed off, then started again. 'Matt and I bought a place together a couple of years ago, just off Drayton Road, but then he moved in with his girlfriend, so now it's just me.'

'Oh, I'm not far from there,' Annie told him. 'In Hellesdon.'

'That's really close,' Jamie agreed. 'I'm surprised I haven't bumped into you.'

'Well, I'm usually here,' Annie laughed. 'And then we bump into each other in the kitchen.'

Jamie laughed too. 'You're obviously a hard worker.'

Annie shrugged. 'I enjoy it. I suppose it's true what they say – it doesn't feel like work if you're enjoying it.'

Jamie nodded. 'I know what you mean. Although I'd rather work from a Caribbean beach than an industrial estate in Norwich.'

'Mmm, I'll join you there,' Annie grinned. 'Take me with you if you win the lottery.'

'I will,' Jamie promised, his eyes sparkling. 'I'll give you a job as my number one games tester.'

'It's a deal.' Annie smiled, then checked the time once again and groaned. 'It's been fun, but I think I need to head home now.'

'Yeah, I need to make a move too. I'll just finish a couple of things here and then I'll be off.'

'Don't stay too late,' Annie warned him, as she stood up and swung her bag over her shoulder. 'Thanks for tonight, Jamie. I really enjoyed it, and I think you've got a fantastic product.'

'Thanks, Annie. I enjoyed it too. You're a pretty mean gamer.'

Annie laughed. 'Good night, Jamie. See you tomorrow.'

'Night, Annie.'

Annie walked off down the empty corridor, a definite spring in her step despite the late hour. As she pushed open the exit door, she realised that she was smiling away to herself, happiness zinging through her body, as she thought about the evening and the fun she'd had with Jamie.

Woah, what was that all about? she wondered suddenly, stopping dead as she made her way across the car park. It was just Jamie! Jamie, the guy that she saw every day at work, the guy who shared chocolate biscuits and banter during their afternoon tea break. So why was she suddenly grinning like an idiot, feeling as though she could float home instead of drive, and finding herself softly humming 'When You Say Nothing At All' under her breath?

Annie caught herself sharply, feeling emotions start to stir that she hadn't felt in a long time. Well, she wouldn't think about them right now, Annie told herself sternly. She was over-tired – it had been a long and stressful day – and she obviously wasn't thinking clearly. Plus she needed to stop spending her evenings watching *Notting Hill*, then she wouldn't spend the day with cheesy Ronan Keating songs stuck in her head.

No, Annie decided, climbing into her car and slinging her bag onto the passenger seat. She would drive home, go to bed, and when she woke in the morning it would be just another ordinary day. These unexpected, inexplicable feelings of happiness and excitement and promise would have completely disappeared, and everything would be back to normal. Just the way she liked it.

Chapter 15

'Sex is always about emotions. Good sex is about free emotions; bad sex is about blocked emotions'
– Deepak Chopra

'It's great to see another large turnout today,' Annie said, smiling round at the group. It was a Saturday morning and she was back in the boardroom, with eight sets of couples seated in a semi-circle in front of her.

'Today's exercise is going to be all about listening and communicating with your partner. The difference is that your partner isn't going to be the one you arrived with today.'

This announcement caused some murmurings and raised eyebrows around the room.

'That doesn't mean there's going to be wife swapping going on,' Annie quickly clarified, to relieved laughter and sniggers. 'I'm not suggesting you all throw your car keys into a bowl in the centre of the room. But I do want you all to team up with someone else. It doesn't matter how you're mixed – male or female, I don't mind. So, if you could all pair up…'

Everyone eyed each other a little nervously. There was a scraping of chairs as some people pushed theirs back and stood up, moving across the room. Others turned to their neighbour, with a terribly British *'So shall we…?'* and there were grateful smiles all round when everyone was suitably partnered up.

Zoe and Julia were sitting beside each other, but Zoe was somewhat nervous at the prospect of working with Nick's wife; she remembered Julia's behaviour in the previous group session, and assumed she'd be cold and unfriendly. But when Julia turned to her with a hesitant smile and said, 'Shall we work together?', Zoe instantly agreed.

'I'm Zoe, by the way,' she introduced herself.

'Julia,' replied Julia, and the two women grinned tentatively at each other, breaking the ice.

Nick was working with Linda, while Simon and Ray had paired up with some of the other regulars. The rest of the couples mixed themselves up and everyone looked expectantly at Annie.

'Have you all found a partner? Great. Now, for the first part of today, I want you to tell the person you're working with the story of how you met your *actual* partner. Try and give as much detail as you can – really make the person you're with feel as though they're living the story – whether it's funny or embarrassing or just downright romantic.'

'Exactly how much detail do you want us to go into?' Simon asked cheekily. 'I don't want to give away too many secrets.'

Sitting beside Julia, Zoe flushed red. 'Oi!' she exclaimed. 'You make it sound as though you had your wicked way with me on our first date. These sessions are about honesty, not fantasyland!'

Annie smiled at the two of them. 'As I said, *do* go into detail, but preferably not explicit. Try not to embarrass the person you're working with,' she advised, her eyes sparkling. 'Now, the point of this exercise is to get you reminiscing about those early days of falling in love. This is back when the physical attraction between the two of you was strongest; when you were most likely functioning on lust and hormones, and before the oxytocin kicked in. You might not know this, but in the first three years of a relationship, there are all kinds of hormones zooming around your body, literally making your heart race and heightening your sex drive. After that time period, a different hormone called oxytocin – also known as the cuddle hormone – kicks in.

'This does mean an end to those exciting emotions you experienced in the early days of your relationship,' Annie explained, glancing round the room. 'But the upside of this are feelings of security, contentment, and a desire to settle down. And while these are all great, sometimes we want to try and recapture that initial passion, and remember just what exactly made us fall in love in the first place. I'll give you about ten minutes to chat to your partner, and then you can swap over. Any questions?'

Everyone shook their heads, and Annie added, 'Oh, and you don't all have to stay seated where you are – feel free to move about and find a private corner, or somewhere that you feel comfortable, where you can really open up.'

Zoe and Julia moved their chairs a little way from the rest of the group, and Zoe asked, 'Do you want to go first?'

'Er… okay then,' Julia replied, not at all sure that she *did* want to go first. The situation between her and Nick didn't seem to have resolved itself one bit, despite another session with Annie, so remembering how loved up they used to be was the last thing Julia wanted to do.

'Right, so I have to talk about how Nick and I met? That's him over there, by the way,' she explained, pointing to her husband.

Zoe nodded. She remembered the two of them from the last group workshop, but didn't want to bring it up in case Julia felt embarrassed by the way they'd argued.

Julia cleared her throat. 'So, how did we meet? Well, we met at work actually. A bit clichéd, I know.' She rolled her eyes. 'We were working for this advertising company called Skyrocket, back in Derbyshire where we're both from.'

'Oh, I didn't realise you were from there,' Zoe exclaimed.

'Yeah, we moved here just over a year ago when Nick got a new job. It was an offer that was too good to refuse, so we packed up and came to Norwich.'

'And how are you finding it?'

'It's… all right.' Julia sounded uncertain. 'I mean, I don't really know many people yet. It's not like back home, where I grew up, and I had my mum and all my friends around. Plus I've been trying to set up my own business – I'm an events planner – so I've been rushed off my feet, and… Anyway, back to the story,' Julia said with forced brightness, trying not dwell on her problems. 'I was working as a receptionist-cum-PA to the MD of Skyrocket, and Nick was a junior account manager back then. I fancied him straight away actually—'

'That's so cute!' Zoe cut in.

'Yeah, I thought he was really good-looking, and he seemed… I don't know. I mean, every time he passed my desk he would stop and chat, or make a funny comment. He always said hello. Not all of them did – some of the staff were a bit snooty, and didn't have time for you if you were on reception, but Nick always made an effort.

'It got to the stage where I was waiting to see him every day, and when I did my tummy would flutter like crazy,' Julia continued, smiling despite herself. 'We had really good banter too. We could tease each other, and make each other laugh.'

'Did you ask him out?' Zoe wondered breathlessly.

'No, I was too scared! I was pretty sure from the way he talked that he was single, and I guessed he liked me too, but it would have been so awkward if I'd asked him out and he'd said no. We still had to work together after all. But then one day we were talking and he seemed a bit nervous,' Julia remembered, glancing over to where Nick was chatting to Linda. Annie had pulled up a chair and was listening to their conversation, and Julia couldn't help but wonder how Nick was recounting his version of the story. Did he see it the same way that she did? Did he still get misty eyed when he reminisced about their early days, and wonder how everything had gone so wrong for them now?

Julia dragged her attention back to Zoe, who was eagerly waiting for the next instalment.

'Like I said, we were talking, and he sort of steered the conversation round to food and what kind of restaurants I liked. I told him that I loved Italian, and he mentioned this great new place that had just opened, and did I fancy going some time? Of course, I said yes, but I still wasn't sure if it was an actual date, or whether we were just work colleagues socialising.'

'Of *course* it was a date. He obviously fancied you,' Zoe said knowledgably.

'Well, I hoped so,' Julia confessed. 'And I made a massive effort. I went to the hairdressers to get a professional blow-dry beforehand, and I bought a whole new outfit – shoes, handbag, everything. I just really liked him.'

'And was it amazing?'

Julia's face softened as she thought about it. 'Yeah, it was. We had a brilliant evening. It's all a bit of a blur, to be honest, as I was so nervous – I didn't want to spill anything down my new dress, or get something stuck between my teeth! I remember how confident Nick seemed, and he smelt gorgeous. Hugo Boss,' she recalled fondly.

'Five minutes left,' Annie called out, as she stood up from Linda and Nick and moved on to another pairing.

'When we came out of the restaurant, Nick took my hand, and I was ready to explode with excitement. We went to some bars and just had so much fun. We couldn't stop talking, and then we went to a club and danced until two am. You might not believe it, but he's a great dancer,' Julia continued, looking over at her husband once again. 'Well, he used to be. It's ages since we've been dancing now. Too old, I guess.'

'You're not too old,' Zoe scoffed. 'You should definitely go out some time. Hit the town on a Friday night! I mean, Norwich probably doesn't have the best clubbing scene in the world, but there're some fun places, and it's always a good laugh. You should come out with me and Simon.'

'Maybe… I don't think Nick and I are really in that place any more.'

'All the more reason to do it,' Zoe encouraged. 'Recapture your youth.'

'It feels like that's long gone,' Julia replied, with a wry smile.

Zoe paused, unsure how to reply. 'How long have you been married?' she asked eventually.

'Three years.'

'And what was the wedding like? Simon and I have just got engaged – see,' Zoe grinned, holding up her left hand to show off the sparkling diamond. 'So I'm a bit obsessed with weddings, and what other people did for theirs.'

'Oh, it was such a good day. You'll have a ball,' Julia assured her. 'The party afterwards is amazing too. You have all your favourite people – all your family and friends and everyone you love – all in the same room.'

'Everyone keeps telling me it'll go by so fast, and I won't have time to take it all in.'

'That's true. You want to talk to everyone, and make sure they're having fun, and enjoy your new husband all at the same time, so the day just flies.'

'What was your dress like? I can't decide which style to go for. I can't decide on anything really,' Zoe confessed with a giggle. 'I'm trying to pull this whole wedding together so fast and it's a nightmare. I never knew there was so much to organise – the reception, and the catering, and the flowers, and the band. It's endless.'

'Well, if you need a hand, it's what I do for a living,' Julia offered. 'Like I said, I've only been going for about a year, but I've already built up some good contacts and I'm sure I'd be able to help. Having someone to organise your wedding can really take the stress out of it for you.'

'That'd be incredible!' Zoe's eyes lit up, but just as quickly her face fell again. 'I don't think we'd be able to afford it though. We're on such a tight budget.'

'I'd be happy to do you a deal,' Julia shrugged. 'Especially if you'd let me take some photos on the day and give me a testimonial for my website. It's early days still, so I need to build up as much experience as possible. And I can keep my fee really low, as I cut deals with the suppliers and take my commission out of that.'

'That would be unbelievable – if you think it'd be possible?'

'Look, why don't I give you my card?' Julia suggested, searching through her purse and handing over her business card. 'Give me a call some time, and we can chat about your budget, and what you're looking for.'

'That sounds ace,' Zoe squealed, barely able to hide her excitement. 'Ooh, is that you?' she asked, noticing Julia's phone resting on top of her handbag, the screensaver showing a blonde-haired woman in a bridal gown.

'Yeah,' Julia grinned, looking bashful. 'I'd forgotten it was on there. I really should change it.'

'No, leave it,' Zoe insisted. 'Do you mind if I take a look? I'd love to see your dress.'

'Sure,' Julia agreed. 'Here, I've got a few wedding pics saved in a folder…' She scrolled through her photos then handed the phone to Zoe. 'There you go.'

'Ohhh, you look gorgeous!' Zoe breathed, taking in the strapless, mermaid-cut satin gown and sparkling tiara. 'Seriously Julia, you're stunning. Your dress looks incredible. And I love your hair.'

'Thanks, my friend Hanni did it for me.'

'It's beautiful.' Zoe flicked to the next photo. 'Ooh, Nick looks so handsome!' she gushed. 'Some men just really suit formal wear, don't they? Aww, you both look so happy.'

'Do we?' Julia looked sceptical. 'I suppose we were. Funny how things change.'

Her face clouded over once again, then both women looked up as they heard Annie's voice.

'Okay, your ten minutes are up. It's time to switch over,' she announced.

Julia turned to Zoe, forcing herself to smile as she slipped her phone back into her bag. 'Right, that's enough about me. It's your turn now, and I want to hear *all* about how you met Simon…'

Chapter 16

'Man may have discovered fire, but women discovered how to play with it' –
Candace Bushnell, Sex and the City

'Nick, are you coming?'

Nick glanced up to see Nina standing beside his desk. Despite the fact that it was just gone six pm and the end of the working day, Nina still looked as fresh as though she'd just arrived, in a slim-fitting red dress and matching jacket. She was staring at him questioningly.

'Huh?' Nick replied, aware that he sounded stupid.

'I was just saying, a few of us are heading to the pub. Do you fancy coming along?'

Nick hesitated. Right now, he couldn't think of anything better than a pint of cool, crisp lager, a game of pool and a packet of thick-cut steak crisps. But that wasn't really an option for him these days. No doubt Julia would be waiting at home for him, with a sour expression and a new set of lingerie.

'I… I really should be getting home,' he replied eventually, the look on his face making it clear how much he wanted to stay.

'Oh, just come for one,' Nina pleaded. 'It's my two-month anniversary – I've been here eight weeks today! And you've been so good to me, helping me settle in and find my feet. I'd really like to get you a drink, to say thanks.'

Once again, Nick felt himself waver. Over by the door, half a dozen of his colleagues were waiting with their coats on, watching him expectantly. He looked at Nina, hope written all over her face, and tried to remember the last time someone had desired his company so much.

'Okay,' Nick agreed impulsively, as Nina clapped her hands together in delight. 'Just the one.' He grabbed his coat and tapped out a quick text message to Julia.

'Ready?' Nina asked, looking thrilled.

Nick nodded, realising that he was actually looking forward to tonight. It had been ages since he'd gone out after work, and not simply dashed home to a sullen Julia. He looked across at Nina and smiled.

'Let's go.'

✳ ✳ ✳

The kettle clicked off, and Julia poured the boiling water over a bag of raspberry leaf tea, which was supposed to tone the uterus, the pelvic muscles, and aid with fertility in general. She blew across the top of the mug, taking a sip and wincing. It tasted disgusting, but if it was going to help her conceive, then she was willing to try it. She carried the drink through to the living room, picking up a copy of *Mother & Baby* magazine from the coffee table, and flopping down on the sofa.

It had been a long and hectic day at work, driving round the countryside from one beautiful old manor house to the next, trying to find the perfect location for the anniversary party she'd been booked to organise. In between, Julia had been almost permanently on her phone, attempting to placate the demanding mother of a spoilt child whose 'Sweet Sixteen' she was arranging. Julia loved her job, but trying to explain why it would be impossible to source sixteen miniature white ponies and dye them all in different shades of pink wasn't high up on the list of things she wanted to be doing.

She'd hoped Nick would come home on time tonight, but he clearly wasn't back yet. He was always working late at the moment – and leaving early in the mornings too – and Julia strongly suspected that he was doing it on purpose to stay out of the house. The thought saddened her. Tonight, especially, she could really do with a friendly face. Launching her own business was proving hugely stressful, and Julia would have valued her husband's support and advice.

At least she had a potential new job, helping to organise Zoe's wedding, Julia remembered, cheering slightly at the thought. Although Zoe was a few years younger than her, she seemed like a sweet girl, and Julia was looking forward to spending more time with her. She'd been feeling increasingly lonely in recent months, discovering that the downside of working for herself was that she had very little opportunity to meet new people and make new friends. In an unfamiliar city, far away from everyone she knew, there was no one Julia could call for an impromptu coffee; no one to confide in about the problems she was having with Nick, or her difficulty in getting pregnant.

On a whim, Julia grabbed the phone to call Naomi, her best friend from back home in Derby. She quickly dialled the number she knew off by heart, and listened eagerly to the ringtone, hoping her friend would pick up.

'Hello?'

'Hi Naomi, it's Jules. Have you got time to chat?'

'Of course, yes! I haven't heard from you in ages! How are you?'

Julia felt close to tears, hearing her friend's voice. 'Oh, not bad, you know,' she said casually, fighting to hold it all together. 'How about you?'

'I'm good! Alfie's just gone down for a nap, but he'll be up shortly.' Alfie was Naomi's baby son, and he was six months old. Julia had only seen him once since he'd been born, when she and Nick had taken a weekend trip back to Derby to catch up with family and friends. 'I'm okay for at least the next half hour though. Oh, it's so good to hear from you, Jules!'

'You too. How's Nathan?' Julia said, asking after Naomi's husband.

'He's really well. He's up in Glasgow tonight for a work thing, so I'm by myself with the baby. It's the perfect time to talk actually. How about Nick, how's he getting on?'

Julia hesitated before she replied. 'Yeah, he's okay. Busy with work. He's working a lot – we both are actually, but I guess we knew that would be the case when we moved here.'

As she finished speaking, she heard her mobile beep and picked it up:

> *Still at work, shouldn't be too late. Don't worry about food, I'll sort myself out x*

Speak of the devil, Julia thought wryly, noticing how detached his tone was. There was no 'love you' and only one kiss.

'I've actually just got a text from him now,' she told Naomi, forcing a laugh. 'He's working late tonight, as per usual. At least it means I can chat longer.' Julia tried her best to sound upbeat but Naomi, who'd known her since primary school, wasn't fooled.

'Julia,' she began gently. 'What's this really all about? Is everything okay with you and Nick?'

Julia opened her mouth, ready to insist that everything was fine, but what came out instead was a muffled sob. 'No,' she managed, her face crumpling as the tears began to flow. 'No, it's not all right at all. I don't understand what's happening with us. We're trying for a baby – I told you about that, right? – but it's just not happening and we seem to be falling apart...' Julia broke off, unable to speak for crying.

'Oh, love,' Naomi's sympathy reached down the line from a hundred miles away. 'I'm sorry.'

'No, *I'm* sorry,' Julia gulped. 'Forget I said anything.'

'Don't be crazy. Come on, pour yourself a glass of wine, get comfortable and tell me all about it.'

'I can't drink,' Julia managed through her tears, looking sadly at the rapidly cooling mug of raspberry leaf tea. 'I've given up alcohol in case it affects my fertility.'

'Oh, Julia,' Naomi sighed, but there was a smile in her voice, and before long Julia was laughing too.

'Naomi, it's so good to talk to you. I just... I really feel like I'm losing my mind these past few months. And I feel like I'm losing Nick. We don't seem to be able to connect any more. We're having all this sex to try and get pregnant, but the irony is we're so far apart, mentally. I just don't know what to do.'.'

'Maybe Nick's stressed because of work,' Naomi suggested.

'Maybe. I can't help thinking it's more than that.'

'Does he definitely want a baby? He might be having second thoughts, worrying about losing his youth or something.'

'It could be that, I suppose. But you know Nick. He's always been the sensible one – mature and committed. He's always worked hard to ensure we have a good future, and kids are definitely part of that plan.'

'Have you tried talking to him about it?'

'I've tried, but it always seems to descend into an argument. Although…' Julia trailed off.

'Although what?'

'I'm so embarrassed to admit this but…' Julia took a deep breath. 'We've been to see a therapist.'

'Huh?'

'It was Nick's idea. A sex therapist. Please don't tell anyone,' she begged.

'A sex therapist? What do they do, watch you and tell you where you're going wrong?'

Julia burst out laughing. 'No, thank God. Could you imagine? Nick, put your hand there – a bit higher, that's it! Julia, how's that for you?' The two women were in hysterics. 'No, it's more talking about your feelings and your relationship, then the therapist sets us exercises to do at home. Would you believe Nick's complaining that we're having too much sex? He says it feels impersonal, and that he wants more foreplay and more cuddles.'

'Aw, I think that's sweet,' Naomi insisted. 'It does sound like he's making an effort, if he's the one who suggested going.'

'Yeah, I suppose,' Julia agreed, wondering whether she'd been too harsh on him. 'Perhaps I do need to pull back a bit. But I want a baby so badly, you know?'

'I know. Although maybe you should come and look after Alfie for a few days, that might change your mind – sleepless nights, shitty nappies, constantly looking like crap. And believe me, sex will be the last thing on your mind once you've actually given birth. It destroys what's down there.'

Julia burst into cackles of laughter. 'But it's all worth it, right?'

'Yeah,' Naomi replied, her voice softening. As if on cue, Julia heard the sound of a baby crying in the background.

'Oh, I've got to go, it's feeding time. Listen, don't let the situation get you down, okay? You can always ring me any time you need to. And give Nick a break. You got lucky – he's one of the good guys.'

'He is, isn't he?' Julia agreed. 'Thanks so much, Naomi. Give Alfie a big kiss and a cuddle from me, and send my love to Nathan.'

'Will do. Speak soon.'

'Bye.' Julia hung up, thinking about what her friend had said. Maybe she *was* being too hard on Nick. Like Naomi said, he was one of the good guys. Maybe Julia needed to appreciate him more.

❅ ❅ ❅

Nick was starting to feel pleasantly drunk as he started on his third pint of lager. He'd had nothing to eat except two bags of crisps, which he'd shared with Nina, and he knew that he wasn't going to be able to drive home tonight. Oh well, he thought recklessly, he could just call a taxi.

Right now, he was watching two of his colleagues, Billy and Raj, play a game of darts. It was a tense match; they were down to the final few throws, and there was a whole five pounds riding on the outcome.

Beside him, Nina was sitting quietly, her long legs crossed as she sipped a glass of white wine with soda. They'd been chatting for most of the evening, and Nick was hugely enjoying her company. She was a lot of fun, and he was aware that she was flirting with him, but tonight he didn't care. It had been a long time since he'd had his ego massaged like that, and Nina was undoubtedly a very attractive woman. Hanging out with her was a welcome change from Julia's nagging, and her baby obsession.

'Yeah! Well done Raj!'

Nick heard a shout from across the pub, and realised that Raj had won the darts game. The others were clapping him on the back, whooping loudly, as Billy shook his head and opened his wallet, handing over a battered five-pound note. As Nick watched, they downed the last of their drinks and pulled on their coats, looking over to where he was sitting.

'Nick, we're off now. I'll see you tomorrow. Night, Nina.'

'Sure, Billy. See you tomorrow.'

The group walked out of the pub, leaving Nick and Nina sitting amongst a group of strangers. There was an instant shift in atmosphere, and Nick swallowed, suddenly acutely aware that the two of them were now alone together.

'So, how are you finding everything?' he asked awkwardly. 'You've been here two months now – that's gone quickly.'

'It has, hasn't it?' Nina agreed. 'I'm really enjoying it. And it's been great working with you – you're so good at what you do, and you've taught me so much.'

'Well, I don't know about that,' Nick harrumphed, but he was quietly pleased with the flattery.

'And how's everything with you?' Nina asked casually, flicking her long, dark hair back behind one shoulder.

Nick shrugged. 'Oh, you know. Fine, I suppose.'

'You've just seemed… a little down these past few days. It's probably none of my business.'

Nick smiled ruefully. His phone was sitting on the table in front of him, but he hadn't received a reply from Julia. She was probably still angry at him, he concluded, thinking how petty his wife could be sometimes.

'Just a few personal things going on,' Nick confessed, then immediately wondered why he'd said that.

At that moment, a woman sat down on the other side of Nina, forcing her to shift along the bench towards Nick. Her leg was warm against his, her skirt riding up her shapely thighs as she moved.

'I'm a good listener, if you ever need to talk,' she murmured, leaning into him.

Nick shook his head and sighed. 'You're not married, are you, Nina?'

'No,' she replied, and Nick couldn't help but notice the fullness of her lips as she spoke.

'Then you wouldn't understand.'

Nina reached across, placing a hand on his arm, and Nick looked up at her, startled. Their eyes met and, for a second, something passed between them, something that made Nick's blood race in his veins and his heart beat faster.

'Try me,' Nina whispered softly, an undeniable hint of flirtation in the statement.

Nick's breath caught in his throat. She was so close that he could smell the lingering musk of her perfume, and see the way her pupils dilated as she looked at him. Her lips were partially open, plump and moist, and Nick found that he couldn't stop staring at them.

Suddenly, he felt desperate to confess everything; to tell this vibrant, beautiful young woman how alone and scared and trapped and bored he felt in his marriage. How terrified he was that he'd made a mistake, and his secret fear that fifty years of quiet dissatisfaction was all that lay ahead of him. Nina would listen sympathetically, comfort him and…

Almost before he knew what he was doing, Nick leant forwards, the merest of movements bringing him nose to nose with Nina. His lips found hers – warm, soft, dizzyingly unfamiliar – and for a moment he was lost. A host of emotions rushed through him: relief and pleasure and undeniable excitement. Nina kissed him back eagerly, her body yielding to his, and all Nick could think about was how good it felt. He brought a hand up to her face, stroking her cheek, but the second his fingertips touched her skin he jumped away as though he'd received an electric shock. His eyes were wide, his heart pounding. What the hell had he been thinking?

'Sorry, Nina. I'm so sorry.' Nick scrabbled to his feet, standing up so quickly that he almost knocked his drink over. Nina stared back at him, hurt and confusion clearly written across her features.

'Nick, wait—' she began, but he cut her off.

'I need to go. Need to get home,' he mumbled, shaking his head as though trying to dislodge the spell she'd cast. 'I'm so sorry. I'll see you tomorrow, at work.'

Nick grabbed his jacket and fled, racing outside to hail a taxi and trying not to think about what had just happened. All he knew was that he needed to get out of there right away. He needed to get home, back to his wife.

Out on the street, the cold air hit him. There were no cabs in sight, and Nick began to jog, his only aim to get as far away from the pub as possible. His lips were on fire, his mouth still full of the taste of Nina, and as he ran he felt a new sensation stir in the pit of his stomach, spreading through his body and threatening to overwhelm him. It was a second before Nick could identify the feeling, but as he found a minicab and climbed into the back, his breathing coming hard, he realised exactly what it was.

It was guilt.

Chapter 17

'If you want to have great sex, find a partner who really turns you on' – **Jackie Collins**

Annie was spending her Sunday afternoon in the way she loved the best – chilling out and watching a romantic comedy. This time, it wasn't her extensive DVD collection that she'd turned to. Instead, she'd ventured to Cinema City, the cosy art-house cinema on St Andrews Street, to see the newly released film, *The Tender Night*. It was based on a Nicholas Sparks book, with Ryan Gosling and Amanda Seyfried starring as the leads, and Annie couldn't think of a more perfect combination. The critics had savaged it, of course, calling it schmaltzy, saccharine and unrealistic ('Have your sick bags at the ready' advised one particularly vicious review) but Annie didn't care.

She'd gone to the cinema alone. Having been single for most of her adult life, Annie had a strong independent streak, and wasn't fazed by the prospect of dining solo if she fancied a meal out, or even going on holiday by herself, on the rare occasions that she took a break from work. If the truth be told, she positively relished going to the cinema alone. She felt sure that if she'd asked her sister, or one of her friends, they'd have been happy to come along. But being on her own meant that Annie could selfishly please herself – pick what she wanted to eat, choose where she wanted to sit, and generally be free to drool over Ryan and sigh at the happy ending, without having to worry about whether or not the person she was with hated the film and was falling asleep.

To Annie, it felt like a huge indulgence to have a little quality 'me' time. Some women loved to take a long hot bubble bath with a glass of wine, whilst others liked to shop until they dropped, but for Annie there was no better way to spoil herself than with a trip to see the latest romantic movie.

Right now, she was queuing to get her ticket, leaning over the counter to see what flavour sweets were available. As she moved back, she felt herself knock into someone, her elbow colliding with their rib.

'Sorry,' they both apologised simultaneously.

The other voice sounded strangely familiar, and Annie span round to find herself looking straight at Jamie Kennedy.

'Annie,' he smiled warmly, seeming delighted to see her. 'How are you?'

'Great, thanks,' she replied, feeling the colour rush to her cheeks as she cursed her own clumsiness. 'I hope I didn't hit you too hard.'

'I've had worse,' he grinned. 'The joys of growing up with a brother.'

'Right,' Annie laughed. 'Is Matt with you?'

'No, he's out with his girlfriend today. I actually wanted to go into the office, but Matt insisted that I take a break, so I thought I'd catch a film. What are you here to see?'

'Um…' Annie stalled, wondering if she should lie. She glanced around the foyer, seeing posters for an animated children's film, a serious-looking period drama, a re-run of a classic sci-fi flick, and a French movie with subtitles. None of them appealed. '*The Tender Night*,' she admitted.

A look of recognition crossed Jamie's face and for one brief moment, Annie wondered if he might possibly be there to see it too.

'Yeah, I've heard of it. It's not really my kind of thing though.'

'Oh,' Annie replied, feeling ridiculously disappointed.

'I'm something of a sci-fi geek myself,' Jamie confessed. 'And *Metropolis* is an absolute classic, from the 1920s,' he explained, nodding towards the poster. 'They rarely show it on the big screen, so I thought I'd make the most of it.'

'Why not?' Annie smiled. 'It sounds pretty cool.'

'You don't have to go that far,' Jamie chuckled, as Annie reached the front of the queue and placed her order. 'So who are you here with?' he asked, as the server turned to get Annie her salted popcorn and a small bottle of red wine.

'I'm here on my own,' Annie replied instantly, then wondered whether or not she sounded defensive.

Jamie raised his eyebrows, looking surprised. 'Really? Me too. I didn't want to inflict my geekiness on anyone else, so thought I'd enjoy my afternoon off by myself.'

'Good plan. I thought something similar,' Annie told him, pulling her purse out of her bag and paying for her snacks. She stood uncertainly beside Jamie, waiting while he bought a bottle of beer and a bag of Kettle Chips.

'Well... enjoy,' Annie said finally, as he gathered up his things and stepped away from the counter.

'You too.'

Both of them hesitated, as though they wanted to say something more, but neither of them spoke. Eventually, Annie gave an apologetic smile and went to walk off, but as she turned around she heard Jamie call after her.

'Annie!'

'Yeah?'

'How long does your film last?'

'I'm not sure… I think it's quite a long one. The next showing's at 4.20, so it must be a couple of hours at least.'

'Right. Mine's about the same I think so… I was wondering, if you fancied it, I could wait here for you and we can go grab a drink or something afterwards?'

Jamie seemed nervous, his uncertainty making him adorable, as he ran a hand through his hair and looked at her hopefully.

Annie was taken aback, but she didn't hesitate in her response. 'Sure. Why not. I'd love to.'

'Great,' Jamie grinned, looking relieved. 'See you back here in a couple of hours?'

'You're on.'

❄ ❄ ❄

The film was exactly as Annie had expected – romantic, weepy, and with copious shots of Ryan Gosling without a shirt. But Annie couldn't seem to concentrate. She kept thinking about meeting Jamie afterwards and, for some crazy reason, she felt nervous.

It was just Jamie, she told herself. Jamie, the guy she chatted to almost every day at work when they bumped into each other in the kitchen. Jamie, the techy computer whizz who was into gaming and spent his days developing new apps and other geeky stuff she couldn't even begin to understand. So why did she feel so anxious, butterflies dancing in her stomach?

She guessed it was because she was seeing him outside of work; if they didn't get on, it could make things awkward in future. Yes, that's what was making her nervous, Annie decided, as she swallowed a mouthful of popcorn and tried to get back into the film, where Ryan and Amanda's characters were having an emotional reunion after being kept apart for over a decade.

When the film finished and the lights came back on, Annie stood up and hurried out of the cinema. Usually, she liked to sit and watch the end credits roll, to keep her immersed in the film and avoid breaking the spell until it was completely over. But today, she didn't want to keep Jamie waiting.

She rushed out of the door, and as she made her way back to the foyer she could see Jamie leaning casually against the wall. He was engrossed in something on his phone, his hands flying over the keypad, and Annie studied him for a moment. He looked so different to when she usually saw him at work, wearing his weekend casuals of jeans and a T-shirt, a checked shirt and cosy jacket thrown over the top. He looked good, Annie realised, feeling her cheeks grow warm.

Jamie glanced up and saw her walking towards him, hastily putting his phone back in his pocket.

'Sorry,' he apologised. 'Just sending an email.'

'Working on a weekend?' Annie teased. 'Are you never off duty?'

'Unfortunately not,' Jamie laughed. 'So how was your film?'

'Great, actually. Really good. Totally my sort of thing.'

'Are you a Ryan Gosling fan?'

Annie bit her lip. 'Maybe…'

'Hey, I know all about that. I have a younger sister.'

The two of them were standing round awkwardly, trying to keep out of the way as people streamed in and out of the small foyer.

'Listen, do you fancy going to grab a bite to eat somewhere?' Jamie asked. 'There's a little Spanish place not far from here. They do great tapas, and jugs of sangria.'

'Mmm, sounds perfect,' Annie smiled happily, as the two of them set off walking. 'So how was *Metropolis*? Was it everything you'd hoped for?'

'And more. Can you think of a better way to spend a Sunday afternoon than watching a ninety-year-old, black-and-white German silent film set in a futuristic urban dystopia?'

'Yes,' Annie replied immediately, then burst out laughing.

'Ah, I'm disappointed in you,' Jamie sighed. 'So I can't tempt you away from your rom-coms?'

Annie shook her head. 'I'm afraid not. I think I'm an addict. There isn't a rom-com out there that I haven't seen, no matter how cheesy and clichéd.'

'Oh, I know all of them.' Jamie rolled his eyes. 'My sister forced me to sit through them all when I was growing up. I must have seen *Romeo and Juliet* a dozen times. I swear that's what got me through my English GCSE. Leah had the biggest crush on Leonardo DiCaprio, and she played that Cardigans song, 'Lovefool', over and over again, until the CD got scratched in a tragic accident.'

'I love that song!' Annie exclaimed. 'Sounds like I'd get on well with your sister.'

'Yeah, I think you would,' Jamie said thoughtfully, giving her a sideways glance.

Annie found herself blushing, for some inexplicable reason, but then Jamie announced that they'd arrived at their destination.

'I've never been here before,' Annie told him, as they entered the tiny little restaurant, called La Casita. It was early still, so the place was quiet.

'Neither have I, actually,' Jamie admitted. 'My brother recommended it. He and his girlfriend come here a lot, but I never seem to have got round to it.'

'The menu looks amazing,' Annie commented, her mouth watering at the thought of *calamares* and *patatas bravas*.

'Do you like Spanish food?'

'I like any type of food,' Annie laughed. 'I'm a real foodie. But yeah, Spanish is delicious. What about you?'

'Same. And anything makes a change from takeaway. Matt and I tend to order in a lot when we're working late.'

'It's hard, isn't it,' Annie sympathised. 'Running your own business. It takes a lot of time and dedication if you want to make it a success.'

'Absolutely,' Jamie agreed, as the waiter brought over the bottle of Rioja they'd ordered, and poured out two glasses. 'But at least we're getting to do what we're passionate about, right?'

'That's true. I'll drink to that. To passion,' Annie declared, as she and Jamie clinked their wine glasses together. Their eyes met as they toasted, and Annie realised that her heart was beating a little faster.

'Are you ready to order?' the waiter asked, breaking the moment as Annie quickly looked down at the menu. They requested a few different plates to share, as was traditional with tapas, and the waiter topped up their glasses before moving away.

'So how's everything going with *Coconut Crush*?' Annie asked, keen to change the subject.

'Really well. Surprisingly well, actually. We've had so much interest from the industry, and there are a lot of companies wanting to work with us. It's strange, because for years we've been trying to pitch to people and win business, and now suddenly *they're* contacting *us*. We've even had companies from California interested in what we're doing.'

'Wow,' Annie exclaimed. 'So will you be making the move Stateside? Turn into some Silicon Valley big shot?'

'I doubt that,' Jamie smiled. 'One of the advantages of IT is that you can work from pretty much anywhere, as long as you've got a laptop and internet access.'

'So do you think you'll always stay round here? Even if you had the option of going anywhere in the world, you'd stay in Norfolk?'

'Well, when you put it like that…' Jamie grinned. 'But for the moment I've got no plans to leave. All of my family are here, and I don't see the point in moving to London, or even abroad, just for the sake of it.'

Their food arrived, both of them exclaiming over the delicious-looking dishes of *pulpo a la gallega* and *pinchitos de pollo*.

'So how about your job?' Jamie wondered. 'I know you've told me a bit about it before, but I don't know if I really understand what you do.'

Annie smiled. 'A lot of people don't. They tend to make these weird assumptions, but it's quite simple really. I'm basically a counsellor, and when couples are having problems in their relationship – specifically sexual problems – they come and talk to me and I help them work through it.'

'I don't know if I could ever talk to a stranger about something so personal,' Jamie admitted. 'Don't you get embarrassed?'

'Not really,' Annie shrugged. 'I'm pretty much unshockable these days. I've had men break down and confess to their wives that what they really want to do is dress up in women's underwear. I've had women admit that their husbands aren't the father of their children, and men confess to pornography obsessions,' she continued, as Jamie's eyes boggled.

Annie took a mouthful of *pan de ajo*, and they carried on chatting, the conversation flowing easily. Annie was relieved –

and surprised – that Jamie hadn't made any stupid comments about her work. Most men couldn't resist asking something sleazy or inappropriate, but Jamie seemed genuinely interested and supportive.

'How come you chose that profession?' Jamie asked curiously. 'It's a pretty unusual career.'

Annie sat back thoughtfully, taking a sip of her wine. 'Various reasons, I suppose. I studied psychology because it interested me, then took my degree in it, and for my master's I found I was more interested in relationships and the sexual side of them – how couples interacted with each other, how they overcame problems, and just how common sexual issues in marriages really were. On a lighter note,' she grinned, noticing Jamie's serious expression, 'I think my love of romantic movies made me believe that everyone has their own happy ending out there. I guess I just wanted to help people find theirs and – shit!' Annie swore, clapping a hand over her mouth.

'What is it?' Jamie asked, following her gaze towards the door where a couple had just entered the restaurant and were being greeted by a waiter.

The man was unfamiliar to Jamie, but Annie recognised him immediately.

It was Tom.

'I went on a date with that guy a couple of months ago,' she explained in hushed tones, wincing as she remembered what a disastrous night it had been. 'He was an idiot. Let's just say it didn't go well.'

Annie looked down at the table, letting her bobbed hair fall across her face in the hope that Tom wouldn't notice her. But as the waiter led him past their table, Tom stopped in surprise.

'Well, well, well,' he sneered. 'Look who it is.'

'Hi Tom,' Annie grimaced, trying to pretend that she'd only just noticed him.

'Is this your latest date?' Tom asked coldly, looking Jamie up and down.

'Not exactly…' Annie began, but Tom cut her off.

'I'd watch out if I were you, mate. She's mental this one.'

'Now hang on a minute,' Jamie said, leaping to his feet as Annie shook her head in despair. 'Don't you dare speak about Annie like that.'

'It's just a friendly warning,' Tom continued, sounding anything but friendly. 'You'll end up wearing that wine instead of drinking it.'

Jamie frowned, confused, and Annie couldn't resist saying, 'No, Tom, you're the only person I've ever thrown a drink over.'

'See? She's a nutcase!'

'Annie, would you like to leave? I'll ask for the bill,' Jamie said chivalrously, taking out his wallet and signalling to the waiter.

'Yeah, why don't you piss off out of here?' Tom suggested.

Quick as a flash, Jamie turned on him, pressing his face up close to Tom's. 'If you *ever* speak to Annie like that again, you'll have more to deal with than having a drink thrown over you. Okay?'

A flicker of fear crossed Tom's face; he might have been muscular, but Jamie was a head taller than him, and Annie suspected that Tom was a coward at heart.

'Yeah, whatever,' he sneered, but he took a step backwards towards the woman he'd arrived with. 'Come on, Nicki. Let's go sit down.'

Annie exhaled slowly, too shaken up to protest as Jamie insisted on covering the bill. As they stepped out into the chilly evening air, Jamie looked at her thoughtfully and asked, 'Did you really throw a glass of wine over him?'

'Yeah,' Annie admitted guiltily. 'But he totally deserved it. He's a dickhead.'

'I can see that,' Jamie smiled.

They walked along in silence for a few moments, Annie pulling her jacket more tightly around her. 'Thanks for defending my honour back there,' she said eventually. 'I really appreciate it.'

'Any time,' Jamie replied. He grinned at her, and Annie found herself grinning back, a warm glow of contentment spreading through her body.

Chapter 18

'I'm as pure as the driven slush' – **Tallulah Bankhead**

Simon was sitting at the water's edge, dressed in tracksuit bottoms, a hoody and painter's overalls. It was a beautiful spring day – chilly, but with a dazzling blue sky so bright that Simon needed to wear sunglasses – and he was painting one of the company narrowboats, the *Belle of the Broads*. Now that the weather was warming up, it was a race to get all the boats prepared for the forthcoming season. They were almost fully booked over Easter, and he needed to have everything in pristine condition by then.

Simon hadn't planned to work for the family business. He'd tried his hand at various jobs after he left college, including admin work in a hospital and telesales for a bank, but the corporate environment didn't suit him at all. Simon loved to be outdoors, working with his hands, and with no set routine every day. Today, for example, he was by the canal, only the occasional low of a cow, or the gentle hum of machinery on a nearby farm to break the peace and quiet.

After he'd finished painting, he'd need to replant the flower tubs then check the interior of the boat, ensuring nothing was broken or missing, before making his final inspection of the engine and the machinery. But there was still plenty of time for all of that over the coming days and weeks, and Simon worked steadily, ensuring that he did a thorough, professional job.

He would just get to the end of this bit, and then he'd break for lunch, Simon decided. He dipped his brush into the red paint he was using, and carefully traced a line along the lower edge of the boat, making sure to keep it neat. His forehead was narrowed in concentration, sweat beading on his brow, when he heard his phone beep from deep inside his overalls. Not wanting to stop until he'd finished the section he was on, he carried on painting for another few minutes, before pulling out his phone and seeing that he had a message from Zoe:

Hey handsome, what are you up to? xxx

Simon set his brush down in the paint tray, and wiped his hands on the rag he kept nearby, before replying:

Not much. Painting the Belle. What about you? xxx

He barely had time to pick up his tools before his phone beeped again:

Thinking about you and what I want you to do to me

Simon almost dropped his paintbrush. Instinctively, he cradled his phone closer to hide the screen, even though the nearest living creature was probably the cow two fields away. He realised he was breathing a little faster, his body tense with anticipation. Did Zoe mean what he thought she did? Had he misread the text? Without giving himself too much time to think about it, Simon quickly tapped out a reply.

❅　❅　❅

Zoe was at work in the vet's, pulling on her coat as she prepared to go on her lunch break. Her mobile was clutched in her hand, and she felt deliciously naughty, wondering what she'd started. At their last therapy session, Annie had taken Zoe aside and given her a secret mission, challenging her to send a series of sexy messages to Simon at some point over the forthcoming week. It was all to do with building anticipation, Annie had explained, and even functioned as a form of foreplay, ensuring that your other half was raring to go when you next saw them.

Zoe had taken Annie up on the challenge but, while she was game for most things, she felt a little uncertain about this. How explicit did they have to get? What if Simon thought it was all a big joke, or didn't understand what she was trying to do?

The phone in Zoe's hand vibrated, and she eagerly read the text:

Oh yeah? Tell me all about it ☺

Zoe broke into a triumphant smile. Simon appeared to have got the message, and he understood exactly what she was doing! Now came the difficult part – what was she going to send back? Zoe wanted something fun and teasing, not graphic and crude.

'I'll see you in an hour,' she called out to Jackie, who worked on reception, as she stopped to stroke a beagle with a bandaged paw.

'Bye, Zoe. Have fun.'

'Oh, I will,' Zoe replied with a wicked grin, wondering what Jackie would say if she knew exactly how much fun Zoe was intending to have.

The door clanged as she walked out, and Zoe looped her scarf around her neck as she walked briskly along Princes

Street towards the cathedral. When the weather was fine, she loved to sit in the grounds and eat her lunch.

Zoe marched through the gate, barely stopping to admire the splendour of the magnificent building soaring above her, and quickly found an empty bench, where she sat down and tapped out a reply:

Remember that hotel on our anniversary? I loved what you did to me that night...

Then she pulled her lunch box out of her bag, took out an egg mayonnaise sandwich, and waited for the reply.

❄ ❄ ❄

Simon had forgotten all about work. His paintbrush lay abandoned, the bristles stiffening in the sunshine, as he stared at his phone, waiting for Zoe's next message to come through.

As soon as his phone lit up, he immediately pressed the 'read' button, his eyes devouring the words on the screen. Then he broke into a wide grin.

Simon remembered all too well the night that Zoe was referring to. It had been their first anniversary, and he'd taken her to Hambledon Hall, a beautiful country house hotel up near Fakenham. After spending the afternoon in the spa, getting hot and steamy in the Jacuzzi, they'd ordered a bottle of Prosecco from room service and proceeded to do some very naughty things indeed. Simon had taken a mouthful of the sparkling liquid as he disappeared between Zoe's thighs, and the sensation of the bubbles against her most intimate parts had left her panting for more.

I can do it again whenever you want – just say the magic word. I've got the Prosecco on ice ;)

When the message was sent, Simon lay back on the grass, looking up at the clouds scudding across the sky. He could feel himself getting horny, that telltale stirring in his trousers. This celibacy thing was far harder than he'd expected – no pun intended. More than once, he'd thought of suggesting to Zoe that they call it all off, but she was adamant that they would stand by their decision. Simon wasn't sure he'd last until the wedding night. And if he did… Well, if he was being honest, Simon was secretly terrified that it wouldn't be the amazing experience Zoe was hoping for. There was a worrying possibility that it could all be over within minutes. Seconds even.

And if Zoe was going to send him suggestive texts like this, it was going to make things even harder – literally.

Simon groaned out loud at the thought, throwing one hand over his face to shield it from the sun, as he waited for Zoe's response.

❋ ❋ ❋

Zoe was eating her lunch, enjoying the feel of the warm sun on her face, and waiting for Simon's text. She looked out across the church yard, watching people pass through – tourists staring up at the beautiful cathedral; young mothers with children in pushchairs using it as a convenient cut through; other workers, like herself, grabbing five minutes of relaxation on their lunch break.

Zoe noticed that someone was making their way towards the bench where she was sitting. The figure was dressed all in black and, as they drew closer, Zoe realised that it was an elderly nun. Her hair was tucked up beneath her habit, and she wore a pair of oversized spectacles, with a gold cross around her neck. She smiled at Zoe as she sat down beside her and

Zoe smiled back, gathering up her lunch box and moving along the seat to give the woman some space.

Just then, Zoe's phone beeped, and she snatched it up, grinning as she read Simon's reply. She certainly wouldn't mind a replay of that night at Hambledon Hall. Zoe sat thoughtfully for a moment, chewing on her sandwich as she composed a reply. Sexting Simon was a lot of fun, but so far they were both playing it safe. She needed to spice things up a little, inject some filthiness into the conversation.

'Excuse me?'

Zoe looked round, realising that the nun was speaking to her. 'Yes?'

'I'm so sorry to disturb you, but do you have the time?'

Zoe glanced down at her phone. 'It's just gone half past one.'

'Half past one?' the woman repeated slowly. 'Thank you. I'm afraid my watch has stopped working,' she told Zoe, holding up her arm to show her the ancient-looking watch on her wrist. 'I'll have to get a new battery, I suppose.'

'I think there's a shop on Wensum Street that fits replacements,' Zoe advised her helpfully, before going back to her text. Struck with a sudden burst of inspiration, she quickly typed:

I've been having this fantasy where you

'It's a beautiful day, isn't it?'

Zoe's head shot up, colour infusing her cheeks, as she realised that the nun was chatting to her once again.

'Yes. Yes, it's lovely,' she agreed.

'I think this is my favourite time of year,' the woman said contemplatively. 'Spring, when everything's renewing itself. It makes me realise I've survived another winter,' she chuckled.

Zoe wasn't sure how to reply. She smiled heartily, and said once again, 'It really is lovely.' Then she put her head back down to read what she'd written so far, carefully angling her phone away from the nun.

Hmm, Zoe wondered. Which fantasy should she text to Simon? The bondage-themed one? Or the one involving a threesome…?

'Can you believe this is over nine hundred years old?' The nun's voice broke into Zoe's thoughts. She was staring in disbelief at the mighty cathedral in front of them. 'It makes me feel positively young!'

Zoe smiled politely, feeling increasingly awkward. The nun was a very sweet old woman, who clearly just wanted to chat, but it was extremely difficult to think raunchy thoughts when sitting beside a servant of the Lord. Taking decisive action, Zoe clicked the lid on her lunch box and pushed it back into her bag.

'Have a lovely day,' she said brightly to the nun, swinging her handbag onto her shoulder as she stood up. 'I need to get back to work now.'

'Right you are. Have a nice day,' the woman replied contentedly, showing no signs of moving.

Zoe walked away, along the path that led out of the cathedral grounds. Quickly, she tapped out the message that came to her so easily now:

> *I've been having this fantasy where you tie me up and spank me hard xxx*

She smiled to herself in satisfaction, pressing send as she passed through the main gate.

❄ ❄ ❄

Simon was still lying on the grass, daydreaming about his fiancée. He really was madly in love with her, he thought happily. She was absolutely gorgeous, and with a naughty side that meant she was always up for trying new things. Most of all, Simon loved how sexy she made *him* feel. Zoe craved and desired him, just as much as he wanted her, and that was the biggest turn-on of all.

But, if the truth be told, Simon couldn't help but feel a little insecure at times. His previous girlfriend – his childhood sweetheart, in fact – had cheated on him and broken his heart not long before he met Zoe. And whilst he'd had very little in the way of past relationships, he knew that Zoe was far more sexually experienced than him. Simon found himself wondering whether she'd done this with other people, sexting previous boyfriends, and realised that he hated the idea. What if he didn't live up to the other men she'd slept with? What if Zoe thought his replies were dull, or that he wasn't as exciting in bed as her former lovers?

Simon shuddered, hating the idea of Zoe having sex with someone else. And he *really* hated the idea of Zoe having sex with someone who was *better* than him. It was every man's secret fear, and Simon was no different, worrying that—

Zoe's text came through, and Simon immediately forgot all of his concerns, blown away by what she'd written. Wow! Did Zoe really fantasise about being tied up and spanked?

Reading over the message again, the link from Simon's brain to his crotch was instantaneous. He glanced around guiltily, wondering if anyone could see his growing excitement. He was hugely aroused, and it would be patently obvious to anyone who happened to be nearby. Fortunately, Simon was alone, and he let out a long, shaky breath, trying to slow his racing pulse. By now he'd forgotten all about work;

there was no way he could concentrate on anything apart from his conversation with Zoe. Quickly, he hit reply:

Sounds amazing. I'll do whatever you want. Ready right now with my handcuffs ☺ ☺

Simon immediately pressed send, but the message icon circled before flashing up the 'failed' symbol.

'Bollocks,' Simon swore out loud. He tried once again, but it timed out after a couple of minutes, and Simon let out a frustrated groan. One of the hazards of working out in the countryside was that mobile reception could be very unreliable. He waved his phone aimlessly above his head, hoping to pick up something, but nothing happened. Zoe was going to think he was ignoring her, Simon realised. Or she'd worry that she'd gone too far and freaked him out.Simon jumped to his feet, jogging along the riverbank and waving his phone in the air, but the screen still showed *SOS Emergency Calls Only*.

This is *an emergency!* Simon thought in frustration.

He ran back towards the house, doing a strange dance which involved skipping from side to side and waving his arms, desperately trying to find reception.

'Is everything all right, Simon?'

Simon span around in alarm to find his dad, Brian, watching him curiously. Simon had been so distracted, he hadn't even noticed him, and he felt his cheeks grow crimson.

'Oh, yeah,' he said sheepishly, hanging his head. 'I was just… trying to send a text. No reception,' he explained lamely, waving the phone.

'Right.' His dad raised a sceptical eyebrow. 'Must be an important one. I've been watching you jumping about like Billy Elliot for the past few minutes.'

'Oh,' Simon said again. 'I was trying to send Zoe a message. She's on her lunch break.'

'Someone's under the thumb,' Brian teased. 'Anyway, how are you getting on with the *Belle*?'

'The what? Oh, she's fine,' Simon said quickly, embarrassed to admit that he'd forgotten all about the boat he was supposed to be painting. 'I'm just taking a quick break.'

Brian frowned once again. 'Fair enough. Let me know if you need any help.' And with that, he strode off in the direction of their storage shed.

As soon as he was out of sight, Simon looked down at his phone to see that he now inexplicably had four bars of reception. Before he could lose them again, he quickly pressed send on the text, then scrolled through his contacts to call Zoe.

'Hello lover,' she purred, as she picked up the phone.

'Hi,' Simon replied, suddenly feeling shy.

'I got your text. I was just messaging you back.'

'I can't wait,' Simon groaned. 'You don't know what you're doing to me, Zoe. This is such a turn-on.'

At the other end of the phone, Zoe smiled. 'Good.'

'It's not good,' Simon protested. 'I can't concentrate on work. My dad thinks I'm going mad. And my reception keeps cutting out, which is the most frustrating thing in the world.'

'Well, my lunch break's nearly over too,' Zoe sighed, sounding disappointed. 'I guess we could press pause on this, and pick up where we left off later.'

'I don't know if I'll last that long.'

'Exercise some self-discipline. I'll see you tonight, lover,' Zoe replied. The last thing Simon heard before she hung up was a naughty little giggle.

Chapter 19

'The problem is that God gives men a brain and a penis, and only enough blood to run one at a time'
– Robin Williams

Nick and Julia were halfway through their therapy session with a somewhat distracted Annie. She was doing her absolute best to concentrate fully on her clients, but Annie found that her mind kept drifting elsewhere, a goofy smile appearing on her face at inappropriate moments.

The cause of this rare unprofessionalism was a certain Mr Jamie Kennedy, who'd appeared in her office at midday, leaning casually against the doorframe and enquiring about her lunch plans. On learning that Annie's next client wasn't until three pm, he'd insisted on whisking her away for a couple of hours, driving her out to a charming country pub for a delicious Ploughman's and a cheeky glass of wine.

It had all felt thrillingly illicit, like playing truant from school, as they sped through the countryside leaving the office far behind. Hidden away in a corner booth, the conversation and laughter flowed easily. Annie opened up about her profession, and her career aspirations, whilst Jamie had told her more about his business and his family. Annie watched him as he talked, suddenly finding herself fascinated by every little detail: the stubborn piece of hair above his right ear that would never quite lay flat; the tiny scar cutting across his left eyebrow; the small patch of stubble that he'd missed when shaving that morning.

While Annie insisted to herself that she was simply an exceptionally observational person, the strange fluttering sensation in her stomach told her there might be another reason why she was paying such close attention to Jamie. A reason she really didn't want to think about right now...

They'd talked for so long that the time had flown by, and they'd ended up racing back to the office, Jamie putting his foot down to ensure that Annie wasn't late for her appointment. She'd arrived moments before Nick and Julia, ushering them through to her office where the three of them had been talking for thirty minutes now, working honestly and openly through a variety of tough topics.

Annie was proud of them; Julia, especially, had come a long way. She seemed receptive and responsive, with a clear desire to solve their issues. Surprisingly, Nick was the one who was being distant; his answers were evasive, his body language awkward, and he struggled to make eye contact, one leg jiggling up and down nervously when he spoke.

'Julia, we touched a little on your background,' Annie continued, glancing at her notes and trying to push all thoughts of Jamie out of her head. 'I'd like to expand on that. What sort of words come to mind when thinking about your childhood?'

'Um...' Julia hesitated. 'Insecure, maybe? Anxious. Lonely? I don't want to make it sound too depressing. Mum did a great job trying to bring me up but... I was an only child, so I didn't have that support system of siblings,' she explained to Annie. 'And my dad left us when I was tiny. It just made life really unstable, I suppose. Things were always tight with money, and I was really aware at school – when you had to draw pictures of your family and stuff – that I didn't have the typical mum, dad, brothers and sisters like everyone else seemed to.'

Annie was nodding. 'And can you remember wanting to have a family from a young age?'

'Yes, absolutely. I created my own little gang of dolls and teddy bears, and I would look after them, pretending to be the mummy. I always felt sure that I'd have a big family – definitely more than one child – and I desperately wanted a happy marriage. One that was stable, and secure, and where I could be sure I was with a good man who wouldn't walk out on me.'

She glanced across at Nick with a hesitant smile, but he wouldn't meet her gaze, his eyes fixed steadfastly on the floor.

'And do you think it might be possible that you put that desire for a child above maintaining that stable relationship?' Annie suggested.

Julia thought for a moment before she eventually spoke. 'Yes. Yes, I can see that perhaps I did. I've been so caught up in this desire to create the perfect life – the image that I had in my head, with the career and the kids and the man – that I probably neglected my husband. I *did* neglect him,' Julia realised, looking across at Nick once again. 'But to tell you the truth, I just felt so scared that if I *couldn't* have a baby, everything would fall apart. My dream wouldn't come true the way I planned it.'

She looked close to tears, and Annie smiled supportively.

'Here,' she said, pushing a box of tissues across her desk towards Julia. Annie always made sure to keep a supply, as clients regularly needed them.

'Sorry, I'm being silly,' Julia sniffed, as she dabbed at her eyes, worried that her mascara had run.

'No, you're not at all,' Annie insisted. 'You're being extremely honest, allowing yourself to be vulnerable, and you've taken some huge strides forward.'

'Thank you,' Julia murmured, looking visibly relieved.

'Nick.' Annie turned to him. 'Julia's just shared a lot with you. How does that make you feel?'

Nick grimaced, looking as though he was waiting to be executed. His expression indicated that he wanted to be anywhere apart from in that room, and Annie was surprised. He'd always been the one who was so enthusiastic about therapy, the one who'd taken the lead in fixing their relationship.

'I don't know, really,' he shrugged, still refusing to look directly at Annie.

'Can you understand now why Julia's been behaving the way that she has? Why having a baby is such a priority for her?'

'Yeah, I guess.'

Annie stared at him, her frustration building. 'Is everything okay with you today, Nick?'

'Yes, of course. Why wouldn't it be?' Nick sounded irritated.

'I don't know,' Annie replied honestly. 'You don't seem as open as you usually do. You seem like you don't want to be here.'

'Is there something the matter?' Julia asked worriedly.

'Everything's fine. Can we just drop it?'

The truth was that Nick was feeling hideously guilty over what had happened with Nina, and hearing everything that Julia had to say only made it worse. The fact that she saw him as some kind of saviour figure – a good man, who she could trust, and with who she desperately wanted to start a family – merely served to make him feel ten times worse.

It had only been a kiss, Nick tried to tell himself. Just one, very brief, kiss and he'd stopped it before they went any further. It wasn't as though the situation was wholly his fault either; Nina had been blatantly flirting with him, practically offering herself to him on a plate and—

No, Nick realised, shaking his head. However he tried to spin it, he knew that he bore the brunt of the responsibility. He was older than Nina, her senior at work, and he'd been the one to make the first move. If he was being honest, he knew that he'd enjoyed the flattery and the admiration of an attractive young woman. But he'd been bloody stupid, he could see that clearly, and now he had to deal with the consequences.

Nick looked up to find Julia and Annie both staring at him, confusion and accusation written across their faces, and suddenly he felt trapped, imagining that both of them could guess exactly what was going through his mind.

'We can change the subject if you're not comfortable, Nick,' Annie said softly. 'But it's a shame, as I thought we were really getting somewhere. What would you like to talk about instead?'

Nick took a deep breath, running his hands tiredly across his face. All he knew was that keeping this secret was destroying him, and that Julia deserved to know the truth.

'I kissed someone else,' he mumbled, the words spilling out before he knew what he was doing.

Uncertainty flashed across Julia's eyes, wondering if she'd misheard him. 'What?'

Even Annie was unsure. 'Could you repeat what you just said, Nick?'

'I kissed someone else, okay? Did you get that? I kissed someone else!' Nick's voice was getting louder with every word.

Julia stared at him in disbelief. 'Who? When?'

Annie watched, equally shocked, but trying to maintain her professionalism. She'd had all sorts of bombshells dropped in her office, from couples demanding divorces to one man announcing his intention to change gender. Her instinct was to try to let Nick and Julia work it out for themselves, and step in if needed.

'Someone at work,' Nick admitted. His posture slumped, and he looked utterly defeated, his head in his hands.

'Nina,' Julia said knowingly. 'It was her, right?'

Nick looked up in shock. 'How did you…?'

'I'm not stupid, Nick,' Julia lashed out. 'You've mentioned her so many times. It was pretty obvious you had a crush on her.'

'*She* had a crush on *me*! She was the one who encouraged me. She put her hand on my arm, and she said—'

'Oh, save it, Nick,' Julia snapped, her face a picture of hurt. 'That's pathetic.'

'I pulled away, told her we couldn't do it.' Nick was babbling desperately. 'I told her I needed to get home to you.'

'Oh how bloody clichéd. Home to the frumpy, miserable, nagging wife?' Julia shot back, coming uncomfortably close to the truth.

Nick swallowed, saying nothing.

'When did it happen?' Julia knew that she was torturing herself, wanting to know every detail, but she couldn't help herself.

'The other week, when I texted you to say I was working late. I went to the pub instead. Everyone else went home, and it was just the two of us left. I'd had a bit to drink, hadn't eaten…'

A tear slid down Julia's cheek as she listened to Nick's explanation. He looked utterly wretched, but Julia didn't feel any sympathy for him. She felt completely devastated. She'd longed for a happy, stable family life, with as many children as she could physically pop out, and now her husband had cheated on her.

'You lied to me,' she realised. 'You said you were at work.'

Nick nodded slowly. 'You made me feel like I had to,' he protested. 'You make me feel guilty if I'm not with you 24/7, trying to make babies. I'm not allowed to do anything normal like go out for a drink with my colleagues.'

'Tell me what happened,' Julia whispered, her voice breaking as she spoke. 'Why did you do it?'

'I've been so unhappy, Julia,' Nick confessed, feeling a huge sense of relief despite everything. 'I feel like you don't care about me any more – that all you care about is having a baby and, quite frankly, I could be anyone as long as they can get you knocked up.'

Julia looked as though she'd been slapped. 'I never meant to make you feel that way,' she stammered. 'You know I didn't. Most men would be grateful that their wives wanted them, not run off with the nearest floozy.'

'But you *didn't* make me feel wanted. You made me feel like a bloody sperm donor, not a loving husband.'

'And what? This *Nina* –' Julia practically spat the name '– made you feel like a big man, so handsome and so clever. Is that it?'

Nick closed his eyes, sighing heavily. 'She was… She was fun. Easygoing. And yes, she paid attention to me, flattered me. I can't remember the last time you and I shared a joke,

Jules. The last time we had a laugh, or went out for a drink. I know what I did was wrong, and you have to believe me when I tell you it meant nothing… but all it did was remind me of how much we've lost.'

'You still see this woman every day at work' Julia burst out, her eyes filling with tears at the realisation. 'I bet it's all cosy little chats in the canteen and long, lingering glances across the office. Oh my God, has it happened more than once? Did you want it to?' The questions came tumbling out, as Nick shook his head, frantically trying to reassure his wife.

'No, of course not. Nothing like that. I spoke to her afterwards – I *had* to,' he explained, seeing the look on Julia's face. 'I apologised for my behaviour and said it should never have happened. I told her that I'd been confused and stressed and had acted completely out of character, and that I was married and it could never happen again,' Nick continued, recalling the excruciatingly awkward conversation he'd had with Nina. She'd been gracious and understanding about the whole situation, and the two of them had kept their distance ever since. 'She's working with a new team on a different project, so we barely see each other. And I promise you, Jules, I have no desire for it to happen again.'

'This is… It feels like a nightmare,' Julia managed, her voice rising as the tears began to flow once again. 'I wanted this perfect marriage, and perfect family, and you've spoilt everything for a quick ego boost with some slapper.'

'Julia,' Annie stepped in, seeing how upset she was getting. 'No relationship is perfect, and if you want to move forward you need to accept that you're not going to create something perfect. If that's what you're expecting, you'll only be disappointed. The question is, do you want to move forward and move past this?'

Julia looked at Nick. 'Well, do *you*?' she demanded. 'Or do you want to run off with your bit on the side?'

'Of course not,' Nick said desperately. 'It meant nothing to me, really Jules, you've got to believe me. A moment of madness, that's all. But if anything, it's shown me just how much work there is to do, and how right we were to come and see Annie.'

'It wasn't my fault, Julia rounded on him. 'You can't blame it on me, and say that if I'd paid you more attention that you wouldn't have done it. Are you claiming I drove you into the arms of another woman? That's ridiculous.'

'I've said what I did was wrong, but I don't believe if everything was right between us, then I would still have done it. I'm admitting we have a problem, and maybe it's bigger than we thought. What I'm saying is that we need to sort it out.'

Julia turned to Annie. 'What do you think?'

'I think both of you make some valid points,' Annie began diplomatically. 'And everything we've been discussing in these sessions has led up to this moment. We really are at crisis point, and it's up to the two of you to make a decision about how you want to carry on.'

Neither of them spoke, both staring at her helplessly.

'Nick's explained and apologised, and what you have to do, Julia, is decide whether you're ready to accept that explanation and apology, and move forward. And Nick, you have to be absolutely certain that you're not going to put yourself in a situation like this again, however tempting it might be.'

'I won't. I know I won't,' he insisted. 'Julia's the woman I love, and I want to be with her.'

'Then tell her, not me,' Annie said softly.

Nick swallowed, turning in his seat to face his wife. 'I love you, Julia. I really do. You're the only woman for me. I'm so sorry, but I promise you that I'll never do anything like this again. I really want things to get better for us, and I'm willing to do whatever it takes to make things right.'

Julia was watching him, her expression dispassionate in the face of Nick's pleading.

'I…' She opened her mouth, then thought better of it and fell quiet. A few moments later, she tried again. 'I'm sorry, Nick. I need some time. I don't know what I think right now, and it's all so fresh…' She paused, looking up at him with grief-stricken eyes. 'I'll let you know when I've made my decision.'

Chapter 20

'Flirting is a woman's trade, one must keep in practice' – **Charlotte Brontë**, **Jane Eyre**

Annie was in her bedroom, scrutinising her reflection in the wardrobe mirror. She was currently wearing a long skirt with a loose, cream top, and on the bed behind her lay a pile of discarded clothes. It was very unusual for her to spend so much time getting ready, but she didn't want to look too overdressed. Then again, she didn't want to look as though she hadn't made an effort either, and getting the balance right seemed to be impossible.

'What do you think?' she asked Harry and Sally, as she jogged downstairs and into the living room. 'You like?'

The goldfish looked at her glumly, their mouths gawping, their eyes bulging.

'Hmm, thanks for your enthusiasm, guys,' Annie told them moodily, wondering whether she should throw on jeans and a light jumper instead.

Oh, for heaven's sake, Annie reprimanded herself. She was only meeting Jamie after all. It wasn't a big deal.

After she and Jamie had bumped into each other at the cinema a couple of weeks ago, Jamie had casually suggested one day that they should make it a regular thing. He knew that she was passionate about rom-coms, whilst he loved sci-fi, so perhaps they could introduce each other to a whole new genre? Annie had agreed, thinking it sounded like a fun idea, and today they were due to meet up at Cinema City.

She'd been thinking about Jamie a lot recently. They kept running into each other at work – well, it wasn't quite so accidental any more. After their pub excursion, they'd arranged to have lunch together a couple of times last week, and they seemed to have mutually agreed to both take a break at three pm every day, if Annie didn't have a client, and meet up in the kitchen for tea and HobNobs.

Jamie seemed like a great guy, and Annie realised that she was in serious danger of developing feelings for him. But right now, she was in denial, insisting to herself that they were friends and nothing more. She couldn't help but remember how badly things had turned out the last time she'd fallen for someone, and she was still dealing with the emotional scars. A therapist would probably tell her that she had trust issues, Annie thought wryly, appreciating the irony.

There was also the fact that Jamie had never given her any real indication that he saw her as anything more than a friend. They were just two work acquaintances with a shared interest in movies and pub lunches, and there'd been no suggestion at all that this was a date. Which was totally fine with her, Annie told herself firmly.

She glanced up at the clock and realised that she should have left five minutes ago and was now running late. Damn, there was definitely no time for a change of clothes. Slipping on a pair of embroidered ballet pumps, she grabbed her bag and blew a kiss to Harry and Sally.

'Wish me luck!'

The fish stared at her dolefully, and Annie hurried out of the door.

❄ ❄ ❄

'Hi,' Annie said, rushing up to Jamie. He was already waiting for her outside Cinema City, and he looked gorgeous in loose jeans and a long-sleeved T-shirt, his blond hair more styled than he wore it for work. Had he always been this attractive? Annie wondered idly, then quickly tried to suppress those sort of thoughts.

'Hi Annie,' Jamie grinned, bending down to kiss her on the cheek. 'Are you okay?'

'Fine. What makes you say that?' Annie replied, then realised she was speaking far too fast.

'Nothing,' Jamie looked amused. 'You just seem a bit… flustered maybe? As though you've been rushing.'

'Oh, well I did set off a few minutes late,' Annie explained, grateful to have been given an explanation for her flushed face and frazzled appearance. 'My goldfish were taking too long to give me their opinion on my outfit.'

'Your what were what?' Jamie frowned, and Annie wondered why on earth she'd said that.

'Nothing!' she breezed, smiling brightly.

'Well, I think you look great – even if your goldfish couldn't decide,' Jamie grinned, making Annie blush even deeper.

'So are you ready to go do this?' she asked, changing the subject as they walked into the cinema. 'Ready to be inducted into the world of romantic comedies?'

'I think so.' Jamie looked up uncertainly at the poster. '*Where the Heart Is,*' he read out loud. 'The story of a big city girl who left her heart in a small town.'

'Sounds wonderful, doesn't it,' Annie said dreamily.

'Sure you don't fancy *They Walk Among Us*?' Jamie suggested, staring longingly at the advert on the opposite wall, which showed an alien face amongst a crowd of people.

Annie shook her head. 'Nope. But you can choose that when it's your turn, if you like.'

'Those were the terms of our agreement, I believe,' Jamie teased. 'Now, what snacks are we getting? I'm going to need a lot of food if I'm going to sit through two hours of a syrupy, girly cheese-fest.'

'It's not syrupy and girly,' Annie protested. 'It's about real issues – feelings and love and romance. And, since you asked, I'm putting in a vote for salted popcorn.'

'You're on,' Jamie grinned, as they ordered their drinks and bought their tickets.

'I'll pay,' Annie told him, reaching for her purse. 'You got the tapas last time.'

But Jamie shook his head. 'Don't worry about it. I invited you, so it's my treat.'

'At least let me get the drinks,' Annie offered.

In the end, they compromised, with Jamie buying the tickets and Annie buying the wine. One of her favourite things about Cinema City was that they sold alcoholic drinks, and the seats were so comfy it was almost like being in your own living room.

'I love it here,' Annie sighed, as they made their way into the screening room.

'It's a great little place, isn't it?' Jamie agreed.

They sat down beside one another, with Annie acutely aware of just how close they were. Jamie smelt delicious, as though he'd just showered and splashed on a spicy, musky aftershave, and Annie's heart began to beat faster. She reached for a piece of popcorn and Jamie did the same, their hands accidentally brushing. Jamie turned and grinned at her, and Annie felt her stomach flip, as though she'd just driven over a hill at ninety miles an hour. This was crazy! She'd worked in the same building as Jamie for months now, yet suddenly she was melting into a puddle if he so much as looked at her.

The lights went down, and Annie breathed a sigh of relief, grateful that Jamie couldn't see her in the darkness. She felt sure that everything she was thinking must be written plainly across her face.

As the film started, Annie realised that there was no way she could concentrate with Jamie sitting beside her. She was far too aware of every movement he made, every time he sighed or shuffled or took a sip of his drink. Annie found herself fantasising about just what exactly they could do in the shadowy cinema, wishing that Jamie would lean over and kiss her passionately, the two of them making out like teenagers under cover of darkness. Surely no one would notice if he moved closer and slowly slid a hand over her knee, disappearing beneath her skirt and up her thigh towards—

Stop it! Annie reprimanded herself, feeling her face flame in the darkness.

'Are you enjoying it?' Jamie leant across to whisper.

His face was next to hers, his warm breath caressing the exposed skin on her neck. It felt wonderfully sensuous.

'Mmm hmm,' Annie replied, not trusting herself to speak.

In truth, Annie had no idea what was happening in the movie. Even though it wasn't the most complicated of plots, she was struggling to pay attention. The current scene showed the heroine alone in her office at night. She was staring wistfully out of the window, gazing at the New York City skyline. It looked fabulous, the skyscrapers all lit up, as the full moon shone over the Empire State Building.

Then suddenly the scene switched, showing a semi-naked couple rolling around on a bed. It was a raunchy flashback, as the heroine recalled losing her virginity to her childhood sweetheart back home in Texas. Annie cringed inwardly, wondering what Jamie was thinking. Shit, what if he thought that she was some kind of sex maniac – doing the job she did, and watching films with scenes like this? Or worse, that she had an ulterior motive in bringing him to see this movie, trying to suggest that *she* wanted to roll around on a bed with *him*, and now he was sitting there mortified and—

Stop it, Annie, you're over-thinking this!

Annie sank lower in her seat, trying to hide her embarrassment and, as she moved, her knee brushed against Jamie's.

'Sorry, sorry,' she whispered hastily. 'It was an accident.'

She heard Jamie laugh quietly. 'It's fine.'

Annie sat stock still for the rest of the movie, resolving to focus fully on the plot. She was slightly calmer by the time the end credits began to roll, as she and Jamie stood up and made their way back through to the foyer.

'So did you enjoy it?' Jamie asked.

Annie wrinkled her nose. 'It was good, but I don't think it's destined to become a classic. How about you?'

'It was… bearable,' Jamie conceded, and the two of them burst out laughing.

'Do you, um, fancy getting a drink, or some food?' Annie suggested, summoning her courage and surprising herself with her boldness. 'They've got a great restaurant here, and—'

'I'm really sorry, Annie, but I can't,' Jamie interrupted.

'Oh.'

He saw the way her face dropped, and quickly added, 'I'd love to, I really would but… I can't.'

'Oh,' Annie repeated, feeling crushed. 'No problem.'

'It's just that I have to… well, it's a bit complicated actually. But I'd love to do this another time. We could grab a drink after work, or I could take you out for dinner – one night next week?'

'Sure, that's fine,' Annie rambled, doing her best to sound bright and breezy even though she didn't feel bright and breezy at all. What on earth had she been thinking? Once again, she'd totally misread the situation, scaring him off with some ill-judged comment.

'I'll walk you to your car,' Jamie offered. 'Are you parked nearby?'

'A few streets away. Don't worry about it, it's fine,' Annie insisted, not wanting to prolong her humiliation any further.

'I'd like to,' Jamie said softly. Annie looked up and met those dazzling blue eyes, and knew that resistance was futile.

'Okay,' she agreed.

They set off walking, both of them deep in thought. Annie was cursing her own stupidity, whilst Jamie was thinking something very different.

'How's everything with work?' Annie asked, eager to break the silence and get back to a safe topic.

'Huh?' Jamie asked, looking confused for a moment. 'Oh, yeah. It's going well, thanks. Really well actually. I don't think I told you – we only found out on Friday – but Matt and I have a really important meeting coming up.'

Annie looked at him questioningly.

'It's with this company called Gamejacker, who are pretty massive in the gaming world right now, and we're pitching for a contract to develop new ideas for them. If we get it, it's the big time for us.'

'Wow, that sounds exciting,' Annie told him genuinely.

'Yeah. I'm a little bit terrified to be honest,' Jamie admitted. 'It's not my natural territory, schmoozing the big execs. But needs must, I guess.'

'You'll be wonderful,' Annie assured him. 'You always have this calm, confident aura about you.'

'Do I?' Jamie looked surprised. 'That's really nice to hear – especially coming from you.'

'Me?'

'Yeah. You're the expert at this kind of thing, aren't you? You know, spotting personality traits and following your intuition.'

Annie smiled. 'If you say so. It doesn't seem to work once I'm out of the office though. Professionally, I've got it together. Personally…' she trailed off.

'You shouldn't be so hard on yourself,' Jamie insisted. 'You're clearly a very good judge of character – that's why you've come out with me,' he grinned, as Annie laughed.

'Well, this is my car,' she said, indicating her Mini as she came to a stop beside it.

'Right.' Jamie stopped too, both of them turning to face one another. 'Honestly, I'm really gutted that I can't do tonight. I've already organised something that I can't get out of. But we'll definitely do it another time. I really like spending time with you, Annie.'

'Me too,' Annie admitted shyly. 'But don't worry about it. Another time.'

'I'd like that, Annie. I really would. It's just that…' Jamie paused, as though he was about to say something more, then came out with, 'Have you ever seen the movie *Paul*?'

Annie shook her head, a little thrown by the unexpected change in the conversation. She wasn't sure what she'd been expecting him to say, but it certainly wasn't that.

'It's a sci-fi movie, with Simon Pegg, but it's a comedy too, so it's a good intro to the genre.'

'Sounds great. Is Cinema City showing it? We could go see it next time.'

'No, it came out a few years ago, so it won't be in the cinema. I've got it on Blu-ray though…'

'Well, how about instead of going to the cinema next time, you come over to mine and we'll watch *Paul*? I can always cook us some food, get a bottle of wine in…' Annie trailed off, realising what she'd just suggested. It sounded as though she was trying to seduce him, and she looked up in panic, expecting to see an expression of horror on his face.

Instead, Jamie looked genuinely pleased. 'Yeah, I'd love to. It's a date.'

'Is it?' The words were out of Annie's mouth before she could stop herself. 'Oh, I didn't mean—'

But Jamie simply grinned at her, shrugging his shoulders. 'Sure,' he said easily. 'Look, I've got to head off now, but I'll see you at work on Monday. Have a great evening, Annie.'

Annie swallowed, wishing that the ground would swallow her up. 'You too,' she managed, as she climbed into her car and quickly drove off.

Chapter 21

*'I know nothing about sex, because I was always married' – **Zsa Zsa Gabor***

It was a Saturday morning and the three couples, together with half a dozen of Annie's other clients, were once again gathered in the boardroom. They'd just completed a rather terrifying trust exercise, which involved closing your eyes and falling backwards into your partner's arms, relying on them to catch you.

Annie had hired a crash mat from a local gym, just in case, and it turned out to have been a wise decision. Whilst Zoe let herself drop into the safety of Simon's muscular arms without batting an eyelid, Julia couldn't bring herself to trust Nick at all, and kept squatting down on the floor the moment she overbalanced. Nick, in turn, was becoming increasingly frustrated, which didn't help the situation one bit.

When the couples swapped round, Ray leant his full weight back onto Linda without hesitation, sending both of them crashing into the safety of the mat, their limbs entangled as Linda lay crushed beneath Ray. A flustered Linda, and a slightly hysterical Ray, finally emerged unscathed after much flapping and flailing.

'Right, after all that excitement,' Annie began, doing her best to calm the giddy, adrenaline-fuelled couples around her, 'we're going to finish with a brief verbal exercise.'

'Is that the same as an oral exercise?' Zoe whispered to Simon, and the two of them started giggling.

Annie rolled her eyes at them – it had been that kind of morning – which only made the two of them laugh even harder. 'I need you to pair up with someone who's not your usual partner,' she continued. 'And find a seat together in the room.'

When everyone was settled, looking expectantly at Annie, she went on, 'Okay, now this is going to be fairly quick. You only have five minutes each—'

'I can be quick. I reckon five minutes is about all I'd need right now,' Simon muttered to Zoe, who let out an undignified snort.

'But you're going to take it in turns and I want you to tell the person you're working with three things that you love about your husband or wife, boyfriend or girlfriend. These can be physical – for instance, you might love their bottom,' Annie suggested, which raised a few sniggers. 'Or it could be something simple like, "I love the fact that they bring me tea and toast every morning".'

'Chance would be a fine thing,' Ray piped up cheekily, and Linda shot him a look across the room.

'Whatever you want really,' Annie smiled. 'It's just a tool to get you thinking about all the reasons you appreciate your other half.'

Linda and Simon paired up together, and were surprised to find that they got on rather well. Simon reminded Linda of her son, Robbie, and she enjoyed listening to him talk about Zoe and their upcoming nuptials. Seeing the two of them so young and full of optimism gave her a sharp pang of nostalgia.

'Do you want to go first?' Linda asked.

'Sure,' Simon nodded agreeably.

'All right, what are your favourite three things about Zoe?'

'Boobs and bum,' Simon responded instantly. 'And… um… personality?' he finished, clearly struggling for the third.

'Ah, yes, can't forget the personality,' Linda laughed. 'So are those your three?'

Simon shrugged. 'Yeah, I think so. That pretty much sums it up! How about you? That's your husband, isn't it?' he asked, nodding across the room at Ray.

'Yes, that's him,' Linda replied, in a tone that Simon couldn't quite read. 'Hmm, well, I might have said "bum" once upon a time too, but probably not any more. That all went south a long time ago,' she chuckled. 'Not that I'm any better. Gravity gets us all in the end, I'm afraid.'

'Nah, you look great still,' Simon grinned flirtatiously. 'If I wasn't engaged, I'd be after you myself!'

'That's very sweet of you, but I don't believe a word you're saying! No, for Ray I'd say… his sense of humour. He can sometimes be quite funny, I suppose. And, um, he's very practical. He's good at fixing things – changing light bulbs and putting up shelves and so on. That'll do, won't it? And the third…'

Linda paused, desperately racking her brains. Could she really not think of three things she liked about her husband?

'Our children,' she finished finally. 'He gave me three wonderful children.'

'Uh uh.' Simon shook his head, making a noise like a quiz show contestant giving the wrong answer. 'That doesn't count.'

'Yes it does,' Linda argued.

'Sorry, no. Do you want me to check the rules with Annie?'

Linda pretended to glare at him. 'Okay, okay. Well then I'd have to say… his eyes,' she finished finally, sounding very underwhelmed. 'Don't look at me like that!' she protested. 'It's all right for you and Zoe, you're love's young dream, but it's much harder when you get to our age. Come back to me once you've been married thirty-odd years and had three children, then we'll see how enthusiastic you feel.'

She saw Simon's face drop and immediately felt bad.

'All I'm saying is don't take each other for granted,' Linda told him softly. 'It's wonderful to see you two so happy and in love – I've no idea why you're coming to these sessions, but that's your own business. And I know you probably think I'm a daft old bat, but I'm speaking from experience, and I don't want to see another couple make the mistakes that we did. If you love Zoe, tell her every day. Cherish her, make her feel special, and let her know that she's the centre of your world.'

Simon smiled. 'I will. You know, your husband's a very lucky man.'

Linda stared across the room at Ray, deep in conversation with Nick. She wondered what he was saying, what the three things he loved about her were.

'I just wish someone would tell him that,' she finished ruefully.

❄ ❄ ❄

'It's clever, isn't it?' Linda said. She and Ray were in the car, heading back from their group session with Annie.

'What's that, love?' Ray asked, slowing down to overtake a woman on a horse. She held up her hand in thanks as Ray drove safely past.

'These sessions. Well, Annie really. It certainly gives you food for thought, the questions she asks.'

'So you're feeling a little more well disposed towards the idea of therapy?' Ray couldn't resist asking.

'I suppose I am. I wouldn't have thought it was for me in a million years, but I can see that it has its value.'

Ray smiled, knowing that was the closest Linda would come to admitting he'd been right, and acknowledging that there was a problem between them.

'You know, you gave Annie a pretty hard time at that first meeting.'

Linda pulled a face, looking embarrassed. 'I know. I really should apologise to her. But I suppose she's used to it – not everyone who goes to see her can be open and embracing from the start, can they?'

Ray said nothing, just carried on driving, and they lapsed into silence.

'So what did you say?' Linda asked eventually, curiosity getting the better of her.

'Hmm?'

'What did you say to that chap Nick – your three things that you loved about me?'

'Oh, that,' Ray chuckled to himself. 'I'm not really sure if I should tell you. Aren't these workshops supposed to be confidential?'

Linda leant across and hit him with her handbag.

'Hey!' Ray protested. 'I'm driving. That's dangerous be-haviour.'

'I'll do something even more dangerous in a minute if you don't tell me,' Linda threatened, as Ray laughed even harder.

'Okay, okay, I'll tell you. First of all, I said your creativity. I really admire what you do with the flowers – how you make those bouquets look so beautiful – and I'm so proud at how you've built up your business. I could never do that.'

'Really?' Linda was surprised. 'You've never, ever told me that before. You've never said you were proud of me.'

'Haven't I? Well, I suppose I've always thought it. The occasion didn't really arise to mention it.'

'I suppose not,' Linda replied, feeling quietly pleased with his response. 'Number two?'

Ray's grin got even wider. 'Your legs,' he told her, taking his eyes off the road for a cheeky glance. 'Never seen a better pair in all my days. I was raving to Nick about when we first met, and how good you looked in that little tartan skirt with the long socks.'

'Yes, well, I think my mini skirt days are long gone.'

'Ah, but you've still got cracking legs,' Ray insisted. 'I manage to get a glimpse when I can!'

'Do you think so?' Linda couldn't help asking, as she stared down at her trouser-covered thighs.

'Absolutely,' Ray insisted, noticing the way Linda was soaking up the flattery. 'I wouldn't mind seeing a bit more of them. In fact, I wouldn't mind spending a bit of time between them now and again.'

'Raymond Anderson!' Linda burst out, sounding shocked. For a moment, Ray wondered whether he'd overstepped the mark. They'd been chatting away, communicating better than they had done for months, and he hoped Linda didn't clam up again. Instead, she burst out laughing, wiping the tears from her eyes.

'You're a devil, you are,' she insisted. 'My mother always warned me about men like you.'

'We're the best kind,' Ray winked. 'And there's still number three to come.'

'Let's see you top the last one, then. What's number three?'

'Your smile,' Ray said softly. 'You always look beautiful to me, but you're at your most beautiful when you smile.'

'I feel all self-conscious now,' Linda protested, putting a hand over her mouth.

'Don't be,' Ray told her. He took a deep breath before adding, 'But, like your legs, it's something I don't see very much these days. You don't smile as often as you used to, and I'd give anything to change that.'

Linda paused for a moment, taking in what her husband had said. Then she leant across to where his hand was resting on the gear stick and clasped it with her own. Ray held onto it tightly, their fingers linking together as he stroked her hand with his thumb.

They were almost home, about to turn off the ring road towards Little Plumstead, when Ray suddenly hit the brake, pulling over to the side of the road.

'What are you doing?' Linda asked in alarm.

'I've had an idea! It's only early still – not even midday yet – so why don't we go out somewhere for the day, just the two of us? We haven't done that for years.'

'I don't know,' Linda began reluctantly. 'I promised Rose I'd pop into the shop this afternoon, and then I've got bits to do around the house.'

'Rose'll be fine,' Ray insisted. 'You know she will, and she's got Katie there to help her today. And any jobs you've got at home can wait until later. I'll give you a hand with them tomorrow, if you want.'

'Wonders will never cease,' Linda said tartly, raising an eyebrow. 'Would you really know what to do with it if I gave you a duster?'

Ray ignored her. 'Come on, love. Why don't we have a ride out to Cromer?' he suggested, mentioning the pretty seaside town. 'We haven't been there for years. It'd be lovely to have a look round.'

'We can't!' Linda insisted.

'Why not?'

'We're not teenagers. We can't just go running off as though we've got no responsibilities.'

'But we *don't* have any responsibilities,' Ray replied calmly. 'We don't have anywhere we need to be, or anything we need to do, so we might as well please ourselves.'

He looked over at his wife, who seemed far from convinced. 'So what do you say?'

Linda shrugged helplessly. 'Cromer it is then.'

❋ ❋ ❋

It took them just under forty-five minutes to reach the seaside resort of Cromer. They stepped out of the car to a chorus of crying seagulls, and the smell of fish and chips, candyfloss and waffles floating on the air. The day was overcast, but not raining, and the breeze from the North Sea was light, for once.

'Ah, smell that sea air,' Ray exclaimed, as he took in the view stretching out ahead of them. They'd managed to get a parking space right along the front, and below them lay the blue-grey sea with its foamy white waves. On the beach, dog walkers were out in force, along with half a dozen families picnicking, and a handful of hardy children playing in the shallows. Further out, wet-suited paddle boarders tried to catch a swell, whilst a few big ships lurked on the horizon.

'So what do you fancy doing?' Ray asked. 'Shall we have a quick dip in the sea?'

'I don't want to get hypothermia, thank you very much,' Linda retorted, pulling her coat more tightly around her. 'Let's walk along the esplanade, past the pier.'

'Your wish is my command.' Ray held out his arm and, after a moment's hesitation, Linda took it, linking her arm through his as they strolled along.

'The kids used to love it here when they were little, didn't they?' Linda reminisced, as she watched a young boy, only a few years old, fill a bucket with sand and turn it upside down, his face lighting up with joy as he pulled the bucket off to reveal the lopsided castle beneath.

'They did,' Ray agreed. 'I remember our Rose playing for so long in the water that her lips turned blue. She still didn't want to get out, even though she was freezing!'

'And do you remember when that seagull tried to steal Marianne's ice cream? It was a huge thing, and it flew right at her. She couldn't stop crying. She's always been a bit nervous of birds ever since.'

The pair of them laughed, and Ray instinctively knew that he'd done the right thing by suggesting that they come here. Already, they felt closer than they had in years.

They passed by the pier, with its adverts for the upcoming summer show, and completed the loop of the esplanade, walking back up towards the town itself. As they passed a row of tall townhouses overlooking the sea, Linda stopped suddenly.

'What is it?' Ray asked.

'That one there,' Linda replied, nodding at a pink-coloured house in the middle of the block. The paint was peeling and the windows were shabby; a sign outside read 'Robin's Nest Guest House'. 'Don't you remember?'

Ray stared at it for a moment, frowning.

'Of course, it's changed its name. It was called "Sunnyside B&B" back then,' Linda prompted him.

The penny dropped for Ray, and his mouth fell open. 'Oh my goodness! I can't believe I forgot! That's where we stayed, isn't it? Back when we were dating.'

Linda was nodding her head. 'I had to lie to my mother – I told her I was going away for the weekend with Margaret Scott. She'd have had a fit if she knew I was going away with you!'

'And then we had to pretend to the B&B owner that we were married, otherwise she wouldn't have let us stay. Right old battleaxe she was.'

'We spent the weekend calling each other "Mr and Mrs Anderson",' Linda chuckled.

'Ah, we had a great time, didn't we?'

'Do you know, our Rose was probably conceived in that building,' Linda said thoughtfully.

'And I don't regret a single minute of it,' Ray told her. 'Any of it.'

'Don't you?' Linda asked, unable to keep the note of bitterness out of her voice. 'You never think what life would have been like if I hadn't got pregnant? You'd have been free to chase Susie Townsend, or whoever you wanted, and we wouldn't have been forced into some shotgun marriage.'

Ray sighed. 'Linda, I don't know how else to convince you of this, but I didn't want to go chasing after Susan, or anyone else for that matter. The only person I've ever wanted is *you*. How can I regret you getting pregnant when we've got our Rose – not to mention Marianne and Robbie? I couldn't be more thrilled that you're my wife, and I hope you're just as happy that I'm your husband.'

Linda went quiet for a moment, seemingly taking in everything that Ray had just said. Then she leant across and kissed him, her eyes closed, leaving her lips on his for several seconds. When she pulled away, Ray looked shocked, but thrilled, unable to believe what had just happened. He couldn't even remember the last time that he and Linda had kissed, and it was a struggle to keep the smile off his face.

'Well, Linda Anderson!' he exclaimed. 'My mother warned me about forward girls like you.'

Linda hit him playfully on the arm. 'Oh, shut up, you silly old thing,' she laughed affectionately. 'Now come on. If you're really good, I'll let you treat me to fish and chips.'

'You're on,' Ray replied, grinning happily as he took his wife's hand and they walked contentedly up the hill towards the town.

Chapter 22

'Make love when you can. It's good for you' –
Kurt Vonnegut

Julia stirred in her sleep, as Nick slowly pulled back the duvet and climbed out of bed. It was a Sunday morning, and the two of them were enjoying a much needed lie-in. Julia was due to meet Zoe and Simon later, for a cake tasting appointment, but for now she luxuriated in the comfort of her pillows and the warmth of the duvet as she drifted back to sleep.

Some time later – possibly minutes, possibly hours – she became aware of the smell of freshly ground coffee and buttered toast filling the room. Then Nick was shaking her gently, murmuring: 'Wake up, sleepyhead. I made you breakfast.'

Julia kept her eyes tightly shut. 'I'm not hungry,' she replied petulantly. She knew exactly what Nick was doing, and it was going to take more than coffee and toast for him to get back in her good books.

'I'll leave it on the side, then.'

Julia heard him put the tray down on the dressing table before slipping back beneath the duvet and cuddling up against her. He wrapped an arm around her, pulling her close as he began kissing her neck.

'Sunday morning… Nothing to do…' he whispered. 'The perfect time to make a baby.'

Julia tensed, wriggling out of his grasp. 'Not now, Nick.'

She felt his body freeze and knew he'd be confused; usually Julia couldn't get enough of her husband, eagerly seizing any opportunity to try to conceive.

Nick's arm retreated, and he sighed. 'Julia…'

'No, Nick,' she shot back. 'I don't want to do this right now. I don't want to have this conversation.'

'Well, we have to have it some time.' Julia could hear the frustration in his voice. 'We can't go on like this. We've talked it out, and I've apologised until I'm blue in the face. Like Annie says, we either have to move past it or—'

'Or what?'

'Or… not,' Nick said slowly. He didn't need to spell out what that meant. Both of them knew that if they decided their relationship was irreparable, they were on the slippery slope to divorce. Despite the vicious arguments and hurtful accusations, neither of them wanted it to come to that.

Julia rolled over to face her husband. She didn't speak, but simply stared at him for a moment. Their faces were almost touching as she took in the familiar features: the deep lines that had appeared on his forehead in recent weeks; the weekend stubble peppering his jaw line; the pale blue eyes that seemed to have lost their sparkle. Then she stared at his lips. Lips that had whispered words of endearment to another woman, kissed her and…

Julia squeezed her eyes closed. She couldn't think like that. It was going to be the end of them – the end of their marriage – if she did. Like Annie, and Nick, had said, she needed to make a decision.

'It's just hard for me, Nick,' Julia confessed. She opened her eyes, and Nick saw that they were shining wet with tears.

'I know it is. And I know it's all my fault. I've been a total and utter idiot, and I'd do anything to take back what I did. But all I can do is tell you a thousand times that you're the woman for me. I love you, I want to be with you, I want to have babies with you.'

'Do you?' Julia swallowed. 'Because it's not looking that way at the moment.'

'Of course I—' Nick began, then hesitated. He's been about to insist that he *did* want children, and that Julia was imagining his reticence, but Nick realised he needed to be honest with her. 'You know something,' he tried again. 'I honestly did want kids. I mean, *do*,' he hastily corrected himself. 'But I think it hit me harder than I expected when we started trying for a baby. It suddenly became real, that this was something that was going to massively change our entire lives.'

Julia bit back a dozen sarcastic retorts and stayed silent, listening to what her husband had to say.

'And then I think – and I'm not blaming you for this – but it all just became so much pressure. It didn't seem as though making a baby was something we were doing together. It was like it was your little project, and I was pushed out.'

'That's not fair,' Julia protested.

'Maybe not,' Nick acknowledged. 'But I'm just telling you how I felt. I didn't say it was logical,' he said, with a tentative smile.

Julia didn't smile back, frowning as she thought about his words. 'So what are you saying? That I pushed you towards Nina?'

'No,' Nick insisted, wishing Julia would stop saying her name. 'I'm not making excuses. I know I have to take responsibility for what I did – however bloody stupid it was.

But I regret that moment more than anything I've ever done. It could have ruined everything. Everything we've built together. Everything we've planned for the future.'

'Do you still love me?' Julia asked, her voice trembling as she looked at him from beneath lashes heavy with tears.

'Jules, I love you so much, I really do,' Nick sighed, moving closer and taking her in his arms. It was heartbreaking, listening to his wife ask him those questions, with such uncertainty in her voice. 'And I understand, too,' Nick continued. 'Since we've been seeing Annie, I know why having a family is such a huge thing for you. And I know how badly I must have hurt you because of that.'

'You were a dickhead,' Julia told him fiercely, her voice muffled from being pressed into his chest.

In spite of her words, Nick smiled, recognising that they were turning a corner. 'Yeah,' he agreed, kissing her on top of her head. 'I was a dickhead.'

Julia lay quietly, wrapped up in Nick's arms, their bodies intertwined. In spite of all that had happened, it still felt safe and secure. Everything about the situation was reassuringly familiar: the cosy softness of the duvet, the feel of Nick's body against hers, the smell of his skin.

Julia exhaled slowly, suddenly realising that she was tired of everything – all the arguments and recriminations, the holding of petty grudges, the silent treatment and the ever-present tension between them. She wanted their relationship to be back to how it used to be, but Julia knew it could never be the same again. One of the many things she'd learnt from Annie was that you always had to keep moving forward – you could never go back – and trying to recapture a particular moment in time was impossible.

If Julia wanted her and Nick to move forward, she needed to let go of her anger and resentment, and forgive her husband for the mistake he'd made.

'Make love to me,' Julia murmured softly. 'No agenda, no trying to get pregnant. Just you and me, slow and gentle and loving.'

Nick propped himself up on one elbow, scrutinising Julia's face. 'Are you sure?' he asked, his tone serious.

Julia lay back and smiled at him, reaching out a hand to gently caress his cheek. 'I've never been more sure of anything.'

❋ ❋ ❋

More than a dozen cakes were laid out on the table, and they all looked incredible. There was red velvet smothered in cream cheese; lemon drizzle coated in sweet, white icing; traditional vanilla sponge with a strawberry jam centre; dark chocolate ganache shot through with cherry liqueur.

Zoe stared at them longingly, embarrassed to hear her stomach give off an almighty rumble.

'They smell delicious,' she sighed, inhaling the sweet scent of icing sugar and cocoa that permeated the air of the cake shop.

'What time is Julia supposed to be arriving?' Simon asked, for the third time in as many minutes. His mouth was hanging open, and he fully expected to look down and see a little pile of drool on the table in front of him.

'She said one o'clock,' Zoe replied worriedly, checking her phone again and noting that it was now almost quarter past.

'Well, I don't think it's very professional,' Simon harrumphed. 'It's the first meeting she's arranged for us, and she can't even be bothered to turn up on time.'

'Don't say that,' Zoe shushed him. 'She's organising this whole wedding for next to nothing, and she can get us a really good discount on whichever cake we choose. We wouldn't even have known about this place if it wasn't for her, let alone got them to open on a Sunday.'

The two of them were in 'Truly Scrumptious', a traditional bakery in the pretty little market town of Fotheringham, just outside Norwich. The elderly owner, Molly Macdonald, was one of Julia's contacts, and she'd arranged for Zoe and Simon to have a private tasting when the shop was closed, so that they could decide on the filling for their wedding cake. Julia had offered to accompany them, but so far she was nowhere in sight.

'I'm sure there's a perfectly good explanation as to why she's running a bit late,' Zoe insisted.

Molly, who'd been standing at the window watching for Julia, turned and smiled at them. 'There's still no sign of her, I'm afraid,' she said, in her gentle Scottish accent. 'Would you like to get started anyway? I can always cut you a couple of samples to be going on with.'

Zoe and Simon looked at one another.

'Maybe we should just hang on another few minutes...' Zoe suggested, biting her lip longingly.

'No,' Simon burst out, overcome by the sight of the moist, juicy carrot cake topped with creamy mascarpone. 'I'm not waiting any longer. Do you mind if we try that one?' he asked, pointing to a white chocolate and raspberry gateau.

'Of course not,' Molly smiled. Simon almost whimpered as she slid the knife into the cake, the chocolate cracking and splintering as the raspberry filling oozed out. Molly had just plated up two small portions when Julia came dashing through the door.

'I'm so sorry,' she apologised breathlessly. It looked as though she'd got ready in a hurry: her hair was a mess, her blouse was buttoned up wrongly, and the label was sticking out of the back of her skirt. On the other hand, her skin was positively glowing and her eyes were shining. 'I was just… that is… Nick and I, um, overslept and then… I can't apologise enough. I'm never normally like this, I promise.'

'Don't worry about it,' Zoe smiled easily. 'We'd just given in and decided to try the cakes, but you're here now.'

'Yes.' Julia sat down, smoothing back her hair then pulling a notebook and pen out of her bag. 'What do you think? Initial impressions?'

'It looks amazing,' Zoe gushed. 'Thanks so much for bringing us here. I'd never heard of this place before.'

Julia looked pleased. 'Good. Molly's the best kept secret in Norfolk,' she grinned, smiling at Molly who was cutting a third slice of cake which she handed to Julia.

'Mmm, that's divine.'

'Incredible!'

Simon said nothing, letting out a long, slow moan of pleasure instead. 'We'll have that one,' he managed finally.

'We haven't tried the others yet,' Zoe giggled.

'I don't care. Nothing can taste as good as that.'

'Well, my red velvet's pretty tasty too,' Molly smiled, as she cut three generous slices and handed them round.

Julia poured them each a glass of water from the jug on the table, and they all took a sip to cleanse their palates, before taking a forkful of the red velvet.

'I think this is even better,' Simon wailed. 'How are we supposed to choose?'

'We could have a tier of each?' Zoe suggested. 'If we keep them small, we might be able to afford three.'

'Then bring on the next,' Simon beamed, as he scraped his plate.

'You're not supposed to eat the whole portion, you'll be sick,' Zoe told him, laughing. 'I can handle it,' Simon shrugged. 'I'm a big guy.'

'Vanilla sponge next?' suggested Molly. The knife sliced deftly through the cake which was light as air, jam and cream sandwiched in the middle.

'I think we've found our third tier,' Simon grinned.

'Your wedding cake's going to be twenty tiers high at this rate,' Julia chuckled.

'You do know the cake's for our guests as well,' Zoe told Simon. 'We don't get to eat it all ourselves.'

'Really? Oh.' Simon looked crestfallen.

'Although maybe there'll be other things to look forward to on our wedding day.' Zoe leant in close as she whispered, 'Like our wedding *night*.'

'Oh, yeah…' A wide grin spread across Simon's face as he savoured the prospect. 'Maybe we could combine the two? My new bride, covered in chocolate ganache,' he suggested, as Zoe giggled naughtily.

It was another hour before they'd worked their way through all of the samples, and by then they all felt thoroughly sick and full to bursting.

'I don't ever want to see another cake again,' Simon groaned, as he reached for the water jug.

'I warned you,' Zoe admonished him, although she was feeling pretty nauseous herself. It turned out that it *was* possible to have too much of a good thing.

'So have you made your final selections?' Molly asked pleasantly, looking at them from behind her wire-rimmed glasses.

'I think so,' Zoe replied, looking across to Simon for confirmation. 'We're going to go for a layer of red velvet, coated in cream cheese, on the bottom.'

'That's the biggest one right?' Simon asked, as Zoe nodded. 'Just checking.'

'Then a layer of vanilla sponge with buttercream, and just a small traditional fruit cake layer on the top, covered in white icing – our parents will like that.'

'And you'd like pink rose petals decorating all three tiers?' asked Molly, as she wrote everything down carefully.

'Yes, please.'

Zoe, Simon and Julia all stood up, scraping back their chairs as they surveyed the messy remains of the cakes on the table.

'I'll give you a call later in the week to confirm everything,' Julia said to Molly, as she hugged her goodbye.

'Thank you so much,' Zoe added. 'Your cakes are amazing!'

'You're very welcome,' Molly told her, pressing a small white box into her hands. 'And here're a few extra samples, just to take home.'

'Are you trying to kill me?' Simon joked.

'What about me?' Zoe said, as they made their way out of the door. 'I'm supposed to be fitting into a teeny tiny wedding dress in less than three months.'

'Ooh, that reminds me,' Julia said. 'Are you still okay to do a trying-on session next week?'

'Absolutely. I can't wait!'

'Me neither. And I promise I won't be late for that one,' Julia assured her, her cheeks turning pink as she remembered the exact reason *why* she'd been late today.

'Oh, don't worry about it,' Zoe insisted. 'I hope you were doing something fun.'

Julia's turned even redder. 'You could say that,' she managed, as they reached her car. 'Anyway, I'll see you both soon, and I'll give you a call about next week,' she promised, as she hugged them both goodbye.

'Well, we've got the whole afternoon ahead of us,' Zoe mused, waving as Julia drove off. 'What shall we do?'

'Hmm, I'm thinking you, me, that chocolate ganache…'

'I thought you couldn't eat any more?'

Simon leant across, pulling Zoe to him and pretending to bite her on the neck, which made her squeal with delight. 'Looking at you, I'm feeling hungry all over again!'

Chapter 23

'A liberated woman is one who has sex before marriage and a job after' – **Gloria Steinem**

Annie was in her kitchen – a room in her house where, ordinarily, she didn't spend a huge amount of time. Right now, she was feeling extremely stressed, nervous adrenaline racing round her body, her face red and blotchy from the heat. Steam was blasting from pots simmering on the hob, the oven was pumping out hot air, and the work surfaces were littered with sticky mixing bowls and the remnants of chopped vegetables.

Annie opened the window to try to cool the room down, staring round in bewilderment at the mess she'd created. The kitchen was not her natural territory; being so busy with her job, Annie often picked up a takeaway on her way home from work or popped a ready meal in the microwave, and her culinary skills didn't really extend much beyond that. When she'd invited Jamie over for a film night, she'd casually offered to cook something simple, but now she felt as pressured as though she were competing on *Masterchef* and doing her utmost to impress a harsh panel of critics.

As she and Jamie had planned to chill on her sofa and watch a film, Annie hadn't wanted to cook a formal, sit-down meal. In a moment of optimism, she'd opted to make American diner-style cuisine: hotdogs with mustard and fried onions; homemade sweet potato fries; mac 'n' cheese in little ramekins; barbecue chicken wings; with chocolate brownies and vanilla ice cream for dessert. Now Annie was starting to think that she might have been a little overconfident in her choices. She was essentially trying to cook five different things at once, and it was all starting to fall apart.

'Shit,' Annie swore under her breath, as she noticed the time on the oven clock. Jamie would be here any minute. She dashed upstairs and into her bedroom, catching sight of her reflection in the wardrobe mirror. Urgh. Her face was flushed, her neatly blow-dried hair had gone frizzy, and her white T-shirt sported a remarkable variety of cooking stains.

Quickly, Annie pulled on her blue skinny jeans and a Breton striped top, which she hoped might lend her an air of French sophistication. As she hastily applied a touch of make-up, Annie found herself thinking about Jamie's words after their last cinema outing, as he'd walked her to her car and she'd stupidly asked whether or not this was a date. He'd simply shrugged and replied, 'Sure', those blue eyes dancing in the way that made her stomach flip. Was he merely humouring her? Or was tonight really a proper grown-up, I-like-you-you-like-me, potential-for-romance date?

Annie wasn't even sure what she wanted the answer to be. She definitely liked Jamie. More than liked, in fact. If the truth be told, she was starting to develop real feelings for him. But the fact remained that she was terrified; she was scared of getting hurt again, and making another colossal life-changing mistake. How did you know when your feelings for someone were genuine, she wondered. How could you be sure that all the lust and excitement wouldn't fade and disappear over time? Maybe the difference was that when you had a good relationship, you didn't just walk away, like she had with Mark. You knew that you had something worth fighting for, and you did everything in your power to keep it.

The doorbell rang and Annie's heart lurched. She counted to three and exhaled slowly, before jogging down the stairs and opening the door.

'Hi Jamie,' she smiled, trying her best to sound cool and composed.

'Hi Annie,' he grinned, leaning over to kiss her on the cheek, a gesture that made her body fizz at the skin-on-skin contact. Jamie looked gorgeous in his usual jeans and a casual shirt, and he was holding a bunch of flowers, a beautiful arrangement of roses and freesias. 'These are for you.'

'Thank you!' Annie exclaimed. 'You really didn't have to.'

'I know, but I wanted to,' he replied, which made Annie's smile grow even wider. She didn't think a man had ever bought her flowers before – certainly not Mark, who'd viewed them as a waste of money. But Annie thought they were a wonderful, romantic gesture, and she delightedly inhaled their sweet scent.

'And I brought this too,' Jamie continued, holding up a bottle of Malbec. 'You prefer red, right?'

'Well remembered!'

They stood there for a moment, simply smiling at one another, luxuriating in the moment and the anticipation of what tonight might bring.

'Come through,' Annie told him, guiding him swiftly past the kitchen and into the living room.

'You've got a beautiful house, Annie,' Jamie said admiringly, as he stared round at the well-kept room. It was decorated in relaxing, neutral shades, with her goldfish bowl set on a chest of drawers beside a framed photograph of her parents. There was an overflowing bookcase in one corner, and shelves containing all her DVDs on the opposite wall. Jamie strolled over, reading the titles with a grin.

'*Shakespeare in Love... Moulin Rouge... The English Patient.* You really have got them all.'

'Naturally! And tonight I get to experience some sci-fi.'

'I'm planning to convert you,' Jamie teased.

'Well, I'll let you get everything set up. It's pretty straightforward,' Annie said, gesturing towards her DVD player. 'I'll just go and check on the food. Can I get you a drink? Wine? Beer?'

'I'll start with a beer, thanks.'

Moments later, Annie brought it through, Jamie chinking his bottle against her glass of Malbec. 'Here's to tonight,' he toasted.

'And to losing my sci-fi virginity,' Annie joined in, then immediately blushed scarlet. She took a sip of her drink to cover her embarrassment, pretending not to notice the way Jamie was laughing.

'The food smells delicious,' he commented, taking another slug of his beer. 'What are we having?'

'American-style finger food. I thought it would be easy to eat whilst watching TV.'

'Great plan,' Jamie grinned, and Annie felt her stomach do a long, slow flip. He looked even more handsome when he smiled, his eyes crinkling at the corners, his whole face lighting up. There was a quiet confidence about him, Annie reflected, sneaking a sideways glance at him as she took in his handsome profile. Jamie never seemed to feel the need to show off in front of her, or try to impress her; he was just very comfortable in his own skin, and it was very attractive. It was *sexy*, Annie realised, feeling tingles where she hadn't felt tingles for a very long time.

'Can you hear something?' Jamie asked with a frown.

The sound of a pan boiling over startled Annie out of her reverie, and she dashed back through to the kitchen to discover it had turned into a disaster zone in her absence. Smoke was billowing from the oven, and when she pulled open the door she discovered that her sweet potato fries were now nothing more than charred black lumps. The chicken, in contrast, still looked worryingly pink, whilst her mac 'n' cheese appeared to be little more than gloopy lumps of pasta swimming in milk. Annie felt like crying.

'Is everything okay in there?' Jamie called.

'Fine,' Annie lied, alarmed to hear her voice come out strangely high-pitched and strangled. 'Just a couple more minutes.'

She was desperately trying to rescue the hotdog sausages from their watery grave, when she heard a noise in the doorway, and turned to see Jamie standing there, shock written across his face.

'Maybe another few minutes?' Annie suggested, knowing that she'd been rumbled.

She watched as Jamie looked around at the carnage of the kitchen, taking in the smudge of cheese sauce on Annie's cheek and the barbecue marinade splattered all over the worktop. Then suddenly, he began to laugh, a small snigger that gradually turned into a deep, rumbling belly laugh.

Annie stared at him in disbelief, but the more she thought about it, the funnier it seemed, and soon she was laughing too, the two of them in hysterics at the state of their meal.

'I'm so sorry,' Annie apologised through her giggles, as she tried to catch her breath. 'I wanted to make something really delicious and simple – just a few little dishes – but I forgot

I'm not exactly Nigella Lawson in the kitchen. I've totally messed it up.'

'Don't worry about it,' Jamie insisted. 'Honestly. It's the thought that counts.'

'I've got the number of a good pizza place,' Annie suggested.

'That might not be necessary… First things first, drink this,' Jamie instructed, topping up Annie's wine glass and handing it to her.

Annie did as she was told, gratefully taking it from him and noticing that after a few large mouthfuls, things didn't seem quite so bad any more.

'Right, let's take this off the heat,' Jamie murmured, as he turned off the hob and removed the saucepan containing the hotdog sausages. 'We can always fry them later with the onions. And what's this supposed to be?' he asked, peering nervously into a large Pyrex dish. 'Rice pudding?'

'Macaroni cheese,' Annie shot back indignantly.

Jamie's lips twitched once again, and he made no attempt to hide his smile. 'Do you have any flour? It might just be salvageable…'

Annie rooted round in her cupboards and passed it to him, as he picked up the tray of charcoal lumps that had once been fries and promptly dumped them in the bin.

'Do you have any more sweet potatoes?' he asked.

'No, but I've got ordinary ones.'

'Perfect,' Jamie winked, taking the bag from her.

Annie watched admiringly as Jamie got to work. He seemed to be an expert in the kitchen, quickly taking control as he added flour and grated cheese to thicken the macaroni mix, re-coating the chicken in barbecue sauce and placing it under the grill. Annie stood back and drank her wine, not wanting to cause any more damage. Perhaps it was the influence of the alcohol, but she couldn't help gazing at Jamie, watching the way his well-defined arm muscles pulsed and flexed as he moved around her kitchen. He seemed completely calm and unflustered, confident and capable as he gradually got their meal back on track.

'You're so good at this,' Annie told him, clearly impressed.

'I told you, I like to cook.'

'But I feel so bad. I invited you round here, and now you're the one who's doing everything.'

'It doesn't matter. Teamwork. Here, will you give me a hand with these potatoes? The trick is to season them well…'

Annie followed Jamie's instructions to the letter, slowly gaining in confidence with each successfully completed task. To her surprise, she found that under Jamie's guidance she was making good progress, and the two of them worked extremely well together. Annie's kitchen was only small, forcing them to work in close proximity, and the chemistry between them was undeniable.

Finally, more than an hour after Jamie had first arrived, they sat down on Annie's sofa to eat their food, an impressive spread laid out on the coffee table in front of them.

'This is incredible,' Annie gushed, taking a bite of her mustard-smothered hotdog. 'There's no way I'd have been able to do this by myself.'

'Nah, you were great,' Jamie insisted. 'I just helped out a little at the end.'

Annie smiled gratefully at him; they both knew he was being modest. She picked up the remote and pressed a button, and *Paul* began to play on the TV, but despite Annie's attempts to concentrate, she and Jamie kept breaking off from watching the film to chat. She felt so comfortable with Jamie,

Annie realised, and hugely enjoyed his company. She was rapidly getting the impression that he felt the same way…

The movie was soon forgotten about as the two of them talked about everything, from work to family to food to travel, childhood memories and funny stories, favourite books and songs that made them cry. By the time the end credits rolled, they were both sprawled out on the sofa, their bodies inches away from one another. The bottle of wine lay empty on the table, and as Jamie drained his glass he turned to look at Annie. His eyes were soft, his lips full, and Annie's pulse began to race, sensing a distinct shift in the atmosphere.

'You know when you asked me if this was a date…?'

'Forget it,' Annie cut in, waving away his words. 'I didn't mean it to come out like that.'

But Jamie pushed on, regardless. 'Did you want it to be?'

Annie hesitated. 'I… I don't know. I don't have a very good history with dating.'

'Maybe it's time for that to change.'

Annie stared at him, wondering what he was trying to say.

'Look, Annie, I'm not a teenager any more and I don't like playing games. If I like someone, I have to say it. And I really like you, Annie.'

Annie inhaled sharply, her heart hammering in her chest as his words set off a flurry of emotions inside of her – happiness, and excitement, and sheer, unadulterated fear as well. She swallowed hard, her voice little more than a whisper as she admitted, 'I like you too, Jamie.'

And it was true; she'd been trying to deny it for too long, but now it was out there, Annie thought, feeling a sense of exhilaration. As she sat there, her heart thumping wildly, Jamie slowly moved towards her, and Annie realised that she wanted him badly. His lips touched hers, and in that instant all the chemistry and excitement and pent-up frustration crystallised into that one incredible moment, sparks shooting through her veins, fireworks exploding in her body. Annie kissed him back, loving the feeling of his lips against hers, running her hands through his hair, over his strong shoulders and muscular chest.

When they eventually came up for breath, Jamie pulled away, looking at her hesitantly as though requesting her permission to carry on. Annie didn't say a word, simply leant forward and kissed him once again, their lips finding each other as though they'd been made to fit together.

It felt right. It felt perfect. And Annie never wanted it to stop.

Chapter 24

'For women the best aphrodisiacs are words. The g-spot is in the ears. He who looks for it below there is wasting his time' – **Isabel Allende**

Julia was browsing the beauty department at Jarrold's, Norwich's famous independent department store. There was so much choice that she felt baffled: creams for day time, separate creams for night time, products with caviar and seaweed and ones with technology developed by NASA. There was even something called an 'age-defying micro-dermabrasion sonic cleansing roller', which sounded completely terrifying.

Once upon a time, Julia had kept up with all these new products. When she was first dating Nick and working on reception at Skyrocket, she'd believed it was an important part of her job to look attractive and well-groomed, and thought nothing of blowing a chunk of her salary on spa treatments and designer make-up.

These days, Julia's priorities had shifted. Now that she and Nick were homeowners with a mortgage to pay, and the very real possibility of a baby on the way, Julia had learnt to be far more sensible with her money. She was still establishing her events business, meaning her income was small and fluctuated from month to month, so blowing her money on expensive clothes and shoes simply wasn't an option any more.

She strolled past the brow bar, where a woman was reclining on a chair having her eyebrows threaded, and stopped at the Chanel counter. Above it was an enormous picture of a famous actress, looking flawless and irresistible in a glossy lipstick. Julia sighed, looking longingly at the array of make-up in front of her. Surely a little treat was okay, she insisted to herself. After all, she didn't want to let her standards slip completely, and now that Nick was making an effort to come home early and spend more time with her, Julia wanted to look good for him.

Impulsively, she picked out a vibrant pink lipstick in its distinctive black and gold packaging, and handed it to the assistant.

'This one, please.'

'Oh, that's gorgeous, isn't it?' the young woman said, as she scanned the box then popped it in a bag. 'It'll go wonderfully with your colouring. And of course that shade is just perfect for summer.'

Julia smiled, feeling a surge of happiness and optimism flood through her. It seemed silly, but that one small purchase somehow left her feeling light and positive, able to believe that everything was going to be okay again.

'Treating yourself?' came a voice from behind her.

Julia span around to see a grinning Zoe.

'Hi, Zoe! Yeah, I thought I'd buy myself a fancy lipstick. It's been ages since I've had anything new.'

'Tell me about it. It feels like any spare money I have is being sucked into the wedding budget. Everything's so expensive! I can't remember the last time I bought anything for myself.'

'Oh, but it'll all be worth it,' Julia assured her. 'Come the big day, all the sacrifice will seem worthwhile. So, shall we head straight up to the bridal department?'

'Let's do it!'

Zoe had booked the afternoon off work to go wedding dress shopping with Julia. She'd already visited a few shops one weekend when her mother was visiting from Chester, but Zoe had yet to find the elusive perfect dress.

'Do you know what kind of thing you're looking for?' Julia asked, as they headed to the escalator.

'Something quite classic – nothing too outrageous. But it has to be that little bit special, you know?'

'Absolutely,' Julia nodded. They got off at the third floor, following the signs to bridal wear, which took them through the children's department.

'Oh, look at that,' Julia exclaimed, with a wistful sigh. 'Isn't that just the cutest thing you've ever seen?'

She was pointing at a tiny pink babygro, with a bear motif and the slogan 'Mummy Loves Me'.

'Yeah, it's sweet,' Zoe agreed. She went to move on, but Julia seemed mesmerised.

'And these are amazing too,' she breathed, taking a pair of blue stripy dungarees from the rail and holding them up.

Zoe watched her in confusion. 'Are you shopping for someone in particular?'

'No, not really. Just looking.'

'Do you and Nick have kids?' Zoe pressed. 'You never mentioned…?'

'No, we don't,' Julia replied quietly. 'We're… we're trying though.'

'That's so exciting! Me and Simon have talked about having babies, but I think we're going to spend a couple of years just enjoying being married before I start popping them out.'

Julia smiled sadly. 'It's not always that easy, unfortunately.'

'Oh, I'm sorry,' Zoe apologised, noticing the expression on Julia's face. 'Have I said something I shouldn't?'

'No, no, of course not. It's just that… Well, we've been trying for a while, and nothing's happened yet. We'll probably give it a couple more months and then go and see the doctor, but… It's not having the greatest effect on our relationship. That's actually why we're seeing Annie,' Julia admitted, feeling a huge amount of relief to have finally got it off her chest.

'Right,' Zoe nodded sympathetically. 'And are the sessions helping?'

Julia shrugged. 'I don't know to be honest. I was very reluctant to go to them at first, and gave Nick a really hard time. Annie too, come to think of it. It's given me an opportunity to say the things I wanted to say, but then it's thrown up a whole heap of other stuff too. Some days it's like we're on different planets, with no way of connecting. But then other days are better…' Julia stared, unseeing, at the dungarees, then quickly put them back on the rail. 'Anyway, enough about me,' she said, with forced brightness, not wanting to go into her marital issues right now. It hardly seemed appropriate when shopping for Zoe's bridal gown. 'This is about you. Let's go find you the dress of your dreams.'

Julia turned her back on the children's clothing, and the two of them set off again, passing through the lingerie section that was situated next to bridal wear.

'Maybe we should pick up something for your wedding night too,' Julia suggested cheekily. 'There's some gorgeous stuff in here.'

'Oh, I can't wait for my wedding night!' Zoe exclaimed, with such passion that Julia looked at her in surprise.

Zoe saw her expression and burst out laughing. 'Well, as you've told me why you're seeing Annie, I suppose it's only fair that I tell you too. Me and Simon have taken a temporary vow of celibacy,' she explained, the words tumbling out in a rush. 'We're not having sex until the wedding, but when we do it's going to be amazing! So Annie's given us all these exercises about discovering each other's bodies, and acting out fantasies, and building up the anticipation.'

'Wow,' Julia replied, looking gobsmacked. 'I don't know what to say! Is it difficult?'

'It's a bloody nightmare,' Zoe admitted. 'But, you know, we're finding other ways to satisfy each other, shall we say. There are a few things that aren't off limits, and we're making full use of those.'

'Wow,' Julia said again. 'I never knew that—' Suddenly she stopped short, staring across the shop and squinting. 'Wait a minute, isn't that...?'

Zoe followed her gaze, her eyes opening wide with shock. 'That's Linda, isn't it? From the group sessions?'

Julia nodded, neither of them speaking as they stared across at Linda. She was browsing a selection of slinky silk negligees, her hands running over the soft fabric. As they watched, she plucked a champagne-coloured one from the rail and held it up against her experimentally.

'Should we say hello?' Zoe whispered.

'I don't know. She might be embarrassed that we've seen her shopping for sexy underwear.'

'Oh my gosh! Do you think she might be a nymphomaniac? Maybe that's why she's seeing Annie.'

'Her husband did look pretty exhausted,' Julia whispered back, as the two of them burst into giggles.

Linda seemed to sense that someone was watching her and turned round, colour flooding her face as she saw Julia and Zoe.

Hastily, she shoved the nightgown back onto the rail, calling out an awkward, 'Hello!'

'Hi, Linda. How are you?' Zoe asked brightly, as she and Julia walked towards her.

'Fine thanks!' Linda replied, her voice unnaturally high. 'I was just… um… shopping for my daughter. She asked me to pick something up for her. She's busy working, you see.'

'Right,' Julia nodded suspiciously.

'What about you two? I didn't realise you two knew each other outside of…' Linda trailed off, not wanting to mention the place where they'd all met.

'We didn't – initially,' Julia laughed. 'We got chatting one week, and as I'm an events planner, I offered to help with Zoe's wedding.'

'She's great,' Zoe put in loyally.

'Oh, how wonderful!' Linda explained. 'Yes, I'd forgotten you're getting married soon. I had a lovely chat with your fiancé last week. He's such a nice young man, isn't he?'

'*I* think so,' Zoe grinned.

'Well, I won't hold you up any longer,' Linda smiled, hitching her handbag onto her shoulder and starting to walk off.

'You can come with us, if you like,' Zoe called out impulsively. 'We're just going over there, to try on some wedding dresses, if you fancy giving your opinion.'

'The more the merrier,' Julia encouraged.

'I… well…' Linda hesitated. Then she broke into a wide smile. 'Why not? That would be lovely.'

They made their way across the store and under a white archway, into a section of the shop that was specially cordoned off for bridal wear.

'Oh, aren't they all beautiful,' Julia breathed, gazing round at the rails of white dresses in silk, lace, organza and tulle.

Zoe couldn't stop grinning. 'This is so exciting!' she exclaimed.

Just then, an immaculately presented woman wearing a smart burgundy skirt-suit approached them. 'Can I help you?' she enquired.

'We have an appointment,' Julia explained. 'In the name of Zoe Miller. I'm Julia Crawford, her wedding planner.'

'Oh yes, here it is,' said the woman, as she scanned down her list. 'Two pm, right on the dot. My name's Valerie,' she introduced herself, shaking hands with Julia and Zoe. 'And this must be the mother of the bride,' she continued, smiling at Linda.

'Oh no,' Zoe giggled, realising her mistake. 'This is my friend, Linda. She's going to help me out today.'

'Ah, I see,' Valerie chuckled. 'My mistake, I do apologise. Now, what size are you? I'd say about an eight to ten,' she continued, standing back and scrutinising Zoe's figure.

'I remember those days,' Linda murmured to Julia.

'Me too. I can't see that I'll ever get into a size eight again,' Julia whispered back ruefully.

'And do you have any ideas about what styles or colours you'd like?' Valerie continued.

'I really like ivory, but I'm not too fussy. Cream suits me too.'

'Oh yes, that would go beautifully with your hair.'

'And I've tried on some empire-line dresses, which I loved. I prefer slim-fitted, with a narrow cut. Nothing too voluminous. I don't want to look like a toilet roll holder!'

Valerie nodded, frowning thoughtfully. 'Okay, I have a few that you might like,' she said, as she moved over to a rail and pulled out a sleeveless column dress, with a high neckline and delicate beadwork.

'Ooh, I love that one,' Julia squealed, nudging Zoe. 'It's very classy.'

'Would you like me to put it in the changing room for you?' Valerie asked. 'I'll select a few more, and if you'd like to have a look yourself too. Just let me know if you need any help.'

'Thank you, we will,' Zoe told her, excited as a child at Christmas. 'Oh, look at this,' she breathed, as she pulled out a beautiful cream dress with a lace overlay. It had a deep V neckline, with a ribbon sash that tied beneath the bust, and a delicate train that flared out at the bottom.

'It's gorgeous,' Julia agreed, her eyes lighting up as she gazed at the incredible gown. 'And how about this one? Look how pretty the back is…'

Between the four of them, they pulled out half a dozen dresses, as well as a selection of veils, tiaras and shoes, before Zoe disappeared into the changing room. Valerie went in to help her, while Julia and Linda sat outside in anticipation, like proud parents.

When Zoe emerged a few minutes later, entering princess-like through the white curtain, Julia and Linda gasped in amazement.

'Oh Zoe, you look stunning,' Julia gasped.

'Beautiful,' Linda echoed, dabbing at the corners of her eyes.

Zoe was wearing an ivory-coloured dress, classic and deceptively simple. It was strapless, and cut straight across the bust, with a jewelled sash at the waist before it fell gently to the floor. She'd paired it with a delicate veil, edged in a cream trim, and she looked absolutely incredible.

Zoe bit her lip, peeping up at the two women from beneath her long, pale lashes. Her eyes were shining, her face glowing. When she spoke, her voice was low, as though she hardly dared to break the spell.

'I think this is it,' she whispered, looking stunned but exhilarated. 'I think I've found the one.'

Chapter 25

'I'm a trisexual. I'll try anything once' –
Samantha Jones, Sex and the City

'Oh my gosh, I can't believe it!'

'No way – you've got to be kidding me.'

'Have you gone *crazy*, Annie?'

'No, I haven't gone crazy,' Annie replied happily, as she took in the sight in front of her. 'I did tell you all to wear sporty clothes.'

'But I never imagined… *this*!' Nick exclaimed.

'Well, I like to keep you on your toes – or should that be your bottoms?'

Annie was running her regular Saturday morning group session, and had asked the couples to meet her not at her office, but in a car park at the entrance to the Mid-Yare Nature Reserve. Five couples had signed up and were currently staring, open-mouthed, at the contents of the minivan that had just pulled up.

'Well, at least it's not dogging,' Simon couldn't resist saying. 'I did wonder what we were in store for, when you asked us to meet in a remote car park…'

He shut up quickly, as Zoe hit him on the arm.

'What do you think?' Annie asked. 'Are you all willing to participate?'

The group looked nervously at the minivan marked 'Thompson's Cycles', where five tandem bikes were being unloaded, gleaming in the late spring sunshine. One by one, all of the couples answered in the affirmative, as Annie explained:

'What could be better on a beautiful May morning? This exercise is obviously all about the importance of working together. I don't want any of you sitting at the back and letting your partner do all the hard work up front – you have to put in equal effort. It can be a little bit tricky getting used to the tandem, so you'll have to master that together too. You'll need patience, and a sense of humour. Plus, exercise releases endorphins, which should get you ready for a steamy session in the bedroom later.'

'I don't know about that,' Ray cut in. 'I think I'll be exhausted – if I haven't collapsed of a heart attack first.'

'I'm sure you're fit and raring to go,' Annie teased. 'With all that golf you play.'

Ray harrumphed and grunted. As Annie had told them to come in sportswear, he'd put on his golf clothes, and was currently wearing golf trousers and a polo shirt, with a diamond-pattern jumper over the top.

'There are helmets and cycle clips available too. Just line up and see the guys from the hire company,' Annie explained, as she began handing out high visibility jackets.

'Do these come in any other colours?' Nick asked, eyeing the fluorescent yellow doubtfully.

'What I didn't mention is that today's session is all about overcoming embarrassment too,' Annie grinned.

'What about you?' Julia asked Annie, as she wrestled her high-vis jacket over the hoody she was wearing. 'Who are you going to pair up with?'

'Ooh, is that hot guy from the obstacle course session coming back?' Zoe asked excitedly. 'What was his name?'

Annie felt the colour flame in her face, and tried to keep her expression neutral as she replied, 'His name was Jamie, and no, Zoe, he isn't coming with us today. I'll be riding solo, and cycling alongside you on my mountain bike.'

'I don't think I've ever looked so unattractive in my whole life,' Julia muttered to Nick, as she tugged awkwardly on her cycle helmet.

Nick looked down at his wife, her green eyes peeking out from beneath the helmet, her blonde hair tied in a ponytail that stretched down her back. 'You look cute,' he winked.

Julia smiled back, enjoying the almost-forgotten sensation of flirting with her husband.

'When you're all ready, climb aboard,' Annie instructed.

As everyone was mounting their tandems with much giggling and shrieking, Annie headed over to the bike hire men. 'Thanks, guys, if you could meet us at the pick-up point at two pm.'

'No problem. See you then,' they nodded, before getting into their van and driving off.

'Right, are we ready to go?' Annie called out. 'Then follow me.'

The roads around Postwick were quiet, and Annie pedalled out of the car park, swinging easily onto the road. She glanced back and pulled to a stop, noticing that whilst some of the couples were doing okay, others were struggling to find their rhythm.

Simon and Zoe went flying past her, yelling, 'Sorry, we can't stop or we'll never get started again!'

Julia and Nick looked to be having a minor disagreement at the back, whilst Ray and Linda had found their rhythm, and were pedalling along steadily looking particularly proud of themselves.

Eventually, all five couples got going, and they sailed along the country roads, puffing and panting. The county of Norfolk was famously flat, so there were no major hills to navigate, and the countryside around them was beautiful. Cars slowed down to overtake them, surprised to see a convoy of tandem bikes, while children waved at them from back seats and some drivers beeped their horns in greeting.

'How's everyone doing?' Annie asked, when they stopped for a rest break. She'd advised each couple to bring a rucksack to store their personal possessions, along with a bottle of water.

'Hanging in there,' Ray gasped.

'I'm really enjoying it actually,' Zoe grinned. 'I think Simon and I should add "tandem bike" to our wedding gift list.'

'How much further are we cycling?' Nick asked, trying not to show how much he was sweating. Being so busy at the office, he rarely had time to get to the gym these days, and was shocked to discover how unfit he'd become.

'There's still quite a way, but you can do it.'

'Where are we going?' asked Linda.

'It's a surprise,' Annie grinned. 'Wait and see…'

They remounted their bikes and followed the path alongside the canal, past fields of wheat and barley stretching as far as the eye could see. Flowers bloomed in the hedgerows and swallows danced overhead, as they passed dog walkers and horse riders and even an old windmill, picturesque against the hazy blue skies. They continued through pretty villages, and past a country pub.

'I'd kill for a pint of Wherry,' remarked Ray, referring to the local bitter, as Linda, on the front of the tandem, rolled her eyes.

But they didn't stop at the pub, leaving it far behind as they carried on deep into the heart of the countryside. Annie felt inexplicably happy as she pedalled along, her legs pumping, feeling the sun on her face. It felt good to get some exercise. She'd spent so long sitting behind a desk that she'd forgotten how glorious it was to do something like this.

Of course, her good mood might have something to do with a certain Mr Kennedy, Annie realised, unable to stop smiling at the thought of Jamie. After a rocky start, their movie night had all the hallmarks of the beginning of something special. The chemistry between them had been undeniable and they'd kissed for hours, getting hot and heavy on Annie's sofa. She sincerely hoped Harry and Sally hadn't been watching – they'd certainly done enough to make a goldfish blush.

It had been at Jamie's insistence that things didn't go any further; Annie had lost all sense of self-control, but Jamie had been the one who'd reluctantly pulled away, saying that he needed to get home. It had been half an hour before he'd made it out of the door, Annie recalled, smiling at the memory as she cycled along, gazing round at the scenery.

Eventually, she spotted their destination and slowed down, glancing behind to check that everyone was still with her. She came to a halt at the side of a field and dismounted, the rest of the group doing the same. They'd been riding for over an hour, and there was a mixture of glowing, energised faces and bright red exhausted ones.

'You'll be pleased to know that you've all made it, and that's all the cycling we're doing for today. We've ridden over ten miles, so some of you have done exceptionally well. And now we're here!'

'Where?' queried Nick, looking round at the empty field that led down to the River Yare.

'The location for the next stage of the day's activities.'

'Please don't tell me we're doing a triathlon, and now we have to swim five miles,' Simon begged. 'I didn't bring my trunks anyway.'

'Then you have to go skinny dipping,' Annie teased. 'No, the hard stuff is over for today. The good stuff comes…' she checked her watch '… right about now.'

She stared off into the distance, and the others followed her gaze. As they watched, another van came into view, this one smaller than the vehicle that had carried their bikes.

'Hi Jan,' Annie greeted the driver excitedly, embracing her as she got out of the car. 'Thanks so much for doing this.'

'You're very welcome,' Jan replied, as she went round and opened the back doors. 'I hope you all enjoy it.'

'And *voilà*,' Annie announced triumphantly. 'Lunch is served.'

In the back of the van were half a dozen wicker hampers, along with cool boxes and picnic blankets.

'If you could all grab something, that would be really helpful,' Annie called out.

Everyone did as they were asked, carrying the hampers into the middle of the field, where they spread the rugs on the ground and began unpacking the food.

'This is amazing!' Zoe exclaimed, as she held up freshly baked baguettes and smoked salmon. The others were pulling out Scotch eggs, potato salad, couscous and olives, along with sparkling water, chilled white wine and cans of ready-made Pimm's.

'You deserve it,' Annie smiled round. 'You've all done brilliantly.'

'I don't think I'll be able to cycle after all this,' Ray groaned.

'I certainly won't be able to cycle in a straight line,' Simon agreed, as he grabbed the bottle opener and cracked open a beer.

'You don't have to,' Annie announced. 'The journey ends here. The van will come to pick up the bikes, and you'll all be dropped back at the car park.'

A cheer went up from the group.

'You've thought of everything,' smiled Linda.

'The perfect woman,' chuckled Ray.

They all tucked in, eating and drinking, satisfyingly warm and tired in the sunshine. Annie moved over to talk to Michael and Carolyn, and Jennifer and Richard joined in, leaving Ray, Linda, Nick, Julia, Simon and Zoe in their own little group.

Linda was watching Annie with interest. She looked young and healthy, attractive in knee-length work-out pants and a loose vest top. 'Do you think she's married?' Linda mused.

'Who?'

'Annie.'

'I don't know,' Nick shrugged.

'She doesn't wear a ring though,' Julia added.

'I noticed that,' said Ray. 'Maybe she takes it off for these sessions.'

'Why would she do that?'

Ray shrugged. 'I don't know.'

'We could ask her?' Zoe suggested.

'Maybe we should,' agreed Julia. 'I mean, how can she comment on our marriages if she's never been married herself?'

'It's probably better that way,' Nick said thoughtfully, as he chomped on a slice of pork pie. 'She can bring an outsider's perspective. Anyway, it's not all about being married, is it? She's got loads of certificates on her wall, so she clearly knows her stuff.'

'Speaking of marriage, your engagement ring really is beautiful,' Linda commented to Zoe, looking admiringly at her left hand as she leant over to scoop some prawn salad onto her plate.

'Thanks,' Zoe beamed proudly.

'You know, I really don't understand why a young, engaged couple like yourself are going to relationship counselling,' Ray wondered out loud, as Linda rolled her eyes at her husband's indiscretion.

'We've taken a vow of celibacy until the wedding,' Zoe announced, not embarrassed in the slightest.

'Zoe!' Simon began sharply. 'It's supposed to be confidential.'

'We can tell people if we like,' Zoe said defensively. 'It's up to us.'

'Well, I didn't expect that,' Ray chuckled.

'We thought it would be exciting and romantic, waiting until our wedding night. Didn't we, Simon?'

Simon nodded, not looking convinced.

'And how are you finding it?' Nick asked, reading his expression.

'Pretty tough,' Simon admitted, and everyone laughed.

'Sounds like an understatement, if ever I heard one,' Nick grinned, helping himself to a handful of strawberries.

'If you need a florist for the wedding, I can recommend a good one,' Ray chimed in.

'We do, actually,' Zoe told him. 'We're getting married in July, and we only got engaged in February, so it's all a bit of a rush, although Julia's been a lifesaver sorting everything out.'

Ray nodded towards Linda, who took up the conversation. 'I don't think I mentioned it before, but I run Expressions, the florist on Pottergate. If you're still looking, that is.'

'Oh, that's not far from where I work – I'm on St Andrews Street, at the Vet Centre.'

'I always wanted to be a vet when I was a little girl,' Julia commented, with a wistful sigh.

'Well, I'm a veterinarian assistant, not actually a vet,' Zoe explained. 'But I love it.'

'I gave up the idea when I realised I was no good with blood and gore,' Julia laughed.

'There'll be a lot of blood and gore when you have a baby,' Nick warned.

'Oh, are you pregnant?' Ray asked innocently.

He saw the look that passed between Nick and Julia and instantly realised that he'd said something wrong.

'We're trying,' Julia explained quietly. 'Nothing yet though.'

The group fell silent, but Zoe came to the rescue, quickly changing the subject. 'I'll definitely pop in and see you,' she promised Linda. 'I've no idea what I want, or how much anything costs though.'

'Well, I'd be happy to help. Roses are always beautiful for a July wedding, and lisianthus go perfectly with those. Or if you want something more elaborate, there's always calla lilies, or zinnia. Anyway, I'm in there most days, and if I'm not you can speak to my daughter.'

'She's supposed to have taken semi-retirement but, like she says, she's in there most days,' Ray couldn't resist adding.

Linda shot him a look as Annie made her way over, a smile on her face. 'So how have you all enjoyed today? I hope you got a lot out of it.'

'It's been great,' Zoe assured her enthusiastically.

'I'll certainly sleep tonight,' Linda chuckled. 'All that fresh air and exercise.'

'The vans are due any moment,' Annie explained ruefully. 'So I think we'd better start packing up now I'm afraid.'

With sighs and groans, the group got to their feet, folding up their blankets and picking up their rubbish.

'Feel free to take any leftovers with you,' Annie told them, as Ray eagerly scooped up all of the sausage rolls, and Simon slipped a couple of bottles of beer into his rucksack.

As they picked up the empty picnic baskets and walked back across the field, the bike hire van and a minibus pulled up.

'Time to go,' Ray said sadly, as they all climbed, exhausted, into the minibus that was to take them back to their cars.

'I've had such a lovely day,' Zoe said, as she snuggled up to Simon. 'Thanks so much, Annie.'

'You're very welcome.'

Across the aisle, Linda slipped her hand into Ray's, lacing their fingers together. Ray looked up in surprise, then gave her hand a gentle squeeze.

Sitting behind them, Nick rested his hand on Julia's knee, leaning across to give her a spontaneous kiss.

Annie saw it all, and smiled.

Chapter 26

'Men marry women with the hope they will never change. Women marry men with the hope they will change. Invariably they are both disappointed' –
Albert Einstein

'I really do feel that we're making progress,' Linda was explaining enthusiastically to Annie. 'I feel so much happier than I did three months ago.'

'That's great news. I'm so pleased,' Annie beamed, sitting back in her chair. The room was warm, sunshine streaming in through the window, and she could feel that summer was on its way. Ironically, the warmer months usually meant less business for her; people always felt more romantic and, frankly, horny when the sun was out. Whereas the stresses of Christmas, and the darkness and depression of winter, meant that Annie always had an influx of new clients in January, as couples resolved to try to fix their broken relationships. 'Ray, how do you feel everything's going?'

'Oh, we're definitely making huge strides,' he agreed, beaming at Linda. He reached out and took her hand, squeezing it tightly. 'We're so much closer than we've been in a long time. Years in fact.'

'And I've particularly been enjoying the group sessions,' Linda added. 'Those workshops are such a good idea, and it's been so nice to chat to some of the other couples, and hear their stories. I bumped into Zoe and Julia the other day in fact,' she told Annie. 'They were shopping for Zoe's wedding dress, and asked me for my opinion.'

'How lovely! Did Zoe manage to find anything?'

'She did, actually. She found a gorgeous dress, and she was so excited, bless her.'

'I'm so pleased,' Annie smiled. 'She and Simon are a great couple. They're such fun to work with.'

'Unlike us, in the beginning,' Linda said, looking slightly ashamed of herself.

'Oh, I didn't mean—' Annie began, but Linda cut her off.

'No, I owe you an apology, Annie,' she said quietly. 'I was very... resistant to the idea of coming to these sessions, and I believe I was very rude to you when all you were trying to do was help.'

'Thank you, Linda, that's good of you to say. Believe me, you're not the first person to be somewhat sceptical of therapy. But let's forget about it, and concentrate on you two,' Annie smiled. 'You've both said that you're much happier, and you certainly seem far more in tune and more comfortable with one another. Have you managed to make any progress with the more intimate aspects of your relationship?'

At this question, the atmosphere in the room suddenly shifted. Ray and Linda both looked at the floor, and Linda slipped her hand out of Ray's, dropping it in her lap instead. There was a long silence.

'Well, we're definitely more tactile than we were...' Ray offered.

'But you haven't re-established a sexual relationship?'

Ray shook his head. 'No. No, we haven't.'

'That's not a problem,' Annie assured them. 'As I said, you've made great strides so far, and I wouldn't necessarily expect you to have re-established a full-on sex life by now. But given that you have – by your own admittance – grown closer, what are the barriers that you still need to overcome in order to start making love once again?'

'Well, I'm ready to go!' Ray tried to joke. 'No barriers on my part.'

'Oh, so it's all my fault, is it?' Linda snapped back. 'Thanks for making that clear.'

'Ray, I don't want us to get into the habit of apportioning blame,' Annie said carefully. 'You might not feel that there are any barriers on your side, but you have to understand that Linda isn't at that stage yet. Her reservations need to be taken into consideration and respected by you.'

Ray looked chastened. 'Sorry. I see that now. I was only trying to make a joke.'

'That's fine,' Annie assured him. 'And it's great to have a sense of humour when dealing with these topics. As long as the joke doesn't make someone else feel uncomfortable.'

Ray nodded in understanding.

'So, Linda, why do you feel you're not ready to have sex with Ray quite yet?'

'I just… I don't know,' Linda replied awkwardly, trying her best to be truthful. 'The idea makes me want to freeze up. I feel far too self-conscious.'

'Self-conscious?'

'Yes. I feel like there's so much pressure on me. Because we haven't… made love,' Linda continued, forcing herself to say the words. 'For such a long time, it seems like it's a really big deal. As though there's a huge build up to the act itself. And, yes, I *am* self-conscious – about being undressed, being exposed. I'm not twenty-one any more.'

'But I've told you before, that doesn't matter to me,' Ray interrupted. 'You're still the same woman I married, the same woman I've always loved. I'm not twenty-one any more either.'

'But it's different for you,' Linda protested.

'Why? You don't think that I get self-conscious too? I know that I've lost most of my hair, and I've got a sticky-out gut and those bandy legs that you see on old men. But I hope you still love me despite that.'

Linda smiled, reaching across for his hand once again.

'And is this something you'd like to achieve?' Annie asked Linda. 'Would you like to get back to having regular sex with Ray?'

Linda paused, really thinking about the question. 'Yes,' she decided eventually, looking across at him. 'Yes, I would.'

Ray looked visibly relieved, grinning as he exhaled.

'Great. That's fantastic news,' Annie smiled. 'What I'd suggest we do is take this in stages — step by step, ensuring that Linda feels comfortable all the way, and only progressing to the next level once she does. Does that sound okay?'

Both of them murmured their assent.

'Linda, that means you're in control, so hopefully once you know that, it should take some of the pressure off. You're in charge, okay, and things are only going to go as far as you want.'

'Yes, that sounds good,' Linda agreed.

'I'll outline a series of steps for you — we can talk through them today and make sure you're happy with them. I'll also give you a document to take away and work through at home. The steps will be things like massaging one another; having a bath together; being comfortable around one another in just your underwear, or swimwear. And I want you to talk through all the different areas on both of your bodies that you're self-conscious about – whether it's stretch marks and a saggy bottom, or your sticky-out gut and bandy legs, Ray. I want you both to reassure each other the whole time.'

'Can we stop going on about my sticky-out gut and my bandy legs,' Ray said, with mock-annoyance. 'If I'd known they were going to cause this much excitement, I'd never have mentioned them.'

'Aw, I hardly even notice them,' Linda teased, reaching over to pat him on the stomach.

'So does all that sound acceptable?' Annie queried.

'It sounds like hard work,' Linda laughed.

'Relationships are,' Annie said wryly. 'If it feels effortless then there's probably something wrong. But as long as you're fighting for it, and experiencing strong emotions, then that's important as it means you're not giving up.'

'She speaks a lot of sense, that one,' Ray said to Linda, nodding at Annie.

'Oh, and I do hope you'll be able to come to the next group session, as you've enjoyed the others so much,' Annie added. 'I'll send more details round nearer the time, but I have something very special planned...'

After the session had finished, Annie needed a break. She got up to go to the kitchen, lost in her thoughts as she strode down the corridor. Ray and Linda had come so far, and had one final hurdle left to clear. Like she'd told them, they'd made huge strides with their relationship, and she really hoped that—

'Sorry!' Annie burst out, as she collided with someone in the corridor. 'I wasn't paying attention to where I was going,' she gabbled, at the same time as the other person said:

'It's completely my fault, I was in a rush!'

Annie realised she'd run into someone tall and slim, who was wearing a suit – she was face to face with a silk tie and a crisply pressed shirt – and who smelt delicious. There was something very familiar about that toned torso and that musky aftershave and, as Annie slowly raised her head, she found herself staring straight into Jamie's devastating blue eyes.

'I'm so sorry,' she repeated, feeling hugely flustered. Her heart was hammering at the sight of him, and Annie couldn't help but remember that the last time she'd seen him, she'd been crushed beneath his body as they kissed with wild abandon on her sofa.

'Not a problem,' Jamie said easily, as he gently brushed a stray hair from her face. The gesture felt thrillingly intimate, completely out of place in the work environment. Annie found herself suddenly fantasising about dragging him into her office and locking the door, letting him throw her over the desk and have his wicked way. *Very* wicked, hopefully.

'I was going far too fast. Are you okay? I didn't hurt you, did I?' Jamie asked solicitously, looking concerned.

'No, no, I'm fine,' Annie managed, as she somewhat unwillingly disentangled herself from him. She could feel her cheeks growing warm, a delicious tingling sensation spreading all around her body as she took in Jamie's appearance. He usually looked smart for work, but today he'd pulled out all the stops in a dark grey suit that fitted him to perfection, teamed with a crisp, white shirt and a dark blue tie. He looked composed and professional, like a   high-flying city type, or a movie star at a film premiere. He looked… *hot*, Annie realised, feeling a sudden burst of lust.

'You look… smart,' she said carefully, terrified that she was going to say 'hot' instead.

'Thanks. I'm glad you approve,' Jamie grinned, his eyes sparkling as though he knew exactly what she was thinking. Then his expression grew soft, his voice gentle as he asked, 'So how have you been?'

'Good, thanks,' Annie replied shyly. 'You?'

'Busy, hence all the rushing around. You remember I told you about that important meeting Matt and I had lined up? Well, we got the contract!'

'Oh, that's wonderful news,' Annie burst out, genuinely pleased for him. 'It's a big deal, right?'

'A *huge* deal,' Jamie confirmed. 'We're meeting the money men today to go over some of the finer details – they should be here any minute.'

'I'm so pleased for you,' Annie beamed, but Jamie didn't return her smile. 'What's the matter? It's good news, isn't it?'

'Yeah, I suppose so. I mean, financially, it's great news, and it's what we've always dreamt of for our business. Gamejacker wanted to buy us out, or for us to go and work for them, but we were adamant we didn't want that. So, for the moment, we've signed a massive deal with them, and we still get to work independently.'

'Sounds perfect!'

'Yeah,' Jamie said half-heartedly, not looking as though it was perfect at all. 'The thing is… Well, like I said, it's going to be a huge project – far too much for just the two of us – so we'll need to take on more staff… and move to a bigger office.'

'Brilliant. Sounds like an amazing opportunity.' Annie's mouth was moving on autopilot as her brain tried to register what Jamie was saying. He was moving to a new office? Leaving the building where Annie worked?

'I suppose it is. But it means we're going to have to leave this place. We've had some good times here,' Jamie said wistfully, not breaking eye contact with Annie as he added, 'And, of course, the neighbours are pretty cool.'

A sad smile spread across Annie's face, as she realised what he was saying. 'So how long until you go?' she asked, trying to keep her tone neutral, although her stomach felt as though she'd swallowed a ball of lead.

'Matt's already handed our notice in to the management company, but we can move into the new office straight away. We're planning to be out of here fairly soon…'

'Right.' Annie bit her lip, as she and Jamie stared at each other, a long moment of silence stretching out between them. There were a thousand things that Annie wanted to say, but she didn't seem to be able to get the words out. She knew that if she was counselling one of her clients, she wouldn't hesitate in advising them to be proactive and go for what they wanted. But when it came to her own life, she just couldn't do it.

'Listen—' Annie began, at the same time as Jamie said:

'Annie—'

The two of them started to laugh, and Annie indicated that he should go ahead.

'I've been so busy, I haven't even seen you,' Jamie began apologetically. 'Matt and I have been in back-to-back meetings, and we've been offsite most days, which is why I haven't been around. Look, are you free tomorrow night?'

Annie shook her head. 'I've got clients up until nine pm, so I won't be out of here until at least ten. The day after?'

Jamie pulled a face, grimacing apologetically. 'I don't think I can. It's the only night Matt and I both have free, and we've agreed to sit down and work through everything in the new contract. He'll kill me if I cancel it. Friday?'

'I'm staying at my sister's. Her husband's away, and she doesn't want to be on her own.'

Jamie nodded in understanding. His mobile buzzed, and he looked down at the phone in his hand, noticing the time. 'Damn, I've really got to hurry or Matt's going to freak out. These people will be here any second.'

For a moment they looked at each other, clearly wanting to say something more, but it wasn't the place or the time, Annie realised.

'Go,' she insisted. 'We'll catch up later.'

'I'll give you a call, okay?' Jamie told her hurriedly, as he sprinted off down the corridor.

'Sure. Congratulations again,' Annie called after him. He turned and grinned at her, that sexy smile that made her heart skip a beat, before he disappeared round the corner.

Dammit, she was really falling for this guy, Annie realised, terror and excitement flooding through her in equal measure, as though she was standing on the edge of a cliff preparing to dive into the dazzling blue water below.

And all she needed now was the courage to jump.

Chapter 27

*'I remember the first time I had sex – I kept the receipt' – **Groucho Marx***

'Hello, you two,' Annie grinned, as Zoe and Simon made their way into her office, flinging themselves down on the armchairs like it was a second home. They were rapidly becoming two of Annie's favourite clients; their easygoing and open nature made them a lot of fun to work with.

'Hi Annie,' Zoe replied, beaming. 'How are you?'

'I'm good, thanks. How about you two? What have you been up to?'

'We've had such a great week,' Zoe gushed. 'We've finally got the date and the venue confirmed – July eleventh, at two pm.'

'Congratulations,' Annie smiled. 'Where's the ceremony going to be?'

'St Stephen's, which is Simon's local church,' Zoe explained. 'It's in the village where he grew up, and his mum and dad are regulars, so the vicar was happy to marry us at short notice.'

'That sounds wonderful.'

'It's a gorgeous venue,' Zoe enthused. 'So quaint and old-fashioned. And Linda – you know, from the Saturday sessions – is going to do the flowers and she's giving us a really good rate, so the church'll look incredible when it's all decked out.'

'Sounds perfect,' said Annie. 'I bet you can hardly wait.'

'I certainly can't,' Simon commented wryly. 'I just want to get the ceremony over and get her into the marital bed.'

'Simon!' Zoe exclaimed, going pink with pleasure. 'Oh, and we wanted to give you this,' she said to Annie, rummaging in her handbag, then passing her a crisp white envelope with silver writing. 'It's a wedding invite,' Zoe explained eagerly, before Annie even had a chance to open it. 'You've done so much to help us, and we'd love it if you could come.'

'Aw, thank you,' Annie told them, looking genuinely touched. 'I'll check my diary, but I can't see that will be a problem.'

'And you have a plus one, in case there's anyone you'd like to bring,' Zoe couldn't resist adding.

'Thank you,' Annie said primly, not giving anything away as she tucked the envelope inside her notebook. 'Now, how did you both get on with the exercise I set you?'

Last week, she'd given them a creative task, asking them both to write an erotic story using themselves as the main characters, and then to read them aloud to each other.

'It was so much fun,' Zoe squealed. 'I wrote a piece about being kidnapped and locked in a tower. Simon came to rescue me, fighting off the guards then having his wicked way with me.'

Annie grinned. 'It sounds fabulous. How about you, Simon?'

Simon pulled a face. 'Writing's not really my thing.'

'Oh, but you did such a good job,' Zoe insisted, turning to Annie and adding, 'I loved his story. We were both so horny by the end!'

Simon fidgeted awkwardly in his chair. 'It was about how I get this mysterious note to go to a big, fancy mansion, and when I get there, Zoe opens the door, all dressed up – you know, in sexy clothes – but I'm not allowed to touch her. She invites me up to the bedroom, and tricks me, so that I'm naked on the bed, tied up by my wrists and ankles. And then she does whatever she wants with me…'

'There was more detail than that in the actual story,' Zoe added helpfully. 'My favourite bit was where I danced for you, and you wanted me so badly, but you couldn't touch yourself because you were all tied up.'

'Wow, sounds like we might have the next *Fifty Shades of Grey* on our hands,' Annie teased.

'Ooh, I loved that book,' Zoe giggled, as Simon shook his head.

'So the reason I set you this particular exercise,' Annie continued, 'is because it's a great way to lead into the subject of fantasies. One way to keep your relationship fresh and alive, once you've been married for a few years, is by acting out fantasies. And by sharing them now, it will give you a deeper understanding of your other half – what really turns them on, and what are their deepest desires. Are you both comfortable discussing that with me today?'

Zoe and Simon nodded, Simon looking far more enthusiastic than he had done about the writing task.

'Simon, we'll start with you.' Annie turned to him. 'Looking at your story, there were elements of S&M in there, of being tied up, and a theme of bondage. Is this something you fantasise about? Something you'd want to try?'

'I suppose so…' Simon began carefully. 'I mean, nothing too weird – I'm not really into kinky stuff – but the idea of being tied up like that is a turn-on, yeah.'

'The idea of relinquishing control? Of letting Zoe take charge?'

Simon nodded, as he and Zoe looked at one another and grinned.

'And is this something you've already tried?' Annie continued. 'I know you said before that the two of you had been fairly experimental in the past.'

Simon shuffled uncomfortably. 'Well, I have tried... I mean, not with...' Zoe stared hard at him, and Simon swallowed. 'No, I haven't,' he finished quickly.

'No, Simon, what were you going to say?' Zoe's voice had taken on an angrier tone.

'Nothing. I wasn't going to say anything.'

'You started to say that you'd tried it before, but not with me, didn't you?' Zoe pressed, her voice growing louder with every word, as Simon looked hopelessly at the floor, wishing that the ground would open up and swallow him.

'Calm down, Zoe,' Annie interjected. 'Simon's trying to be honest with you, and you need to respect that.'

But Zoe wasn't listening. 'Oh, I suppose it was with *Emily*, wasn't it?' she drawled, almost spitting out the name.

Annie looked from Zoe to Simon. 'Who's Emily?'

'My ex,' Simon managed, still keeping his gaze firmly fixed on the carpet.

'His childhood sweetheart, who he dated through high school, and they lost their virginity to each other,' Zoe burst out furiously. 'Tell her, Simon.'

Simon swallowed, looking deeply uncomfortable. 'We... um... we went out for a few years, but then she cheated on me, so we split up. I met Zoe a few months later.'

'She broke his heart, and I'm not sure that he's ever got over her,' Zoe told Annie, looking close to tears.

'Everyone has a past,' Annie began gently. 'Simon's with *you* now, and he's marrying *you*. It sounds as though he's been very upfront with you about this girl, and you have to trust that he's over her. She's his past, but you're his present and his future.'

'Hmm, well it's hard to forget about the past when she lives just down the road, and still keeps in touch with his mother,' Zoe shot back.

'Well, how do you think I feel?' Simon contended. 'At least you've only got one person to worry about. Every time we go to the pub I worry that we'll bump into one of your exes. You've slept with half of Norwich!'

Zoe's mouth fell open in shock. 'How dare you!'

'Simon, that's out of order,' Annie warned him.

'It's true!' Simon retorted. 'I've slept with one other person, and she won't shut up about it. Do you know how many people she's slept with? Sixteen!'

Zoe turned scarlet. 'It's really not that weird. I went through a bit of a wild phase at uni,' she explained to Annie. 'But everyone was at it – one night stands were no big deal, and I always used condoms. I had a few relationships, but none of them lasted more than a few months. And none of them really meant anything either. It's not like I'd been going out with the same person since I was fourteen, and still keep a secret stash of photos hidden in the bottom of my underwear drawer.'

Now it was Simon's turn to look stunned. 'I can't believe you found… It's just memories, that's all! We were together for ten years. I can't help it if she's in pictures of my cousin's wedding, my holiday photos, my family Christmases.'

'I've never loved anyone apart from you, Simon,' Zoe burst out, looking close to tears. 'But every day I feel like I have to compete with pretty, perfect, blonde *Emily*, and I'll never be good enough.'

Annie watched them anxiously. It wasn't unusual for arguments to flare up when couples were discussing sensitive issues, but she hated to see the two of them at each other's throats like this. Zoe was usually so positive and upbeat, Simon so funny and laidback; to see them like this was a real shame.

'This is clearly something that the two of you feel very strongly about, and that affects you both deeply. Remember, it's perfectly natural to have feelings of jealousy, or insecurity, but the trick is not to let them override everything else. The two of you have chosen to get married – to be together for the rest of your lives – and that's a commitment you've never made to anyone else, so it seems clear that neither of you have ever felt like this before. Don't let anything spoil that, or come between you.'

There were a few seconds of silence. Annie waited for one of them to speak, and eventually Simon broke the tension.

'I'm sorry, Zoe, I really am. I didn't realise… I mean, I knew you didn't like me mentioning Emily, but I didn't know how upset it made you. Emily's my past,' he insisted, as he leant across and wrapped his arms around Zoe. 'I love you, and I want to marry you.'

'Even though you think I'm the town bike?' Zoe protested, through snuffles.

Simon forced a smile. 'I didn't say that. But you have to understand that I get insecure too. I'm the man. I'm supposed to be the one with all this experience and history, and I don't have that. I can't help but worry that all these other blokes were better than me in bed, that they could all show you a better time, and – quite frankly – that they were packing more in the underpants department than I am, and I just hate thinking about all of that.'

'Simon,' Zoe murmured, as she snuggled up against him. 'You know that I love the contents of your underpants just as much as I love the rest of you. We've spent many happy hours together – you, me and the contents of your underpants.'

All three of them burst out laughing, and Annie was relieved to see them smiling once again.

'You've made huge progress,' she told them. 'Both of you were able to talk honestly about your feelings, which is so important, and together you moved past the issue. I'm proud of you.'

'We're such good students,' Zoe smirked, looking pleased with herself. 'Now, is it time to talk about my fantasies? Because I know exactly what I want…'

And she looked at Simon and winked.

Chapter 28

*'Your naked body should only belong to those who fall in love with your naked soul' – **Charlie Chaplin***

It was the hottest weekend of the year so far, and Ray and Linda were making the most of it. They'd invited their family for a barbecue, and the back garden was filled with the excited shrieks of their four grandchildren, who were chasing each other round the lawn and searching for insects in the bushes. Adam, Rose's husband, was manning the barbecue, and the last of the meat was sizzling nicely. Ray was relaxing in a garden chair, discussing golf with Marianne's husband, Daniel, whilst Linda was standing with her two daughters, sipping a glass of rosé.

'It's been such a beautiful day,' she sighed contentedly. 'I can't believe this weather.'

'It's gorgeous, isn't it?' agreed Marianne. She looked very similar to her sister, Rose – the two of them were less than three years apart – and she was wearing a brightly coloured sundress with strappy sleeves. 'Alfie, let go of that scooter right now and give it back to your sister,' she bellowed across the lawn.

'Anyone for another burger?' asked Adam, as he flipped them for a final time, before moving them onto a serving tray.

'I couldn't manage any more, I'm stuffed,' Rose replied.

'I'll squeeze one in,' Daniel offered, as the others all shook their heads.

'It's a no to the burger, but I'll have another beer though, if you're asking,' Ray said cheekily, as Adam levered the top off a bottle of Kronenbourg and brought it over.

'Ray, are you sure your head's not burning? It looks a bit red,' Linda fussed.

'I'd be more worried about his knees – I'm not sure Dad's legs have seen the sun for a very long time,' Marianne giggled, indicating the shorts that Ray was wearing.

'Oi! I can hear you, you know,' Ray shouted good-naturedly. 'I'm just fine, thank you very much. Don't you all go worrying about me.'

Linda shook her head affectionately, turning back to her daughters. 'So what are your plans for this evening?'

'We'll probably head off shortly,' Rose replied. 'I want to get the kids in bed at a decent time, then we can have a bit of peace and quiet this evening. I'm sure they'll pass out in the car after their exciting day at Granny and Granddad's.'

'Same here really,' Marianne added. 'And I've got to try and keep the kids out of the way tomorrow, as Daniel's got work to do before he's back in the office on Monday. He's got a really big project on, and he'll go mad if they disturb him.'

'Well, we could always have them,' Linda offered. 'They can stay here tonight, and we'll drop them back to you tomorrow evening.'

'Would you?' Marianne asked gratefully. 'That would be such a huge help, if you're sure it's okay.'

'Of course,' Linda insisted. 'We'd love to have them, wouldn't we, Ray?'

'What's that?' he grunted. He'd been deep in conversation with Daniel about Europe's prospects in the next Ryder Cup.

'I was just saying to Marianne, we don't mind having the kids this evening, do we?'

Ray frowned, easing himself out of the lawn chair and getting to his feet. 'Sorry, Marianne love,' he said, putting an arm around his youngest daughter. 'We can't do tonight.'

Linda looked at him in confusion. 'Of course we can. Why not?'

'Tonight, we have plans,' Ray explained with a wink.

Linda immediately realised what he was talking about, and blushed, waving away his words. 'Oh, that doesn't matter. We can do that any night.'

'No,' Ray said firmly, much to Linda and Marianne's surprise. 'We've made our plans, and we're going to stick to them. Hope you don't mind,' he continued, directing this comment at Marianne. 'But we have the kids over a lot, and we never turn you down, and for once your mother and I are going to say no, and spend some quality time together.'

Marianne couldn't help grinning at the way her father was behaving. 'Isn't he masterful, Mum,' she giggled, nudging Linda. 'I never knew he could be like this. Okay, I'll leave you both to your secret plans. I guess I'll just take them out of the house tomorrow – maybe we'll go over to Fairhaven, as it's supposed to be another sunny day.'

'I'm so sorry.' Linda looked awkward. 'You know we'd usually have them…'

'That's fine,' Marianne insisted, not looking at all put out. 'Like Dad said, you have them all the time. We'll probably get going soon anyway,' she continued tactfully. 'Come on, Alfie, Mia, start getting your toys together. It's time to go home.'

'We'd better make a move too. Leave Mum and Dad to their secret plans,' Rose added, her eyes twinkling, and her voice loaded with meaning. She didn't know exactly what had been going on with her parents over the last few weeks, but her mother was in a far better mood recently. She kept taking time off from the shop, and had even suggested hiring someone else part-time so that she could scale back her hours even further. Whatever the reason, it was good to see her parents happy for a change.

Half an hour later, Rose, Marianne and their respective families were climbing into their cars, laden down with Tupperware boxes filled with leftovers and carrier bags full of kids' toys. Ray stood with his arm around Linda as the vehicles pulled away, the children waving frantically from their car seats.

'I can't believe you did that!' Linda exclaimed, as the cars rounded the corner and disappeared from sight. 'What are they going to think?'

'Who cares?' Ray replied recklessly. 'They need to understand that we're not just here as a babysitting service and a cashpoint. We've got our own lives to lead as well.'

He squeezed Linda to him, planting a kiss on top of her head as they went back into the house. Linda immediately headed for the kitchen, running the hot water and rinsing the plates, before loading them into the dishwasher. The place was a mess; they'd brought in everything from outside, but now the work surfaces were full of empty salad bowls, plates covered in congealed tomato ketchup and sticky barbecue utensils.

Ray sneaked up behind her, snaking his arms around her waist, and turning off the taps. 'Leave that for now,' he told her, planting a kiss on her neck.

'I need to get it out of the way. This grease will stick like glue if I don't—'

'I'll do it later,' Ray promised, taking the empty potato salad bowl from Linda and placing it back on the side.

'Ray,' Linda began. She turned to look at him, her eyes full of hesitation. 'Maybe we should leave it for tonight. It's been a long day, and I'm tired, and I really need a bath…'

'If you don't want to do this, then I'm not going to force you into anything,' Ray replied softly, trying to hide his disappointment. 'But we told Annie we'd try. I understand that you're nervous, but the whole point is for us to get over this. I'll be with you all the way,' he reassured her, before taking her hands in his, bringing them to his lips and kissing them. 'Do you want to come upstairs with me?'

Linda didn't reply. Gently, Ray tugged at her hands, and she took a couple of steps forward. Ray smiled, and they continued like that, Ray leading her out of the kitchen, up the stairs and into the bedroom.

'Give me ten minutes,' Linda pleaded, as Ray began drawing the curtains. She fled across the hall to the bathroom, and moments later Ray heard the sound of the bath being filled. He switched on the bedside lamps and plumped up the pillows, trying to make the bed look as inviting as possible.

Now that the moment was near, Ray had to admit to feeling a pang of nerves himself. Although he and Linda weren't planning to do the deed tonight, they'd agreed with Annie to spend time exploring each other's bodies, talking through their fears and hang-ups, and reassuring one another. The focus had all been on making sure that Linda felt comfortable, but now Ray realised that he wasn't overly confident either.

Standing in front of the mirror, he saw an ageing man, with everything that entailed – grey hair, wrinkles, sagging skin and gnarled hands. His belly hung over the waistband of his shorts, and no matter how much he sucked it in, it wouldn't lie flat. His posture was poor, he realised, as he pulled back his shoulders and stood up straight, noticing for the first time how knobbly his knees were. He untucked his shirt, wondering if he should strip down to his underwear, or whether that would be a step too far.

As Ray bent down to take off his socks, feeling his back groan in protest, he heard the bathroom door open with a click. Linda emerged, swaddled in her dressing gown, biting her lip anxiously. She hesitated for a moment, as though scared to step into the bedroom.

'So,' she asked nervously. 'What do we do now?'

'I don't know,' Ray admitted.

He caught Linda's eye, and suddenly the two of them began to laugh uncontrollably.

'Honestly, what are we like?' Linda managed, through her giggles. 'Married over thirty years, and all of a sudden I'm shy about you seeing me in my dressing gown.'

Ray was shaking his head, wiping away tears. 'Come here,' he said, sitting down on the bed and motioning that Linda should join him. She did as she was told, crossing her legs and clutching her gown more tightly around her.

'It's not fair – you're fully clothed,' she pointed out.

'I took my socks off,' Ray argued, and the two of them burst out laughing once more.

'They're not the prettiest feet, are they?' Linda commented, as she looked at them. His big toes were hairy and the nails were yellow.

'So you don't want to suck my toes then?' Ray couldn't resist asking.

The expression on Linda's face was all the answer he needed. 'Annie didn't suggest that, did she?' she wondered, looking horrified.

'No, she didn't,' Ray admitted. 'But you are supposed to give me reassurance on the areas of my body I'm self-conscious about. So,' he continued, a wicked gleam in his eye, 'do you love my feet?'

Linda paused, searching for the right word. 'Well, I wouldn't exactly say *love*…'

'No.' Ray was shaking his head. 'That's what you have to say. I've got the sheet Annie gave us if you want me to prove it.'

Linda couldn't help but smile. 'Okay then, I love your hairy, ugly feet.'

Ray frowned. 'I'm not sure that's exactly right.'

'It's as good as you're going to get,' Linda grinned.

'Okay then. What about you?'

'Me?' Linda thought for a minute. There were plenty of body parts that she hated, but she didn't want to reveal any of them to Ray right now.

'How about if I open this?' Ray suggested wickedly, tugging at the belt of her robe.

'No!' Linda screamed, clutching it to her. 'I'm not ready for that. Okay, okay, I hate my legs,' she confessed, kicking them back and forth beneath her dressing gown.

'What?' Ray looked outraged. 'You've got amazing legs. I'm always telling you that.'

'Not any more I don't,' Linda said sadly. 'The skin's gone all slack, and my thighs are all dimply, and I've got a horrible varicose vein right here,' she said, indicating the back of her knee. 'Which means I hate wearing skirts.'

'Linda,' Ray told her seriously. 'I absolutely love your legs. You know I do. They're long, and luscious, and supremely sexy,' he insisted, making a grab for them.

Linda shrieked, and swatted him away. 'You daft sod!' she chuckled. 'Anyway, now it's your turn.'

'Me? What is there to dislike about the way I look? I'm a man in his prime,' Ray joked, flexing his biceps like a muscle man.

'Sorry to burst your bubble, but you're hardly giving Brad Pitt a run for his money,' Linda replied archly.

'Hey, I thought you were supposed to be making me feel better about myself!'

'Sorry,' Linda apologised, with a giggle. 'You're right.'

'So to make up for it, how about we both strip off?' Ray suggested, a naughty grin on his face as he began unbuttoning his shirt, throwing it recklessly to one side. Then he unzipped his shorts and slid off his underpants, looking expectantly at Linda.

'Oh, stuff it,' she exclaimed, unfastening her robe and letting it drop from her shoulders. It felt strangely liberating, and she wondered why on earth she hadn't done it sooner. Suddenly, it didn't seem to matter about her less-than-pert breasts, her flabby tummy, or her hated bingo wings.

'Look at us,' she murmured softly, taking in her husband's naked body. 'We're not exactly hot young things, are we?'

'I suppose not,' Ray agreed, taking hold of his wife's hand. 'But it doesn't matter, does it?'

Linda looked at him and smiled. He was right, she realised. They had each other, they had three wonderful children, and they were blessed in so many ways. 'No,' she agreed, as she leant across to kiss him. 'It doesn't matter at all.'

Chapter 29

'Sex is the consolation you have when you can't have love' – **Gabriel García Márquez**

'Look at you,' Annie cried, as she spotted her sister waiting for her. She was sitting on a bench outside the Castle Mall shopping centre, her face turned up to the sunshine. 'You've got a bump!'

'Are you sure it doesn't just look like I'm fat?' Holly questioned, as she stood up to hug Annie. 'I'm in that really awkward in-between stage where I look like I've eaten too many pies.'

'Of course not, you're absolutely glowing. And your boobs are enormous!'

'I know. Greg's thrilled.' Holly rolled her eyes. 'He wants to keep playing with them, but doesn't seem to realise how painful they are. They feel so swollen.'

'Well, you look amazing,' Annie assured her.

'Thanks. I wish I felt it.'

'But you're okay generally though? Everything healthy with the baby?'

'Yeah, we're both fine. The morning sickness stage seems to have passed – it's supposed to, once you're out of the first trimester. I'm feeling pretty exhausted most of the time, but you just keep on going, don't you?'

'Make sure you get plenty of rest,' Annie told her, looking concerned. 'We can just go and sit in a cafe or something and you can put your feet up, if you want. We don't have to go shopping.'

'Don't tempt me. I could spend the afternoon stuffing myself with cream cakes, insisting it's what the baby wants,' Holly giggled. 'No, I'm excited to have a look round. It'll be more fun with you than with Greg – he's not really into nursing bras and sterilising sets.'

'So where's our first stop?' Annie asked, as the two sisters walked into the mall.

'Shall we try Mothercare? I don't know if I'm going to buy anything today, but I just want to see what's out there, and start and get some ideas for cribs and car seats.'

'Sure,' Annie agreed.

It was a Saturday afternoon, and the centre was busy, with teenagers aimlessly hanging out with their friends and busy families doing their weekly shop.

'That'll be you soon,' Annie grinned gleefully, as she noticed a woman struggling to manoeuvre a pram up an escalator. A man stopped to help her, and the woman thanked him gratefully.

'Hmm, well, that's one way to get some male attention when you're a new mum,' Holly quipped, as the two of them made their way into Mothercare.

For Annie, it was like entering another world; a world filled with breast pumps and maternity pads and other terrifying objects that she couldn't even begin to identify.

'Nipple cream,' Annie read out loud, as she picked up a tube and stared at it. 'Is this like they sell in Ann Summers?'

Holly stared hard at her sister. 'No, Annie. No, it's not. That's something very different.'

'Oh, okay,' Annie replied meekly, putting it back on the shelf.

They moved onto the bedding section, which was filled with Moses baskets and traditional cribs.

'Aw, isn't that cute,' Holly sighed, pointing out a white painted cot decorated with Beatrix Potter characters.

'Are you going to find out the gender?' Annie wondered, looking from Peter Rabbit to Jemima Puddle-Duck.

'I think so, yeah. We have the twenty-week scan coming up soon, but we're doing the nursery in white and buttercream regardless. We're getting someone in to do it – Greg's a bit useless at that kind of thing – and he's gutted that we're losing the spare room. He's got all sorts of rubbish in there that I've told him to get rid of.'

'Poor Greg,' Annie laughed. 'Oh look, isn't this sweet,' she exclaimed, picking up a squashy, pastel-coloured elephant.

'Getting broody, are we?' Holly teased, as Annie blushed.

'No,' she insisted. 'I'm just excited for you.'

'So when's it going to be your turn?'

'Stop it with the questions! I don't know! For now, I'm just going to concentrate on being the most amazing auntie ever. In fact, why don't I buy the baby its first present?' she suggested, giving the elephant a little squeeze.

'Thank you, that would be a lovely gesture,' Holly smiled. She wandered into the pram section, as Annie headed for the till.

Waiting in the queue, Annie couldn't help but think about what her sister had said. Would she ever have a baby of her own? Right now, she was perfectly happy with her career but, at the risk of sounding like her mother, that might not always be the case.

Annie was well aware that with her thirty-fifth birthday approaching, she needed to get a move on if she wanted to start a family, but with no husband and no serious boyfriend on the scene, the decision seemed to have been taken out of her hands. Still, there was always the sperm bank…

'Someone's in their own world,' Holly teased, as she joined the queue behind Annie, carrying a maternity bra and a set of newborn babygros.

'Yeah, I was just thinking about hiring a sperm donor.' Holly looked at her in shock, and Annie started laughing. 'Well, not really, but it makes you think, doesn't it?'

'Oh Annie,' Holly said softly. 'I didn't mean to make you feel bad.'

'No, you haven't at all,' Annie insisted. 'I'm so excited for you, and I know you're in exactly the right place in your life. You've got Greg, you're married, the natural next step is to have a baby. I'm just not there yet,' she sighed. 'I don't know if I'll ever have a baby, or if I even want one.'

They reached the front of the queue and paid for their purchases.

'I think Tom's still available,' Holly said, as they collected their carrier bags and walked back out into the mall. 'You know, if you're looking for a sperm donor.'

'I'm not that desperate,' Annie snorted.

'Think about it – the baby'll have great abs,' Holly giggled. 'In fact, Greg said he's been talking about you a lot recently.'

Annie frowned. 'Tom? That's weird! What's he been saying? Calling me a crazy, forty-year-old psycho again?'

'No, he's been saying nice things apparently. He seemed quite taken by your "feistiness",' Holly explained, putting quote marks around the word. 'Greg said that Tom saw you out with some guy, and it's made him jealous.'

Annie burst out laughing. 'That's ridiculous!'

Holly shrugged, looking intently at her sister. 'So who was the guy?'

'What? Oh, it was just Jamie.'

'Really?' Holly was increasingly suspicious. 'And who's "Just Jamie"?'

'Just a guy who works in the same building,' Annie explained, trying to sound as nonchalant as possible. 'We bumped into each other at the cinema, then went to grab a bite to eat afterwards, and that's where we saw Tom.'

Holly's eyes were wide, her love antenna on full alert, sensing there was something Annie wasn't telling her. 'And do you like "Just Jamie"?'

'Stop calling him that,' Annie complained, attempting to change the subject. But Holly wasn't going to be distracted quite so easily.

'Well?'

'Holly, don't ask me that.'

'Why not? I'm your sister, and I need every last detail.'

Annie took a deep breath, ready to make her confession. 'Okay, yes, I do like him,' she admitted, as Holly squealed and clapped her hands together.

'Hallelujah! Break out the bunting! So are you seeing each other?'

'I think so,' Annie began, and found that once she'd started talking, she couldn't stop. She told her sister all about how she and Jamie often bumped into each other at work, and how they'd agreed to make their cinema meetings a regular thing. She told her how Jamie had come over to hers the other week, and the kitchen disaster that had ensued, before the two of them had finished the night kissing passionately on Annie's sofa.

'You *kissed* him,' Holly shrieked, her eyes as wide as saucers.

'Yes! Keep your voice down! And I've no idea what's going on between us, but now he and his brother have got some amazing new contract with a big company, which means they have to move offices, so I might never even see him again,' Annie finished, feeling exhausted. It was a huge relief to finally be able to talk to someone about everything that had happened.

'Of course you will. He *soooo* likes you. He's totally into you, I can just tell,' Holly told her confidently.

'But it's as though he's holding back somehow, and I don't know why. There's definitely chemistry between us, and kissing him was incredible, but I don't know where we stand.'

'Maybe he's shy?'

'He doesn't seem like he is.'

'So why don't you ask him? March into his office, grab him by the tie, snog his face off, and tell him you fancy the arse off him.'

Annie raised an eyebrow at her sister.

'Okay, maybe not the snog-his-face-off bit. Or the grab-him-by-the-tie bit. But you can tell him how you feel at least.'

'I can't do that!'

'Why not? Maybe he's saying the exact same thing about you – "*I think she likes me, but I'm not sure how she feels…*"'

'Yeah, but he's the—' Annie began, then broke off suddenly.

Holly stared at her triumphantly. 'What were you going to say? That he's the man, so he should take the lead? Annie Hall, I'm surprised at you! Emmeline Pankhurst would be spinning in her grave. Is that what you tell your clients, hmm? That the man should do all the running? Exactly! It should be fifty-fifty, and the woman has to make an effort too.'

Annie was squirming uncomfortably, knowing that her sister had a point. She could be sensible and logical when advising her clients, but when it came to taking that advice herself, it was much harder.

'We were supposed to be meeting up this afternoon, actually,' Annie admitted. 'But he cancelled. Something came up apparently.'

'It happens,' Holly shrugged. 'Give him the benefit of the doubt.'

'Maybe,' Annie sighed. 'Can we change the subject now please? We're supposed to be shopping for you.'

'Hmm, okay then,' Holly agreed. 'You've given me lots of good stuff today, so I'll stop interrogating you. But the moment anything happens, you have to let me know.'

'I will,' Annie laughed, grateful that her sister was in an understanding mood. 'So where to next?'

'Let's head to the Early Learning Centre. I want to check out their baby toys, plus I need a present for Greg's niece. It's her birthday on Wednesday, and we're going to her party next weekend.'

They carried on chatting as they made their way over to the toy shop, and they were almost there when Annie stopped suddenly. Through the crowd of people, she'd spotted someone she recognised. Her first thought was that she must be mistaken, but as she blinked and looked back again, she realised it was definitely him.

Annie's heart began to pound, the colour rising in her cheeks.

'What is it?' Holly asked, noticing how strangely her sister was behaving.

'Talk of the devil. That's him.'

'Who?'

'Jamie,' Annie whispered urgently, unable to tear her eyes away from the familiar figure.

Holly's mouth fell open. 'Where?'

'Just there.' Annie tried to point discreetly. 'The tall guy with the blond hair, wearing a blue jacket.'

'The one heading towards us, walking with that blonde woman?'

'What? Oh, I don't think they're together.' Annie squinted, looking closer. She'd been so busy looking at Jamie that she hadn't noticed the woman. Now that Holly had mentioned it, they did seem to be walking beside each other. Then Jamie turned and said something to her, and the woman laughed. Yes, they were very definitely together, and they seemed worryingly at ease in one another's company.

Annie swallowed; she had a very bad feeling in the pit of her stomach. 'Maybe it's his sister,' she said in a small voice. 'He mentioned he had a sister.'

'It could be,' Holly agreed, looking worriedly at Annie. 'What do you want to do? Shall we go and say hi?'

'No,' Annie said quickly. 'Not yet.'

The two of them watched for a moment as Jamie and the mystery woman continued walking towards the Early Learning Centre, in the direction of Annie and Holly. They were barely metres away when the crowd in front of Annie parted, and she had a clear view, allowing her spot something – or some*one* – she hadn't noticed before. A young girl, who looked about seven or eight years old, was walking in between Jamie and the blonde. They were each holding one of her hands, and she was swinging their arms happily.

As they approached the toy shop, the little girl turned her face up to Jamie, her pigtails swinging as she moved. 'Daddy, will you buy me something, please?'

Her voice was loud, the words clear and unmistakeable as they carried across the mall. Annie gasped, turning on her heel and instinctively hurrying away.

Holly immediately ran after her. 'Sis, are you okay?'

Annie shook her head. 'No. No, I'm not.' She looked utterly shell-shocked. 'Do you mind if we leave now? I don't think I can…'

She trailed off, and Holly instantly understood. 'Of course, that's fine. Let's go.'

Annie felt utterly stunned, grateful for her sister's support as Holly took her by the arm and steered her towards the exit.

Chapter 30

'Some things are better than sex, and some are worse, but there's nothing exactly like it' –
W.C. Fields

Annie was standing at the front of the minibus, feeling a little bit like a tour guide, or a teacher on a school trip. It was a glorious day in early June and, ever the optimist, she was wearing shorts and a vest top, with a pair of jewelled sandals.

'Come on, Annie, tell us where we're going,' pleaded Nick.

'Yeah, don't keep us in suspense,' added Simon, from where he and Zoe were cosied up on the back seat.

Annie was running one of her Saturday group sessions, and there were eight couples seated on the minibus, looking at her expectantly. She'd told them that this would be an all-day event, and that it would be something a little bit different, but other than that, she'd kept them in suspense. Until now...

'So today we're going to...' Annie stared around, dragging out the drama.

'Get on with it,' Ray heckled, as everyone laughed.

'The beach!' Annie exclaimed. 'Specifically, Great Yarmouth. More specifically, the Pleasure Beach.'

'The Pleasure Beach? Sounds filthy!' Zoe quipped.

'Not that kind of pleasure, I'm afraid,' Annie grinned. 'Although hopefully it might lead to that later, if you play your cards right.'

'Do you mean all those big rides and the rollercoasters?' Linda asked, looking terrified. 'I'm not sure that's my kind of thing.'

'You don't have to go on them, if you don't want to. Although maybe we can get you on something gentler, like the carousel?'

'Maybe…' Linda didn't look convinced.

'You see, one of the main aims of today,' Annie explained, as the minibus bumped its way out of the car park and onto the main road. 'Is to get your adrenaline flowing, and also to release endorphins into your system.'

'Is this the science bit?' Zoe wondered.

'Yes, it is,' Annie smiled. 'Bear with me here. All of you are in long-term relationships and, as I've explained to you before, after three years oxytocin – also known as the "cuddle hormone" – kicks in, making you get comfortable with your partner.

'In some ways, this is great, because it boosts your trust in your other half, helps you fall in love and increases overall happiness. But, as we know, getting too comfortable can be a dangerous thing, so every now and again we need to give ourselves a kick up the backside.

'When you're scared, and in danger – as in an amusement park, for example – your body gives off all kinds of hormones. And if you and your partner have just survived what your brain perceives as a "near death experience", then the outcome really can be to bring you closer together and ramp up your sex drive. If you've narrowly escaped death, your body's natural instinct is to try and reproduce. So fun times all round!'

'Are you saying that we should regularly put ourselves – and our partner – in danger?' Simon asked curiously. 'I'm just wondering whether I should push Zoe off a high building once a week?'

'Maybe not that extreme,' Annie acknowledged with a smile. 'But it's good to put yourselves in a new situation from time to time. Even something as silly as going to the park and playing on the swings can have the same effect.'

The couples all laughed, chattering amongst themselves as Annie took her seat at the front of the bus, crossing her long legs and staring straight ahead. In spite of her bravado around her clients, she felt utterly wretched. She was grateful that she'd been so busy with work these last few days, as it had kept her mind off Jamie and the sight that she'd witnessed whilst out shopping with her sister.

Annie exhaled slowly, recalling the scene she'd played over and over in her mind since it had happened. The little girl with the pigtails and the princess dress had clearly called Jamie 'Daddy', and he'd looked pretty cosy with the woman too. Did he have some sort of secret family that he'd been hiding from Annie? Was he living a double life?

It seemed obvious to Annie that Jamie had completely misled her – that she'd been nothing more than a bit on the side; a bit of fun. How many times had she counselled women who'd been faced with the same situation? Annie thought of Nick and Julia, and the pain she'd felt on Julia's behalf when Nick had admitted his fling with Nina. Annie had never thought that would happen to her; that she would be 'the other woman'.

Right now, Annie never wanted to speak to Jamie again. She didn't care what he had to say, and she was hurting too badly to listen.All Annie knew was that she felt completely devastated and humiliated. It was the Mark situation all over again – she'd fallen for a seemingly great guy, only to find out that he wasn't the person she'd thought he was. She'd built Jamie up in her mind, turning him into some Hollywood-style hero, when in reality he was just a liar and a cheat. What was wrong with her? Annie wondered miserably. Why did she keep doing this – picking bad men and making the wrong choices?

Annie turned her face to the window, staring with unseeing eyes at the view that rushed past outside. Well she wouldn't allow herself to get hurt ever again, she vowed. She would cut off all contact with Jamie, ignore the gaping hole where her heart had once been, and pay no attention to the overwhelming sense of longing when she woke in the night, restless with dreams of him. In time, Annie would learn to live with the crushing sensation in her chest that made it hard to breathe whenever she thought of the feel of Jamie's lips against hers, his hands on her body, and instead, she would put the focus back on building her career, just as it should be.

She just wished it didn't hurt so very badly.

❄ ❄ ❄

'I can't wait to go to the Pleasure Beach,' Zoe exclaimed, as she cuddled up to Simon. 'I love rollercoasters.'

'What do you think?' Nick murmured, as he leant across to Julia. 'Sounds fun, doesn't it?'

'Maybe,' Julia shrugged. 'Although do you think it's safe for me to go on all those fast rides? I mean, what if I *am* pregnant?'

'Up to you,' Nick said easily. 'Like Annie said, we could just go on the carousel. Or maybe the teacups, if that's too much for you.'

In spite of herself, Julia smiled. 'We'll see how brave I'm feeling. Oh, I've just remembered…' Julia span around in her seat to chat to Zoe who was sitting behind her. 'I wasn't able to book your first choice of band – Swagger Jagger, right? They've already got a gig on the eleventh. But the good news is that The Hot Shots *are* available, so I've put the deposit down on them.'

'Brilliant! Thank you so much, Jules,' Zoe beamed. 'They were my favourite anyway – Simon wanted Swagger Jagger, and I let him get his own way for once.'

'Given that you're getting first choice over everything else in *our* wedding…' Simon couldn't resist adding, as Zoe blew him a kiss.

'You're still coming to my hen do, right?' Zoe turned back to Julia. 'Linda's coming, but I'm not sure about Annie. I guess she thinks it would be unprofessional to fraternise with the clients.'

'By "fraternise with" do you mean "get ridiculously drunk and do bad karaoke with"?' Julia giggled, as Zoe nodded. 'I'll definitely be there. I could really do with a fun night out.'

'Oh, this'll be fun,' Zoe promised. 'Don't you worry about that!'

❄ ❄ ❄

Just over half an hour later, the minibus pulled up outside the entrance to the Pleasure Beach.

'We'll see you back here at five, is that okay?' Annie confirmed with the driver, as everyone climbed down from the bus, stretching their limbs and smoothing out their clothes.

'No problem, Annie. Have a great day,' he replied, tooting his horn as he drove off.

The day was bright and breezy, the sun beaming down overhead, with a brisk wind whipping off the North Sea. The beach was packed, with everyone in the local area apparently turning out to enjoy the good weather. Already they could hear the shrieks and cries coming from the Pleasure Beach, the noise blaring from the machines and the pop music playing on the rides.

'Oh, I can't wait,' Zoe squealed. 'What are we going on first?'

'What do you fancy?' asked Annie. 'We don't all have to stay together, by the way. Just make sure you're back here at five to be picked up. But what I'd suggest is that we spend the first hour or so together at the Pleasure Beach, head for fish and chips at lunch, then you've got free time to do whatever you want in the afternoon.'

'Sounds good to me,' Simon grinned, as the others murmured their assent.

'Ooh, look, there's a pirate ship!' Zoe shrieked. 'Can we go on that?'

'You do realise I'm nearly sixty, don't you?' Linda laughed. 'Are you trying to give me a heart attack?'

'Don't worry, you'll love it!'

'What do you think?' Linda asked, looking at Ray.

'I'm up for it if you are,' he grinned gamely.

'Oh, stuff it,' Linda shrugged. 'You only live once, after all.'

The group made their way over to the pirate ship, with Zoe excitedly leading the way. As they joined the queue, Annie felt her bag vibrate. She pulled out her phone and read the message:

Hey Annie, I've been trying to call but you're not picking up. Are you free tomorrow? J x

Annie hesitated for a moment, then quickly deleted the message and pushed the phone back in her bag. Her face was ashen, and she took a deep breath, trying to maintain her composure. 'Hey, Annie!' Annie glanced up to see Zoe looking at her in concern. 'Are you okay? Come on, we're up now!'

Zoe scrambled eagerly over the metal walkway, making her way onto the pirate ship beside Simon. Annie and the others followed, taking their seats on the ride.

'I feel sick,' Linda muttered, despite the fact that the ship hadn't started moving yet. The bar was down over her lap, and she was gripping it so tightly that her knuckles had turned white.

'I'll look after you,' Ray grinned, taking one hand off the bar and wrapping his arm around her.

'That's what I'm afraid of.'

The pirate ship began to move, with a huge squeal of metal, and Linda let out a yell, gripping tightly onto Ray's knee.

'Oh, my stomach just turned over,' she cried, as the ship rolled back in the opposite direction.

Ray couldn't help laughing, clearly thoroughly enjoying himself. 'It's years since I've been on one of these things. I think I went on with the kids at Alton Towers, do you remember?'

'I'm not listening,' Linda told him, her eyes wide. 'If I stop concentrating, I might fall out. Oooh!' She squealed as the ship rose even higher, giving them an impressive view right out to sea.

'Look at me, no hands!' Ray chuckled, as he took both hands off the bar and waved them in the air, causing Linda to shriek even louder.

'Stop it, you'll fall!'

Behind them, they could hear Zoe's excited squeals, whilst along the row from them, Julia and Nick were laughing loudly, Julia's blonde hair streaming out in the breeze.

Gradually the ride slowed down and they all stumbled off, chattering and giggling.

'I'm so glad to be back on solid ground,' Linda exclaimed.

'You did very well. I was proud of you,' Ray grinned, pulling her to him and kissing her on the top of her head.

'So everyone's up for the log flume next?' Zoe asked eagerly, looking around the group.

'Give me a minute to catch my breath!' Linda pleaded.

Nick was standing with his arm around Julia, his hand caressing the soft curve of her waist. Things were gradually getting back to normal between them, and both of them were really making an effort.

'Did you have fun?' he murmured, his mouth close to her ear as he bent down to speak to her.

'I really did.' Julia gazed up at him, her eyes sparkling. 'It's so long since we've done anything like this.'

'I know. It was a really good idea of Annie's,' Nick agreed. 'Sometimes you get so tied up in all the adult stuff – the mortgage, the bills…'

'…The trying to have a baby,' Julia cut in.

'That you forget about just spending time with each other and having fun.'

They'd set off walking towards the log flume with the rest of the group, when they passed a shooting gallery, laden with teddy bears to be won as prizes.

Nick tapped Annie on the arm. 'We'll catch up with you in a minute,' he told her, as she turned round. 'I just want a go at this.'

'Nick, what are you doing?' Julia asked, with a giggle.

'Proving my manhood,' Nick said seriously, as he handed over his money and picked up a rifle. 'I'm going to win you a bear.'

'You really don't have to,' Julia insisted. 'And I'm sure these things are rigged anyway.'

'Are you doubting my abilities?' Nick asked, with mock-seriousness. 'Just you watch.'

He raised the rifle to eye level, squinting through the sight at the row of bears in front of him. They were moving on a conveyor belt, and they each had little targets above their head. Nick watched them for a moment, getting used to the speed, before he gently squeezed the trigger. There was a loud crack, and the target disappeared.

'Oh Nick, you got one, well done!' Julia cried, clapping her hands excitedly.

Nick didn't look up, not wanting to lose concentration. He fired again, and a second target went down, as Julia suppressed a squeal. By now a small crowd had gathered, passersby stopping to watch. If Nick was feeling the pressure, he didn't show it. He pulled the trigger a third time, and unbelievably a third target bit the dust.

'And we have a winner!' shouted the woman behind the stall. There was a small round of applause from those standing nearby, and Nick bowed his head, holding up his hands in acknowledgement.

'You did it!' Julia exclaimed, throwing her arms around him.

'You should never have doubted me,' Nick joked, as the two of them embraced.

'You need to pick your prize,' the stallholder told them. 'For three targets, you get to choose between a Winnie the Pooh or a Scooby Doo.'

'Nick, they're huge!' Julia gasped, as she saw them. They were almost half the size that she was, and just as wide. 'I'll take Winnie the Pooh, please. I can't believe I've got to carry this round all day,' Julia giggled, as the giant bear was handed over.

'Now, don't be ungrateful,' Nick joked. 'I won that especially for you.'

In spite of herself, Julia grinned. 'Thank you,' she said, leaning over to kiss him.

'No problem. Hey, you know what? We should put it in the nursery. Save it for the baby.'

Julia smiled, a warm glow spreading through her at Nick's words. 'Good idea, honey. That's exactly what we should do.'

Chapter 31

'Sex isn't all that important, but it is when you love someone very much' – **Ava Gardner**

By the time Nick and Julia had made their way over to the log flume, the rest of their group were almost at the front of the queue.

Zoe spotted them and waved. 'Quick, come and join us.'

Julia looked at the long line of people and didn't think they'd appreciate her trying to push in. 'Don't worry about it,' she shouted back. 'We'll wait for you.'

'Where did you get that bear?' Zoe yelled. 'He's amazing!'

'Nick won him for me,' Julia replied proudly.

'I want one! Simon, you need to win one for me too.'

'No problem,' Simon insisted, feeling a primal sense of competition roused within him. 'We'll go get you one afterwards.'

The queue moved forward, and Nick and Julia found a bench to sit down on where they could watch the ride and wait for the others. Winnie the Pooh sat next to them, taking up a full seat by himself.

The amusement park was busy, with excited children charging past them, followed by harassed parents, while too-cool-for-school teenagers were out on dates, their arms slung casually around one another. The smell of waffles and doughnuts drifted deliciously in the air, mingling with the scent of sizzling hotdogs and fried onions.

'Oh, my stomach's rumbling,' Julia groaned. 'It feels like ages since we had breakfast.'

'I think we're going for food soon,' Nick replied. 'Didn't Annie mention something about fish and chips for lunch?'

Julia gazed up at him pleadingly. 'Yeah, but I could always squeeze in a tiny bag of candyfloss before then. It's mostly air anyway.'

'Is this what it's going to be like when you have cravings? Okay, I can take a hint,' Nick joked getting to his feet and heading to one of the stalls to buy an enormous bag of the bright pink spun sugar.

'Thanks,' Julia said gratefully, as she broke into the bag and pulled out the fluffy contents. 'Mmm, it's good. Do you want some?' she asked, taking another handful and feeding it to Nick.

He grinned, as he ate the candyfloss out of her hand, and Julia began to giggle.

'Ooh, look!' she yelled suddenly, pointing up at the log flume. 'They're at the top. You can see Annie.'

Nick squinted. 'Oh, yeah! Linda's just behind her – she looks terrified.'

'She's doing well. I'm amazed she's going on these rides.'

'Do you think we'll still be doing this kind of thing in thirty years' time?' Nick wondered.

'I hope so,' Julia replied softly, a slight sadness in her voice. They'd talked about Nick's indiscretion with Nina many times in the sessions with Annie, and they'd finally moved past it, but it still made Julia sad that Nick had behaved like that. And despite what he said, Julia couldn't help but blame herself for pushing him away.

'There they go!' Nick cried, as the ride suddenly dropped and the carriage plunged down the steep slope. They could hear Zoe's excited screams, her distinctive hair flying in the wind. Then they hit the water, spray flying all around them.

'I can't see them any more. Did they get wet?' Julia wondered.

'I can see Annie… She's absolutely soaking,' Nick laughed. 'I hope she brought a change of clothes.'

'She can't be that bad, can she?' said Julia disbelievingly. A few moments later, the group walked towards them, and Julia's mouth fell open in astonishment. 'Oh wow. I'm *so* glad we stayed here!'

They were all utterly bedraggled and dripping wet. Annie's pale yellow vest top had turned completely see-through, while Zoe looked as though she'd just taken a shower, and Linda's sandals were squelching. The rest of the group were in a similar state of disarray.

'At least the sun's shining.' Annie tried to look on the positive side. 'We should dry out quickly.'

'Let's hope you do, before you get arrested for flashing,' Simon laughed, nodding at Annie's bra which was clearly visible beneath her T-shirt.

'I think that's me done for the rollercoasters,' Linda announced. 'I'd like something more sedate now.'

'Aren't you feeling those endorphins pulsating round your body?' Ray demanded. 'Aren't you desperate to leap on me right now?'

'No, I'm desperate for a change of clothing and a hot cup of tea,' Linda shot back.

'That does sound like a good idea,' Annie agreed. 'Is anyone else hungry?'

'Starving,' Simon nodded.

'How about we head for a cafe, grab some food and dry off. Then it's up to you all what you want to do for the rest of the afternoon.'

'Sounds like a plan,' agreed Nick, as they all trooped out of the Pleasure Beach, heading towards the nearest cafe.

❄ ❄ ❄

The sun was still blazing in the middle of the afternoon as Nick and Julia walked along the beach, hand in hand. They'd taken off their shoes and were wandering through the shallows, trying not to wince every time the chilly sea water broke around their ankles.

After their fish and chip lunch, the group had all gone their separate ways. Zoe had invited Nick and Julia to go back to the Pleasure Beach with her and Simon, but the two of them had wisely decided to spend some time alone together. Julia felt more content than she had in a long time, as they strolled along, watching families relaxing on the sand and toddlers smeared in sun cream playing happily in the shallows.

'Do you think that will be us one day?' she asked wistfully.

Nick followed her gaze to where a young couple were cooing over a tiny baby, both looking exhausted but incredibly proud and happy. 'I know it will be,' he said fiercely, wrapping his arm around her shoulders and pulling her close as though he never wanted to let go.

'I hope so,' she whispered, surprised by the intensity of Nick's reaction.

'Look, Jules,' Nick began awkwardly. 'I know we've been over and over this, but I really can't say it enough. I'm so sorry about what happened. Sorry, and ashamed of the way that I behaved.'

'It's fine,' Julia assured him. 'I probably wasn't the easiest person to live with either.'

But Nick wasn't ready to drop the subject just yet. Since he'd been attending the sessions with Annie, he'd found it considerably easier to open up to his wife, and right now he felt as though he needed to explain himself.

'That doesn't excuse anything,' he insisted, shaking his head. 'I need to tell you why.'

'No, you don't.'

'I do,' Nick burst out. 'I need you to understand. I felt scared and trapped and insecure and… jealous. This baby, which hadn't even been conceived yet, was taking up all of your time and all of your energy. And I could just see the whole life we'd built together disappearing. I don't want to turn into one of those dull, boring couples whose life is over as soon as they have children, who never go out and who never have sex any more.'

Julia linked her arm through his, kissing him on the shoulder. 'We won't. I promise you.'

'I know that now,' Nick acknowledged. 'There was just so much going on that it was hard for me to articulate how I felt. I didn't even *understand* how I felt at the time – except that I was angry and resentful and you were the person I took it all out on.'

'I never meant to make you feel pushed out,' Julia said softly. 'We'd talked about having children, and agreed it was what we both wanted, and I just took that decision and ran with it. My entire focus was on getting pregnant, and I didn't want anything to get in the way of that. And to be honest,' she said, taking a deep breath, 'I think I've felt quite lonely this past year, since the move. You were always working, and I don't have any family here. I don't really have any close friends either,' she admitted. 'Although that's changed since I met Zoe and Linda. They've both been great. And I guess I thought having a baby would help with all of that.'

Nick listened to what his wife was saying. 'I never even thought of that. I guess this move's been harder on us than we expected.'

'True. But we're starting to properly make a go of things now, aren't we? We're building a new life for ourselves, and everything's getting back on track.'

Nick stopped walking, turning to face Julia. 'You know, you're absolutely the most important thing in my life. I lost sight of that for a while, but I don't want anything to jeopardise that ever again. I want you to be happy, and I'll do anything I can to make sure you are.'

'I am happy,' Julia whispered, wrapping her arms around Nick's neck and pulling him close. 'I'm happy as long as I'm with you.'

Nick let his arms encircle Julia's waist, and the two of them kissed, lost in the moment and each other, utterly oblivious to the presence of hundreds of people on the packed beach.

Held in Nick's arms, Julia felt safe, secure and a huge sense of relief. They'd weathered the worst of the storm and come through it stronger; everything that came afterwards would be plain sailing.

❄ ❄ ❄

Ray and Linda were sitting in a cafe overlooking the seafront, two cups of tea and a Chelsea bun to share on the table in front of them. They'd decided not to go back to the Pleasure Beach after lunch, and had instead spent the afternoon looking around the town itself, browsing in the shops, and just generally enjoying pottering around with no particular place to be.

The clock on the cafe wall read 4.45 pm. Linda drained her teacup and looked at Ray.

'I suppose we'd better make a move. We've got to be back at the bus by five, and we don't want to be late.'

Ray bit his lip, looking at Linda with a strange expression on his face. 'About that…'

'What?' Linda demanded, narrowing her eyes suspiciously.

'Well, I have a bit of a surprise,' Ray confessed. 'I hope it's a good one.'

'What have you done…?'

'I've… Well, I've booked us into a hotel for the night.'

Linda almost dropped her teacup. 'You've done what? When?'

'It's all arranged – Annie knows about it,' Ray explained hastily. 'She's not expecting us back at the minibus. Unless you'd rather go home tonight, that is.' The look in his eyes gave away how much Ray wanted them to stay.

'So you've planned some sort of dirty weekend?'

'Don't think of it like that! I thought it might remind you of that first night we spent away together, in Cromer.'

'What's everyone going to think when we don't get back on the bus?'

'It doesn't matter what they think. This is about you and me.'

'Well, how are we going to get home if we miss the bus?'

'We can catch the train. Look, Rose printed the timetable out for me,' Ray explained, pulling a sheet of paper from his back pocket.

'Rose knows about this?' Linda said incredulously. 'She helped you plan it?'

'I think she thinks it would be good for us.'

'But I don't have anything with me,' Linda realised suddenly. 'No toothbrush, no change of underwear.'

'We've got just over half an hour before the shops shut. I'm sure we can grab a few essentials before then.'

Linda clapped her hand over her mouth as she realised something else. 'I don't have a nightgown – and you don't have any pyjamas. We can't go buying a whole new set of nightclothes.'

'We could always… sleep in the buff,' Ray suggested, his eyes twinkling at the suggestion.

Linda flushed bright red, her mouth falling open in shock. 'Ray Anderson, you're a real devil you are.'

'But you love me for it,' Ray teased, trying to keep his tone light, but hoping for confirmation.

'Yes. Yes, I do,' Linda acknowledged. She knew what it meant if they stayed here for the night – she'd be expected to do the deed. They'd be making love for the first time in over a year, and the thought made her extremely nervous. Nervous and yet… excited, she realised, butterflies dancing in her stomach as though it was her first time all over again.

'So what do you say?' Ray asked, as he checked the clock. 'We've got ten minutes before the bus leaves. Or do you want to stay here and have a dirty weekend with your husband?'

Linda paused for a moment, a smile twitching at the corners of her mouth. 'I think… we should go buy me a toothbrush and a fresh pair of knickers,' she smiled.

Ray winked at her. 'That's my girl.'

Chapter 32

'I think women are sexy when they got some clothes on. And if later they take them off then you've triumphed' – **Groucho Marx**

'Oh my,' Linda exclaimed. 'I can't believe you booked The Grand. You are splashing out!'

The Grand was situated on Marine Parade, part of the Golden Mile that ran alongside Great Yarmouth's seafront. It was a stately Victorian building, built when the British seaside holiday was at its height of popularity. It had faded somewhat since the glamour of its heyday, but it was still a sight to behold, and the finest hotel in the town.

'Nothing but the best for you,' Ray replied.

'It's a little different to that tiny B&B back in Cromer,' Linda murmured, as they walked into the reception. The inside reflected the outside, with a grand, sweeping staircase, Roman pillars and ornate chandeliers. Once again, it had clearly seen better days, but there was a beautiful sense of faded grandeur.

'Mr and Mrs Anderson,' Ray announced to the young woman on reception. As she checked the booking, Ray leant over to whisper to Linda, 'Do you think she believes that we're married?'

'I'm not sure,' Linda giggled. 'Maybe she thinks I'm your bit on the side.'

'So you've booked our honeymoon suite, is that correct?' the receptionist asked, looking up expectantly.

'Yes, that's correct,' Ray confirmed, as Linda's mouth fell open in shock.

'That's on the top floor, with a sea view. You'll find a complimentary bottle of sparkling wine in your room, and breakfast is also included in the tariff, served between eight and ten in the dining room,' she finished, handing over the key.

'Thank you very much,' Ray smiled, as they walked away.

'*Honeymoon suite?*' Linda hissed.

Ray shrugged. 'Why not? I thought I'd splash out.'

They took the lift up to the top floor, following the corridor right to the end, where there was just one single door.

'Oh, this is lovely,' Linda breathed, as Ray entered the key card and they walked in. 'I think it's bigger than our living room at home!'

The room was extremely large and decorated in an old-fashioned, chintzy style that reflected the era of the property. There was a grand four-poster bed in dark wood, a flowery bedspread and matching curtains with a pelmet and tie-backs. One of the windows was open to air the room, and they could hear the screeching of gulls, and smell the fresh, briny tang of the sea.

'So, Mrs Anderson, should I open the bubbly?' Ray grinned, as he pulled the bottle out of the fridge.

Linda shook her head, suddenly feeling self-conscious. They were alone, together, and she knew what came next. She just didn't know if she was ready for it.

'This feels silly,' she giggled. 'What on earth are we doing?'

Ray looked crestfallen, and Linda instantly regretted being so flippant.

'I didn't mean… Go on then, pour me a glass,' she said brightly, thinking that it might help her nerves.

Ray uncorked the bottle with a pop, then looked round in confusion. 'I can't find any glasses,' he laughed in disbelief. 'We could use the mugs?' he suggested, looking at the two teacups sitting on a tray beside a selection of teabags and instant coffee sachets. 'Or I could ring down to reception?'

Linda wandered out of the bathroom, where she'd been admiring the large whirlpool bath. 'Don't bother them. There are a couple of glasses in here,' she said, bringing out two plastic tumblers that had been sitting by the sink.

Ray poured out the bubbly, and they sat down beside each other on the edge of the bed, clinking their tumblers together.

'This is the life, eh?' Ray chuckled. 'Drinking cheap sparkling wine out of a tooth mug in a hotel that's seen better days.'

'Don't say that!' Linda chastised him. 'I think it's absolutely perfect.'

'Do you?'

Linda nodded. 'I'm here with you, and that's all that counts.'

Ray leant over and softly kissed her. He felt Linda instantly stiffen up, and sat back again.

'Sorry, sorry,' she apologised. 'I'm just so nervous. It's ridiculous, isn't it?'

'No,' Ray shook his head. 'But I don't want to rush you, and we've got all the time in the world, so we can take things at your own pace. If you want to, that is?'

He looked so hesitant and so hopeful that Linda couldn't help but feel a surge of love for him. 'Yes,' she said. 'Yes, I do want to.'

'And no more silly talk about whether I wanted to marry you, or whether I wanted to chase after whatshername. None of that's important. I married you because I loved you, and I still do. In fact, I love you more than ever.'

'I love you too,' Linda whispered, feeling close to tears. 'And I want this to be a fresh start for us. I feel like we've missed out on so much.'

'It will be,' Ray promised. 'And we're not going to miss out on any more. We've got a lot of catching up to do,' he murmured, bending his head closer to hers.

Linda gazed at him. He was no longer the young, handsome man she'd married; he'd lost most of his hair, and the little that remained was grey and sparse. His face was lined, and his body was soft and sagging, where once it had been hard and firm. But he was her husband, and the father of her three beautiful children, and she loved him.

Linda knew that she was no longer the woman he'd married either – the skinny young livewire in the short skirt with long, luscious hair and a smooth, unlined face was gone forever. In her place was a soon-to-be pensioner, with a thicker waist and rounder hips, her stomach criss-crossed by stretch marks. But she knew that Ray loved her too, and that his love was unconditional.

This time, when he moved to kiss her, Linda didn't resist. She kissed him back, feeling the passion stir, all the long lost emotions that she'd kept buried for so long slowly resurfacing. Slowly, deliciously slowly, Linda fumbled with the buttons on her husband's shirt, as Ray bent down to kiss her neck and she let out a contented sigh. Outside their window, the evening grew dark, the moon rising over the sea. But Ray and Linda paid little attention, oblivious, as they were, to anything apart from each other.

❄ ❄ ❄

Linda was woken by the light streaming through a gap in the curtain. For a moment, she couldn't remember where she was, but then it all came flooding back. She rolled over in bed, shocked to find that she was wearing nothing at all – the last time she'd slept naked had been about thirty years ago, on holiday in Spain when the heat had been unbearable. The sheets were rumpled and warm against her skin. As she remembered the events of the night before, she couldn't help but break out into a wide smile.

Beside her, Ray stirred, blearily opening his eyes. When he saw that Linda was already awake, he broke into a smile that mirrored her own. 'Morning, gorgeous.'

Linda giggled, knowing that she was behaving like a teenager, but too happy to care. 'Morning, handsome.'

Ray moved across to kiss her, and Linda responded straight away, sliding her leg between his.

'You know, we've got a lot of catching up to do,' she murmured seductively.

'Are you sure?' Ray wondered. 'We're going to miss breakfast.'

'Who cares?' Linda grinned. 'I've got everything I need right here.'

❄ ❄ ❄

When they checked out a couple of hours later, it was a different receptionist on duty to the one who'd checked them in the night before. Linda was relieved – she was all too aware that they were looking pretty dishevelled, and wearing the same clothes that they'd worn yesterday. Both of them stood there holding hands, with silly, soppy grins on their faces.

'How was your stay? I trust everything was to your satisfaction?' the receptionist smiled, as she took the key from them.

'Oh yes,' Ray nodded, with a knowing wink at Linda. 'Everything was absolutely perfect.'

Chapter 33

'Life is like sex. It's not always good, but it's always worth trying' – **Pamela Anderson**

'Julia! Over here! Oh, and Linda's here too!'

Zoe stood up, wobbling dangerously on her stilettos as she waved her arms to try to catch the women's attention across the crowded bar.

'Zoe!' Julia exclaimed, as she spotted her. 'You look stunning.'

Zoe was wearing a short black skirt paired with a gold sequinned top, and the tight-fitting outfit showed off what a great body she had. Her copper hair had been left long and loose, while a cheap, glittery tiara was perched on top of her head, and a pink sash across her shoulder read 'Bride To Be'.

Zoe hugged Julia and Linda tightly. 'Thank you so much for coming,' she beamed, looking just the tiniest bit drunk. 'Everyone, this is Julia and Linda,' she bellowed across the table at the dozen girls seated there, who all waved and said hi.

'Here you go,' smiled a pretty brunette wearing a 'Chief Bridesmaid' sash, as she handed Julia and Linda 'Hen Party' sashes of their own. 'You've got to wear them – it's compulsory,' she grinned, as the two women gamely wriggled into them.

'This is my friend Claire,' Zoe introduced them. 'She's my *best* friend, and she's come down all the way from Chester, specially for me. We've known each other since we were four, and we used to sing *Grease* together. I was always Frenchy, because of my hair,' she rambled happily.

'Nice to meet you, Claire,' Linda smiled, as Julia hugged her.

'Come and sit down here, you two,' Zoe insisted, patting the banquette seat beside her. 'Sit right next to me, and we'll get you both a cocktail.'

'Oh yeah, how did the cocktail making go?' Julia asked.

Zoe had been to a class that afternoon with the rest of her hens, but Julia and Linda had agreed to turn up later in the evening, worrying that they'd feel a little out of place amongst a group of twenty-somethings.

'I had so much fun! They were all totally delicious. Here, Linda, try this one.'

'What is it?' Linda asked suspiciously, as Zoe pushed a lurid green concoction across the table towards her.

'Vodka and blue Curacao mixed with pineapple juice. Turns out if you mix the blue and yellow, you get green. Just like painting at primary school!'

Cautiously, Linda took a sip. 'It's very… sweet,' she finished, but had to admit it tasted better than it looked.

'I've drunk quite a few of them already,' Zoe admitted, as Linda passed the glass to Julia and she took a large gulp, wincing slightly afterwards. 'Let's get something else if you don't like that. How about Sex on the Beach? Or a Screaming Orgasm? God, I'd kill for either of those right now,' Zoe groaned, and Julia realised she wasn't just talking about the cocktails.

'It won't be long until you can have both,' Julia giggled. 'Only two weeks left before the wedding.'

'I'm counting the days. Both of us are going out of our minds, but we're determined to do this.'

'Good for you,' Julia told her. 'Has it been worth it?'

'I'll tell you after my wedding night,' Zoe winked. 'Nah, it's been a really interesting experience. One that I don't ever want to repeat...'

'Funny how things work,' Linda mused. 'There's you and Simon desperately trying not to... you know... and then Ray and I...' Linda trailed off, looking as though she wished she'd never started speaking. 'Well, the opposite.'

'Really?' Zoe's eyes widened, as she beckoned over one of the bar staff and ordered another round of cocktails. 'So that's why you were going to see Annie?'

Linda nodded, playing nervously with the hem of her top. She was wearing smart black trousers and a matching tunic, teamed with a glittery cardigan.

'We did wonder, didn't we, Julia?' Zoe continued. The more alcohol she drank, the less discreet she became. 'When we saw you in Jarrold's looking at sexy underwear, we thought you might be a nymphomaniac.'

Linda almost choked on the Woo Woo the barman had just handed her. 'No, quite the opposite in fact. Wait until I tell Ray, he'll think it's hilarious!'

'So are the sessions with Annie helping?' Julia asked, sipping her Cosmopolitan through a suggestivelyshaped straw. She'd wondered whether or not to drink alcohol tonight, but decided that one wouldn't hurt. Or possibly two, depending how the evening went...

'Yes, they are, as a matter of fact,' Linda admitted. 'Annie keeps telling us what good progress we're making, and I know myself that there's been a huge change in our relationship. To be honest, I'm not sure how much longer we'll keep on seeing her for.'

'I know what you mean,' Zoe chimed in. 'Simon and I have got one final session scheduled before the wedding, but then we won't need them any more. Well, not if everything goes well,' she giggled. 'If you see me back there in six months' time, you'll know we're having major problems!'

'It might be worth going to the occasional meeting still,' Julia suggested. 'You know, just to keep things on track.'

'Or the group sessions,' put in Linda. 'I think they're great. We might keep attending those, as I find the exercises really helpful.'

'They're fun, aren't they?' Zoe grinned. 'And Annie's great. I wish she'd come tonight.'

'Yes, why isn't she here?' Linda wondered. 'Did you ask her to come?'

Zoe nodded. 'I invited her along – and to the wedding too. She's RSVP'd to the wedding, but I don't think she thought it would be quite right to mingle with us all like this!'

'It's such a shame,' Julia shook her head. 'It would have been great to see her.'

'Yeah, I reckon she's really good fun on a night out,' Zoe said, her eyes sparkling. 'I bet she's got a really wild side to her!'

The music was loud, the bar filling up, and they all had to raise their voices to be heard. The DJ in the corner was playing cheesy pop tunes, coloured lights strobing across the black and white chequered dance floor. Outrageously dressed girls and casually attired guys streamed through the door, all single and excited, wondering what the night ahead might bring.

Julia and Linda finished their cocktails, and decided to split a bottle of wine, as they mingled with Zoe's friends and even got up to dance as the DJ played some classic songs.

'Are you having a good time?' Zoe asked them, as she shimmied her way across the floor to Beyonce's '*Crazy in Love*'.

'I'm having a lovely time,' Linda assured her, looking slightly tipsy. 'I thought I might feel a bit out of place, but everyone's so welcoming!'

'I'm glad you're enjoying it,' Zoe beamed. 'You'll have to get Ray to take you out some time.'

'I might just do that,' Linda nodded. 'He's always wanting us to try and recapture our youth – I should play him at his own game and take him out to a nightclub.'

'You can get down and dirty on the dance floor!' Zoe giggled.

'Stranger things have happened…'

'Oh, I can't believe you're getting married,' Julia told Zoe, as she enfolded her in a spontaneous hug. 'You still look so young! But you and Simon make a great couple.'

'Thanks, Julia.' Zoe hugged her back. 'You've been the best wedding planner a girl could ask for. I really don't know what I'd have done without you.'

Julia waved away her compliments. 'I've had so much fun working with you. Honestly, I think you…' Suddenly she trailed off, her face changing as she looked past Zoe.

'What?' Zoe demanded, turning to follow Julia's gaze. A muscular 'police officer', wearing aviator sunglasses and a highly dubious-looking uniform, had just entered the bar. 'Oh my God!' she squealed, as she whipped round to face her friends. 'Tell me you didn't?'

The man strode across the bar to where Zoe was standing, open-mouthed. He stopped in front of her, spreading his legs and planting a hand on each hip.

'Zoe Miller?' he asked, in a low, sexy voice.

Zoe could hardly speak, she was laughing so much. She managed to nod in confirmation, and the man seemed satisfied with that.

'I'm Officer Hotrod,' he began, as he whipped out a pair of handcuffs. 'And you are under arrest… for being too damn sexy!'

He nodded in the direction of the DJ, and 'I'm Too Sexy' came over the speakers, as Zoe shrieked and hid her face.

The guy began to bump and grind, pulling off his cap and settling it on Zoe's head. Her face had gone bright red, as her friends crowded round her, cackling with laughter. Then, in one swift movement, the man ripped open his shirt to expose his tanned, toned chest.

'Wow,' Julia leant across to comment to Linda. 'Not bad.'

'I'm definitely glad I came tonight,' Linda grinned, as she turned back to watch the floor show.

By now, a crowd had gathered, circling the stripper with a chant of 'Off! Off! Off!'

The guy seemed unfazed by the attention, producing a bottle of baby oil which he raised in the air then squeezed all over his chest. He grabbed Zoe's hands, pulling her towards him and encouraging her to smear the oil all over his body. Zoe squealed, screwing up her face as she carried out his instructions, her hands wet and sticky.

'Don't put photos on Facebook, Simon'll go mad,' she shrieked through her laughter, as her friends eagerly snapped pictures on their mobile phones.

Julia and Linda were laughing along with everyone else, enjoying watching the hilarious scene, when Zoe turned around and beckoned for them to join her.

'What? No!' Julia yelled in alarm, trying to hide behind the crowd. But Zoe reached out and grabbed her arm, pulling her closer and pushing her hand onto the guy's chest. Julia cackled with laughter as she ran her hands up and down his oiled torso.

Linda, however, didn't need quite so much persuasion. She gamely marched up to the stripper and quickly got stuck in, her hands clashing with Zoe's and Julia's, as they all smeared and stroked.

'I might never get the chance to do this again,' Linda cried gleefully.

'I'm sure Ray'll let you do that if you ask him nicely,' Julia shot back.

The crowd were watching incredulously, fascinated by the sight of the three women rubbing oil over the stripper's naked chest. As they whooped and cheered in approval, the man took a step backwards, placing his thumbs teasingly inside the waistband of his trousers. They had Velcro panels down the side of each leg, and in one swift movement, the trousers fell away, leaving the man wearing nothing but a pair of dazzling white, extremely tight, underpants.

Zoe screamed, as he advanced towards her, circling his hips in a way which drew attention to the unmissable bulge in his underwear. Then he dropped to the floor, putting on an alarming display of pelvic thrusting, before finishing with a few one-handed press-ups, which drew the admiration of the crowd.

He leapt to his feet, kissing a giggling Zoe on both cheeks, before standing back and saluting her.

'Zoe Miller, I've been Officer Hotrod. Now enjoy the rest of your evening,' he told her, blowing her a final kiss before grabbing his clothes and heading out of the door.

'I can't believe you guys did that,' Zoe yelled accusingly at her friends, her cheeks aching from laughing so much. She saw Julia and Linda watching her, their hands still sticky from the oil, and threw her arms around all of them in a group hug.

'Thank you so much for coming,' she screeched, her face flushed and her eyes wide. 'I love you all so much, and this has been the best night ever!'

Chapter 34

*'Women are meant to be loved, not to be understood' – **Oscar Wilde***

'One thing's for sure: the more pressure you put on trying to achieve an orgasm, the more difficult it becomes. This is why we have to take the focus off the end result, and instead concentrate on enjoying the sexual act – whether it be intercourse, fellatio or even—'

There was a knock on the door, and Annie frowned. No one should interrupt her when she was with a client; it was a rule she insisted upon, and always ensured that the 'Do Not Disturb' sign was prominently displayed when a session was in progress.

'I'm so sorry,' she apologised to Oliver and Liz. This was only her third session with them, and Annie was aware that it looked extremely unprofessional.

The knock came again, and Annie stood up from her desk. 'I do apologise, I'll just go and see what the issue is.'

She strode quickly across her office and opened the door to see Jamie standing there. Annie felt her pulse quicken at the sight of him, that familiar leap in her stomach. Then she remembered what she'd seen the other week, and her face hardened.

'Jamie, I'm with a client right now.'

'I know, Annie. I'm really sorry, but I just wanted to let you know that Matt and I are leaving today. Moving out of the building.'

Annie hesitated for a moment, before stepping into the corridor and closing the door behind her – partly to protect the privacy of her clients, and partly to make sure that her conversation wasn't overheard.

'I've been trying to contact you, but I haven't heard anything,' Jamie continued. Annie could hear the anguish in his voice, see the confusion in his expression, but she resolved to stay strong.

'I can't speak to you right now. I'm in the middle of a session.'

Annie turned to go, but Jamie placed a hand on her arm. His touch sent bolts of electricity racing through her body, memories of the night they'd spent together at her house flashing into her mind, and she hastily pulled away.

'*Please*, Annie,' Jamie whispered.

'Do you realise how unprofessional this makes me look?' Annie hissed, all of her emotions crystallising into anger. She kept her voice low, but she was clearly furious.

'I know, I know, and I'm so sorry. I just didn't know how else to get in touch with you. I really wanted to see you before I left, and… I don't understand what's happened between us.'

His voice cracked on the final words, and Annie raised her eyes to look at him. He seemed utterly exhausted; there were deep bags under his bloodshot eyes, his hair was a mess, and he clearly hadn't shaved for a few days. The stress of moving offices – *and keeping a secret family*, Annie thought angrily – was obviously taking a toll on him.

'I'm sorry, Jamie,' Annie said coldly, as she grabbed the handle and pushed the door open. It was taking all of her willpower to walk away from him like this, and she knew she couldn't betray any sign of weakness. One last word, or one last look, would be all it took for him to see how badly she wanted him. 'Please don't bother me while I'm working.'

'Will you call me?' Jamie asked desperately.

Annie didn't reply. She stepped back into her office and closed the door firmly, sitting back behind her desk and turning to Oliver and Liz with a bright smile. 'Please accept my apologies for the interruption. It won't happen again. Now, where were we...?'

Later that day, Zoe was curled up on the sofa in her flat, watching television. The window beside her was open, letting the fresh evening air blow through, whilst across the hall Simon was taking a bath. Zoe could hear him singing to himself – a Kings of Leon track – and she smiled.

She would miss this place, Zoe thought sadly to herself. She'd lived here since finishing university – first with her friend, Hannah, and then with Simon – but just the other day they'd received a letter from their landlord, explaining that he was selling the property and giving them two months' notice. It had thrown the pair of them into a panic – on top of the pressure of preparing for the wedding, they now had to start looking for somewhere new to live. They couldn't afford to buy a place of their own just yet, and had even started talking about moving in with Simon's parents, just until they'd got a deposit saved up. Zoe hoped they didn't have to do that. She got on well with Brian and Jill, but she didn't want to start off her married life by living in someone else's house.

But the idea of having their own home at some point in the future was incredibly exciting. They'd probably move outside the city, where prices were cheaper. It would mean a longer commute for Zoe (currently she could walk to work every morning), but a shorter one for Simon. And after a couple of years of married bliss, they planned to start trying for a baby.

Fingers crossed, thought Zoe, remembering Julia with a pang. Perhaps it wasn't always so easy to get pregnant.

All the same, she couldn't help smiling at the prospect of having little Zoes and Simons running around. Ideally, she'd like one of each – the boy born first, so he could look after his sister. Maybe a third baby, if there was time, and she felt up to it. In some of their more soppy moments, she and Simon had already picked out potential names…

Zoe sat back on the sofa with a satisfied sigh. She really was a very lucky girl. She could hear Simon now, splashing about in the bathroom. He'd been cleaning machinery at work today and come home absolutely filthy, so she'd run him a deep, hot bath with lots of Radox to soothe his aching muscles.

Maybe she should go and join him, Zoe thought naughtily. Obviously they couldn't actually have sex, but she was pretty sure they could find other ways to have a lot of fun in there…

She'd stood up from the sofa and was moving towards the door when she heard a soft pinging noise. It was Simon's phone, she realised, and he had a text message. She'd take it through to him, in case it was something important.

She crossed back to the coffee table and picked up Simon's mobile, then noticed the name that had popped up on the screen: Emily.

Zoe's heart began to beat faster. She felt strangely nauseous, her stomach churning unpleasantly. Without even stopping to think what she was doing, she tapped on the message to open it:

Hey Banana, it was great seeing you the other day. We should do it again some time. I miss you. Love Pooky xxx

Zoe saw red – literally. It was as though a coloured mist had descended in front of her eyes, fury coursing through her body.

She stormed out of the living room, slamming the bathroom door open. Simon was soaking in the tub as she burst in, lazy and relaxed, but he sat up instantly when he saw Zoe's face, sending a wave of water sloshing over the side.

'What?' he asked anxiously, just as Zoe yelled furiously:

'What the hell is this?'

She held up his phone, her face contorted with anger.

'What's what?'

Zoe narrowed her eyes, fixing him with a steely glare, as she spat out the word, 'Emily.'

Simon's cheeks reddened unmistakeably, and he looked nervously at Zoe. 'What did she say?'

Zoe raised an eyebrow and began to read. 'Hey *Banana*,' she began furiously, knowing that it was Emily's pet name for Simon. Emily and Simon had gone on holiday to Majorca together and Simon, for some reason, had bought a pair of yellow swimming trunks. They turned rather revealing when he jumped in the pool, and Emily had called him 'Banana' ever since.

'"It was great seeing you the other day",' Zoe continued, her voice dripping with sarcasm. '"We should do it again some time. I miss you. Love Pooky. Kiss kiss kiss". What the hell does she mean by, "It was great seeing you the other day"?' Zoe demanded.

Simon's mouth flapped open and closed. Despite his bulk, he suddenly looked smaller than usual, and infinitely more vulnerable, sitting naked in the rapidly cooling water.

'She came over to the house the other day when I was working. She'd been out shopping with Mum.' He winced,

knowing how much Zoe would hate that. 'But then she…
She came and sat with me for a bit while I worked. I was fixing the *Aurora*, and she just sort of hung around, chatting.
But that was it, I swear,' he added hastily, as he saw the look
on Zoe's face.

'Oh, how cosy,' Zoe shot back. 'What were you doing?
Reminiscing about old times? About how great it was before you met me? All the fun you used to have, and all the
great sex, while you were tying each other up and doing God
knows what to each other?'

'It wasn't like that! We were just chatting about rubbish.
She was a bit down because she'd just split up with Lee, her
boyfriend.'

'Oh, poor Emily. And what, you were trying to make it all
better, rubbing her back and telling her how gorgeous she is,
and how any man would be lucky to have her?'

'Don't be ridiculous, Zoe.' Simon was getting annoyed
now. 'Why are you making this out to be something bigger
than it is?'

'Oh, I'm being ridiculous am I? My boyfriend – fiancé in
fact – has been seeing his ex behind my back, and I'm not
supposed to be concerned?'

'I know it looks bad, but it wasn't like that at all, I swear. I
don't know why she's texting me.'

'I think it's pretty bloody obvious why she's texting you. *I
miss you. Let's do it again some time*,' Zoe mimicked, in a high,
sappy voice. 'Do what again, exactly?'

'I don't know because nothing happened!'

'She used three kisses, Simon. *Three*,' Zoe repeated for em-
phasis. 'And we all know what that means!'

'Do we?' Simon looked utterly bewildered.

'Have you been in touch with her before?'

Simon squirmed uncomfortably, looking guilty all over again.

'You have, haven't you.' Zoe bit her lip, suddenly feeling as though she might cry. It felt as though the bottom had dropped out of her world.

'No, not exactly,' Simon scrambled to speak. 'You know she still sees my mum, and occasionally she'll comment on something on Facebook. But you know all that anyway – there's nothing to hide.'

'Well, if it was all so innocent, why didn't you mention it to me at the time?'

'Because I knew you'd react like this!'

His argument made sense, but Zoe wasn't behaving logically. 'Oh, how convenient!'

'I've had enough of this,' Simon muttered, as he pulled himself out of the bath, his body dripping. Angrily, he wrapped a towel around his middle and stomped through to the bedroom, leaving wet footprints on the carpet.

Zoe followed him, clearly spoiling for a fight. 'I'm sick of her, Simon. Always popping up, always causing arguments between us. What happens when we get married? Do you want her to come on the bloody honeymoon with us?'

'Don't be stupid, Zoe.'

'Oh, so now I'm stupid, am I? Not like pretty, perfect Emily, with her degree in English and her fancy job in recruitment. I bet you wish you were marrying her now, don't you?'

Simon ignored her, his expression furious as he roughly dried himself and wrenched open the wardrobe door, pulling out a pair of jogging bottoms and a T-shirt.

'Oh my God!' Zoe's mouth fell open, as she suddenly realised something. 'This stupid vow of celibacy – is that what it is? You're not getting it from me, so you're getting it from her?'

'Zoe, you're crazy!' Simon burst out. 'You're just making all of this up from nothing – some idiotic little text that didn't mean anything.'

'If it didn't mean anything, then why didn't you tell me?' Zoe repeated.

Simon rubbed his forehead tiredly. 'We're going round in circles, Zoe.'

Zoe was crying now, vaguely aware that she was behaving irrationally, but unable to stop. 'I can't believe you did this to me.'

'Did what? I haven't *done* anything,' Simon yelled.

'Don't shout at me,' Zoe sobbed.

'I'm not… Listen, Zoe, you have to get a grip. This is ridiculous.' Simon put his hands on her shoulders, but Zoe shrugged them off fiercely.

'Just get off me. Don't touch me!'

'Fine,' Simon snapped. 'You know what? I'm going out.'

'What, with Emily?'

'I'm serious, Zoe. I'm going out now, and I'll come home when you're being normal again.'

'If you walk out now, it means you don't care about us, or this relationship.'

'Zoe, I—'

'I mean it. If you leave now, don't bother coming back.'

Simon glared at his fiancée as he tugged a jumper on over his T-shirt. Without saying a word, he stalked across the bedroom and walked out of the door.

Chapter 35

'The greatest pleasure isn't sex, but the passion with which it is practiced' – **Paulo Coelho**

'You must be so excited,' Annie grinned, reaching out to squeeze Holly's hand as they took a seat in the hospital waiting room.

'It's surreal,' Holly admitted, looking down at her belly and giving it an affectionate rub. She was wearing a pretty patterned maternity dress, which flowed perfectly around her blossoming bump. Her skin was glowing, her blonde hair thick and glossy. After a rocky first trimester with a bad bout of morning sickness, it was fair to say that pregnancy suited Holly. 'But it's one step closer to getting to know the little person that's in here,' she sighed happily.

'And I get to find out whether I'll have a niece or a nephew.'

'Yes, Auntie Wotsit,' Holly teased, as Annie rolled her eyes. 'I spoke to Mum the other day, and she's really disappointed that I'm finding out the gender. She thinks it should be a surprise.'

'I know what she means, but it's so tempting to find out, isn't it?'

'Yep! I want to start making plans – you know, buying clothes in the right colour and so on.'

'Well, as a qualified psychologist, I would have to advise buying gender neutral clothes and toys, rather than imposing societal stereotypes on an innocent child,' Annie said primly.

Holly looked at her in confusion for a few moments, and then the two of them burst out laughing.

'No way,' Holly shook her head. 'If it's a boy, he's getting the cutest little sailor outfits and playing with Thomas the Tank Engine. If it's a girl, I'm smothering her in pink and buying the biggest Barbie doll in the shop.'

Annie pretended to shake her head in disapproval. 'You're a lost cause,' she joked.

A nurse appeared and they both looked up. 'Mrs Watson?' she called. A woman sitting opposite them stood up and waddled off, while Annie and Holly relaxed once more.

'It's such a shame Greg couldn't make it. I bet he's gutted,' Annie commented.

'Yeah, he was pretty annoyed, but this conference has been planned for ages, and he can't get out of it.'

'Where is it again?'

'Manchester. He's supposed to stay overnight, but he's skipping the schmoozing event this evening and racing back as soon as they've finished dinner. I've got to ring him the second we get out of here.'

'Does he have a preference? Boy or girl?'

'He says not,' Holly shrugged. 'And I think he's telling the truth. Whilst I'm sure he'd love a boy to play football with, he'd completely dote on a little girl. Like they say, as long as it's healthy.'

Annie nodded in agreement.

'And the fact that my husband can't make it means I get to hang out with my big sister for the afternoon,' Holly grinned at her.

'Ah, how times have changed. I remember when we used to spend our afternoons hanging out in the pub.'

'You mean you're not having fun?' Holly pretended to be offended, as she glanced around the waiting room. Half a dozen women with various sizes of bump were sitting round on uncomfortable plastic chairs, reading the well-thumbed magazines, or chatting in low voices to their other halves. There were medical posters tacked to the walls, offering warnings against allergies and infections, whilst in the corner a muted television was showing Sky News.

'This is a different kind of fun,' Annie replied carefully.

'Grown-up fun?'

'No, grown-up fun is something else. That's the thing that got you here in the first place,' Annie chuckled, patting Holly's bump as the two sisters started laughing once more.

'Aw, thanks for coming with me, sis. It really means a lot,' Holly told her, leaning across to give her a hug. 'I'm amazed you could take time off.'

'I had to switch a couple of things round, but I wouldn't have missed it for the world,' Annie assured her, squeezing her back.

'So, when's it going to be your turn?' Holly asked cheekily.

'What?'

'You know – marriage, kids, the dream of little girls everywhere.'

Annie let out a heavy sigh. 'Why does everyone keep asking me that? I'd have thought you of all people would give me a break.'

'It's only because I care about you,' Holly insisted. 'You're gorgeous and funny and amazing and clever – I want you to find someone nice.'

'Well, I like the flattery,' Annie smiled.

'Maybe we'll find you a hot doctor here,' Holly suggested. 'Keep your eyes peeled.'

At that moment, a short, thin man in his sixties walked past, wearing an unflattering pair of thick-rimmed glasses. He was wearing a white doctor's coat and carrying a pile of notes, and he was almost fully bald, with the exception of a few random tufts of white hair.

Annie and Holly looked at each other and burst out laughing.

'Maybe not,' Annie laughed.

'You see, Mum always said your standards were too high,' Holly teased. 'I'm sure he'd make a lovely husband.' Suddenly, her hand shot up to her mouth, and she gasped. 'I've just remembered! What happened with that guy Jamie? I can't believe I forgot to ask – I've totally got baby brain at the moment. Did you confront him?'

Annie rolled her eyes. 'No. I mean, it seemed pretty obvious what was going on. He kept trying to call me, but I didn't pick up. Would you believe he even had the cheek to interrupt one of my client sessions to try and talk to me? I was furious. He made me look so unprofessional.'

'So you never found out the full story?'

'I don't want to know,' Annie declared, which wasn't strictly true. 'Honestly, sis, I've had it with men. I don't know why I even bother trying. I'll just stick to fixing everyone else's relationships, as I'm clearly no good at my own.'

'Annie…' Holly sighed.

'What?'

'I just feel… I don't know. That you're giving up too easily or something. You should have at least given him a chance to tell his side of the story.'

'I don't see why,' Annie shrugged. 'Anyway, it's too late now. He's moved offices, so I don't run the risk of bumping into him every day, and he's stopped calling, so I think he's got the message.'

'Right,' Holly said quietly.

Annie could sense her disapproval, but pretended not to notice. Despite the air of indifference she was attempting to perfect whenever Jamie's name was mentioned, and all the stern talks she'd had with herself, Annie couldn't stop thinking about him. Their blossoming relationship had felt so different to what she'd had with Mark all those years ago, and at times she wondered whether she'd made a huge mistake by not giving Jamie a chance to explain himself. She was always advising her clients that communication was key, but, as ever, Annie seemed unable to take her own advice. And the truth was that she missed him. She missed their easy chats and their flirtatious banter, the fluttering in her belly when she caught sight of him and the dizzying sparks when they kissed...

On more than once occasion Annie had sat on her sofa, mobile phone in hand, staring at Jamie's number and having to physically restrain herself from calling him. She would re-read his pleading texts and – 'Mrs Litvinsky?'

Annie glanced up, jolted out of her thoughts, as the same nurse came back down the corridor and looked around the waiting room. A heavily pregnant woman in the corner stood up, and Annie and Holly sat back, disappointed.

'What time are you supposed to be in?' Annie wondered, grateful for the distraction.

'Three thirty, but they usually run a bit late. Hopefully I'll be next.'

Annie opened her mouth to reply, but closed it again as she heard her mobile ringing in her bag. She pulled it out, looked at the number and frowned.

'Jamie?' Holly wondered.

'No, it's one of my clients,' Annie explained. 'Do you mind if I take this? I'll just be in the corridor, so I'll keep an eye out for if the nurse calls you.'

'Sure, go ahead.'

Annie jumped up from her seat and walked quickly from the reception area, pressing the 'answer' button on her phone.

'Hello?'

'Hi, Annie, it's Simon. I'm really sorry to call you out of the blue like this. Are you all right to talk, or are you with someone?'

'I'm not in the office this afternoon – I'm with my sister at the hospital.'

'The hospital? Is she okay?'

'Yeah, she's fine. She's having a baby.'

'She's having a baby?'

'Not right now,' Annie clarified hastily. 'It's just a checkup. So yes, you're fine to talk. Are you okay?'

'Not exactly.' Simon took a deep breath. 'Zoe and I have had a massive row, and she's talking about calling off the wedding. I don't know what to do.'

'Oh, Simon! What was the argument about?'

'I don't even know properly. She found a text on my phone from Emily – you know, my ex – and made it out to be bigger than it was. I probably didn't handle it very well. I walked out and spent the night at my parents' place. Now she's saying she wants me to move my stuff out. But I haven't done anything wrong, Annie. I swear I haven't!'

'Okay, Simon, calm down.' Annie's mind was racing, and she could hear the stress in his voice. 'Are you free to meet me this evening?'

'I can come, but I don't know whether Zoe will. I thought about calling Julia, to see if she can do anything…'

'Yes, that sounds like a good idea,' Annie confirmed. She glanced back into the waiting room to see that the nurse had just called her sister, and Holly was looking around anxiously. 'Look, Simon, I have to go now, but I'll call you as soon as I get out of the hospital, okay?'

'Thanks, Annie. I just love her so much.'

'I know you do. We'll get this sorted, I promise you.'

'Thanks, Annie.'

Annie hung up, dashing back through to her sister.

'Is everything okay?' Holly asked anxiously.

'Relationship crisis,' Annie explained briefly.

'Work your magic,' Holly grinned, as the two of them followed the nurse down the corridor, where she showed them into a small room.

'Hello, Holly, how are you?' smiled the sonographer, as Annie stared round at the unfamiliar equipment.

'Hello, Dr Varshani, I'm very well, thank you. This is my sister, Annie,' Holly explained. 'My husband, Greg, couldn't make it today. He's at a conference.'

'Oh, that's a shame,' Dr Varshani replied. 'Still, at least you have your sister here to support you. So, Holly, if you could just pop up onto the bed here, and pull your top up for me.'

Holly did as she was told, and Annie marvelled once again at how her sister's stomach had changed, the pale skin pulled tightly over the growing bump. It was crazy to think that Holly was growing a baby in there!

'Any concerns, or any changes you've noticed?' Dr Varshani asked, as she washed her hands with antibacterial gel then pulled on a thin pair of disposable gloves.

'I don't think so,' Holly replied. 'Everything seems fine.'

'Wonderful. And you're twenty weeks now, that's right, isn't it?' Holly nodded in reply, as the doctor smeared lubricant over her swollen belly. 'So we may be able to tell you the gender today. Is that something you'd like to find out?'

Holly turned to Annie, her eyes shining. 'Yes, please!'

'Okay,' Dr Varshani nodded. She picked up the transducer, and began to roll it slowly over Holly's stomach. Almost immediately, the noise of a fast, loud heartbeat could be heard, followed by a grainy black and white image on the screen.

'The heartbeat's strong, so that's excellent. And it looks as though baby's sucking its thumb at the moment,' Dr Varshani explained, pointing to the screen.

Annie peered harder at the image, feeling a sudden surge of emotion as she made out the unmistakeable shape of a baby on the screen. She could clearly see its eyes, its mouth – it even looked to have Holly's nose, poor thing! And, like the doctor said, it appeared to be sucking its thumb.

'It's incredible,' Annie gasped, fighting back tears.

'Baby seems to be awake right now,' Dr Varshani noted. 'So let's see if we can encourage it to move a little bit.' She ran the monitor along the underside of Holly's stomach, and the skin there rippled.

'Ooh, there it goes,' Holly giggled, feeling the familiar, fluttery movement.

The doctor peered closely at the screen. 'As I said, we can't be a hundred percent certain, but I don't see any sign of a little winkle there. Congratulations, Mrs Harrington. You're having a girl.'

Annie's mouth fell open, and she looked across at her sister. The two women stared at each other for a moment, joy written across both of their faces, and Annie instinctively crossed the room to take hold of her sister's hand.

'Congratulations, Hol. You're having a girl!'

'I can't believe it,' Holly exclaimed, a tear rolling down her cheek. 'I can't wait to tell Greg. He'll be so excited.'

Both of them stared at the picture on the monitor, hardly able to believe that in just a few short months, the grainy image would be an actual, real person, one that Holly and Greg would love more than they'd ever loved anything in their lives.

'Do you know what you're going to call her?' Annie wondered.

Holly nodded. 'We like Poppy. And then Isabella, after Greg's grandmother. Poppy Isabella Harrington.'

Annie looked back at the monitor, doing nothing to prevent the tears that were spilling down her cheeks. 'Nice to meet you, Poppy Isabella Harrington,' she whispered.

Chapter 36

'Ah, women. They make the highs higher, and the lows more frequent' – **Friedrich Nietzsche**

Zoe was staring around her flat – the flat which until extremely recently she'd shared with Simon – and sobbing as though her heart was broken. Which she thought it might actually be.

She was currently curled up on the sofa beneath the duvet that she'd dragged through from the bedroom, and the TV was playing silently in the background. Her face was puffy from crying, and she had an ice cream stain down the front of her pyjamas, but right now personal hygiene was the last thing on Zoe's mind.

Her emotions were all over the place, and she had no idea what she was feeling any more. Simon had been trying to call her, but she wasn't picking up out of stubbornness, despite the fact that the thing she wanted most in the world right now was to hear Simon's voice. The catalyst for their split had been a stupid row that had spiralled out of control, and Zoe knew that she'd been jealous and insecure, acting illogically as she felt the pressure of the big day looming. Now she was starting to worry that she'd made a huge mistake.

The more Zoe thought about it, the more she realised what an idiot she'd been. Simon was a good guy, and there was no way he would ever cheat on her. His proposal had been perfect, and their whole relationship had been like a fairytale. Plus, Zoe still fancied the pants off him, with his handsome face and big, strong body. Their no-sex vow had been far tougher than she'd expected, but she had to admit they'd had a lot of fun along the way, and really learnt a lot about each other.

And now she'd potentially thrown it all away with one major act of stupidity. She was supposed to be getting married in just over a week, but at this rate it looked as though there'd be no wedding at all. Zoe thought of the beautiful dress she'd bought, sitting inside its protective bag at her friend Hannah's house, and at the thought that she might never wear it she began crying all over again, fat tears rolling down her cheeks and landing on the duvet cover that still smelt of Simon.

She pulled it close, inhaling deeply, breathing in the scent of his aftershave and his shampoo and that indefinable but unmistakeable smell that was… Simon. Oh God, she missed him! Why, oh why, had she reacted so badly to that text? Now she faced spending the rest of her life alone, just a sad, bitter, old—

The door buzzer rang, and Zoe shuffled over to the entryphone to answer it, the duvet wrapped around her waist impeding her progress.

'Hello?' Zoe snuffled.

'Hey love, it's me,' Julia's voice came back.

'Come on up,' Zoe told her, as she pressed the button to let her in. 'I warn you, I look a mess.'

'Oh, Zoe,' Julia sighed, after she'd trudged up the stairs to the first-floor flat and took in the sight of her friend. 'Oh, poor you,' she exclaimed, enveloping her in a hug.

'I think I smell,' Zoe murmured sadly.

'Maybe just a little bit,' Julia said tactfully. 'But nothing that a nice hot shower won't fix.'

'Jules, I've been such an idiot,' Zoe sighed dramatically, as she flopped back down on the sofa, and began to cry once again.

'Don't get upset,' Julia pleaded. 'What's happened? Tell me everything.'

And Zoe did. She told Julia all about Simon's previous relationship with Emily, and the text message he'd received from her, the argument they'd had, and the way she'd thrown him out of the flat.

'He wanted me to go with him to see Annie, ' Zoe managed, through her hiccoughs. 'But I refused. She offered to see us specially, at late notice, but I was too stubborn. And then Simon got really mad with me all over again and didn't come home last night. Oh no,… what if he went to Emily's and spent the night with her?' she wondered, her face falling at the terrible thought.

'He didn't,' Julia assured her. 'Of course he didn't. He stayed with his parents.'

'Right,' Zoe nodded, feeling guilty all over again, and wondering what Brian and Jill must think of her.

'You know what, Zoe,' Julia began gently. 'I think this might be a classic case of cold feet.'

'Do you?' Zoe wondered, looking up at Julia through tear-stained eyes. 'What if it's not? What if it's something else, like women's intuition, or gut instinct?'

'I know both of you. I know how much Simon loves you, and I know how much you love him. Seriously, what is your gut telling you? Is it telling you that you've made a big fuss over nothing and Simon's the man for you, or is it telling you that he's a cheat and a liar who's been double-crossing you the whole time?'

Put like that, Zoe could see how ridiculous it sounded. She started to wonder whether perhaps she *had* overreacted. 'My gut's a bit confused right now,' Zoe mumbled, looking shame-faced.

Julia tried not to smile, feeling that the worst of the crisis had passed. 'Can I call Simon, and ask him to come round and speak to you?' she asked gently.

Zoe hesitated.

'He's going out of his mind,' Julia told her. 'And I'm not exaggerating. He's been calling me, Annie, Linda, even your mum, trying to find out what's going on, and if you're okay. He said you wouldn't pick up the phone to him.'

Zoe glanced at her mobile, where she was currently up to sixty-four missed calls.

'Please, Zoe.'

Finally, Zoe relented. 'Okay then,' she agreed sullenly, as Julia grinned.

'Maybe I should team up with Annie – I reckon I could be a fantastic relationship therapist.'

'No way,' Zoe shook her head. 'You're far too good an events planner to ever change career.'

'Exactly! I've put so much work into this wedding, there's no way I'm going to let you call it off.'

Zoe pretended to glare at her. 'Okay, okay, you've made your point. Now call my fiancé before I change my mind.'

❄ ❄ ❄

Simon was swearing out loud at the vehicle in front of him. 'Pull off the road!' he yelled. 'Pull off the road and let me past!'

But the tractor driver didn't seem to care, as he merrily trundled along at twenty miles per hour, unaware of Simon's frustration behind him.

Simon swerved out wildly into the road, but it was no good – it was impossible to see round the corner on the narrow, twisty lane, and he simply couldn't risk it.

'Move!' Simon yelled again, accompanying the shout with a blast of his horn. Finally, blessedly, the tractor pulled into a siding. Simon put his foot down on the accelerator and roared past, shooting along the quiet country road.

As soon as he'd received Julia's phone call, he'd leapt straight up from the kitchen table where he'd been eating his dinner; despite his insistence that he wasn't hungry, when faced with his mother's homemade chicken pie and mashed potato, he'd finally relented. But he'd dropped his knife and fork when he heard what Julia had to tell him, pulling on his shoes as he raced out of the door.

The journey into the city seemed to take forever, and Simon's heart was pounding by the time he screeched into his usual parking spot round the corner from the flat. He took the stairs two at a time, stopping nervously as he reached the front door. Suddenly, all his bravado deserted him, and nerves took over. What if Zoe hadn't really forgiven him? What if they had another huge row, one that ended everything, for good?

Cautiously, he raised his hand and knocked on the door. He could hear Zoe moving around inside the flat, and then the door swung open.

Simon swallowed. 'Hi,' he said nervously. Something caught in his throat and he coughed to clear it.

'Hi,' Zoe replied, her eyes wide as she looked up at him anxiously. Her hair was dripping wet as though she'd just had a shower – which, in fact, she had – and she was dressed in one of Simon's old T-shirts. At the sight of her, Simon's heart melted.

'Why didn't you use your key?' she asked in confusion.

'I didn't… I didn't know if I was still welcome.'

'Oh Si, of course you are.' Zoe's lower lip was wobbling dangerously, tears brimming in her eyes. She didn't think it was possible to cry any more than she had done in the last twenty-four hours, but it seemed as though she wasn't finished yet.

Simon took a step towards her, and before Zoe knew what she was doing, she was moving towards him too, and the next minute they were in each other's arms and Simon was smothering her with kisses, holding her like he never wanted to let her go. Zoe felt light-headed, dizzy with excitement. Simon's embrace was strong, his chest large and powerful, and Zoe knew one thing with absolute certainty – in his arms was right where she was meant to be.

'I'm so sorry,' she apologised frantically. 'I've been such an idiot. I know you'd never—'

'It doesn't matter,' Simon told her, in between kisses. 'I don't care about that. I just worried that you—'

Suddenly he stopped, pulling away from her, as though he'd remembered something. Zoe looked at him anxiously, wondering what was happening. As she watched, Simon dropped to one knee in front of her.

'Si? What…?'

'I know this seems like déjà vu, but I love you with all my heart, and I would never do anything to hurt you. All I want to do is be the best man I can be to make you the happiest woman in the world.'

Zoe was crying again now, but this time they were tears of happiness.

'I've done this once publicly, and now I want to do it again privately, just for the two of us. Zoe Miller, would you do me the honour of becoming my wife?'

Suddenly, Zoe began to giggle. All the pressure of the past few weeks, all the misery of the past few hours, faded into nothing, and she wanted to laugh out loud from pure joy and relief. 'Yes, Simon, of course I'll marry you! Get up, you idiot,' she laughed, pulling him to his feet.

Simon swept her into his arms once again, kissing her long and hard, as though he couldn't get enough of her.

'I love you,' Simon murmured, as they finally pulled away.

'I love you too,' Zoe whispered back. 'So, so, much.'

'So does this mean that the wedding's back on?'

'Yes,' Zoe confirmed happily, her eyes shining. 'The wedding is absolutely, definitely, one hundred percent back on.'

Chapter 37

'Civilised people cannot fully satisfy their sexual instinct without love' – **Bertrand Russell**

'What if she doesn't turn up?' Simon turned anxiously to his best man Gary.

The two of them were standing outside St Stephen's Church in the little village of Great Walton, the sun beating down on them and making Simon sweat even more than he was already. The day was beautiful, not a cloud visible in the cerulean sky, and the church bells were ringing out in celebration.

'She will. Of course she will,' Gary assured him. 'Why wouldn't she?'

'I dunno. Maybe she'll have another attack of cold feet. Maybe she'll change her mind. Anything could happen.'

'Look, if she doesn't turn up, *I'll* marry you,' Gary offered helpfully.

Simon glared at him. 'Thanks, that's really nice of you.'

'Mate, you love her, she loves you, it's all going to be perfect. And if you could set me up with one of the bridesmaids then this could be the best day ever.'

In spite of everything, Simon burst out laughing. He'd known Gary since they were kids, and would have trusted him with his life. 'Okay, I'll do my best. I think her friend

Kerry is single, so I'll introduce you. She lives in Chester though.'

For a moment, Gary looked downcast, before perking up suddenly. 'There's always Skype,' he remembered, with a cheeky grin. 'I've never had Skype sex before.'

Simon shook his head, giving him a friendly thump on the arm. Gary winced, looking as though he was in genuine pain; he was far smaller and skinnier than Simon, and Simon sometimes seemed to forget this.

'Straighten up, look smart,' Simon told him sharply. 'There's more guests arriving.'

As they drew closer, Simon realised that it was Annie and Linda walking towards him. Annie looked gorgeous in a blue silk maxi-dress paired with a cream pashmina, while Linda was equally lovely in a bright cerise dress and matching jacket. She'd arrived without Ray, as he was going to be the one driving Zoe and her father, Geoff, to the church. Annie had arranged for them to borrow her brother-in-law's vintage Triumph, which Linda had decorated with cream ribbon and a small posy of flowers.

'Simon!' Annie greeted him. 'You look so handsome.'

'He scrubs up well, doesn't he?' Gary grinned.

It was true. Simon looked great in the dark grey suit, with matching patterned waistcoat and silk tie.

'How are the nerves?' Annie asked.

'Out of control!'

'Oh, you'll be fine, honestly.'

'Thanks, Annie. And thanks so much for all you've done for us. You've really helped us out.'

'And tonight's the moment of truth,' Annie couldn't resist reminding him. 'Enjoy yourself.'

'Oh, I will,' Simon assured her, before turning to Linda. 'The flowers look amazing, and you've done such a wonderful job. I know Zoe will be so happy.'

'We aim to please,' Linda smiled, looking thrilled with the compliment. 'Ooh, look, there's Julia and Nick just arriving.'

Nick was parking his BMW outside the church, getting out to open the door for his wife. They strode across the road holding hands, and Annie thought once again what a good-looking couple they made. Nick looked confident and at ease in the classic suit which brought out his dark good looks, while Julia looked stunning in a pretty knee-length floral dress.

'There she is, the woman responsible for this whole she-bang,' Simon greeted Julia, opening his arms wide and embracing her. She'd spent the morning driving frantically between the church and the reception venue, making sure that everything was set up just as it should be, before zooming home to change her clothes and grab Nick. 'You look beautiful.'

'Oi oi, hands off, you're getting one of your own soon,' Nick joked, as he shook hands with Simon, clapping him on the back. 'How are you doing?'

'Not bad,' Simon said uncertainly. 'I'll just be relieved when she turns up and says "I do".'

'Not long now,' Nick grinned.

Simon looked nervously at Julia, suddenly seeming far smaller than his six feet and one inch. 'She is coming, isn't she?' he asked quietly.

Julia laid a reassuring hand on his arm. 'Of course she is. I'll see you in there,' Julia smiled, taking Nick's arm as they made their way along the flagstone path and into the quaint country church.

Simon and Gary turned back to greet the other new arrivals, who were now streaming down the street towards St Stephen's. There were Simon's old school friends, his rugby mates, long lost relatives who he hadn't seen for years, as well as all of Zoe's family and friends, whose names he tried desperately to remember. When everyone was finally seated inside, Simon looked anxiously up and down the road before checking his watch.

'She's late,' he said, unable to hide the concern in his voice.

'It's the bride's prerogative to be late,' Gary assured him. 'Besides, she's probably doing it on purpose, making you suffer. I would.'

'Thanks a lot.'

As Simon checked his watch again, Gary's phone beeped and he pulled it out of his trouser pocket.

'Make sure that thing's on silent. I don't want the "Thong Song" blasting out while we're saying our vows,' Simon warned him, referring to Gary's inappropriate ringtone.

Gary grinned as he pressed a couple of buttons. 'No problem, it's off. But I thought you'd like to know that Ray's just texted me. They're on their way, and they'll be here in five minutes.'

Simon went pale, beads of sweat breaking out along his forehead. 'Okay. Right. Shit. Have you got the rings?'

Gary patted his top pocket confidently. 'All taken care of, mate. Now come on, let's get you inside.'

❄ ❄ ❄

The anticipation had reached fever pitch. People were turning round in their seats every few seconds to see if they could spot anything. From his position at the front of the church, Simon had a clear view straight down the aisle, and he knew that any moment now he would see Zoe arrive on her father's arm.

Then suddenly the mood in the building seemed to shift, and the strains of 'Here Comes the Bride' rang out on the church organ, followed by gasps as the guests caught their first sight of the bride.

Simon looked up and saw Zoe standing at the door beside her father. Geoff looked proud enough to burst, but Simon noticed nothing except his wife-to-be. He didn't think he'd ever seen her looking so beautiful, or so radiant.

She was wearing her dream gown, with its classic, simple silhouette and the jewelled belt that showed off her tiny waist. Her make-up was subtle, and she looked like the quintessential English rose, with a little pink blush on her cheeks and a smudge of colour on her lips. She was wearing the earrings Simon had bought for her birthday, which matched her engagement ring perfectly, and there was no other jewellery to spoil the effect.

Her titian hair had been blow-dried into soft waves, with the front pinned up so that it fell gently around her face, whilst Linda had provided the most incredible bouquet of pale pink gardenias, dark pink roses and gypsophila. There was no doubt about it: Zoe looked breathtaking.

She walked towards Simon, beaming uncontrollably, the very picture of happiness. Simon couldn't take his eyes off her, oblivious to the fact that Linda was dabbing her eyes as she clung to Ray's arm, or that Julia had turned to Nick and the two of them were sharing a small, private smile, both of them lost in memories of their own wedding day.

As Zoe reached him, she smiled shyly.

'You look so beautiful,' Simon whispered, utterly entranced.

'I love you,' Zoe mouthed in reply.

And then the vicar stepped forward, and the ceremony began.

For Simon, it passed in a blur. He found himself saying the words that were so familiar from countless films and television programmes, seeing Zoe's barely concealed look of amusement as he was forced to say his hated second name – Gideon – out loud. He stumbled over a couple of words, and there were sympathetic smiles and good-natured sniggers from his friends and family.

And then the vicar said the famous words: 'I now pronounce you husband and wife. You may kiss the bride.'

Simon and Zoe gazed at each other, smiles of happiness and relief and disbelief on their faces. They were finally married, with rings on their fingers to prove it! Simon took Zoe in his arms and kissed her, tentatively at first, but with the encouragement of the congregation it soon became more intense.

Finally, they were together: for better or worse, richer or poorer, in sickness and in health. And Simon didn't want it any other way.

❄ ❄ ❄

The happy couple emerged from the church to a chorus of cheers and applause, confetti and rice raining down on them. Ray quickly slipped back into his driver role, hopping back behind the wheel of the Triumph. Linda would get a lift to the reception with Annie in her Mini Cooper.

After they'd posed for photos, Simon helped his new bride into the car and the two of them cuddled up on the back seat, holding hands and sharing little butterfly kisses.

'Can you believe that we're married?' Zoe asked Simon, her eyes positively gleaming with excitement.

'It feels amazing,' Simon told her honestly. 'I hope married life is always this good.'

'Of course it will be. And if it's not, then we can go and see Annie,' Zoe giggled.

Simon was staring at her in wonder, hardly able to comprehend that they were finally husband and wife.

He leant towards her, kissing her very gently. 'I love you, Mrs Wright.'

'I love you too, Mr Wright,' Zoe replied. 'And nothing will ever change that.'

Chapter 38

'Healthy, lusty sex is wonderful' – **John Wayne**

'Simon, look,' Zoe breathed, as Ray carefully parked the vintage Triumph in the driveway of Simon's parents' home. 'It's absolutely perfect.'

Brian and Jill owned a large farm-style house, with acres of land running all the way down to the canal where Brian ran his boat hire business. The field leading down to the water was the spot that Zoe and Simon had chosen for their reception, and it was the first time they'd seen it since Julia had worked her magic, transforming it from an ordinary patch of meadow into a breathtaking party venue.

There were fairy lights draped in the bushes and lanterns hanging from ancient oak trees, whilst tea lights in jam jars had been placed around the lawn, giving an enchanting, romantic feel to the whole place. A long trestle table, draped in a white cloth, was groaning with food, and a bar area had been erected where hired waiters were currently making sure that everyone was served with a fruity glass of Pimm's. Scattered throughout the grounds were bunting, balloons and bouquets of flowers, courtesy of Linda, whilst a stage area had been set up just behind the house, to host the band later in the evening.

Even the boats on the water had been specially decorated; one had been painted bridal white with silver trim, then covered in L plates and streamers, with tin cans trailing from the roof and a 'Just Married' sign hanging above the door.

'I know I said I'd surprise you by arranging something special for our wedding night – the place where we're *finally* going to consummate this marriage,' Simon said with feeling. 'And I hope you think it's fitting that I've chosen… this boat.'

Zoe looked at the hesitant expression on Simon's face and burst out laughing, thinking what a perfect choice it was. She didn't need her new husband to waste his money on some grand, impersonal hotel; they'd spent some incredibly romantic nights on the boats, and for Zoe, being out on the water brought back so many happy memories.

'Oh Simon, I don't mind at all.'

'In fact,' Simon continued, biting his lip. 'This is actually *our* boat.'

Zoe frowned. 'What do you mean?'

'Mum and Dad have given it to us. As a wedding present. They know we have to be out of the flat soon so, if you want, we can live here, at least until we've saved up enough money for a deposit on a house.'

'Oh, Simon,' Zoe breathed, her eyes shining as she flung her arms around him.

'And look here,' he said, taking her hand and leading her to one end of the boat. 'It's been re-named. It's now the *Mrs Wright*, in honour of you.'

Zoe gasped as she saw that Simon was telling the truth – the swirly, silver writing did indeed read *Mrs Wright*. Zoe gazed at the boat, hardly able to believe everything Simon was telling her. This was where they would spend their first night as a married couple she realised, suddenly remembering how important tonight was to them both. They'd spent months working towards this evening, refraining from intercourse, and learning everything they could about each other, following Annie's instructions to the letter.

Recalling the new wedding underwear she was wearing, Zoe leant across to her new husband and murmured seductively, 'And after all your surprises, I might have one for you later.'

Simon's eyebrows shot up, a sly grin stealing over his face as he guessed what she was referring to. 'Can we cancel the party? Get straight into bed now?' he joked, his eyes running over Zoe's body. She looked so delicious in her dress, like a parcel ready for him to open.

'We've waited almost six months,' Zoe laughed. 'Surely you can manage another few hours?'

'Ah, my new wife's bossing me around already,' Simon sighed, with a happy grin. 'Whatever you say, darling.'

He took Zoe's hand and the two of them walked across the field and into the party, ready to greet their guests.

❄ ❄ ❄

The sun had set, the day sliding into night as the moon rose and the stars twinkled in the sky above the wedding party. They'd had the speeches, which were both hilarious and touching, and Annie had found herself laughing and crying. She was so proud of how far Zoe and Simon had come. She was proud of how all her clients had done, she realised, glancing at Linda and Ray who were sitting alongside her, holding hands as they watched the guests boogying to the live band.

Opposite Annie were Nick and Julia. Nick had his arms around his wife as she leant back against him, both of them looking happy and contented. Across the field, on the dance floor, Zoe and Simon were dancing with their bodies locked together, completely unselfconscious as they moved with wild abandon in the middle of their crowd of friends.

'It's been a wonderful day, hasn't it?' Linda commented.

'It's been lovely,' Annie agreed. 'And it's so great to see them back together. Those two really belong with each other.'

'They look so happy,' Linda agreed. 'And I'm sure you played a role in that.'

'Me?' Annie looked surprised. 'I don't think I can take the credit for love. I'm hardly Cupid,' she smiled.

'Don't be so modest,' Linda admonished her. 'You've been wonderful with me and Ray. I really can't thank you enough. I feel awful when I think how horrible I was to you in those first few sessions.'

'No harm done,' Annie smiled. 'I'm just pleased to see such positive results. It's undoubtedly the best part of my job.'

Beside Linda, Ray was downing the remainder of his wine. His face looked rather rosy as he leant towards his wife, giving her a little squeeze.

'What do you say we go join the dancing?' he suggested, a gleam in his eye.

The band had just segued into 'Isn't She Lovely' by Stevie Wonder, and Linda exclaimed in delight. 'Ooh, this is one of my favourites. But it's years since we've been dancing, Ray.'

'It's been years since we've done a lot of things,' he shot back saucily. 'But think of the fun we've been having recently.'

Linda blushed, but stood up, smoothing down her dress. 'Go on then, you've twisted my arm,' she giggled. 'See you soon, Annie.'

Annie watched them go, walking hand in hand towards the dance floor and making their way into the crowd of people, where Ray began spinning Linda around as she threw back her head in laughter.

Annie took a sip of her wine, pulling her wrap around her shoulders. After the heat of the day, the air was finally cooling, and there was the slightest of chills in the air. Across the table, Julia slipped away from Nick and walked round to sit beside Annie.

'Are you okay?' Julia asked.

'Yes, I'm absolutely fine,' Annie replied honestly. 'Having a great time. You?'

'Yes, it's been wonderful. I can't help thinking about *our* wedding day,' Julia confessed, blowing a kiss across the table at Nick. 'We've been reminiscing. I think events like this always make you reflective, don't they?' she said, as Annie nodded in agreement.

'And you're getting on well,' Annie pressed gently.

Julia nodded. 'Really well. I feel like we've turned a corner. We were in a pretty bad way for a while back there.'

'But you've come through it?'

'Fingers crossed,' Julia smiled.

'And how's everything going with the baby making?' Annie asked. 'Any progress?'

'No, not exactly. To tell you the truth, we've decided to take a break from it all for a while. It's lovely to be able to drink again,' Julia confessed, nodding at her glass of wine.

Annie's eyebrows shot up in surprise. 'You've stopped trying?'

'Well, not completely,' Julia admitted, with a naughty giggle. 'But we just want to focus on *us* for a while. If it happens, it happens. And if it doesn't, then we'll go and see someone about it – *not* a sex therapist,' she couldn't resist adding cheekily. 'But yeah, for now we're just taking some time to work on our relationship and make sure we're in a good place.'

'That's fantastic. I think you've made a really positive decision.'

'I knew you'd approve,' Julia grinned.

At the other side of the table, Nick looked across at them. 'What are you two talking about?' he asked suspiciously.

'We're talking about you, and how handsome you look to-night,' Julia told him, leaning across and tugging playfully at his tie. Dressed in a dark suit and crisp white shirt, he looked exceptionally attractive.

Nick pretended to run a hand through his hair. 'Naturally,' he said, making the two women laugh. 'Annie, if you don't mind, I'd like to steal my wife away for a little while,' he requested, taking Julia's hand.

'Of course not,' Annie insisted. 'It was nice catching up, Julia. Have fun, you two!'

She waved them off, as Nick wrapped an arm around his wife's shoulders, and the two of them strolled off towards the canal, giggling as they disappeared into the darkness.

Annie sat by herself, watching everyone having fun. She was so pleased with how all three couples had done – they'd come so far, and really worked hard to get their relationships back to a good place.

But for once, Annie found herself wishing that *she* had someone to share tonight with. She was usually fine by herself but, as Julia had pointed out, weddings had a tendency to make you reflective, and Annie couldn't help but feel a little melancholy as she watched everyone else have fun, dancing to the live band who were now playing 'Livin' on a Prayer' by Bon Jovi.

Annie was so engrossed in her thoughts that she didn't notice the person walking towards her, his tall frame silhouetted against the darkness. It was only when he'd almost reached her, and said her name, that she looked up.

'Annie.'

'Jamie?' Annie exclaimed, confusion flickering across her face. 'What are you doing here?'

'Please, Annie, hear me out,' he said quickly. 'Your sister got in touch with me, and told me you'd be here tonight.'

'Holly?' Now Annie was more perplexed than ever. 'How did she...?'

'She looked up the company and gave us a call. She explained why you behaved the way you did towards me before I left.'

Annie's breathing was coming fast, her emotions whirling all over the place. She was furious with Holly, confused as to why Jamie was here and, although she hardly dared admit it to herself, she was thrilled to see him. All the familiar feelings were churning inside her at the sight of him. Her pulse was racing, her mouth dry as she tried to take in the fact that Jamie was standing in front of her, looking incredibly handsome in a suit and tie, his blond hair swept off his face to reveal those soft blue eyes.

'May I sit down?' he asked, and Annie nodded, not trusting herself to say anything.

'Olivia's my daughter,' he explained, with a heavy sigh, as he took a seat on the bench beside Annie. 'She's seven – well, she'll be eight next month. Sara – that's her mother – we're... we're not together any more. We weren't actually together when she found out she was pregnant. We dated for a few weeks, split up and then she found out afterwards that...'

Jamie trailed off. Annie hardly dared to speak. Her eyes were glued to his face, and she was utterly oblivious to the noise and the dancing just metres away from her.

'I was terrified, if the truth be told, but I wasn't going to dodge my responsibilities. Sara decided she wanted to keep the baby, and I said I'd support her. It's the best decision I've ever made. Livvy is... she's just incredible,' he admitted, and Annie saw something in his face that she'd never seen before. Pride and awe and sheer, unadulterated love.

'I should have told you,' Jamie said, bringing his gaze back to Annie. 'I know I should have done. I almost did, in fact, on a few occasions, but I didn't want to scare you off. I liked you – really liked you – and I didn't want to lay this all on you so soon, but in hindsight, that was a really bad decision. I should have just been honest with you from the beginning.'

'I don't…' Annie swallowed, trying to take in everything he was telling her. 'I don't know what to say.'

'You don't have to say anything,' Jamie insisted. 'Just… dance with me.'

He held out his hand and Annie dazedly took it, feeling her skin tingle as their palms met. She stood up, and he led her up to the dance floor. Annie's mind was whirling as the band changed to a slow song – 'Make You Feel My Love' by Adele – and Jamie smiled, wrapping his arms around Annie's waist and pulling her close. Annie let her hands rest on the back of his neck, her heart racing so fast that she felt sure he must be able to feel it through his shirt. Their bodies were pressed close together, and she could smell the fresh, clean scent of him.

'Annie…' Jamie began, but this time he hesitated, seeming more uncertain than before.

'What is it?' she prompted.

'I… I'm just going to say this now before I lose my nerve. And if I'm completely off the wall with this, then you can tell me, and it doesn't matter at all, but…' He took a deep breath, stealing himself. 'I'm absolutely crazy about you. You're gorgeous – and you look especially amazing tonight,' he gushed, taking in the elegant midnight-blue dress that fitted her like a second skin, flowing over her body every time she moved.

'And you're smart and funny and such good company – even if you are a rubbish cook,' Jamie couldn't resist adding with a grin. 'I really like spending time with you, and I'd really like to spend a lot more time with you. Like I said, if I'm saying the total wrong thing and freaking you out, then tell me to get lost.'

'No,' Annie said softly, a smile stealing across her face. 'You're not saying the wrong thing at all.'

Jamie stopped dancing and looked straight at Annie, his blue eyes serious. 'I haven't been able to stop thinking about you,' he admitted. 'Now that we've moved offices, I'm missing you so much. It's crazy, isn't it? I didn't realise just how much I looked forward to seeing you every day and having our little chats in the kitchen, or even just catching a glimpse of you in the corridor. I know I should have said all this before – well, there's a lot of things I should have said before – but I completely messed it up and I was terrified that I'd lost you for good—'

'Sssh,' Annie murmured, laying a finger over his lips. Jamie looked back at her, both of their faces so full of hope and eagerness and anticipation and nerves.

Then, tantalisingly slowly, Jamie leant forward and kissed her. His lips were warm and soft, and Annie closed her eyes, losing herself in the sensations. She was oblivious to her surroundings, to the revellers around them, to the stars dazzling in the night sky. Nor did she notice that Zoe and Simon, Julia and Nick, and Ray and Linda had suddenly gathered around them, so that when she finally opened her eyes and pulled away, a huge round of applause broke out.

Instead of feeling self-conscious, Annie laughed happily, catching Jamie's eye as he did the same. And then they kissed again, and it felt so right and so perfect that Annie never wanted it to end.

Epilogue

'Good girls go to heaven and bad girls go everywhere' – **Helen Gurley Brown**

Five months later...

The city market place looked magical. The pretty little covered stalls had been transformed into snow-dusted chalets, selling everything from knitted hats and faux-fur earmuffs to mulled wine and hot chocolate laced with brandy. At the eastern end of the square, a giant Christmas tree had been erected, with hundreds of tiny white fairy lights twinkling in its branches. Beneath it, a traditional brass band were playing, whilst a chorus of carol singers joined in a rousing version of 'O Little Town of Bethlehem'.

The weather was chilly – snow had been predicted for later that week – but Annie was cosy in her red skater-style coat and chunky snood. She linked her arm through Jamie's and snuggled closer, thinking how gorgeous he looked in his black peacoat and grey woollen scarf. His blond hair was neatly cut to perfectly frame his handsome face, while his cheeks were flushed from the cold, and his blue eyes were sparkling.

'Oh look, isn't that cute,' Annie gushed, as they browsed the stalls on the Christmas market and she spotted a hand-painted bauble that read 'Baby's First Christmas' in swirly red glitter. 'I'm going to get it for Poppy,' she said decisively, pulling out her purse.

'She's going to be completely spoilt by her Auntie Annie,' Jamie grinned. 'You've bought her so many presents!'

'That's exactly as it should be,' Annie replied, not looking the least bit guilty. 'Anyway, Olivia isn't doing too badly either.'

'Believe me, it's much easier to buy for a two-month-old baby than for an eight-year-old girl. Yes to One Direction merchandise, no to Bratz dolls, and Barbie is apparently "totally uncool, Dad". I've no idea when my daughter got so opinionated.'

'She obviously takes after her father,' Annie teased.

'Hmm, I'm not sure about that. Although, of course, she does get her incredible good looks from me,' Jamie added, with a cheeky grin.

'As it's the season of goodwill, I'll let you get away with that one,' Annie laughed, thanking the stallholder as he safely packaged up the bauble and passed the bag across to her.

'Seriously though,' Jamie began, taking Annie's hand as they walked away. 'I hope you get the chance to spend lots more time with Livvy in the new year. She's a great kid, and I want you two to get to know each other better.'

'I'd like that,' Annie replied shyly.

Ever since Jamie had explained everything to Annie at Zoe and Simon's wedding, the two of them had been inseparable. Well, as inseparable as it was possible to be when combining two busy careers and numerous family commitments on both sides. But the situation suited both of them; Annie, especially, was eager not to rush into anything, and over the weeks she was slowly building her trust in Jamie. She felt that as he'd been completely honest and open with her, he deserved the same courtesy in return, so Annie had sat him down one night and, over a bottle of wine and a takeaway, told him all about her history with Mark.

Jamie had naturally been shocked at first. The fact that Annie had been married and divorced at such a young age was a lot to take in, but Jamie felt that he was hardly in a position to judge anyone for their past mistakes. If anything, Annie's confession had brought them even closer together, and it was shortly after that that Jamie made the decision to introduce Annie to his daughter, Olivia. So far, Annie had met her three times, and was increasingly charmed by the bright, sparky, forthright little girl.

Annie and Jamie made their way through the crowds of people, all browsing the stalls and picking up last-minute Christmas presents. The atmosphere was friendly and festive, an excited buzz in the air for the upcoming holidays. Annie had stopped at a jewellery stall and was holding up a delicate pair of silver and turquoise earrings, wondering whether or not she should buy them for her sister, when she heard her name being called.

'Annie? It *is* you, I thought it was!'

Annie whirled round to see a grinning Julia, as Nick strolled up behind her.

'Julia! And Nick! How are you both?'

'We're good, thanks. Really good,' Julia beamed. Her long blonde hair tumbled out from beneath a pink knitted beret, and she looked happy and healthy. 'How about you?'

'Yeah, I'm well, thanks. Just doing a bit of Christmas shopping.'

'Likewise,' Julia laughed, as she held up half a dozen carrier bags.

Annie was suddenly aware of someone appearing beside her, and looked up to see Jamie standing there, a quizzical expression on his face.

'Oh, Jamie, this is Julia and Nick,' Annie introduced them. 'And this is Jamie. My, um… Jamie,' she finished awkwardly, feeling the colour rise in her cheeks. It still felt odd to introduce him as her boyfriend.

'Yes, we met at Zoe and Simon's wedding,' Julia reminded her, a mischievous smile on her face.

'Oh yes, I remember,' Jamie smiled, his face lighting up in recognition, as he shook Nick's hand and leant over to kiss Julia on the cheek.

'So, you two are still going strong,' Julia couldn't resist saying, her eyes dancing suggestively.

Annie found she didn't know how to reply, suddenly remembering the reason why she preferred to keep her personal and professional life separate. It didn't feel natural to have the focus on *her* love life, but Jamie didn't seem fazed. He wrapped one arm tenderly around Annie's waist, bending down to kiss her on top of her head.

'Five months in and she hasn't got sick of me yet,' he joked.

'Well, it's nice to see Annie looking so happy,' Julia told him warmly.

'So how's everything with you two?' Annie gabbled, eager to change the subject. 'Do you keep in touch with anyone? How are Zoe and Simon?'

'We saw them a couple of weeks ago, actually,' Nick cut in, coming to Annie's rescue.

'Oh, they're so sweet, the two of them,' Julia sighed. 'Still completely mad about each other, and acting like typical newlyweds. I see Zoe quite a bit now. We catch up for a drink after work, or meet up at the weekends. Ooh, they had an offer accepted on a house.'

'That's brilliant news,' Annie exclaimed.

'Yeah, they're moving at the end of January if all goes to plan. She showed me the pictures – it's a lovely little two-bedroom place in Trowse Newton, so really handy for Simon to get to work.'

'And are they still on the houseboat?' Annie wondered. 'It must be freezing at this time of year.'

'It's not bad actually – pretty cosy,' Julia replied. 'We went to visit them and Zoe cooked us a meal on the little gas hob. They've got a heater, and a big hot water boiler. It's a lovely little set up.'

'Sounds wonderful.'

'I know they're planning to have a housewarming when they move into the new place, so I'll tell her to invite you. *Both* of you,' Julia added, with a pointed look at Jamie.

'Listen, do you fancy getting a drink or something, then we can sit down and have a proper catch-up?' Annie suggested. 'You don't mind, do you?' she turned to Jamie, who shook his head. 'There's a little stall over there with tables and chairs outside – they sell drinks.'

'Great idea,' Julia smiled, as they all made their way over.

'I'll get these,' Jamie offered, as they found a table and all sat down. 'Then you three can chat.'

'Thanks.' Annie flashed him a grateful smile, thinking once again how sweet and thoughtful he was. She really was a very lucky woman. 'I'll have a mulled wine, thanks.'

'Mmm, sounds delicious, me too,' put in Nick.

'Mulled wines all round?' Jamie asked, looking expectantly at Julia.

'Er…' Julia hesitated, her face flushing as she cast a hasty glance at Nick. 'Just hot chocolate thanks.'

'No problem,' Jamie replied, as he strolled off to join the queue.

But Annie hadn't missed the look that had passed between Julia and her husband, nor could she fail to spot the excited smile that was spreading across Julia's face.

Annie stared hard at her for a moment. 'You're not!' she finally burst out, her mouth falling open in shock, as Julia nodded.

'I am. *We are,*' she squealed. 'You might not be able to tell under all these layers,' she continued, patting her thick coat, 'but I'm five months along.'

'*Five!* I thought you'd planned to stop trying?'

'Funny what happens when you stop worrying, isn't it? To be honest, we think it might have happened on the night of Zoe's wedding.'

'Sounds like it was an eventful night for everyone! Oh, Julia, I'm so happy for you. All three of you!' Annie cried, giving Julia a spontaneous hug.

'Thanks, Annie,' Julia beamed. 'It's so strange to think that this will be our last Christmas as just the two of us. We're going back up to Derby to spend it with our families, as next year we'll want to stay at home with the baby.'

'I bet you can't wait,' Annie smiled. 'The time will just fly by.'

'So will it be your turn next?' Julia asked, nodding at Jamie who'd just reached the front of the queue. 'He seems lovely. And very good-looking,' she couldn't resist adding.

'Oi! I am still here you know,' Nick laughed good-naturedly.

'Oh, I don't know,' Annie shook her head shyly. 'It's early days yet, but it's going well so far. He's great, and I'm really happy,' she admitted, unable to stop a soppy grin from spreading across her face.

'Aw, that's so lovely,' Julia sighed. 'We always wondered if you had some gorgeous man hidden away, and now we know!'

'Do you ever hear anything from Linda?' Annie quickly changed the subject as Jamie came back to the table with their drinks. 'She and Ray came to a couple of the weekend group sessions, but I haven't seen them for a while.'

'Yes, I'm still in touch with them,' Julia replied, as she took a sip of the creamy, delicious hot chocolate. 'Thanks Jamie, this is lovely. Yes, Linda and I have actually worked together a few times, as I've used her for events and she's given me a really good price on the flowers. Although, to be honest, I've mainly been dealing with her daughter, Rose. Linda only works in the shop very occasionally now.'

'That's good to hear,' Annie nodded. 'Ray was always asking her to cut down her hours so they could spend more time together.'

'Well, it sounds like that's finally happening. They're going away this Christmas, to the Caribbean, I think, on a winter sun holiday.' Julia shot a look at Nick, and the two of them began laughing.

Annie frowned, not understanding the joke. 'Why is that funny?' she wondered.

'I don't know what you were teaching them, Annie,' Julia began through her giggles. 'But the last time I saw Linda she confessed that… well, that she and Ray were going to a naturist resort!'

Annie's mouth fell open in shock. 'No! I don't believe you!'

'It's true. She said that they'd got so used to walking around naked at home, and they were so comfortable with their bodies, that they'd decided to give it a whirl. Apparently Ray was thrilled.'

'I bet he was,' Annie laughed, still struggling to take in what Julia was telling her. It was hard to imagine that Linda, who'd once been so shy and self-conscious about her ageing body, was now so completely comfortable showing it off, but stranger things had happened.

'Julia and I were saying, let's hope they take a lot of sun cream with them,' Nick joked.

'And apply it *very* thoroughly,' Jamie chimed in, as they all started laughing.

Annie sipped her mulled wine, savouring the warm, spicy taste, and thinking how contented she felt right now. For once, both her professional *and* personal life seemed to be on track; not only did she have a handsome, sexy, devoted boyfriend, who she was falling for more with every day that passed, but she had the satisfaction of knowing that she'd helped other couples rediscover that same happiness in their own relationships. Zoe and Simon were married and madly in love, Nick and Julia had put their troubles behind them and were expecting their first baby, whilst Linda and Ray were embarking on a whole new stage of their lives together.

'Look,' Julia exclaimed, pulling Annie out of her reverie, as she stared up at the starry night sky. 'It's starting to snow.'

Annie glanced up, feeling a frozen snowflake land on the tip of her nose, where it quickly melted. The flurry became heavier, settling on the roofs of the market stalls, as people stopped what they were doing to watch. Young children shrieked excitedly, jumping up to try to catch the flakes, their faces red with cold and excitement.

The two couples stared happily at the scene in front of them, as the band began to play 'Away in a Manger', and the carol singers joined in, their voices echoing across the crowded square.

Jamie pulled Annie closer, wrapping his arms around her and kissing her deeply.

'Magical, isn't it?' he murmured, gazing into her eyes as a stray snowflake landed on her lashes.

'Yes, it is,' Annie smiled. And she closed her eyes and kissed him back, thinking that the most magical part of it all was that she'd finally found her happy ever after.

Letter from Sophie

Thank you so much for choosing *A Girl's Guide to the Birds and the Bees*. I really hope you enjoyed it, and found it to be a fun and naughty read, with moments to make you laugh and cry.

If you have time, I'd be hugely grateful if you could write a review – I'd love to hear your thoughts, and it would help other readers to find out what *A Girl's Guide to the Birds and the Bees* is all about.

If you'd like to get in touch, I'm @Cafe_Crumb on Twitter and always like to chat! You can also find me on Facebook at: facebook.com/ngbclub

Thanks again for all your support – now I'd better get back to working on my next book...

Sophie x